A Possible Madness

a novel by

FRANK MACDONALD

A Possible Madness

a novel by

FRANK MACDONALD

CAPE BRETON UNIVERSITY PRESS
SYDNEY, NOVA SCOTIA

Cape Breton University Press recognizes the support of the Province of Nova Scotia, through the Department of Communities, Culture and Heritage and the support received for it publishing program from the Canada Council's Block Grants Program. We are pleased to work in partnership with these bodies to develop and promote our cultural resources.

NOVA SCOTIA

Canada Council for the Arts   Conseil des Arts du Canada

Cover Design: Cathy MacLean Design, Pleasant Bay, NS
Layout: Gail Jones, Sydney, NS
First printed in Canada 2011, ISBN 978-1-897009-65-9.

Library and Archives Canada Cataloguing in Publication

Macdonald, Frank, 1945-
A possible madness : a novel / Frank Macdonald. -- New format ed.

ISBN 978-1-897009-78-9

I. Title.
PS8575.D6305P68 2012   C813'.54   C2012-902355-8

Cape Breton University Press
PO Box 5300
1250 Grand Lake Road
Sydney, Nova Scotia B1P 6L2 Canada

For Virginia
with love and gratitude

| 1 |

The last murder to take place in Shean happened almost sixty years ago when Benny Ryan and John Dan MacLean were convicted of throwing Jim Muise through the plate glass window of Murdock's Meat Market. It wasn't a premeditated murder and wouldn't have amounted to much more than another vandalism story in *The Shean Witness* had a large, pointed shard of glass not dropped from the top of the window frame, nearly decapitating Muise. There had been no eyewitness to the murder, but four people testified to seeing the three young men arguing in front of the meat market earlier that evening. That testimony, coupled with the fact that Benny and John Dan could provide only each other as alibis, made the RCMP's case.

No one was surprised. Everyone in town knew those boys, Benny and John Dan, would wind up in real trouble some day, their pasts being littered with drunk-and-disorderlies, break-ins, petty thefts, brawls and a series of thirty-day sentences in the town jail. Proclaiming their innocence, both men served twelve years before being paroled from Dorchester Penitentiary. Benny Ryan died in a car accident a few years later. John Dan MacLean became a patient in the dementia ward of the Shean Manor.

———

David Cameron studied the front-page photograph on a brittle-yellow 1951 edition of *The Shean Witness*. It showed an RCMP officer examining the shattered window of Murdock's Meat Market while behind a police barrier of wooden blockades a crowd watched the macabre scene. Cameron, the current publisher-editor-reporter-photographer of the *Witness*, wasn't even born when the murder occurred, but had grown up aware of it as part of a small town's memory of itself. Now it was front-page news again.

In the palliative care room of the Shean Manor, just opposite the wing where convicted killer John Dan MacLean was living out the rest of his already forgotten life – in a room he could see had he possessed the presence of mind to look through the window – another Manor resident had made a deathbed confession. Eighty-two-year-old Sandy MacArthur, Big Sandy as he was known, infamous brawler, bully, boozer and bootlegger, riddled with cancer and shrunken to less than a hundred pounds, had refused to see a priest but asked to speak to the police.

An RCMP officer was summoned by Rita MacDonald – who had just started her afternoon shift as on-duty nurse – for no other reason than to humour a dying old man. When Corporal Harry Noseworthy came out of MacArthur's room, he asked Rita over a cup of coffee if MacArthur was sane. Rita answered that he was quite lucid considering the amount of pain medication he was getting, adding that Big Sandy tried to save the health care system thousands of dollars by asking her to substitute Black Diamond rum for the morphine feed in his IV.

"He just confessed to killing a man sixty years ago," Corporal Noseworthy said.

"Jim Muise," Rita replied. A statement, not a question.

"You remember that?" the Mountie asked, getting a dark look from the thirty-three-year-old nurse. But her answer also told him he had just heard a murder confession, so with Rita as witness he returned to the sick man's room and recorded the words MacArthur gasped for only the second time in sixty years.

By the time Corporal Noseworthy returned to the RCMP office, the phone was ringing, *Shean Witness* flashing on the caller display. The nurse hadn't wasted any time letting David Cameron know about the confession.

"Hello," the Mountie said into the mouthpiece. "I don't suppose you're investigating the speeding ticket we issued to the mayor's wife last night?"

"I'm always interested in embarrassing His Worship, Harry, but I'm more interested in deathbed confessions. What can you tell me?"

———

While Corporal Noseworthy sent Arlene Jamison, the detachment secretary, into the dusty depths of the storage room filled with boxes of old files to search out the original police reports, David Cameron went down into the *Witness's* basement archives to dig out and read copies of the newspapers that dealt with the murder and trial.

One hand held the newspaper close to his face while the other groped about his desk, probing the paper-covered surface, pulling drawers open until he found the magnifying glass. With it, he studied the aged photograph.

Shoving the glass in his pocket and folding the paper under his arm, he left the office in search of professional help.

| 2 |

David Cameron parked his car across from Memorial Park watching the occupants of the scattered benches. Until a half decade ago, it had been a block of shabby buildings, some still barely open for business, others abandoned.

A fire, one of the *Witness*'s most spectacular front pages under David's editorship, had wiped out the piecemeal architecture, which no one had ever bothered to rebuild. The buildings' charred remnants were hauled to the local dump. Buildings with foundations, and those that had rotting wooden sills, were bulldozed to the ground, leaving a block-long gap like a missing tooth along Main Street.

Squatter grass grew over the rough graves of expired businesses until the day Dan Gillis got it in his head to pick up the garbage that was accumulating there, then push a rotary lawnmower over it all in an effort to imitate a lawn. His grooming gesture caught the attention of the Shean Legion, which was planning to replace its small and crumbling cenotaph with one large enough to accommodate the names of all the veterans who had served in the two World Wars and Korea, not just those who had been killed in action.

Memorial Park came into being the way most things in Shean seemed to happen, through a series of uncoordinated and unplanned actions. David Cameron understood that if there had been an organized effort to create a park on Main Street it would never have happened.

The empty lots that now formed Memorial Park had various owners. One or two lots had been vested to the town through unpaid taxes and absent owners, but most of the properties, he knew, still belonged to whoever held deeds to the buildings, whether they knew it or not. To legally create the park would have taken time, research, money, quit claims, deed transfers, lawyers, surveyors and the paying of close attention to the province's *Municipal Act*, in addition to meeting the demands of an endless litany of bureaucratic regulations. The Legion didn't ignore the rules of law; it just never occurred to anyone to look any deeper than the hiring of one of the town's bricklayers, and there were perhaps a hundred of those, products of various government retraining programs. A truckload of rock and sand was hauled from the beach, and the bricklayer used those to build a cairn in honour of the town's war dead.

The town council never raised the issue of property ownership at any of its meetings, although it did occur to David Cameron, reporter, that there were some questionable legal issues involved in creating the park. But no issue, he felt, superceded the fact that after almost a century the coal town of Shean, for fifty years dying from a terminal economy, now had a green patch in the middle of its dreary woes. Businesses on either side of the park, he observed, had applied a coat of paint or vinyl siding in an effort to look better beside the flowers and lawn, benches and bandstand of the park.

Bit by bit, the greenness of the Legion-sponsored Memorial Park crept over Main Street. The whole town looked better, "a well-laid out corpse instead of a clearly decaying one," *Witness* reporter Tim Donovan wrote at the time of the cenotaph dedication.

Murdock's Meat Market had been one of the businesses in that burnt block on Main Street, although David Cameron had never known the building as such. By the time he was growing up, Murdock's Meat Market was Tony the Turk's restaurant, a high school hangout selling burgers and fries, with pool tables and pinball machines in back. By the time he took over the *Witness* it was just another empty building, tattered plywood covering vandalized windows. Watching and remembering while he sat in his car across the street, David wondered if plywood had even been invented when Mr. Murdock had to cover the blood-stained remnants of his meat market's window back in '51.

On the night of what the town now called The Big Fire, the sound of flames tearing through that particular building was like the rattle of a machine gun as empty wine and rum bottles exploded inside. The building's last occupants had been men, permanent drunks and binge drinkers, who had sought shelter from wind, rain, wives and Mounties inside its broken walls, and it was from within those walls that someone's carelessly tossed cigarette started the fire that helped clean up the sorry block of buildings. Some of those men were now sitting on the park benches, scheming their next drink. Other benches were occupied by the unemployed or retired.

David got out of his car and walked across the street to one of the benches, taking a seat between Don Alex MacInnes and Ronald MacDonald, remembering that he had cracked a smile the first time he'd been introduced to the latter. The older man had seen through the smile, saw the image his name evoked in David's imagination. He then lectured the newspaper editor on the noble history of the MacDonalds and of the name Ronald, a variation of Ranald, Abraham to the largest clan in the Highlands of Scotland, an honourable name passed from generation to generation for centuries until it was trivialized by a chain of hamburger joints and its stupid gimmick of an even stupider clown. Ronald was a frequent writer of letters to the editor at the *Witness* trying to rally all the MacDonalds, Macdonalds and McDonalds of the town into a boycott of the fast food chain.

Easily done since no McDonald's franchise existed within sixty miles of Shean.

"Heard about Big Sandy's confession?" Don Alex asked David, causing the editor to wonder once again why he bothered to publish a newspaper at all.

"Yes. The store was right here, if I remember correctly."

"Murdock's? It was right here, all right," Don Alex confirmed.

"Nope," Ronald interjected. "Alex Joe's Clothes was right here. Murdock's would have been just to the right of here, over there."

"You're wrong there, Ronald. If Murdock's was still in business, we'd be sitting right in his ice room right here."

"You're wrong there, Don Alex…."

David sat and waited until the two men settled their geographical dispute, unable to place the exact location of the building himself though the fire had happened only a few years earlier. It was hard to believe so many buildings had been crammed, shoulder to shoulder, inside this seemingly tiny patch of green.

"Anyway, it was either here or there," Don Alex said finally, a compromise that Ronald's silence obviously accepted so that the conversation could return to its more interesting theme. "Will you be writing that up in your paper? The murder?"

David nodded the obvious answer.

"Going to interview the widow?"

The thought hadn't occurred to the editor of the *Witness*. "I'm not planning on it," he answered, his insides shuddering at the idea of the fallout that could come from that interview, since the widow of Big Sandy was his lifelong nemesis.

"What's the big news anyway?" Don Alex asked. "Those boys were going to Dorchester for something. It just would have taken longer if they hadn't got nailed for Muise's murder."

"They didn't do it, Don Alex. For the love of God Almighty, man, we can't go sticking people in jail just because they might commit a crime," Ronald responded.

"Tell me, what's the point of sticking poor old Sandy in jail now. The man is dying."

"Nobody's going to stick Big Sandy in jail, are they David?" Ronald asked rhetorically. "Good God, man, whether he killed somebody or not, he served his sentence. Look who he was married to. Imagine going on a drunk one weekend way back when and waking up the next morning next to that and her wearing your wedding ring. No wonder Big Sandy was so miserable all his life, but you'd think if he was going to kill anybody it would be … well never mind that unchristian thought. At least John Dan MacLean gets to clear his name."

"Oh, he'll be real happy to hear that, Ronald. Why don't you go up to the old folks home right now and tell him all about it," Don Alex replied.

David Cameron shook his head sadly, visited by the recurring regret that conversations like this were off the record. He'd had to unlearn several rules of journalism when he returned home to purchase the *Witness*, rules that had served him well with the *Toronto Star* but not in Shean, where being able to distinguish between the gossip at the Gulf of St. Lawrence Grill and the stories that could be printed in the *Witness* was a matter of life and near-death experiences. Facing the people he wrote about every morning at the Grill, he had the wisdom – some of it cultural understanding, some of it hard learned – to know what was a genuine news story and what was none of the paper's business. Writing a person's common nickname in the newspaper was one lesson he had learned the hard way.

David had printed a story about Johnny Petticoat donating his late mother's hospital bed to the Shean Manor. As it turned out, Johnny hadn't been donating it at all, as the picture in the newspaper proclaimed. He was returning it. David Cameron didn't find that out until the administrator of the manor phoned about the story in the *Witness*. The manor had loaned Johnny's mother the bed to make her last days at home easier on her and her family. Her last days lasted seven years. The editor and the nursing home administrator discussed the facts and decided to let Johnny Petticoat have his fifteen minutes of generosity. No correction was required.

It was the next phone call that brought a new understanding to David's journalism. Johnny Petticoat's baptismal record showed that he was christened John Alexander MacAdam, not Petticoat, which was a name he picked up in school when a picture of him as a one year old turned up in the classroom. In the picture he was wearing what looked like a girl's petticoat, and that constituted his second baptism. Although Johnny Petticoat had grown into his name, as comfortable as an old coat, he never expected for a second that the *Witness* would present him to the whole world *in print* as Johnny Petticoat and not as John Mac-Adam, Mr. John MacAdam, in fact. After all, he reminded David, donating a bed to the manor was no small thing. The *Witness* should have treated the story and him with more dignity. If it was the mayor making the donation, Johnny Petticoat demanded to know, would David have called him Donald MacNaughton or Donald the Bastard, the generational subtitle of that branch of the MacNaughton family tree? Familiar enough in Shean's kitchen talk, the mayor's nickname had never appeared in the pages of the *Witness*.

Following that experience, David banned the use of nicknames unless specifically cleared by the name's owner, prompting Tim Donovan to complain that the policy forced him to write an extra paragraph in order to explain to readers which of Shean's John MacDonalds he was talking about.

"Anyway, it's going to be a big wake," Ronald MacDonald noted. "Especially if Sandy dies just after the paper comes out and everybody finds out about the murder."

"Everybody seems to know already," David sighed.

"Not the same as reading it in the *Witness* though. That's one paper people'll be saving. They'll want to go to the wake and look at a murderer."

"If it wasn't for Big Sandy killing Jim Muise, Mrs. Big Sandy woulda had to go to the Employment Office to hire pallbearers," Don Alex said. "Now, of course, there'll be lots of volunteers. If it wasn't for my back…."

There were as many bad backs in Shean as there were bricklayers, men on the "burnt-out" pensions. Don Alex had had trouble with the concept of work for as long as anyone could recall, but he'd had to put in his weeks, sometimes months, every year at the highway garage until, after several efforts, he managed to convince provincial doctors on the Workman's Compensation Board that his back was so bad he could never be expected to work again. He was burnt-out, so with the help of the MLA at the time, he qualified for a pension. Being burnt-out, once an honourable profession in Shean, was, like nicknames, a vanishing reality. Government coffers were just too tightly controlled any more for younger men to make the case that they were too burnt-out to work. Don Alex was reminded of his back every time there was a danger he would be asked to use it. "At least it's spring. They won't have to put Sandy in that warehouse up there. They can put him straight in the ground."

"The crypt, you mean?" Ronald asked, knowing what Don Alex meant. "You never had to dig a grave in winter or you won't be so…."

"My back…." Don Alex began to explain.

"Your pension, you mean. Your back never seems to bother you if you have to dig your car out of the driveway to get to a game at the arena," Ronald said.

"You don't know…."

"I know I've seen you walk home with a two-four of Keith's under each arm and one in each hand and never so much as wince."

"What about the crypt?" David asked, interested in Ronald's version of where bodies in coffins were stored from frost until thaw.

"Well the crypt's a damned good thing. In the winter the priest holds all the services, even the graveside service, in the church and then the undertaker and the pallbearers bring the coffin to the crypt. In the spring, when there's a thaw, they get the backhoe and dig as many graves as they need and bury everyone who died during the winter. The family can be there or not, depends on themselves, but the dead have already had a full burial service so there's really no need for the family to be there, going through it all again. It's a damned sight more civilized than making the family stand in the graveyard in the middle of winter listening to frozen clots of dirt falling on their loved one."

"Storage barns and backhoes!" snarled Don Alex. "That's civilized, is it, Mr. MacDonald? There was a time when the people who cared about the people who died dug their graves for them. Now they're contracted out to people who dig foundations for houses. Nothing's been the same around here since they opened that geezley funeral home. But you're right about one thing – Big Sandy is going to have the biggest wake in Shean since they turned the old high school into the funeral home."

David interrupted the argument by producing the newspaper and magnifying glass.

"I wonder if you gentlemen could help me with something related to the story. This is the *Witness*'s story the issue after the murder. Could you look through the crowd there and tell me if there's anyone you recognize?" He passed the paper and glass to Ronald, who took them, arranging the glass for maximum effect, all the while apologizing, "My eyes aren't what they once were, David, so I probably won't recog ... well look at the bastard! It's just like they say in the movies: the criminal always returns to the scene of the crime. Big Sandy right there," he said covering a face with his finger.

"Let me see, let me see," Don Alex insisted, nodding his concurrence immediately upon seeing Big Sandy's much younger face. With the two confirmations, David could go ahead and blow up the face in the picture, superimposing it over the crime scene photo, and perhaps if Big Sandy died before deadline, a photo of the funeral.

"I guess he couldn't live with what he had done any longer," David Cameron observed.

"Bullshit!" spat Ronald MacDonald. "If Big Sandy could live with that witch he's been married to for forever, he could live with anything. My guess is he couldn't wait to tell people that it was him who killed Jim Muise. He was a bully and a braggart. He just didn't want to suffer the consequences."

| 3 |

Sitting at her station in the late evening quiet, Rita MacDonald thought about Corporal Noseworthy and the murder confession. She had gone with him into the room where the shrunken residue of Big Sandy MacArthur, terrorizer of her childhood town, lucidly repeated himself. But it wasn't that moment itself occupying her thoughts; it was the moment that followed.

Once Corporal Noseworthy had left with Big Sandy's confession and her signed confirmation, she had gone to the phone and called *The Shean Witness* and asked for David Cameron, telling him what had happened.

What had possessed her to do that?

Rita sloshed the cooling tea around in her cup, meditating upon the question. Between her time nursing at the Shean Manor and her earlier work at hospitals in Ontario, Alberta and Florida, she has been a silent, professional witness to several venial and mortal confessions, patients begging forgiveness of God or of a wife or a child, without ever sharing with anyone what she'd heard or overheard. So why now?

You're from Shean, girl, you know a good story when you hear one, she teased herself, but there had been other stories since her job at the Manor began. The Manor's residents had once been the familiar adults of her youth and were now aged and for the most part adrift from the lives they had lived, wandering the corridors or strapped into wheelchairs, but their unpredictable antics were enough to keep the staff laughing or exasperated. Funny or sad, those stories were left behind at the end of their shift, never turning the residents into local gossip. And certainly never in the palliative care room, where Big Sandy lay dying, had she or any other Manor employee betrayed the end-of-life rantings, ravings or remorse of those they helped to die as peacefully as possible.

The phone call, she acknowledged, had not been made to *The Shean Witness* itself but to its editor, David Cameron. *Just trying to squirrel away nuts for the winter*, she thought, laughing at her pun.

There weren't many of his and her generation still in Shean, trapped there by circumstances or fear, and David Cameron was definitely the best of a meager lot of males. She suspected that if the town were full of eligible men David Cameron would still be the best of them, and she had been wondering for some time how to get past the nodding familiarity that small towns incubate.

Since David Cameron had been leaving high school as Rita was entering it, they had never really met, so Big Sandy's confession felt like a good place to start. She believed she hadn't violated any ethical considerations since the story was bound to be in the local newspaper as soon as David Cameron called for the weekly RCMP update on crimes and charges.

Rita was certain it wasn't loneliness she felt, not the oh-poor-me country and western music kind of loneliness that dominated Saturday night in Legion, say, but working in the Shean Manor felt very much like she was working in the middle of her own inevitable fate. The company of someone like David Cameron would be a welcome distraction and today's phone call had been bread cast on the waters, a gesture supposed to return buttered with rewards for a good deed done. Like a phone call back....

The clock, reminding her of her rounds, rescued her from herself. Rita buttered a loaf of toast, steeped a gallon of tea, arranged medications and began rolling the mobile medicine cabinet from room to room. Big Sandy's palliative care room was her final call, where she found the large form of Mrs. Big Sandy seated in a chair beside her husband's bed, slightly slumped.

Stepping to the side of Sandy's bed, Rita hooked a new intravenous bag to the pole, checked the flow, took Sandy's pulse and as she fixed the bedclothes and pillow around him sneaked a glance at Mrs. Big Sandy. It was a glance conditioned since childhood, the common property of every child whose parents put them to bed at night with threats of giving misbehaving children away to Mrs. Big Sandy. By the time children grew big enough to stop believing in Santa Claus and witches and even Mrs. Big Sandy's evil eye, they learned to fear her tongue, which had once cursed a priest in the middle of mass because she thought his sermon was about her. The poor man had been speaking about Mary Magdalene.

Rita's surreptitious glance wasn't prepared for the slightly slouching figure of Mrs. Big Sandy with rosary beads slowly passing through her fingers.

Rita left the room quietly, returning a moment later with a cup of tea, placing it on the nightstand beside Sandy's bed, drawing Mrs. Big Sandy's attention to it. The old woman took a moment to comprehend the cup and for whom it was intended but when she did, asked, "Will you have one with me?"

Nervously Rita returned from the tea tray with a cup of her own and sat on the bedside's other chair, staring at Big Sandy MacArthur, trying to think of something to say that would not ignite his wife's legendary temper. No thoughts came because Rita was growing uncomfortably conscious of being a bug under the microscope of Mrs. Big Sandy's scrutinizing stare.

"You're one of Ronald MacDonald's, aren't you?" Mrs. Big Sandy said at last.

"Yes, he's my father," Rita answered.

"I thought so. Same nose. Not so much of it but the same nose. Your great-grandfather had that nose too."

"I never knew him," Rita said.

"I remember him. I was just a little girl, four or five, running home from church. It was Easter Sunday. I tripped and fell into a mud puddle. It was your great grandfather picked me up and took out a very white handkerchief, which was a surprise because coal miners didn't have white handkerchiefs, just those snot-filled polka dot things. It was his Sunday one, I suppose, and he ruined it trying to wipe the mud off my Easter coat. He was killed a few weeks later but he was a nice man. Can't say the same for your grandfather or your father."

This subject wasn't anywhere Rita wanted to go and yet her tea had barely been touched and Mrs. Big Sandy was only now taking her first sip. The phone ringing out at the nurse's station would have been a miracle, but the silence filled corridors and swelled monstrously in Big Sandy MacArthur's room. If David Cameron was ever going to enter her life this would be the right moment.

Rita sipped her tea, quietly gluttonous in her effort to empty the cup and bring the discomfort to an end, her mind trying not to think about what her father's or grandfather's history with Mrs. Big Sandy might be, the effort to avoid the thought sending a montage of X-rated cartoon images to tickle her mind, bringing on a church-urge to laugh at this most inappropriate, and probably dangerous, moment. She buried the urge in a coughing fit.

"Down the wrong pipe," she rasped once she had refocused her forces, rising professionally to go about her duties.

"I suppose it will be in the paper?"

"What will be?" Rita asked, blushing with hypocrisy.

"Sandy's silly confession to that Mountie, I suppose it will be in the paper. That David Cameron just can't wait to put this piece of gossip in that precious little rag of his! If he does, I've got a good mind to go down there to that office and strangle the little shit. What does a town like this need a newspaper for anyway? I'd like to see one goddamned story in that roll of toilet paper that everybody in town didn't already know, but stupid people still pay good money to make that greedy little bastard rich. I never heard of anything so stupid in my life. Well if one word about Sandy gets in that newspaper I'll throw that son-of-a-whore through a plate glass window and see how he likes it.

"I was there you know! I was there when Sandy threw Jim Muise through Murdock's window. He was defending my honour, you know. I was going to defend myself when that drunk little bastard called me Sandy's Candy. 'Here comes Sandy and his Candy and she's just dandy,' he was singing and when you live in little town like this, and I mean little in every way you can think, then a name like that doesn't take long to stick, does it? Sandy's Candy indeed! But Sandy stopped me, saying he better handle it because I'd only kill him. Sandy would've slapped him or something but Jim got even stupider and took a swing at Sandy. My husband had to defend himself, didn't he? He picked Jim up by the shirtfront and lifted him like a bag of marshmallows and meant to hold him up against the window and shake the shit out of him but the window shattered as soon as Jim's back hit it and Sandy dropped him to get out of the way of the falling glass and when it was over we went to the window to help Jim out but he was bubbling blood out of his throat. Then he was dead. You could see that, so there was no sense in staying round because Sandy would be going to prison even though it was an accident. Taught Mr. Muise to call me Sandy's Candy though, didn't it? But now what Sandy did will be all over the goddamn newspaper and I'm going to kill that little Cameron boy. I've wanted to kill him since he was a kid. He shot me once, you know!"

Rita thought of Benny Ryan and John Dan MacLean and the years they had spent in prison but felt this wasn't the time for a discussion on justice and injustice. She just tried to absorb what she had heard, especially what she had heard at the very end of Mrs. Big Sandy's tirade because it seemed to have come to an end now, the woman's interest shifting back to her husband. Mrs. Big Sandy's back was turned to the nurse but her shoulders heaved with anger while she tried to calm herself. Rita glided quiet as the candle-carrying Florence Nightingale from the room to tend to her other sleeping or sleepless patients.

At midnight, Rita MacDonald left the silent seniors' complex and wound down from her shift as she usually did, by driving through Shean. Main Street was lit now by a regiment of new street lamps, part of the town's revitalization vision. This was the same Main Street on which Rita spent a large part of her youth, coming to town from the family's farm every evening she could once her breasts began to assert themselves, hinting at all sorts of other hormonal mysteries. She fought a lot with her father in those days about the street where she and her friends walked and waited for some boys in a car to stop and give them a ride or, failing that, hold an all-gender gathering on a street corner or in the Gulf of St. Lawrence Grill. It was on this street, or because of it, that she and her friends fumbled their way toward sexual awareness. Main Street had looked nothing like it now did, though, brightly blooming in the night.

Passing the newspaper office, she noted there was one lighted desk, David Cameron working on his murder story, she guessed. If she had thought to make coffee before leaving work she would knock on the door and invite herself in, maybe even raise the shooting Mrs. Big Sandy had accused him of, but armed with neither bribe nor purpose, she possessed less courage. What she was not about to raise any time soon were the details of the murder that Mrs. Big Sandy had revealed in the midst of her passionate rant against David Cameron and the *Witness*. David Cameron was desirable but not worth dying for.

Rita's Toyota turned down Beach Road following her head-lights tunnelling through the darkness, revealing nothing until she rolled to a stop at the end of the parking lot. The white tumble of ocean began to play with her car lights, rolls of foamy waves washing ashore, white suds of ocean caught by the wind and lifted up onto the parking lot, onto her car. With more ener-gy, and wearing something warmer than her uniform, she would go walking along the beach, but not tonight. A few moments of watching and she started the car and drove back up to the town.

It was seven miles to her father's farm, her family's farm for about two hundred years, kept in production even after the men in the family, her great grandfather, her grandfather and then her father, started working in the coal mines to earn what money the farm didn't. It was past one o'clock when she turned up the long driveway. The light was on in the livingroom, which now served as her father's study. That man and his Internet! She was a mix of approval and apprehension about the way he had taken to being online. She bought the computer to keep in email contact with her nursing friends working in London or Saudi Arabia or somewhere else in the world that wasn't Shean; occasionally she explored online advertisements for nursing jobs without ever filling out an application. She hadn't become a nurse just to heal people. She became a nurse to travel.

To interest her father, recovering from the stroke that brought her home from Florida, she showed him how to play solitaire on the computer, which he rejected, preferring to play at the kitchen table as he had done since boyhood. "Now if that darn machine could play cribbage...." Rita found an online crib-bage club and introduced her father to it and the first game he played was against a man in Sweden. To date he had beaten crib players in sixty-one different countries and now planned to have someone in every country in the world "pegging for mercy," as he described it. On the wall was a map of the world with victory pins colourfully stuck in every conquered country.

Once he gained keyboard-and-mouse confidence her father began entering other areas of the Internet, including chat rooms, venturing further and further afield while sitting at his living-room table. He had always been interested in the things around him, especially things that gave him a new expertise with which to unsettle his friends, and the Internet was one of those new things. He chatted, he surfed and he worked at his own online project, the Lose-A-Quarter-Pounder-A-Day Club, trying to rally the MacDonalds of the world into a global boycott of Mc-Donald's restaurants. He had learned about fellow MacDonald clansmen who had been sued by McDonald's for simply using their names on their businesses. The clan was clearly under as-sault from the multinational corporation so Ronald MacDon-ald created a blog to promote his boycott and to enlist as many MacDonalds as he could to his cause.

Rita made enough noise coming into the kitchen to alert even her slightly hearing impaired father that she was home and would be coming into the livingroom in a moment. She didn't know where he spent all the time he did spend online, but if pictures of naked women were involved she'd really rather not know.

"Hi Dad," she said, walking up behind him, placing her hands on his shoulders and bending to see the screen.

"I've just been talking to this guy, Mark MacDonald from California, who's been rethinking McDonald's ever since he began reading the stuff on my blog. Three little kids, that's his problem. How do you get a three year old to boycott McDon-ald's when she thinks that's where birthday parties come from? I told him to stop having kids if they're just going to grow up to think like that. How are you, honey?"

"Fine," Rita said, turning her head sideways to study her father's nose as he continued to type with two fingers.

"Hear about Big Sandy?"

"Yeah, Dad, I heard. I'm going to bed. Don't stay up too late."

At the bottom of the stairs she paused, reflected for a moment then returned to the dining room and her father.

"Dad, did anybody ever shoot Mrs. Big Sandy?" Her father paused, confused by the interruption. "Someone said something to that effect tonight and I had never heard anything about it. Do you remember that, or did it even happen?"

Ronald MacDonald's expression began to change, a hint of a smile hovering as he rummaged through his storehouse of small town tales, then bloomed. "For the love of Jesus, I haven't thought about that in years. Yes, somebody did. Lived to tell about it, too. I got the story from Big Sandy himself at the tavern one afternoon. The afternoon after it happened, actually.

"Apparently Sandy and the wife were having breakfast, Sandy at the table scoffing down his bacon and eggs and Mrs. Big Sandy standing with her back to the stove, having her tea. Suddenly she screams and throws her cup up in the air and grabs her arse and when she pulls her hand away there's blood. First they thought she was burnt but that wouldn't bring blood, then maybe a wasp but when she looks out the window she sees these kids on the slag piles with a gun and it dawns on her.

"'I've been shot!' she screams and tears out the door after those kids like she's running the four-minute mile. Sandy checks out the scene of the crime and what he finds, what he thinks at the time, is probably what happened. They had a .22, those boys, shooting at rats or something because everybody used the old mine tailings for a dump so there were plenty of mine rats that came to surface when the mines closed. They were being better fed than half the families because of the garbage. What Sandy figured was that a stray bullet came through the side of the house – he found a small hole in a window sill – hit the cast-iron frying pan and ricocheted into Mrs. Big Sandy's arse. By this time it would have lost all its power, probably didn't do any more damage than a BB, but that didn't matter. Mrs. Big Sandy had been shot and God help the little bastard who fired the gun.

"Big Sandy was just roaring when he was telling that story, tears rolling down his face," Ronald said, losing himself in gales of laughter so fresh and pure that Rita was drawn into the joy of it, joining it with her own melodic laughter. "They never got along after that," Ronald added when the humour had subsided.

"Who?"

"Those boys, Donald MacNaughton and David Cameron. They were what, twelve maybe, best friends, inseparable actually, but they never liked each other much after that, even though they ran in the same circle of friends. They're the mayor and the newspaper editor now. I think what probably drove them apart was that the Mounties confiscated the .22. It was Donald the Bastard's gun but David Cameron was the one who fired the shot and when Mrs. Big Sandy came after them, she chased David to his door; she never got her hands on him, fortunately for him. So she reported the shooting to the Mounties and they came to the Cameron house and took the gun away. Never gave it back to either of them."

| 4 |

Mrs. Big Sandy left the Shean Manor at four thirty in the morning, an hour after her husband of sixty some years had passed away. Still swaddled inside a cocoon of numbness that had enclosed her since the long-ago morning they learned about his cancer, she barely noticed the chilly emptiness of the town at this hour. By the time she had coaxed Sandy into seeing the doctor it had already been too late; he was being devoured alive. Now he was gone. Sometime soon she was going to have to deal with that fact, but not tonight. She just wanted to go home to a large pot of tea and sit and stall time, not think at all.

Reaching Main Street, the town made its presence felt to her, drawing Mrs. Big Sandy's attention to the new street lamps stretching the length of the town like an amber necklace. It made her think of the movies she used to go to where those silly actors and actresses danced and sang on the sidewalk, swinging around lamp posts just like these. "Shean is getting too big for its britches" is what her mother would have said.

Tourism was the future, that's what they all said. First the street lights and a new sidewalk and even a town clock in the park, and now the silly creatures who ran the place, Donald the Bastard and his bunch, were talking about taking the mountains of black and grey mine tailings from another time in Shean's history and burying them under clay and mud and grass next summer. "Over my dead body," Sandy had told the Bastard right to his face, and now Sandy was a dead body.

"Over my dead body now," she shouted into the silent night. She was now the sole owner of the old mine site land.

Strung gaily in its new streetlights, Shean felt like a different world, reminding her of those people who claimed they had died for a minute and went through a tunnel toward a bright light. She stopped and looked behind her and ahead, and found herself amazed that these new street lamps had been in the town for almost a year and every light as far as she could see was still lit. One of these nights, she was certain, her wishful prediction would come true and some bastard of a kid would throw a rock at one of those lights and then people would see how much the town was changing.

There was no bright light at the end of the amber tunnel that was Main Street. Mrs. Big Sandy knew that. At the end of the new sidewalk that reached the edge of the town she stepped onto the unlit shoulder of the road that was the beginning of the path that led to her home. In shadowed moments like these their old, turreted house loomed castle-like. Gloomy and occupied by the very people other people love to gossip about, it was easy to understand why children thought it was haunted. At least it kept the little bastards away, she thought.

Inside, Mrs. Big Sandy turned on the propane stove under a kettle of water and changed out of her clothes into her flannel nightdress. By the light seeping into the bedroom from the hallway she sat before the bureau mirror and braided her life-long length of hair. She liked her face in the dark glass, a charcoal drawing of light and deep lines hinting at a person of character. Under the starkness of the bedroom's overhead light her face was just old.

In the kitchen the tea roiled in its glass pot. Most people didn't like boiled tea but it was all she and Sandy ever drank, fresh handfuls of loose tea added to the old leaves, a splash of milk added to the cup to turn the black tea a dark chocolate. The tea the nurse had brought to her tonight was pitiful, weak as a kitten, but the poor dear meant well. Wallace MacDonald's great-granddaughter! Funny how a face is passed down through the generations. His was one of the few faces from her childhood that stood out sharp as a photograph, although their knowledge of each other was comprised of a few moments standing beside a mud puddle, the little girl crying, the man consoling, his white handkerchief, stiff with starch, rubbing away the tears as he said, "There! There's that pretty face again. Now let's see what we can do about your lovely coat."

There was nothing he could do about the coat but he was right. It was lovely, navy blue with white trim and shiny brass buttons, being worn for the first time to Easter mass. It was ruined and her angry mother threw it in the wringer washer where it shrunk and matted to a secondhand texture and became her school coat. It was no longer lovely and no one ever again mentioned her pretty face. About that Wallace MacDonald had been more kind than right, she knew, and just two weeks later, when a section of the mine roof fell, killing him, she had cried for the kind man.

Wallace MacDonald's children grew up and she always said hello to them although they hardly knew who she was. When one of those children, Angus, had a son he called Ronald, a boy with a face exactly like his grandfather's, defined by a significant nose, she always smiled at him on the street or said hello, but by then she was a big-boned woman who had been styled Mrs. Big Sandy by the town and people were frightened of her. Children yelled her name or called her names from behind the safety of buildings or a distance of street she couldn't cover fast enough to catch them. The anger they instilled in her she vented on anyone within hearing distance, yelling and threatening while her looming presence intimidated them all until she was given wide berth whenever people saw her coming.

And among the teasing youngsters was the familiar face of Wallace MacDonald, inherited now by his grandson, a tormentor of older women. She cursed him along with the others. Ronald's daughter, though, had inherited the kindness of her great-grandfather. When she turned her back to the nurse earlier it was to hide the tears her tirade against the newspaperman had unsuccessfully tried to suppress. She found it strangely consoling that these tears, the first to fall since her Easter Sunday fall decades ago, came in the presence of Wallace MacDonald's great-granddaughter, but when she turned to explain, the nurse was gone.

When the nurse, a different one, lifted the sheet up over Sandy's head in the silence of a room no longer humming with monitors and other life-measuring machines, Mrs. Big Sandy sat alone in numb acceptance of her widowhood for an hour, then rose and left the Manor's palliative care room.

A knock on the door brought Mrs. Big Sandy back from her thoughts to the realization that dawn was spreading across Shean. It was six thirty in the morning.

If that's some stupid bastard wanting to buy a bottle, Mrs. Big Sandy thought as she walked to the door ready to do battle, but when she opened it was surprised and pissed off to see two unexpected guests.

"Good morning, Mrs. MacArthur," Mayor Donald Mac-Naughton said. "I heard about your loss and I wanted to express my sympathies. And this is C.J.M. Lord. I don't believe you've met, but I wonder if we could have a word with you?"

| 5 |

Big Sandy's funeral filled the church and the front page of the *Shean Witness*. The pews brimmed with a Christian audience more curious than prayerful, leaving for those left standing at the back of the church only the front row pews usually reserved for family. No one ventured toward them, not even when the black-clad bulk of Mrs. Big Sandy followed her husband's coffin down the centre aisle, her lone figure quietly drawing Rita MacDonald from her place in a pew beside her father to walk to the widow's side, offering her arm. Mrs. Big Sandy clasped it.

Father Eddie Walker's eulogy skirted the facts of Big Sandy's life to dwell upon the historic significance of his passing. The MacArthurs, he reminded his congregation, were among the first families to settle the land that became Shean, their original land grant encompassing most of what became the town. When coal was unearthed in mind-boggling seams that seemed to run forever under the sea, the family grew wealthy selling off building lots, but keeping hundreds of acres adjacent to the mine works and collecting a royalty for allowing mine waste to be dumped on their property. It had financed the largest house in Shean.

It took a couple of generations for the fortunes of the family, like the fortunes of Shean, to falter and fade, and with the passing of Big Sandy the MacArthur line drew to an end, he and Mrs. Big Sandy not having been blessed with children. This death was an historic loss to the community.

The priest left it to his parishioners to fill in the blanks: how the century-old house peeled away its paint to become a weathered memory of itself. How the family's curiously indifferent attachment to the land would not allow them to sell what remained of it, yet allowed untold tons of tailings to be spread across the hundreds of MacArthur acres. After the mines closed, they allowed much of their land to become the town dump in exchange for an annual stipend. The priest avoided addressing how the family business branched out to involve the selling of liquor, the proprietors drinking more than was profitable, or how the house became surrounded with derelict cars and trucks that someone in the family thought could be fixed up and sold.

The family business may have branched out but the family itself didn't, until all that was left was one male heir to the clay, slag and ash domain. And now he was gone, leaving his widow the family legacy.

David Cameron scribbled atmosphere notes during the funeral ceremony and returned to his office to write a story whose text and reprinted sixty-year-old photographs took up most of the front page. A couple of hundred words in a small shaded box informed readers that Mayor Donald MacNaughton had been hospitalized with a broken jaw following a single vehicle accident.

"You're sure no liquor was involved?" Cameron had asked Corporal Noseworthy, but blood tests at the hospital where McNaughton had driven himself exonerated the mayor, making the story a human interest filler instead of the local political exposé Cameron would have enjoyed reporting.

With the paper out on the newsstands, David Cameron drove over Main Street in a drizzling rain past the empty park, parking in front of the Gulf Grill. Inside, heads at the counter and in the booths were buried in the *Witness*, with its front-page photograph of the original crime scene, including an inserted blow-up showing Sandy's presence at the scene, and another grainy photograph, this one of the victim, Jim Muise. Around those pictures, Cameron's story narrated the facts while inside the paper his editorial used this example of belated justice to argue against the country ever restoring capital punishment, pointing out that two innocent men might have been executed.

Slipping onto a counter stool beside Ronald, with Don Alex reading the paper over his friend's shoulder, David asked what was new. Don Alex began quoting to him from the *Witness*'s front page with "Did you know..." followed by some tidbit from the town's most popular current topic. Obviously Don Alex didn't read bylines, since David's name appeared at the top of the story.

Eavesdropping on the other tables it was clear to David that the jury was still out on Big Sandy's crime, part of the debate being whether it should have been left in the past where it belonged, or brought up now in the newspapers, giving the town a bad name. "The story was in the *Herald* too, you know, not just this paper that nobody reads but ourselves. That means everybody in the province thinks we're just a den of thieves and murderers...."

"Just to change the subject there, David, do you know what surveyors were doing in the park this morning?" Ronald MacDonald asked.

"Wasn't aware they were there," David replied.

"Well I asked them and the head guy says 'surveying,' saying the word like it's none of my business," Ronald answered.

"And was it?" asked Don Alex.

"It's our park, isn't it? Of course it's my business, isn't that right, David?"

"I suppose it is, being a public park, but I don't know anything about surveying it."

"Will you be looking into it?"

"The paper doesn't have the resources to be chasing after every question anybody asks, Ronald."

"Then I'll find out for you. I memorized the name of the survey company and tonight I'll search the World Wide Web and see what I can find out. Let you know tomorrow," Ronald replied importantly. His web findings occasionally provided David with information that he was actually able to use from time to time in the newspaper.

"You and that damn World Wide Web," Don Alex sneered. "The way you talk you'd think it was the greatest thing since fermented hops. I seen it at my sister's, her son's got one of them there World Wide Web things, and there's nothing on it but stupid games. A man your age..."

"Don Alex, I could show you things on the World Wide Web that would make you think you wasted your whole married life. Not just games there, my friend. There's everything on it from politics to girls with dicks, if you'll pardon my Gaelic."

"What in the name of the good Lord is that man going on about, David? Tell me, is this Web thing stupid or what?"

"David's own newspaper is on the World Wide Web, Don Alex. That's where I read it last night before you even got a chance to read this copy without having to pay for it again."

"And did you pay David for reading it last night?" Alex Dan asked.

"I'm going to pay for his coffee so it's the same thing, and besides I sometimes work for the *Witness*, isn't that right, David?"

"That's right," David answered, drinking from the cup he'd paid for when Cheryl placed it in front of him earlier.

"So my next assignment is finding out about those surveyors, is it?"

"Yes, let me know what you find out." David drained his cup and, lifting himself from the stool to leave, opened the door just as Donald MacNaughton was reaching for the outside knob. The town's two combatants stood staring at each other.

"Mr. Mayor," David said. His acknowledgement was met with a slight and very gentle nodding of MacNaughton's immobilized head, jaw wired shut. "A shame something like that has to happen to a politician, Donald. Tends to leave them disarmed, don't you find? Cheryl," the editor called, "fix the mayor the toughest steak in the freezer and send the bill to the paper."

Leaving MacNaughton to snarl inarticulate sounds through his wired teeth, David returned to the office.

| 6 |

Rita MacDonald, wondering why she had come, sat at the table in Mrs. Big Sandy's large kitchen while the old woman went about making tea. On her way to her afternoon shift she left home early and found herself pulling into the MacArthur driveway with no idea whether she would be welcomed or wanted. Something in her hoped vaguely that a chill would meet her at the door, drive her back to her car and away from the draw she felt toward this strange old woman, now utterly alone.

"I'm sorry I didn't bake anything," Mrs. Big Sandy said, placing a cup of dark tea in front of her guest, "but I haven't baked a damned thing since my grandmother died about a thousand years ago. I cook. I don't bake nothing, nothing but biscuits that is, but she had the gift though, and not just for baking. For the teacups, too. She could read, you know."

"Tea leaves?"

"Yes. I don't remember the recipes she tried to teach me but I remember the leaves."

"You read tea leaves?" Rita asked.

"Not any more. Not much anyway. I used to read for people a long, long time ago but all they wanted to hear about was the good things that was going to happen to them. Poor fools thought they had a future but most of those women, mostly it was women wanted to know, well I could take you around this town and point at this door or that door and you tell me if they ever had any future, a pathetic bunch, the lot of them. Probably all dead now and still waiting for a future to find them."

Mrs. Big Sandy lifted her own cup from the counter and sat in the chair across from Rita, waiting.

"I just wanted to see how you were doing," Rita explained, feeling guilty simply because the woman was suspicious of her visit, expecting the nurse to get to the point sometime soon with whatever request or threat had brought her here. "You've lost someone you love, the man you lived with for the past ... how long?"

"A lot more years than you lived, dearie, but don't go asking me to cry for Sandy. I'll be following him down that hole soon enough, but since you ask, I'm just fine. Biggest difference is that I'm talking to myself at breakfast now but I probably always was. Sandy's grunts and snorts didn't amount to a lot of talking but he was there. Now he's not. I can't spend whatever time I have being a weeping or merry widow. I buried him. You were there. You saw. So I'm just fine, thank you very much."

Rita, shaken by the harshness of Mrs. Big Sandy's mourning, regretted whatever impelled her to come here so she sipped hurriedly at the hot tea in her cup, scanning the kitchen as she did so.

The external tiredness of the large house had seeped inside, shaping itself into cracked plaster and dust and dishes stacked in the sink or enclosed in an exceptionally beautiful china cabinet. The dishes in the cabinet probably hadn't been out in the fresh air in the past fifty years. Stacks of magazines and newspapers on chairs, unopened mail piling day by day at the end of the counter, a wall clock whose battery hadn't been changed since it died at 1:29 A.M. or P.M. at some distant date in the past. She speculated that the rest of the rooms would keep the same themes, stacks of this or that climbing the walls, dust, cracks and flashes of elegance.

Rising, she walked to the china cabinet, examining through the glass doors the collection of platters and cups and saucers, glasses that were convincingly crystal. "These are beautiful," she said aloud.

"Dust collectors, you mean. No difference if it cost a hundred dollars from England or fifty cents for a tin cup from the Co-op, they're paid the same to collect dust. Just goes to show you somebody thought they were somebody, if you ask me. Somebody dead."

"Oh, they really are beautiful. Probably rare. I bet this house is full of nice furnishing like this," Rita replied, rubbing a small mahogany table that held a broken lava lamp and a lobster-claw ashtray. "Do you think … I mean would it be possible for you to give me a tour of it sometime?"

"No, I'm not going traipsing up and down stairs I haven't been on since Jesus was a boy scout, but you're welcome to get lost on your own. Feel free. Go ahead."

"Oh no, I didn't mean right now, but thank you. Some day I'll take you up on that invitation." She noticed a clot of loose leaves at the bottom of her empty cup and placed it on the table, followed by a glance at her watch. "I need to be going, Mrs. MacArthur. My shift starts in twenty minutes. Thank you for the tea." She picked her cup back up and stared into it. "If I came back some other time, when I have more time, would you read my cup for me?"

"I don't see a lot of pretty things in the leaves and I don't pretend to see them like the others do. To hear some of the women who read the leaves or the cards you'd think everyone who came to them was going to wind up living in the same house, married to the same handsome man spending the same lottery money, their futures sound so much alike. 'You're going to take a trip and go over water.' Anybody who lives on an island like we do fits that one. And it's the same with the rest of their predictions, the love, the money … the fools. You come by any time and I'll read your leaves."

Rita sat in her car, hand gripping the key in the ignition, wondering why she had arranged for herself a need to return. Tea leaves! She found herself growing curious about what the old woman might see – not that she'd actually see anything, Rita didn't believe that, but she was curious what the old woman might imagine for Rita. She thought about the fact that the cup is empty when people want to peek into their futures. When their cup runneth over people don't think about tea leaves at the bottom and a promise of something more. It had been a while since her own cup had runneth over, Rita thought as she turned the key in the ignition.

"Listen to me, David." The phone call woke the editor past midnight, and Ronald MacDonald's voice rambled on as if it was a natural time to be disturbing people. "Remember when I told you this afternoon about the surveyors and you assigned me to learn more? Well I just got offline. I looked up the survey company first but there wasn't anything there but the company name, Gregor Surveying, and how to get in touch with them. They're from Halifax, you know. What's wrong with our own local surveyors, I ask you? So since they were surveying the park I went to the link to the province's land registrations and the park isn't even owned by the town, did you know that?"

"Yes I knew that," David said. "Can this wait until morning?"

"Did you know the park's made up of a bunch of lots that used to belong to different people? Well they're not belonging to many different people now, I'll tell you that. I went and looked and three of those lots belong to Sylvester MacNaughton, the mayor's own brother, and when did he get his hands on them? I'll tell you when, over the past three months, that's when. Very quiet if you ask me, and those other lots in the park, that's what they were surveying, that's my guess. What's going on, David? Nobody can own the park, can they? Doesn't the town have squatters' rights or something? The whole town's been squatting there for a few years now but it looks like the MacNaughtons have other plans for it. Can they just take that land and not tell anybody?"

"Some of the land's vested to the town through unpaid taxes," David answered. "We'll need to find out what lots those are and what lots Sylvester has deeds to, if that's what's happening." David's tone indicated mild interest while his radar went up. If Ronald was right, and Ronald at his late age seemed to have developed a savant's mastery of the Internet, manoeuvring his way through the virtual terrain the way he once picked and shovelled his way through Shean mines, then there might be a story here. "I'll look into it tomorrow, Ronald. Good night."

Ronald was still listening to the dial tone when a voice spoke behind him. "Who was that on the phone?"

"Oh just David Cameron with an assignment."

"What kind of assignment, Dad?"

"Land dealings. The MacNaughtons scheming again, that's my guess. How was your shift, girl?"

"Fine. I..." Her father waited for her next word but Rita dismissed it with a shake of her head. She thought she was going to tell him about her visit with Mrs. Big Sandy but she grew afraid it might sound like gossip. She kept the experience to herself. "Night, Dad," she ended, walking to his chair to give her father a kiss on the forehead before going up to her room.

| 7 |

David Cameron and Tim Donovan were seated at the editor's desk dividing up the week's stories for the next issue of *The Shean Witness*. When they had settled on the community's coverage, David gave Tim one final assignment.

"I want you to go to the town hall, registry of deeds, and take a look at those lots that make up the park. Tell me what you find."

"What am I looking for?"

"Later. I just want you to look and report back to me," David said. Tim studied his editor for a moment, shrugged and walked back to his own desk. David could sense a questioning bordering on contempt in the young reporter.

Tim Donovan's introduction to journalism had been as a student working summers at the *Witness* but his inspiration had been David Cameron, a former *Witness* reporter who went on to become an award-winning journalist with the *Toronto Star*, the largest paper in Canada. After finishing a journalism degree at King's College, Tim came back to the *Witness* for the experience before moving on. In his first year there the paper's former owner sold it to David Cameron. It was a confusing opportunity for Tim, to be able to work under his idol while wondering why he had walked away from the *Star* to edit a small town rag like the *Witness*.

———

David watched the twenty-four-year-old reporter shoulder his camera bag and leave the building, presumably to go to the town hall and get his mysterious assignment behind him. He slid open the bottom drawer of his desk and glanced down at the plaque resting on top of a stack of papers, a Canadian Association of Journalism award presented for his series on homeless people in the country's largest city, a series that held the promise of a brilliant career. When he first purchased the *Witness* he expected to hang the award on the wall above his desk but it never left the drawer. He couldn't explain why not to Tim or to himself.

Like Tim, summers at *The Shean Witness* had whetted David's appetite for journalism, and like Tim he went from high school to King's College in Halifax, graduating into a job with the *Star*, a stroke of good fortune even if the job description had been trite – filled with happy children and rescued animals – but the strength of his storytelling was soon recognized and he was seconded by the features editor.

One of those features assigned to him was another series on a tired subject exhausted by all major city newspapers but regularly revisited at the edge of each winter: the plight of the homeless. Young and green and walking the streets trying to find a way to connect with someone, anyone, who would talk to him, the nervous young reporter was frightened. And it showed. The streets of the city were strewn with society's castaways, many of them angry men who roared at pointed cameras, who threatened those who would question them. They were there for many reasons – because they were mental health patients abandoned by the health care system, because they were addicted to alcohol or drugs, because they were professional beggars by choice. Because, because, because.

With no experience and no technique, David Cameron spent two days being cursed, ignored, threatened or hustled for money without a scrap of insight for the story he was assigned. On the third day, standing at an intersection amid a crowd waiting for the light to change, he saw on the other side of the street three men leaning against the window of a jewellery store. When the light changed and the crowd of pedestrians made their way across the crosswalk, one of the men peeled himself off the side of the building and moved toward the incoming pedestrians, his eyes never wavering from David, whose own eyes looked everywhere but at the man moving as gracefully as a ballerina through the crowd until he and David were standing face to face on the Yonge Street sidewalk.

"I knew when you couldn't look at me you couldn't refuse me," the man said with a genuine smile that sent David's hand into his pocket for loose change. Midway through that action his hand moved toward his back pocket where his bills were kept and he pulled out a ten-dollar bill, his mind scrambling for a reason why he was doing this.

"You trying to put me into a new tax bracket?" the homeless man asked, and with those words, or more accurately with the inflection of those words, David knew the stranger. Not by name, not by face, but by accent, which he placed as being from Cape Breton. David introduced himself.

"You know there's only a couple of hundred thousand of us on the whole planet," said the man, introducing himself as Dougall, "so it's lucky we bumped into each other."

Standing there on the street corner a desperate David told Dougall about his plight.

"Your job depends on talking to us?" Dougall answered. "Look, let's squander this picture of John A. Macdonald on some holy water and go somewhere where we can talk." David added another twenty to the pool.

With enough wine to get them through the day, Dougall and the other two men, one from Newfoundland, the other from

Manitoba, made their way down an alley and settled in among the trash, using clean cardboard as seats to form a circle, passing the bottle and "helping somebody from home," as Dougall put it.

With his small tape recorder whirling and scribbling with cold fingers, afternoon passed into early evening and eventually he, feeling light from occasionally sipping at the bottles as they made the rounds, went home.

In the Sunday edition, David's story of Dougall and his friends, a narrative spiced and made human with the humour and wit and observations of the subjects themselves, brought letters to the editor, whose orders to David then were to continue pursuing the topic of homelessness.

Dougall was David's password into the hovels of the homeless. Society's castoffs, they were called "the homeless" now, but they wouldn't have been much different than the romanticized hobos of an earlier era. People wrote songs about hobos, and riding the rails was socially accepted by everyone but the railroad bulls who beat them silly. Their hobo jungles at the edges of railyards were communes where the day's take of food was poured into a single, simmering pot of cosmic stew.

It was harder for society to hide its hobos now, with the trains barely running and pricey housing developments sprawling through any corner of a city not already occupied by urban housing, the makeshift shacks of the homeless not considered housing at all. The homeless had no option but to move downtown, become visible as Biblical beggars, occupy street corners and doorways and huddle over warm air vents when the temperature dropped.

Dougall, who like the others he introduced David to, was never identified beyond a first-name pseudonym. He guided David through the six features that ran on consecutive Sundays leading up to Christmas, and David's tales of the street became less and less his own words and more and more Dougall's rambling observations, the experiences of a man without a face because every one of the homeless did not want their pictures in the paper, did not want to be a face a family member or the police or the do-gooders might recognize. The only photos David provided were distant, intentionally grainy shots of backs huddling around barrels of fire.

There was a seventh feature several weeks later, in early March, when the temperature had dropped to minus eighteen and the wind chill factor drove the cold down another thirty degrees. David had been in his apartment, listening like most other city residents to warnings not to go out unless absolutely necessary. But the warmth of his apartment gnawed at his intestines until he acknowledged the guilt, dwelled upon it, meditated upon it, and finally allowed Dougall's face to float up from that clot of unarticulated guilt. David recognized then the root of his guilt, the knowledge that volunteers and city workers were scouring the streets and alleys for the homeless, bringing them into shelters and, when those were filled, churches. But always, advocates for the homeless acknowledged, there were the few who would not come indoors. They were brought more clothes, sleeping bags, hot coffee and soup, wherever and whenever they could be found.

They wouldn't all be found, David knew, because once when he asked Dougall where he lived, the man replied, "My address is unlisted. Wouldn't want Revenue Canada coming after me for unpaid taxes now, would I?" Maybe he wouldn't go into a shelter but he might go home for the night with somebody from home, from the island on the east coast they both still called home in their conversations although it had been more than thirty years since Dougall had ventured that way.

David dressed as warmly as he could, following instruction about layers and not exposing his skin to the cold for any period of time, and set off for Yonge Street and the territorial corner where Dougall peddled his stories for loose change. He wasn't there. David didn't expect him to be, but it was a point on the planet from which to begin looking. He walked along, invading

the privacy of bundles of rags over heating vents asking if anyone had seen Dougall. The question was met with headshakes,
and the same answer was given when he asked where Dougall
was holed up to sleep at night.

He checked shelters to see if maybe Dougall had come in,
but he hadn't. Throughout the night David walked and looked
and called out, fortifying himself with coffee handouts from
other people trying to do the same about these victims of city,
provincial and federal policies that never seemed to address the
housing crisis in the country.

Three people had been found frozen to death he was told
when he went into work the next morning. The assignment was
a natural for the editor to hand to him. At the morgue, David
asked to see the corpses, explaining that he could possibly identify them based on his reporting on homelessness a few months
earlier.

Two bodies he couldn't recall having ever seen, but as he
gazed upon the third tears welled and he told the coroner the
man's name, including his last name, a secret shared late on a
night in early December. He gave a general address for a village
in western Cape Breton and went back to the office to write
an epilogue to the series, lamenting the death of the colourful
character who had been his guide through the dark labyrinth of
homelessness in Toronto.

Those articles, homeless advocates claimed, forced the city
to free up more money than it had in years and the city's churches responded with the compassion of Christ, short-lived though
it was, and school children set up a Homeless People Fund and
gave the money earned from bottle drives, tea sales and even-
splits to the city's shelters. David never flattered himself that his
articles had accomplished anything. He had merely provided a
vehicle for Dougall to speak out on behalf of those who shared
that particular hell with him, although the dead man would
have laughed loud at that compliment. David's final story on
the homeless had been written in a fifty-five-minute fever and

the editor never touched a word. Then David went out and got roaring drunk.

That series led to other assignments that put his byline on the front page, and as David shoved the drawer shut he looked around at what he had traded his career for, ownership of an obscure weekly newspaper that lived perilously close to missed paycheques at the cost of his marriage, and the embarrassment of living with his mother, who tended to his two children amid the unpredictability of the news. David could be called out at any time for a fire, an accident, and knowing that his mother was at home meant he didn't need to make special arrangements for the children to be looked after. Still, he was well aware that he was a grown man living with his mother.

| 8 |

Mayor Donald MacNaughton signalled for the meeting to begin and the councillors broke from their huddle around the coffee machine, taking their seats at the table. Aside from Town Clerk Mable Patterson, Recording Secretary Ann Wilson and David Cameron, the chamber was empty. Monthly town council meetings rarely drew the interest of onlookers. If anything of interest occurred people expected to read about it in the *Witness*. Only crises attracted audiences and nothing alarming was scheduled for Shean's immediate future – no school closures, no increased rates for water or sewer, no angry citizens arguing over property lines.

David had come to the town hall two hours early to scour the minutes of various committees in search of some reference to the park or the lots that comprised it.

"Did you know that Sylvester the Bastard owns most of the land the park's on?" Tim Donovan had asked David that afternoon, returning from his assignment a bit more excited than when he left. "Four lots of the seven, all bought or whatever in the last three months."

"Four?" David asked, recalling the previous night's phone call from Ronald MacDonald, who had reported that three lots were owned by the mayor's brother.

"Yup! One was registered just this morning. Used to belong to Mad Maddie Casey. Those MacNaughtons. Poor Maddie probably happily signed a quit claim on the land for a bottle of wine. Anyway, he owns it now, Sylvester. What do you suppose he's planning to do with them? I could give him a call."

"Not yet," David replied. "Let's watch and see what, if anything, develops. Two of those lots are vested, owned by the town."

"They still are but MacNaughton has them flanked north and south. You don't suppose he's going to start charging admission to sit in the park, do you? Nothing would surprise me when it comes to that clan. But he can't get those lots without them being advertised in the paper, right? The mayor can't make an under the table deal for his brother like that, can he?"

"Not normally, but there are extenuating circumstances for turning municipal-owned land over to someone. Say those lots were crucial to a significant development, then council could vote to offer the lots to a specific someone for their market value without a public auction if it was in the greater interest of the town," David explained.

"Market value's more than Mad Maddie got, I'm willing to bet."

"Yes, well, we'll keep a regular check on those lots. Ask around, as well, Tim. Not as a reporter but as someone as interested in local gossip as anyone else. Maybe you could have a word with the other owners, including Mad Maddie."

"Oh that should be fun," Tim replied, his snarl indicating it would be anything but.

Scanning the council agenda, David Cameron didn't expect to find much to bring out of the council meeting and into the *Witness* except the content of and discussion around the Shean Development Committee's strategic plan for the town.

Getting to that point in the meeting meant listening to the usual issues revisited by council at each meeting, neighbourhoods complaining through their councillor about sewer maintenance or fresh paving, elderly residents terrorized or feeling terrorized by clusters of weekend youth experimenting with liquor or drugs, vandalism in the park, one neighbour complaining about another's unsightly premises. Unless one of the issues flared into a full-grown debate or argument they were minor stories that would serve as fillers if David needed them in the next issue of the paper.

On the other hand, if nothing else at all happened at council or elsewhere in the town in the next few days, one or more of those items could suddenly grow front-page headlines and editorial attention. It wouldn't be the first time.

With his jaw still wired shut from the accident three weeks earlier, Donald MacNaughton spent most of his time scribbling notes to Mable Patterson, who served as the mayor's voice when a question or answer required more than a few words squeezed out between his teeth. Usually MacNaughton had more than enough to say, almost all of it quotable, but his jaw now silenced him.

Mayor Donald MacNaughton presided over a Shean Municipal Council made up of himself and four councillors, two of whom, Jay Morrison and Ralph Malone, had been the mayor's personal candidates in the last municipal election, dependable supporters who ensured a majority vote when the mayor needed something passed. The other councillors, James Jamison and Ted Clarke, did their own thinking, their own deciding, siding with the mayor as often as not but on their own terms, not his. Their lack of servitude frequently forced into public debate issues that MacNaughton might have preferred stay below the surface of public scrutiny as exercised by David Cameron and *The Shean Witness*.

James Jamison, who chaired the Shean Development Committee, rose to present what he hoped would be the final draft of Shean's economic strategy plan. The plan had been dragged through a lost number of public consultations with community organizations, stakeholders and provincial and federal economic development agencies, someone's objections forever sending it back to the drawing board. Still, under Jamison's guidance, a plan was taking shape, a plan that might offer Shean an escape from its treadmill existence as a town floundering at the edge of hopelessness.

Jamison, whose business investments in Shean included one of the town's two motels, which housed a popular restaurant offering a menu different than the Gulf Grill, a gift shop and other tourism-related interests, was suspected by some of trying to shape an economic direction for Shean that assured his pockets would continue to fill. David didn't share that sentiment.

A man in his sixties, Jamison had been involved in efforts to find new opportunities for the town for as long as David could remember. He was a successful businessman, but more important to the editor was the fact that Jamison's volunteer services to the town far exceeded any self-serving interests he might be accused of. Shean had few men or women of his calibre who were willing to give as much of themselves. Expertise gleaned from decades in business might have influenced the direction of the final draft of the strategic plan but there was more altruism than greed in that influence.

Jamison presented a solidly structured plan that contained no new revelations. It did contain appeasements to those who objected to aspects of the plan. But the overall vision aspired toward a transformation of the town, calling for an investment in itself to attract the investments of others.

Parts of the transformation envisioned by Jamison's committee were already in place: lamp-lit sidewalks, gardens in baskets hanging from those street lamps, the sprucing up of public places, including the town hall itself, which housed during the tourist season a visitor's centre staffed by volunteers, Jamison among them. These initial changes were cosmetic but reflected a longing for deeper changes.

Central to the development plan and far from a *fait accompli* was the need to ease this weary old coal-mining town toward a time when, with enough local, provincial and federal investment, the Shean beach, a golden strip of sand that stretched from Noss Head to Hughie's Point, could become a major provincial tourist attraction. Noss Head and Hughie's Point reached far out into the Gulf of St. Lawrence, cradling between them a broad bay that held two of Shean's greatest treasures: its beautiful and unblemished beach and the breakwater and channel leading into Shean's sheltered harbour. In the strategic plan's view, the harbour, which depended on mooring fees to cover maintenance, could be expanded into a marina, visiting craft tying up alongside local lobster boats.

The most important part of the plan was the proposed reclamation of the old mine tailings. Those large mounds of grey clay and red ash created by decades of mine waste would always be a deterrent to making the town attractive, sprawling as they did across private and public land, pushing up against the magnificent dunes and wetlands those dunes protected.

The Shean Economic Development Plan argued forcefully for the capping of the mine tailings, proposing a thick carpet of heavy clay be laid over the unsightly and possibly unhealthy site, which would then allow the development committee to pursue plans for a golf course, one unique in Canada and modelled on the Scottish links. If it could be pulled off, Jamison predicted, then opportunities would grow for local businesses to expand, and for people to offer new services to visitors. Coupled with the thriving Celtic cultural arts that fiddled and sang and danced their way through Shean's summers and falls, the town and surrounding county had a lot to offer, Jamison added, moving to adopt the strategic plan.

Jamison's presentation was made in the tone of contained excitement. The vision may have been millions of dollars and years away from reality but the first steps in the town's journey in that direction were clearly laid out.

If nothing else, the development plan was a masterpiece of hope, and David's mind toyed with thoughts of the mysterious land grab at the park, and whether Sylvester MacNaughton might be dabbling in a bit of insider trading. The park itself and its popularity as Shean's outdoor gathering spot and amphitheatre was a small-scale example of what was possible for Shean, a solid argument that change for the better was possible, even probable if all the pieces could be coaxed into place. He sat poised to record for readers the councillors' vote on the plan, expecting unanimity.

"It all sounds very good to me but there's a lot in here that needs further study, I think. I'd like time to take a closer look at this," Jay Morrison said. "I'm not saying I'm not supporting the plan, just that before we go off half-cocked we should be sure that this is what people in Shean want."

"A public meeting, you mean?" Ralph Malone asked.

"Everybody in town who cares has been consulted already," Jamison countered.

"Maybe, but I move that we table the plan until the fall meeting, give people a chance to digest it," Malone motioned.

"But this is our last meeting before we break for the summer. If we're not going to get back to it until sometime next autumn, we can't even begin approaching government departments or private investors," Jamison argued.

"I agree," Ted Clarke said in support of Jamison. "Our committee has put a lot of work into this plan and it deserves better treatment than this. Nobody's come up with a better one that I'm aware of, but if we don't start moving on it right away we could lose momentum."

"What momentum?" Morrison asked. "Have you already been pushing this plan without even getting our approval?"

"No, of course not. I just mean..."

Clarke was interrupted by Donald MacNaughton's fist pounding on his desk. He passed a note to Mable Patterson. "The mayor says that considering the differences of opinion and the fact that nothing gets done in the summer anyway, not in Shean and not in Halifax and not in Ottawa, nothing will be lost by tabling the motion until September."

The tied vote, two councillors to two, was broken by Mac-Naughton, who sided with those wanting to table the strategic plan for the time being.

"What the Christ was that about, David?" James Jamison asked as they left the council chamber.

"Weren't expecting it, Jamus?" David asked, using the Gaelic pronunciation of Jamison's first name.

"Hell no. It was an ambush! MacNaughton's been growing pretty cool to the strategic plan for months now but I had no idea how cool. He hasn't attended a meeting in I don't know how long. He seems to have just lost interest. David, if we wait until fall that will back up any possible progress on this by a year. Donald's been muttering about how we need something bigger, but we all know that. This town could use a hundred year-round jobs but it's not going to happen next week. Right now tourism is the only game in town." Jamison shook his head in frustration.

"Let's talk about this formally," David said, taking his notebook from his camera case.

David walked along the sand in the fading light of a saffron sunset and settled himself on a log that had drifted to this shore from who knew where, not unlike the people themselves that had washed ashore in Shean. First came a handful of Highlanders who were granted land here, the MacArthurs among them. Later, with the discovery of coal and the development of the mines, the rural solitude of the region was shattered by the arrival of hundreds of miners who came from across the Atlantic, from England, Scotland, Wales and Ireland, from Belgium, from Poland, from Italy, from Germany, migrants who drifted from boom town to boom town and moved along when the seams were exhausted. But in Shean, in the town that rose up around the coal boom, something changed for many of those miners.

In his university studies, David searched church records and town records and in a history thesis made a case for why the town continued to possess a sense of itself long after the coal – its *raison d'être* – had been depleted. He argued that the original Highland families abandoned their subsistence farming in large numbers for the cold hard cash of the coal mines, some moving into town, some to the pits, while others opened businesses. Cross-cultural pollination was a common phrase in the twenty-first century, but the people of Shean had been practicing it a century earlier. Intermarriages between the miners and the people for whom the region in and around Shean had been home for more than a century created families whose children were raised knowing that this was the home of their ancestors, and their home as well. Many of the miners who came to Shean chose not to move along to the next coal boom, whether it was across the island in New Waterford or across the country in Alberta. They, like him, David believed, had come home.

This was the concept David found difficult to explain to Tim Donovan or anyone when queried about why he had left "big time" journalism for the dubious pleasure of sitting through school board or town council meetings, or any of the scores of mundane events that needed to be reported if the *Witness* was to bear the responsibility as the newspaper of record for Shean and the county beyond.

The sense of home that had been forged in the fusion of migrant miners and rooted Gaels had been passed down to David Cameron through his genes or his mother's cooking or his own experience of growing up here. Whatever the factor or factors, they had created an irrepressible ache in him, a longing, a loneliness, during those years when he was away. If circumstances had not unfolded as they did to bring him home, he could have remained where he was, doing what he was doing, for his entire working life. But he knew Toronto would never have become home to him. At best, it would have become a poor substitute for the place he left behind.

His, their decision, Alexandra's and his, to return to Shean had not been blinded by homesickness. He knew then that he was coming back to a town that most of his friends had already left and that had been profoundly down on its luck for more than fifty years. He knew he was coming back to a business that had miraculously survived in the hands of its previous owners, the last of which had advised him at the time of sale that the newspaper could be nursed along as long as David didn't ask too much from it. Lately, he found that he had to ask less than he needed from the paper, and spent what time he could in the role of publisher racking his brains for new revenue ideas. Fortunately the *Witness* staff of manager Cheryl Horne, accountant Helen MacKinnon and graphic designer Mary Agnes MacIsaac were more creative in that field than he was and he recognized his dependence on them.

His return home had coincided with the election of Donald MacNaughton as mayor. Were they enemies? David often wondered. Until they were eleven years old, they had been the best of friends, then came the day Mrs. Big Sandy was shot. Tensions grew between them after that, were still growing between them. Yet, growing up in a town the size of Shean they shared the same friends, travelled in a gang of buddies who liked them both equally. Even with four or five of them walking together over street, Donald would be at one end of the group and David at the other. Any closer and the result was an argument.

There seemed no point upon which they could reach agreement, settling at best for accommodation of each other. It began with David as a fan of the Toronto Maple Leafs and Donald as a fan of the Montreal Canadiens. This wasn't an uncommon chasm between sports fans, many families shared similar, but with David and Donald it was indicative of deeper fault lines.

In high school, their differences had turned first historical and then political. Donald felt that war was nature's way to control population, that the society they were living in at the time was the result of the survival of the fittest. His outlook drew him to political conservatism and the belief that private enterprise held the solution to the world's problems, and that poverty, like wealth, was a condition of one's own making.

David found himself on the far side of the political spectrum, whether by nature or by his resistance to anything and everything Donald thought, felt or expressed. He argued that everyone was his brother's keeper, and that governments should act out of that understanding.

In university they had been assigned as roommates, probably the registrar's thoughtful idea of allowing two boys from home to feel less alone while they were away. It wasn't a room they shared but a ring, and after three fistfights and a short suspension for both they were assigned different rooms in different campus houses.

Coming back to Shean, David found himself once again in frequent opposition to Donald, newspaper editor verses local politician. It wasn't wholly acrimonious, nor was it uncommon for the two to share a cup of coffee at the Gulf Grill, their understanding of where each stood with the other making them almost comfortable in their differences. "Maybe we're growing up," David once said to Donald in a lighter moment. "Not growing up, David. With the way you write it's more like throwing up." Both men laughed a laugh that tried and failed to reach each other across a canyon-wide void.

It dawned on David that he was now listening to the waves that he had been watching slap their peaceful way ashore earlier. Darkness had dropped around him and by squinting at his watch he could see it was already well, well past the children's bedtime. But in listening to the waves he knew that he had also been listening for something deeper, for some inarticulate sense of foreboding to express itself. Nothing rose out of the darkness to inform him.

Making his way back to the parking lot he saw Rita MacDonald's car parked beside his. She must have walked in the other direction, toward the breakwater, he thought. It occurred to him to walk that way, maybe feign an inadvertent meeting with the off-duty nurse. "Yeah, like she's looking for a man with two children who still lives with his mother," David chided himself as he got into his car and pulled away.

| 9 |

Rita MacDonald sat in the cool sand, her back against one of the breakwater boulders, wishing upon a sky full of stars that she were anywhere else. It wasn't a bitter wish because she had accepted these circumstances two years ago. By then she had worked in a number of cities, Toronto, Calgary, Miami, and had applied for and was accepted as an onboard nurse for a cruise line bound for the Caribbean. When she was hired she was told the company had ships cruising all corners of the world and transfers between ships was easy.

Two days before her departure, amid the excitement of preparations, the phone rang. Her father had had a stroke. While asking questions of her sister, Rita walked around the room continuing to place clothes in the half-full suitcase, packing more slowly now because her destination had changed. There were brothers and sisters, none living any longer in Shean, all with families, and all working on the same assumption that if you didn't have children you didn't have a life, that a single person and a nurse was fair game for drafting into family service. It never occurred to Rita to resist. Her widower father needed her care.

Stargazing beside the breakwater, Rita knew that there was nothing now to keep her in Shean except her father's health. He was doing just fine since his stroke, suffering no impairment that being aged sixty-seven couldn't account for, but her faith in his immortality had faltered the day she arrived home and walked into that hospital room.

Tubes and monitors, a web of technology breathing for him, feeding him, threatening to let go of that slender hold at any moment. All her knowledge and experience fled as her hands flew to her face, stifling her horror. He was going to die and she knew that she would be at his side all the way through it. She composed herself quickly as years of bedside training returned to her, and she was glad when he opened his eyes and she could look into them one last time. It took awhile to register that they didn't close. Her faith in him was restored. Her father was never going to die. She felt little-girl safe again.

Ronald MacDonald credited his recovery to his daughter's presence and the fact that he had never entered a McDonald's restaurant. Except to move his bedroom downstairs and install a downstairs bathroom not much else changed when he came home from rehab. The fact that Rita was home to stay was the biggest change of all. The loneliness vanished from his house.

Maybe it was because she was the one who least needed him, always knowing what she wanted. Or maybe it was because she was the one for whom he found himself pacing the living-room floor at two in the morning when she was in high school, worrying about where she was, imagining all sorts of tragedies, and being so grateful when she reached the front door that he simply slid off to his bedroom leaving no sign of himself behind. The one thing that hurt him was knowing that this was the last place on earth she wanted to be, though his guilt didn't extend all the way to sending her on her way again.

He would deteriorate pretty fast, she felt, if he was left to fend for himself, leaving her to take command of the family castle, ordering his life. "That's what you're eating, so learn to like it."

When he grew reluctant about exercising, Rita began their trips to town by saying, "I'll wait for you at the brook," leaving the house and driving away, parking two kilometres down the road beside Colin's Brook. She knew her father would rather make the unhappy walk than miss out on a coffee at the Gulf Grill or basking in the gossip at Memorial Park. He didn't know yet that she was growing confident that his fitness had progressed to the point where she was considering driving down the road another kilometre. Someone would drive him home later in the afternoon where, in his livingroom/study he would log on and explore what was happening to the world. By the time she got home from her regular night shift to their cup of tea together, his chatter was filled with quirks and facts gleaned from the World Wide Web.

Rita wouldn't allow herself to be governed by the bitterness that frequently tried to assert itself when she grew acutely aware that Shean, a place she had always imagined escaping from, had snared her, probably for good. She had always thought of it as the place she was born and a place she would return to for the occasional family Christmas, but she had not planned on ever coming home to stay again.

Often after work she would drive to the beach, walk along the sand and settle in her favourite spot at the breakwater, staring up into the midnight sky. She tried to decipher a Morse code of glimmering stars, searching for a destiny elsewhere.

When she had pulled into the parking lot she noticed David Cameron's empty car parked nearby and along her walk to the breakwater hoped they would run into each other. But such was pure fantasy and best left in that realm. She didn't kid herself about the attraction she felt but she wasn't about to risk becoming entangled in a life that involved divorce, two children and a man who lived with his mother. David Cameron had a lot going for him and because of it Rita MacDonald decided that even the fantasy was dangerous, more dangerous to her becoming trapped here in Shean than even her father's unfailing health.

Following publication of the next issue of the *Witness*, David Cameron made his usual way to the Gulf Grill to sip a cup of coffee and relax in the company of whoever was present. Unlike Big Sandy MacArthur's murder confession, the kind of story that comes along once in a dozen blue moons, the most recent edition primarily dwelt upon the town council's reluctance to adopt the strategic plan James Jamison's economic development committee had placed before it.

Other stories caught the interest of Gulf readers, notably Tim Donovan's tale of the black bear that walked into the Shean Hospital through the emergency doors while paramedics were unloading a suspected heart attack and the story of Mad Maddie (Matthew Casey in the *Witness*) being arrested for assaulting a video lottery terminal in the Legion, claiming it ate seven hundred of his dollars.

"And where would Mad Maddie get seven hundred dollars?" Gulf readers asked of the sudden wealth claimed by the town's premiere panhandler.

David turned on the stool to the sound of his name to encounter an ashen-faced Ronald MacDonald, with a cautious Don Alex walking beside him. *Another stroke*, was the first thought David had upon seeing his friend. "I'm not ill, David, just sick. We need to talk." He pointed toward the empty back booth where the three men soon sat, a fresh round of coffees in front of them.

Ronald MacDonald's mouth twisted and stretched but no words poured forth, as if he were afraid that merely speaking of something would bring it into being. Finally he got the courage to pronounce, "Sylvester is opening a McDonald's in the park!"

David gave a moment for this unlikely information to sink in. "You found this out online?" he asked incredulously.

"No, David, I found this out at the post office from Mr. C." Mr. C. was the name pinned on the postmaster many years ago, short form for Mr. Confidentiality, for his ability to whisper to an individual news that he had gleaned from letter addresses and postcards. This individual confidentiality extended to just about everyone entering the post office. "The Bastard has been getting packages from McDonald's Restaurants. That's what's going on, David. That's what's coming to the park. You've got to stop this foolishness before it goes any further. Your newspaper needs to make people aware of this, rally the clans against it."

"That's exactly what David wants to do," Don Alex said, speaking for the first time. "The last thing he wants to see in Shean is another advertiser."

"You wouldn't let them advertise, would you? Not in your paper?"

"Now Ronald, why don't you tell David everything Mr. C. said about Sylvester's mail." Then, turning to David he spared Ronald the task. "Sylvester has been getting all kinds of packages from companies that offer them-there franchises. Is it true he bought the park like Ronald says?"

David nodded his head in assurance while his thoughts tried to make sense of what he was hearing. Shean, nearly de-populated by diminishing births and increased deaths, by gradu-ating high school classes of forty or fifty students while primary school enrolments the past couple of years were less than twenty, by a middle-aged population virtually vanishing into the rest of the country, was a town in trouble. It had neither the population nor the prosperity to sustain even an outlet for Canada's favourite institutional franchise, Tim Horton's.

"You know what will happen, David. If Sylvester opens a McDonald's here, this here restaurant right here," he emphasized by tapping the booth table with his forefinger, "won't last through its first breakfast. It'll be gone."

David couldn't disagree with that diagnosis and a silence fell in their booth as the men contemplated the consequences of Ronald's nightmare coming to town. In that silence, commentary from the next booth floated into their space.

"...because this whole strat...strat...this whole plan for the town is a stupid idea. Tourism! All that means is that people get minimum wages jobs cleaning the arses of rich tourists. Golf courses! It's too bad we couldn't get at the Beaton Seam, then we'd see some real prosperity around here." David recognized the voice as belonging to the generally unemployed by choice Hatter Jones. "Tourism's only for a season, but the Beaton Seam..."

David allowed himself a quiet smile while he eavesdropped. The Beaton Seam was Shean's lost economic lottery, the "what if" that people like Hatter Jones looked hopelessly back upon when they hadn't the imagination to look forward. David Cameron was probably as informed as any living soul about the legendary coal seam, having written about it or referenced it a forgotten number of times in the *Witness*. The seam was real enough. In fact, it contained a quality of coal rarely found in most of North America, but it was located so close to the seabed that every effort to mine it had resulted almost immediately in flooding. Four miners drowned in the last attempt, 1917.

"...and it's not just my personal feelings about McDonald's, David. It's about supporting the local economy. That's what everybody says we should do but how many people do it? Do you? Take the grill here. Best hamburgers in the town, the county, hell I'd say the province but don't ever tell my daughter I know this from experience. And they're the best because they make their patties from fresh meat straight from the Co-op and put them right on the grill. Those hamburgers you get at that other place whose name we shall not mention are frozen little pucks of meat that will come here from God knows where, not fresh hamburg from the Co-op. And," finger waving like an instructor, "and the Co-op, I can tell you as a member, sells nothing but prime Atlantic beef, all raised right here in the Maritime provinces. How much more local can you get than that? But this here little restaurant that's been in business since sometime in the 1930s will be gone in thirty minutes if Sylvester MacNaughton gets his way."

"Tell me this, Mr. Local Shopper," Don Alex broke in. "If it was one of those other television advertisements we see every night, one of those other hamburger places, that A&W King's Burger thing, say, would you be saying the same thing or would you be saying they'll hire more people than work here at this here grill here, and if they hire more people that's good for the economy, isn't it? Isn't it? Isn't it?" he repeated, the last aimed at Cameron.

"That's the theory," David conceded, avoiding any chance of being lured to any side of Ronald's war with the fast food industry.

"David," Ronald lowered his voice to a confidential level. "We've uncovered a conspiracy here, didn't we? Sylvester stealing the park to open his own burger joint to put local businesses out of business. That's got to be next week's front page, if you ask me."

"Ronald, right now Sylvester is buying up the lots that make up the park but there's nothing illegal about that if he has the legal deeds, and according to the land registration office, he does. What he plans to do with it is speculation, probably as much on his part as ours, but more important, until there's an official announcement I don't feel the paper has any more right to investigate Sylvester than it does any other person who's buying or selling property."

"What you're telling us, David, is that you need a big reason to report on the conspiracy."

"What I'm telling you is that there is no indication of a conspiracy, Ronald." David was emphatic, more emphatic than a dark, unarticulated niggling in the corner of his mind told him he should be.

| 11 |

Mrs. Big Sandy picked up the cups from the table and set them on the kitchen counter. That nurse was becoming a habit, twice this week and this time she brought egg salad sandwiches and an apple pie she baked herself, probably showing off because the widow told her she didn't bake at all, if you didn't count biscuits. She shouldn't tell anybody anything. That's how she survived in this pathetic little town for as long as she did, not telling anybody anything unless she was telling them off. But that nurse had a way of wheedling things out of her that she never meant to say.

"Well, she'll get a piece of my mind if I ever hear anybody repeating the things I told to that one," Mrs. Big Sandy thought aloud. "What business is it of hers if I'm eating or not eating enough? That's probably why she brought those damned sandwiches, because she thinks I'm too old to feed myself. If there's one thing living as long as I have should let me do is decide when and what I want to eat. Oh, I shouldn't have ate them! Egg sandwiches always make me fart like an old cow. I shouldn't have ate any of them, not that fourth one anyway." She slammed the pie plate onto the counter, grabbing at it immediately to prevent it falling into the sink. There was still more than half a pie in it.

"There's no need of it going to waste. I'll have a piece of it with my afternoon tea, but that was my afternoon tea. Tonight then," she added, taking a fork and scraping loose apple filling from the plate where two pieces had been removed. "Maybe one little piece right now while I still have some peace and quiet in this house."

She picked up the teapot. It was empty except for a couple of fistfuls of loose tea at the bottom. She sloshed them out in the sink and flushed who knows how many futures down the drain, filled it with water again and put it on the kitchen's propane stove, making certain that the action rattled through the room, announcing her angry impatience. "No tea in the pot in the middle of the afternoon! Sandy would throw a fit! How much tea did that nurse drink? If she thinks she's going to be coming here whenever she likes to drink my tea, she's got lessons to learn, that girl. I'm nobody's fool. She's going to have to bring her own tea, that's what I'll tell her. 'Oh, you came for another cup of free tea, did you dearie? Well I hope you brought your own and not those god-awful bags but good strong loose tea like we've been drinking in this house for the past fifty years. Longer.' She'll be coming on Wednesday, I bet. I bet she's going to be as predictable as the moon. She'd be better off finding a man for herself, that's what she should be doing instead of sticking her nose into somebody's business that doesn't care to have anyone's nose stuck in it. I've broken noses that have stuck themselves in my business and if you don't believe me just ask Sandy. So she better not start pretending to be my friend. I know where she works. In the old age home and if she thinks for one minute she's going to sweet talk me into going in there she's got another thought coming and it will be coming on the end of my fist or my frying pan if she or anybody tries to make me move into that place. That place's nothing but an open grave, that's what Sandy called it when they took him in there to die. An open grave."

Steam poured from the teapot spout and Mrs. Big Sandy flicked back the lid, reached into the tea can for a handful of leaves and threw them into the boiling water. She picked up her cup and rinsed it in readiness. Then she picked up the nurse's cup, the pattern of tea leaves still pasted to the bottom. Waiting for her own tea to steep she brought the nurse's cup to table, sat and studied it. She had already read the dregs and although the nurse never said anything Mrs. Big Sandy could tell she hit the nail on the head more than once. People have a way of telling a reader that, even if they think they aren't. There's a shift in the air or in the way their eyes look at or away from the leaf reader. That nurse's eyes thought they weren't telling Mrs. Big Sandy anything the way they didn't blink when she heard the old woman tell her that she had already missed her boat, but her eyes brightened – with wonder or fear she couldn't tell, but that girl had missed the boat somewhere in her life, and she knew it. It was in those very eyes she was looking through.

"At least she wasn't like those other women who wanted to know the future. She didn't ask any questions at all, just listened, then left. She didn't want to know. The things I could have told that woman…."

She got up to pour her own tea, taking the nurse's cup back to the sink, and cut herself a slice of the pie, lingering over the first bite, coming close to savouring the taste of it, wondering why the girl would waste years in nursing school when a gift for cooking like this could get her a man in a single weekend.

"There's more to that one than she lets on. That's why she's got no man. She's not exactly the fainting kind and men hate that in a woman, that's what Sandy said. I wasn't the fainting kind and that's what he liked about me. Not many other men would put up with me, he said, meaning it in a nice way but even if it was an insult it didn't matter because of the men I'd seen it's me who wouldn't be doing the putting up with. But I didn't have to put up with Sandy and he didn't put up with me, we just sort of met in the middle of somewhere and stayed there with each other for sixty years. Sixty-one. But there aren't a lot of Sandys in a rundown place like this goddamned town. That poor woman may wind up living alone because there's more to her than she lets on. She's not fooling me, not about that and not about the sneaky way she left her pie plate so she'll have an excuse to come back."

| 12 |

Her father was gone when Rita woke and came downstairs. She guessed that he'd left, walking to town expecting somebody to pick him up. The morning sun poured on her back as she stood looking out to sea, sipping from the cup in her hand. From their farm Ronald and Rita could see a long way up the coast. The ebb and flow of tides. The golden ribbon of sand that was the Shean beach. The town itself, church spires rising through a tree canopy, a pretty image that didn't hold up all that well under scrutiny. Mountains ringing the valley that ran back from the town toward the rest of the world. Beautiful and peaceful, somewhere in her past it used to be enough. At moments like this it still was, but it wasn't a feeling she wanted to nurture beyond the length of a cup of tea.

The memory of yesterday's tea with Mrs. Big Sandy returned, how when her cup, drained of liquid, made a pattern of leaves up the porcelain sides and the old woman took it from her and stared into it. No, gazed into it, her eyes seeming to glaze over. What she said chilled Rita. "You've missed the boat, girl." She couldn't possibly have known about Rita's near miss with the cruise line. Who had she told? No one, not even her father, for fear that his guilt about it might contribute to another stroke.

"Is that right?" was all Rita could say, rising before the old woman could go on, saying she needed to get to work early to catch up on some charts. She left quickly, a near panic overtaking her in the car. She knew she had missed the boat, literally and figuratively, that she had been spirited back to Shean by the harnessing forces of family love and duty. She had almost laughed when her sister called to tell her about their father's stroke, almost accepted the sadistic humour with which life played itself out, but bitterness was never far off, and needed to be fought back. "Right here, right now," was her mantra, a reminder not to look back, not to look ahead, just deal with the moment she was in. But to have heard Mrs. Big Sandy's words, through whatever guesswork she employed, reaching toward a central loss in Rita's life brought her close to bitter tears.

Leaving the morning sun and yesterday's sadness behind, Rita went back into the house, checking her email, grabbing an hour for novel reading, catching up on a few chores that needed doing around the house. Sooner than she expected, it was time to get ready for work.

The park seemed unusually busy as she drove past, and a glance in her rear-view mirror confirmed that she had not glimpsed a mirage, causing her to slam on the brakes and pull to the curb. From her car she could see David Cameron moving through the figures on the sidewalk, snapping pictures of her father in full-kilted MacDonald Clan Ranald battle dress, holding a sign warning that Shean was about to lose its park. Behind Ronald in the park's bandstand stood Jeremy MacDonald, no relation, recruited from the Legion's pipe band, piping laments while Ronald predicted the park's disappearance. Several men and a couple of women in Legion blazers and tams stood near the cenotaph.

In the warm June weather there was no lack of audience for any spectacle and Ronald MacDonald was holding sway with his crony, Don Alex, at his side, basking in the attention. *War Memorial, YES! Hamburgers, NO!* Ronald held the sign while explaining to anyone willing to listen that there were plans afoot to level the park and open a restaurant whose name and iconic clown were an insult to the Celtic cultural identity of Shean. He ignored the fact that half of his audience were named LeBlanc, Polanski, Donovan, Llewellyn, Hess.

"Dad, just what the hell do you think you're doing?"

Rita's question came out in a low hiss in hope of carrying on a private conversation with her father while the gathering crowd eavesdropped on the family spat.

"Rita, I told you last night what Sylvester's up to and that somebody needed to do something to save this park from becoming another Glencoe."

"Glencoe? Dad, Glencoe was a slaughter of the MacDonalds in Scotland two hundred years ago. A new restaurant in town doesn't compare..."

"It's all relative, dear."

"It's all your relatives, you mean. God, Dad, can't you just write another letter to the editor or something? I don't want to see this park disappear either, nobody does, but if somebody else owns the land there's nothing you can do about it."

"If nobody wants to see it disappear, then why is it going to disappear? Because that's the kind of government we have here in Shean, that's why! It's a dictatorship, that's what it is!"

"Just like your Highland clans, do you mean, with their chieftain or laird or whatever?"

"It's your clan, too, girl."

Rita wheeled away from her father and walked toward David Cameron, who was busy snapping pictures of their family feud. "Do you need to do that? Can't you find something else, somebody else, to make look like a fool in your newspaper?"

David lowered the camera, allowing it to swing on a strap around his neck. "Your father is the person who phoned the paper," he explained. "You may have noticed that he also got the Legion involved. He talked to me yesterday about this park and I told him that whatever Sylvester MacNaughton is up to, it isn't really the *Witness*'s business, not really a news story, so he's decided to make it a story. And he's making it a damned interesting one, but I have no interest in making a fool of your father."

"Well don't make one of me either," Rita said, her tone low but more emphatic than a shout, and walked away toward her car while David Cameron, only slightly scorched by her fire, watched with interest.

When Rita MacDonald's car pulled away from the curb another pulled into its place, followed by Sheriff John Thurber's four-wheel drive. Donald – his jaw recently released from the wires that had kept him quiet of late – and the sheriff got out of their respective vehicles. Together they walked toward the park and toward Ronald. David joined the convergence, sensing that his elderly friend was indeed going to get the story he wanted in the *Witness*.

"There's a by-law against what you're doing," the mayor informed MacDonald. "I need to ask you to put down that sign and leave the park."

The piper fell silent.

There was a slow, hushed movement as Legion members and standers-by formed a ring of curiosity around the two men.

"What by-law is that, Donald? One you made up this morning?"

"No, one that was passed when the park was formed, and it was passed at the request of the Legion, that there be no politics, no preaching and no protests allowed in Memorial Park. You're breaking that by-law."

"So you brought the sheriff along to arrest me, did you. David, be sure to get a good shot of me being handcuffed and dragged off to jail."

"Nobody's going to jail, but Sheriff Thurber is responsible for by-law enforcement in Shean," MacNaughton informed MacDonald.

"Only the RCMP are going to take me to jail, not that boy scout."

"It's not RCMP responsibility to enforce municipal by-laws," MacNaughton said. "I've merely requested the sheriff be here when I remind you people of the by-law. It's my responsibility as mayor to see that by-laws are enforced and I believe this is a very important by-law, one the Legion insisted on so that the cenotaph wouldn't become a gathering place for nonsense like religious nuts or political rallies or illegal protests like this one."

"So Sheriff Thurber is here for crowd control?" David probed.

"I just don't want things to get out of hand so I asked."

"Asked for police protection is what you asked for, isn't it Donald?" Ronald accused. "You think I'm going to organize a riot or something? Afraid maybe these Legion members came armed to stop your brother's plans? That's what this is about, isn't it? What your brother's planning for this park, and what's that going to do to the cenotaph?"

"I'm not my brother's keeper," MacNaughton said. "He doesn't have to share his plans with me, if he has any."

"And do you share any of the town's plans with him, mayor?" David asked. "Or don't you know that he's bought three of the lots in this park?" Notebook and pen at the ready, David was anxious to scribble whatever MacNaughton answered.

The mayor fell into thoughtful silence before answering, which Ronald immediately interrupted. "You should be your brother's keeper and you should keep him in jail to keep him from desecrating this monument to our heroic fallen with grease from his hamburgers. But you don't know anything about that, do you, Mr. Mayor. Like hell you don't. You're all just a bunch of bastards if you ask me," Ronald shouted, the redness of his face sending a signal of concern through those gathered there.

David stepped in front of Ronald, easing him back from the precipice of a dangerous rage, then returned his attention to the mayor. "Do you know of any plans by your brother or anyone else to open a fast food franchise here, one that will replace Memorial Park?"

| 13 |

David Cameron had already chosen the photograph for the next issue's front page, one of Ronald MacDonald and Mayor Donald MacNaughton going nose to nose, Sheriff Thurber at the mayor's shoulder, but he studied the on-screen image of one of his other choices, Ronald MacDonald and his daughter Rita in a tense exchange. No one wants to see her father making a spectacle of himself although she was the only one who thought that. Ronald's kilt-clad warning about the fate of the park took on an aura of truth when the mayor refused to flat out deny that the park belonged to the people of Shean, noting that there was private ownership of some of the land on which the park was located. The mayor's warning led to Legion members taking an on-the-spot petition to town council to protect Memorial Park from any commercial development.

It wasn't often that David conducted an interview with anyone while surrounded by such an interested audience. The exchange between the mayor and Ronald and David had turned into a formal interview in which the reporter questioned the mayor about council's position regarding Memorial Park.

"Mr. Mayor, the land the park stands on has been zoned as commercial property going back long before the Big Fire and that didn't change when the park was created. Will council be considering the removal of that commercial zoning and classifying it as green space instead?"

"I can't speak for what council will do but, personally, I would have to think long and hard about such a decision. Shean's been in an economic sinkhole for a long time now and council has been dedicated to finding new ways to stimulate investment and growth here. Taking a large section of the main street out of any potential development formula, and I'm not saying I'm personally aware of any such existing plans, would in my opinion be shortsighted. Besides, the fact remains that much of the park land is privately owned so I don't see what council or anyone can do to prevent owners from doing what they want with the land."

"Considering the role the park now plays in the town's life, from the site of the community Christmas tree to outdoor summer concerts, not to mention the cenotaph itself, would yourself or council consider expropriation of the properties in question to ensure that the park remain forever a public place?"

"Expropriation?" The word, or the idea, seemed to enrage the mayor. "Of private property? Is that what you're proposing? I see where this is leading. You're only interested in a story that will sell more of those damned papers of yours. I told you from the start that a by-law is being violated here and it's my responsibility to act in the public interest. You're stretching my intent into another one of your sensational headlines, and I won't play your game. Expropriation of private land needs to be for a just reason, but all you're doing is trying to put words in my mouth."

"Then you won't ensure people here today that the park will be protected?" David called to the mayor's vanishing back, his question met with an angry, dismissive wave.

Here they were again, David thought, he and Donald MacNaughton on opposite sides of another issue. There seemed to be no place where they found common ground. It's wasn't just politics. Their dislike of each other had been festering since boyhood. They clashed compulsively in the classroom over anything from theories of history to the meaning of poetry. When the subject of girls began to surge and outshine all others, one boy's interest became the other boy's challenge.

Yet throughout their school years, there had been moments of pure harmony between Cameron and MacNaughton that thrilled Shean fans. On the summer ball field, they formed a pitcher-catcher battery that dominated opponents from Port Hawkesbury, Sydney, Antigonish. Donald, crouched behind the plate, masterfully called for whatever pitch in David's arsenal best exploited a batter's weakness. In winter, the two athletes elicited howls of delight, even disbelief, from the Shean hockey fans that packed the arena for high school games. With David on left wing, Donald on right wing, gliding along the ice in an almost mystical harmony, they brought victory after victory for the Shean Miners, and nurtured fan fantasies that one or both boys would be drafted, eventually making their way into the NHL. Their on-ice magic carried them through varsity hockey even as they fist fought with each other as roommates. That synchronicity still flashed on the ice when the men laced up each winter for the local gentlemen's hockey league.

Now those long ago classroom arguments about current events occurred regularly in the pages of *The Shean Witness*, where MacNaughton's political leadership of the community found itself in constant conflict with Cameron's sense of which direction that leadership should be taking the town. The park was just another example, and the two men would again brawl in print for the enlightenment and, in the greater reality, entertainment of readers.

There was something else about the day's events at the park that stirred David's interest, which was why he studied the picture of Ronald and Rita MacDonald. It was by far the finest photograph he had taken that afternoon and it, too, would have made a fine front-page picture except that the father-daughter argument wasn't really relevant to the story, although there were plenty of other newspaper people he knew who would disagree with his assessment of the photo's news value. There was also her implicit threat to consider, which reminded him, and he must never think this thought again lest it get said aloud, of Mrs. Big Sandy, who had honed threats to a fine art. There the similarities ended. Rita MacDonald, caught in this photogenic moment by his camera, revealed herself as a strikingly intense and beautiful woman, her brown eyes and dark complexion accented and strengthened by her classic nose. It was the face of someone anyone would wish to know.

He cropped the picture then, removing Rita MacDonald's image from the context of the protest in the park and the heated exchange with her father, and what he was left with was a candid portrait, an accident of photography that he probably couldn't recapture after hours of studio work. Saved among the paper's archive of photos titled Personalities, this picture of Rita MacDonald would never find its way into the *Witness* unless the nurse ever became the subject of a news story. The *Witness* had hundreds of similar photographs gleaned from each week's pictures, people whose image might need to be used following the winning of some award, some tragic occurrence, an obituary. In fact, David's professional hobby was trying to have on file photographs of everyone in Shean for just such occasions, so weekly he sifted through his and Tim Donovan's photo files for faces to be cropped, named, dated and stored in the paper's electronic archives.

The usual detachment with which he culled the weekly photographs wavered and weakened with Rita MacDonald's picture, his awareness of being a man alone brought forcibly into focus by a beautiful woman. It wasn't just her facial beauty that his camera had caught but the fire in her eyes, recalling for him the passion in her voice. It occurred to him during their own brief exchange that she may have been the most alive person he had encountered in ages. Most alive woman.

It seemed a long time since his attention had last been grabbed by an interesting woman. There was too little time for emotional or sexual musing with the paper absorbing so much of his time, and his children all the rest. It was a fact of community newspapers like his that most of the news takes place during evenings and weekends, when other people aren't working. Volunteers, their organizations, their efforts, their hopes, their events make small towns like Shean function. Any spare moments he had left called for his attention to the business of running a newspaper, more boring and ulcer-producing than covering and writing about each week's stories. Just arranging a weekend for himself or his family required forethought and planning, and usually it was just easier to go ahead and do a reporting job than go through the trouble of arranging not to do it.

Underlying those legitimate excuses lay a deeper truth, an emotional exhaustion that had come with separation and divorce, and with raising Tony and Mary, of making enough time to be there when they needed him, and to be there when he needed them. One of the appeals of coming home to buy the *Witness* was the very nature of small towns, of this small town in particular, where neighbours and friends and families and even familiar enemies mattered in a way he found absent from larger, anonymous newspapers. With a weekly or community newspaper, the lives of neighbours and friends and family were front-page news every single week, and no other newspaper anywhere in the province or country had the time, interest or care to record those lives – not unless the town was struck by tragic or scandalous events. Provincial papers, national papers, covered "the big picture," but David Cameron's interest had always been in the smaller, more intimate pictures, that microcosm called the small town.

He also needed to remind himself frequently that in recording the life of that small town he mustn't forget that he was also part of it, that he and his were some of those neighbours, friends, families, enemies even. That his family needed and de-served as much of his time as any other in Shean. So there was this woman he encountered from time to time with her father, a woman he'd spoken with on the phone when Big Sandy died, but barely knew, never thought about. A woman who until this afternoon had been an attractive stranger and who he would never see again as merely attractive but as achingly beautiful. And she as good as told him to take his camera and shove it up his arse. David laughed aloud and closed Photoshop, relegating the picture to the archives, thinking it was time to give some time to his family.

| 14 |

An hour later David Cameron was back in Memorial Park seated on a bench, watching as five-year-old Mary joined several other children who had gathered at the front of the bandstand while Alex Burton's fiddle reeled off scores of tunes. The children took up the music's challenge to dance, their enthusiasm oblivious to the rules. They were just children jumping for joy.

In his short absence the atmosphere of the park had transformed itself, vibrating now with the presence of people enjoying being there. His son Tony was in a mock free-for-all wrestling match on the lawn. Elsewhere clusters of people sat on benches or sprawled on the grass, in many cases talking to each other for the first time since the weather last allowed this to happen, sometime last year. Even in a town as small as Shean people can grow huge distances between themselves and others simply because they don't work in the same places, or turn up at the same volunteer or addiction get-togethers. Seasons can pass without paths crossing. With its invitation to sit or listen or lounge on a beautiful day, Memorial Park was a place for people to banter and catch up, chatting while a soundtrack of fiddle tunes whirled around them.

It was such an ideal afternoon in the park, so quickly following the earlier protest, that David was tempted to believe the moment had been orchestrated in support of the Save the Park movement, except that he knew that organizing anything this seamless in Shean wasn't in the realm of possibility.

Shean possessed no blueprint to its future, no vision of its own economic and cultural aspirations. Not that there weren't occasional forays in that direction. Councillor James Jamison's committee had a plan that was heading in that direction. It wouldn't be the first, and it probably wouldn't be the last time a Shean winter was wiled away wildly imagining a future that some would cheer, some would scorn, most would ignore. The resulting reports vanished into the archives, hurried there by enemies of whatever it proposed, or by the disinterest of provincial and federal funding agencies, but most often by the town's general apathy. Between political rhetoric and newspaper editorials there was an illusion of action toward economic solutions, and many were content to leave it there. Besides, there were better things to do, like hang out at the park listening to music or bitching about anyone who dared suggest the town even had a future. For everyone, it felt as if Memorial Park had always been there, proof enough that with or without a blueprint, things got done.

Not that there were no plans for Shean. It was just that there were so many plans for Shean. Everybody knew exactly what Shean needed. Solving the town's problems was something that was done every day by just about everybody in the town. David himself did it almost weekly in his editorials, as others did it over coffee in the Gulf Grill, in their talks here in the park, in their homes. Conversations veered from tourism to a federal penitentiary to the legendary Beaton Seam to the idea of extending to the Japanese an invitation to invest in the town, just to piss off the Americans.

This was why, David supposed, James Jamison's hard work on the virtually rejected economic strategy was met with not much more than a shoulder shrug, because everybody had a plan.

The mayor had plans but few people knew what they were. Whatever they were, David speculated, they were self-serving, and nothing made David more certain of those suspicions than Sylvester MacNaughton's land grab. The mysterious plan might even be something good for the town, genuine jobs, but it would be good for the Bastards too, of that he was certain.

Donald MacNaughton was mayor, everyone said, because nobody else wanted the job. That was true of ninety-nine percent of the population, who saw the job as one of presiding over the slow death of the town, a job less interesting than the delightful one of criticizing whoever took on that palliative task. But there are always one or two or a few who gravitate toward, and eventually fill, a power vacuum, no matter how small a world it might govern. Donald MacNaughton wanted to be mayor, and nobody was interested in getting in his way.

If there had been an election, David mused, MacNaughton would have won it. Helping people in need unsolicited was his *modus operandi*. He would dispatch one of his unimpressive entourage to shovel the walk of a woman he just passed in his car trying to dig her snowbound car out of her driveway. "MacNaughton sent me over to do that for you," the agent would say, gently drawing the shovel from her hands and turning upon the snowbank with the power and speed of a superhero. The woman is naturally grateful. Few were those in Shean upon whom no favour has been bestowed by Donald MacNaughton, mayor by acclamation and now into his second four-year term.

While he didn't doubt that MacNaughton would like to deliver an economic winner, live up to his own reviews of himself, David believed the man lacked the imagination to pull off something so dramatically appealing, and so dramatically unlikely. Nothing more imaginative than one of those migrant call centres that tour the world, panhandling for government cash to set up temporary operations, was David's guess, a guess that appeared in print in the *Witness* on more than one occasion.

What were they up to, the MacNaughtons?

Sylvester, like his brother, was a bright man, bright enough to take advantage of an advantage if one was handed to him, such as getting from his brother a preview of something the town doesn't yet know about itself. The coffee or hamburger franchises he was looking into called for the investment of a small fortune by most people's standards. A person needed to do a lot of business to get that investment to turn into the proverbial goose of the golden eggs.

Adding to that suspicion was surprise that the Jamison committee plan had been tabled by the town council. MacNaughton and his supporters had killed it without even hearing the details read into the public record. David Cameron shook his head free of speculation and looked around for his children, one dancing, one fighting. They seemed to have mastered the art of belonging to a culture where each of those activities was considered a traditional value.

On the ground in front of the bandstand lay a level plywood platform where an elderly couple stood among the dancing children, holding hands. A long-married couple, visitors might think, or the budding of a November-November romance, but Patrick Donaldson and Sally Hart were both happily married to other people, people who liked to square dance much less than either of them, so they stood on the platform patiently listening to the fiddler and waiting. It was a fairly short wait, and soon they were joined by another couple, then a third and a fourth. Once the four couples had assembled Alex Burton brought the set of tunes he was playing to a close. When he started up again it was for the first figure of a square set. The children eased back from centre stage to watch and copy.

David Cameron reached into his ever-present camera bag and began snapping pictures of the dancers, pictures that might or might not matter come the next edition, depending on how many holes he had to fill. He had learned early in journalism the truth behind the saying, "a picture is worth a thousand words." If, during the editing of the paper he found himself facing a large hole, he knew he could fill it with a last-minute, thousand-word essay on some meaningless topic or a four-column photograph of square dancers in Memorial Park. He preferred having lots of spare pictures handy.

A flash of colour took a seat beside him, Ronald MacDonald in his kilt.

"Well, David, do you think we stopped Sylvester?"

"Hard to say, Ronald. He wasn't here so I haven't had a chance to talk to him myself, if he'll talk to me at all about the land or his plans."

"Yeah, but he's going to see that everybody's against it. That should tell him something, don't you think."

"I think that if that famous MacNaughton temper comes into play he'll go ahead and bulldoze this place, all the while holding his middle finger up in the air waving it at us while he does it. Donald certainly would."

"Will you be talking to him?"

"I intend to, if he'll talk to me."

"He has to, doesn't he? You're a reporter."

"Some people think that a reporter has a right to ask questions, and he does. What most people don't realize, thank God, is that nobody, and I mean nobody, is obligated to answer any reporter's questions. Not Sylvester, not you, not even the mayor. That most people assume they have to talk to reporters makes my job easier, even possible. But don't worry, with or without quotes from Sylvester MacNaughton you've managed to get your worry about a McDonald's franchise onto the front page."

All the while he spoke, David kept his eyes shifting from one child to the other until Mary turned away from watching the dancers and ran over to her father, signalling for him to bend his head so she could whisper. David listened and burst out laughing. When Ronald raised his eyebrows, David explained, "Mary asked me why you're wearing a dress when you have no boobies."

"You let your children talk to you about things like that?" Ronald asked, partially amused, partially embarrassed by the child's candid talk.

"I saw the way you let your children talk this morning, Ronald, so I wouldn't be in a hurry to criticize other parents," David teased.

"Rita! She's my youngest you know. Love them all the same, my children, but you know how it is, there's always one in the litter that can break your heart with a smile. Dropped her whole life and came home the moment she heard about my stroke. Been with me ever since. I tell her to find herself a good man and settle down but she'll make up her own mind about that, not me. But she can heat up faster than her mother could when ... well, you saw, you heard. Don't suppose her old man embarrassed her, do you David? I guess I won't find that out until tonight when she gets home from work."

A small boy stood in front of Ronald trying to lift the edge of his kilt. Behind him a group of boys giggled as Ronald brushed the hand away and tucked the kilt tightly under his legs. "Go away!"

"Tony, don't bother Mr. MacDonald," David said to the lad whose face was flushed and whose clothes were mud and grass stained.

"I'm hungry Dad. Let's get something to eat," Tony urged.

"Your grandmother has a vegetable soup on the stove. We can go home right now and have some."

Tony made a face. "No, let's have some real food like they have in a real restaurant."

"Oh," David said. "Do you mean something good like a Big Mac or a Quarter Pounder with fries like they serve at McDonald's?"

"I wish!" the boy said while Ronald MacDonald glared at him.

| 15 |

Rita MacDonald felt herself whitening and withering under Mrs. Big Sandy's glare, the widow's large body vibrating with rage that the nurse feared would momentarily erupt into a lava of verbal violence.

The afternoon visit had begun amiably enough over tea and buttered biscuits, with discussions about the fine weather, Ronald MacDonald's picture on the front page of the newspaper and the fate of the park. Rita was now firmly on her father's side, won over late that night after work when she came home to confront Ronald about his kilted protest and learned about Sylvester MacNaughton's purchase of land in the park, and Ronald's fear that Donald MacNaughton would make it possible for the other properties, owned by the town, to be transferred to his brother.

Ronald's rumours that the ultimate goal in this conspiracy was to open a McDonald's restaurant right in the middle of Shean was something she worried about because her father had begun to believe his own stories and she worried they might actually bring on another stroke. Her own opposition to McDonald's was tepid despite a lifetime of listening to her father's propaganda, although in deference to him she had never in her life or travels darkened a McDonald's doorway. It was the potential disappearance of the park itself that appalled her, so used had she gotten to the fair-weather presence of people basking on sunlit benches, the occasional presence of children playing, the sound of music coming from the bandstand, the bright spot in midwinter when the community Christmas Tree blazed there.

By contrast, her girlhood memory of that stretch of Main Street was one where men huddled in doorways and she and her friends hung out on concrete steps on weekend nights wishing there was something to do, aching to be far away from the despair of the dark street. A park to hang out in might have made for different memories.

"I don't see anything wrong with a store there," Mrs. Big Sandy said in her turn to comment on the future of the park. "That park was just built for hoity toities to show off their daughters when they crown the Shean Gathering princesses, as if any of them is a princess. Or a queen! Besides, people are just waiting for that park to be destroyed. Not everybody likes it you know. Not the children. I've seen how many mornings the flowers have been pulled up or one of those skinny new trees broken or the railings on the bandstand kicked out. That's where that park is heading, into becoming a dump."

"I know there's been vandalism, Mrs. MacArthur, but what's remarkable to me is that every morning when something's destroyed, someone from the Legion is there planting new flowers, replacing the bandstand spindles, putting splints on broken trees. Eventually the kids will just get bored and stop vandalizing it."

"Stupidity never gets bored! I've lived in this town a lot longer than you, and I can tell you that first hand. I've been dealing with the stupid people in this town my whole life and none of them ever got any smarter by growing up, let me tell you. And if you think for a minute that park's a place for everybody to enjoy, then you come with me and watch me walk into that park all by myself and sit beside somebody on a bench. They's be gone before my arse flattens on the seat!

"No different there than at the post office. I go every day just on the dot of two when the mail has all been sorted and it's not just to get the mail. It's to watch those lazy tramps that loaf there all day waiting for the mail like it was a job, most of them never having had jobs anywhere anyway. But when I come through that door you never saw so many busy men, looking everywhere but at me as if they were scared to look me in the eye, thinking maybe I'd say, 'what do you think you're looking at?' and I would, you know, I would say it. So they get busy enough to make a person think they're working hard, trying to stick their keys back in their boxes. Oh I hope they have better aim with their wives. And what do they expect to find in there that hasn't been there the last ten times they opened their post office boxes? What they expect to find is not me in there when they're squinting in those little square holes, waiting for me to get my mail and go. Not much a woman can do to have fun around here, but going for the mail's one of them."

Mrs. Big Sandy's story drew Rita's attention to the stack of unopened mail on the kitchen counter. On the very top was an important-looking letter from Service Canada. No matter how much of a front Mrs. Big Sandy put on about being in charge of her life, the unopened mail, Rita surmised, was Mrs. Big Sandy's way of refusing to deal with her husband's death.

Then another thought came to Rita, unbidden and unfortunately uttered before she had time to assess its consequences. "Mrs. MacArthur, can you read?"

Now she sat across from the trembling rage of a woman she had been raised from childhood to fear, and felt everything from her bones to her bowels go slack. If ever Mrs. Big Sandy possessed the evil eye then she did now. Her eyes glowed with rage. Rita raised her hands protectively in front of her although she sat across the table and beyond physical reach of the angry woman. Her gesture seemed to startle the old woman. The snorting through her nose began to subside into a heavy but regular breathing, the rhythm growing calmer with each breath. "Of course I can read!"

"I was asking because your mail hasn't been opened since the funeral and I noticed some important letters there," Rita explained, almost faint with relief.

"I lost my glasses."

"I can loan you ... oh, I know, I can read them to you, if you don't mind me seeing your mail."

"What important letters?"

"The one on the top, for example. Just a second, let me go get it. Yes, this one on the top is from Service Canada. That's the department that handles pension cheques and other stuff, like deaths when a pensioner dies. This is a form and if you fill it out you will get a cheque from the government to help with Sandy's funeral costs."

"They're that happy about it, are they? Now that Sandy's dead the government's making money from not paying him and so they bribe his family to go away and shut up. This isn't bounty money, is it, because Sandy's been caught for killing that silly fool?"

"No, Mrs. MacArthur, it's not a bounty."

"It better not be!"

"I think everyone who dies gets some help with funeral costs. I could help you fill out this form then all you need to do is sign it and mail it. You should get a cheque for I don't know how much in a week or two."

"Sign it? Trying that trick on me now, are you? See if I can write. Well I can sign my name I'd like you to know. Sandy taught me. He taught me to make a big letter and a long squiggle and another big letter and another long squiggle and that's what my name is. So what business is it of yours, I'd like to know."

"It's none of my business, Mrs. MacArthur, and I'm sorry I brought it up. It's just that this mail..."

"No, I can't read."

Rita hadn't been looking Mrs. Big Sandy in the eye while she had been talking, afraid of making contact with the unknown. She looked at the old woman now, as weary and naked as she probably had ever been in front of a stranger, and thought carefully before she spoke.

"I'll never know what kind of relationship you and Sandy had but if it lasted for more than fifty years you must have gotten to know each other pretty well. I take it he always wanted what was best for you. He helped you get by not knowing how to read or write by teaching you tricks to fool people into thinking that you could."

"That's not what he did at first. At first he got these little books, they're still upstairs, about dogs and children and Granny's house and all that foolishness and tried to teach me the letters and words in them, but I was just too stupid. Everything he got me to write came out backwards, just like me. He slapped me once just like that – a backhander across the face because I said that, that the words I wrote were backwards just like me. That was the only time he ever hit me, although this town thinks this house was Madison Square Gardens, the stories I've heard from Sandy. People'd tell Sandy things about him and me that they would never say a word of in front of me or I'd have shoved their prim little heads up their tight little arses. He just thought it was funny, and if I had known for a fact, which I never have, that Sandy helped those stories along by adding to them, then he would never have lived as long as he did. There's different ways of getting along, Sandy said, but whoever spied on our lives was getting it all wrong, as if we wouldn't die for each other if we had to. I never thought about that until he said it but when he did I knew it was true, that I'd die for Sandy. This house," Mrs. Big Sandy said with a sweep of her head, "Sandy used to call it our country club for two. This table's where he tried to make me learn my words, but he never could. So there you go, I can't read or write so what's the big deal? Going to broadcast it all over town?"

"No. But the biggest deal, Mrs. MacArthur, is that you need to be able to go on living here, and to do that you're going to need money. I don't think you're rich, so you'll need to have your pension coming in, and you'll get part of Sandy's as well. You get that because you're his widow. But forms need to be filled out and mailed away and we need to find birth certificates and a death certificate and other documents. I can help you with that, if you'll let me. Will you?"

"If I don't get Sandy's cheque then the government just gets to keep it, doesn't it? We better get busy, girl. Bring that pile over here."

Side by side, with a pot of tea under a greasy cosy, the two women began the task of whittling the mail away. Most of it was junk mail, glossy pitches for credit cards or pizza specials. Two cheques and two utility bills surfaced, then another government department letter, which Rita opened. She began to read aloud but her voice trailed off into silence while the old woman watched her. "Well!" Mrs. Big Sandy ordered. Without answering, Rita put the letter aside and began rifling quickly through the rest of the pile, extracting two more unopened letters from the same department. Frightened now not for herself but for the old woman's heart, she explained what she thought the letters meant, setting off Mrs. Big Sandy's gift for verbal fireworks on a scale worthy of July first. At the end of her tirade she asked Rita what they were going to do.

"We need to go see David Cameron," Rita answered, the only person she could think of who might be able to make sense of what she discovered. She gathered the relevant letters and tucked them in a magnetized letter holder on the fridge. She would have liked to go right away but this visit, like most others, was an hour taken on her way to work, where she needed to be in a few minutes. "Tomorrow, we'll go to see him at the *Witness*," and noticing the old lady's lower lip curling with stubborn contempt, added, "I know you don't like him, but please come with me."

After establishing her independence of decision with a solid minute's silence, Mrs. Big Sandy nodded her head.

| 16 |

There was a letter waiting for David when he got home, Toronto postmark. He recognized the handwriting and the fact that it was a letter and not an email gave him pause. While his mother, Alice Cameron, prepared a pork chop supper with potatoes and turnips, and the children bickered over which cartoon to watch on television, he extracted the contents, scanned it, then read more slowly.

Alexandra, the children's mother, wrote that she wouldn't be able to bring Tony and Mary to the city once school closed, as they had agreed and in accordance with the custody agreement. Her job had "morphed" into a new opportunity that would absorb her full time for the next few months. Could David express her apologies? She promised to phone and speak with the children once he acknowledged via email that he had received her letter. She apologized if this inconvenienced David and his summer plans.

David's summer plans.

He buried his delight because the children would be disappointed. The plan had been that when school ended, he would pack them into the car and drive them to Toronto. The trip would take a few days, with them exploring parts of Nova Scotia, New

Brunswick and Quebec along the way. Once in the city they would spend a day watching a baseball game at the Skydome. David stubbornly refused to acknowledge that in the corporate culture of the times, the name had been changed to the Rogers Centre. He refused to goosestep along with that foolishness. He loved the Skydome – he could never feel anything for the Rogers Centre. Ronald MacDonald would be proud of him, he felt.

After delivering the children to their mother, David would return to Shean and let Tim enjoy the heart of the summer vacationing on the beach. He would chase the season-long litany of parades, concerts and festivals, letting the tiresome politics of school boards and council lay dormant.

He made a mental note to email Jim Turner and Bethany Burke, two friendships that had survived his departure from the *Toronto Star.* They had stood as Tony's godparents at the boy's christening, and it was they he usually got together with when he was in the city. He would miss that, the industry banter, gossip and catching-up over several glasses in their favourite drinking spot until they ended the night in some English or Irish pub. Maybe he would send an invitation by email suggesting they come to Cape Breton, check out this "mysterious East" of his that had lured him away from the headlines and bylines of the country's biggest city and newspaper.

He told his mother first, since the impact on her plans would be immediate, but she simply smiled. "I'm packing a lunch on July first and the three of us will walk to the beach and come back home on Labour Day, David. You can feed yourself in the meantime, and you can tell Tony and Mary to come and be fed right now."

"Give me a minute to let them know or let them down or whatever."

The children were sprawled in front of the television, pillows piled between them like a demilitarized zone, watching replays of *Curious George*, the tattered shape of Mary's own Curious George clutched under her arm. It wasn't Tony's choice and he impatiently aimed the remote control at the television, clicking the channel changer, unaware that Mary had the control's two batteries concealed in her hand.

David walked over to the television and manually turned it off, wondering how low-tech a guy could get. "We need to talk," he said, taking a seat on the couch while his children squirmed around on the floor to face him.

He told them about their mother's change of plans. Sadness filled Tony's face and tears welled in Mary's eyes, their winter-long expectations shattered more profoundly than David had imagined or anticipated. No outbursts or tantrums, just a simple, heartbreaking acceptance that brought a lump to his own throat. It seemed as if they had been expecting it, and yet Alexandra, who had been gone close to a year, had never given them any reason to doubt her promises, aside from her carefully worded explanation that she was going away and they would be staying behind with their father. But there was no possible way to avoid the implicit brutality of telling Tony or Mary or any child that their mother, or father, was leaving them behind. Or that their mother didn't want them to come see her this summer.

Tony turned his attention back to the remote control, clicking more and more aggressively and pointlessly until in frustration he flung the gadget at the television, dinging Curious George on the forehead before bouncing off the screen and onto the floor. Mary lowered her head into her arm and began to cry quietly, shoulders convulsing. David reached down and placed his hand on her head only to have it shaken off as the little girl snaked away beyond his reach.

The words that might have healed the moment eluded him, as the children's hurt became his own. They were the victims of the dream Alexandra and he had composed together when they left their jobs, packed their children and their belongings into the SUV and waved goodbye to Toronto in the rear-view mirror and drove off together into the sunrise.

Barely three years had passed before tensions between them led to sniping, foiled expectations and separation. The children, they promised each other amid the disintegration of their marriage, would not become victims. A pointless vow. Watching the fiercely controlled disappointment in children much too young to be so stoic, David acknowledged the folly of adults pretending they could be mature enough even in their differences to transcend the kind of behaviour and words that would hurt children. Tony and Mary were the young casualties of his and Alexandra's failure. They had inflicted the children with a pain neither child could comprehend, not for some time to come.

This was not the time to try to talk his children through whatever they were experiencing, abandonment or betrayal or some other unarticulated loss. Leaving them to their isolation he went back into the kitchen and explained about the letter and the children's disappointment.

"See how lucky you are?" Alice Cameron asked her son.

"Lucky! My children are devastated and I don't know what to say to them, what to do for them."

"Yes, but lucky you still have your mother to run to when you have a scrape on your knee or your heart. The best thing to be doing now is just what you're doing, letting them be, but don't let them be alone with that disappointment for too long before you talk to them about it."

"How do I tell when it's the right time, Mrs. Wisdom?"

"You won't be able to tell the right time by looking. You need to listen for it. I'm just sharing with you a little trick I picked up practicing on a young boy you remind me of, in fact. Now call Tony and Mary to dinner."

The children spent their table time sculpting potatoes and turnips and some animal parts into something utterly inedible. David decided not to notice, and talked about how they could get the best out of what summer has to offer right here at home. A little known, world-class beach practically in their backyard was really something, the kids knew, but compared to their winter-long anticipation of Canada's Wonderland with its rides and fancy ice cream and Kidzville, it was just a beach their father took them to. It was fun, but Canada's Wonderland was the country's largest sand castle and they were going to see it, be there. And then they weren't.

David needed to find ways to be with them or perhaps better still ways for them not to be with him while he hovered over them from a distance. The summer had already been divvied up into vacation blocks at the paper and his name wasn't to be found anywhere between the beginning of July and early September. He had magnanimously foregone a summer vacation, preferring autumn when the kids would be back home from Toronto and they could have weekend vacations together. Not such a great idea after all. He knew he couldn't go into the office and bump someone's vacation. He might own the paper but Conrad Black he wasn't. If he tried to pull rank with the staff his life could get seriously mauled in the process. There wasn't a single person on the staff who counted hours on the days when they laid out the newspaper. Nor when they were dealing with some of the paper's other problems.

There were also business decisions that he was unprepared to make because the staff knew better than he what was good for the business, and, by default, for him. What it essentially boiled down to was that the staff was protecting the business from its owner. He got a paycheque at the end of almost every week. He learned about financial crises from Helen MacKinnon as they arose and did what he was told in order to soothe the situation. This business strategy depended on him pretending not to know the score, while the staff understood that he was more aware of what was going on than they liked to give him credit for. It worked perfectly if not particularly profitably, and David was not going to disturb that equilibrium by declaring "I'm the boss!"

The alternative was to stay alert for opportunities for the children, scour the ads in the paper for distractions and hopefully keep them busy until they'd forgotten all about Toronto and began to just enjoy themselves. In fact, most of the stories he had to cover over the few weeks involved music or dance or food or storytelling or workshops. Hell, he'd hire them.

"Since you two are going to be home here all summer don't think for a minute you're going to have a free ride. Since you're not in school there's no reason why you can't pay room and board while you're living in this house. You're going to need jobs, both of you, and you're in luck. There happens to be an opening at the *Witness* for a couple of apprentice photographers. Since there's no school tomorrow there's no reason why you can't start work in the morning, unless of course you don't want the jobs. In that case, we may have to ship you out to Fort McMurray..."

"I want a job!" they shouted in unison.

"Then be ready to leave here with me at eight o'clock. On our way to work we need to detour to Lake John. There's a farmer up there whose cow just had three calves. I need to take a picture of them, or maybe one of my assistants might want to click the camera."

"I'm your assistant for that, Dad," Tony shouted, and Mary asked, "Can I come anyway?"

"Yes, Mary, but only if you promise me one thing. I've already spoken to Glenn Skye and he told me that triplet calves might make a good picture but that's all they're good for. He's a dairy farmer and for one reason or another, these calves won't grow up to be milk cows. I don't know why that is..."

"Maybe they're all boys, Daddy," Mary interjected, startling David that his daughter was already so familiar with the biological functions of boys and girls.

"You're probably right, but what I do know is that Glenn is offering the calves to anyone who wants one for free and no matter how tempting the offer is, Mary, Tony, neither one of you is to look at those cute little animals and say you want to bring one home. Is that understood?"

The children nodded.

"Good."

"Dad, how much are you going to pay us?"

"Son, you are going to be on the same pay scale as those immigrants that come to Canada to work in sweat shops of one form or another, at least a dollar a day."

"Wow!"

| 17 |

Tim and David were clicking through a collection of pictures Tim had uploaded to the office's computers, interesting angles of street corners, oddities including a dog perched behind the driver's wheel of a parked car, and an assortment of "can't lose" shots of children, one of slumbering twins in a grocery cart. David was looking for anything for the front page more interesting than a grip-and-grin of Mayor MacNaughton presenting the Business Person of the Year plaque to William Storey, the only significant businessperson in Shean who had never spent a dime on advertising in the *Witness*. It was too much publicity for either creep, according to David, who was about to point out his choice when he glanced over Tim's shoulder and muttered, "Oh, Jesus!"

Tim cast a glance over the same shoulder and saw Mrs. Big Sandy and Rita MacDonald bearing down on the editor's glassed-in cubbyhole and, picking up his camera case, made for the door, getting there just in time to hold it open for the two women, nod his welcome, then close the door behind him, whispering to David, "Think lions and Christians."

The *Witness* staff was hyper-vigilant this morning, heads down, phones tucked between ears and shoulders or captivated by computer screens, but at any given moment there was at least one set of eyes casually glancing in his direction. Over tea in the lunchroom the staff pieced together the whole encounter.

"What can I do for you ladies?" David asked, standing behind his high-backed office chair.

"We need to talk to you..."

"*She* needs to talk to you," Mrs. Big Sandy interrupted.

"We need to talk to you," Rita began again. "I don't know who else might know."

"Might know what?"

"Why the province has expropriated Mrs. MacArthur's house and land. It looks like it's already a done deal, David." Rita passed a group of letters across the desk to him.

David picked up the official-looking stationary and read the notice of expropriation. Hundreds of acres were under mine tailings containing an unknown amount of contamination, most notably PCBs from old mine generators that may have been buried in the tailings. The letter bearing the attorney general's letterhead and signature stated it was the Minister's responsibility to act to protect the safety of Nova Scotians.

Mrs. MacArthur would be compensated for the land at market value, but what was market value, David wondered in silence, considering the potential environmental problems and the cost to taxpayers to rehabilitate the property.

"There were two prior notifications over the weeks since Sandy Mac-Arthur died, but they went unnoticed and so Mrs. MacArthur wasn't able to challenge the expropriation," Rita explained.

"Unnoticed?" David asked, curious.

Rita remained silent.

"Well you might as well tell him so he can tell the whole goddamned world in that rag of his that I can't read or write," Mrs. Big Sandy snapped.

"You're illiterate?" David asked her.

Mrs. Big Sandy's face grew stroke red. "I am not! My parents were married for years before they had me and if you think you're going to write something like that in that newspaper of yours I'll feed your balls to my dog!"

"She doesn't have a dog. Mrs. MacArthur," Rita said, speaking softly, naturally so the old woman had to calm down to listen to her. "David's not saying you're illegitimate. He asked if you are illiterate, which means a person who can't read or write. It's nothing to be ashamed of and it's certainly not going into the newspaper..."

"It better not," Mrs. Big Sandy warned. "But I've seen the lies you put in that paper of yours, the one in that paper, the same paper that was about Sandy's funeral."

"There were no lies, Mrs. MacArthur, just the facts that were given to me by the RCMP and what had been written at the time the crime took place," David said, stepping from behind his chair, prepared to defend his professional integrity.

"I don't mean the story about Sandy. I mean the other story you wrote on the front page saying Donald the Bastard broke his jaw in a car accident."

"It was no lie. The mayor's car went off the road and his face hit the steering wheel. I thought you couldn't read?"

"Maybe I can't but I can tell when somebody is laughing at what they're reading and I saw her father," nodding toward Rita, "and that Don Alex fellow reading that front page and laughing. I went aboard them with a piece of my tongue. They were just lucky it was just a piece of my tongue but I couldn't stand anybody laughing at Sandy. Not one of all the cowards in this town would laugh at him when he was alive. It was Ronald MacDonald who told me they were laughing at the mayor's car accident, saying that the worst thing that could happen to a politician would be breaking his jaw so he couldn't speak ... Car accident my arse!"

"Do you know something about the accident?" David asked.

"No, because there was no accident. Ask me how he got his jaw broke, though, and I might have something to tell you."

"Tell me about the mayor's jaw," David asked, hitting the "On" button on his desk recorder.

"The night Sandy died, the very next morning, six o'clock in the morning if you can believe that, comes a knock on my door. It was the mayor and this other man."

"Who was the other man?"

"Oh, Lord, I don't know. I never seen him before ... oh, that's right, Lord. His name was Lord, something, something, something Lord, a stiff little prick with no hair and a necktie as tight as a noose. The Bastard, Donald that is, not the other bastard, offered me money for Sandy's home. Poor Sandy was still warm in his bed at the Manor when this bastard comes trying to steal his land. So I slapped him!"

"Slapped him? You slapped the mayor and broke his jaw?" David asked, caught between incredulity and awe.

"Well maybe I had the cast-iron frying pan in my hand at the time but I slapped him and his jaw broke, and that was in my kitchen, not some ditch beside the road."

Hours after Rita MacDonald and Mrs. Big Sandy left his office, hours after Tim Donovan had come and gone from the office several times, long after the staff had shut down the computers, put out the lights and left for the day, long after the sun set, David Cameron was still at work, sifting through copies of the expropriation documents that had been delivered to Mrs. Big Sandy, lying unread week after week while bureaucratic forces closed around her.

He had downloaded and read the province's *Expropriation Act*, talked to whatever public servants he could contact, most of them remote from their respective ministers, all apparently oblivious to the issue he was pursuing, the expropriation of the late Sandy MacArthur's substantial property that lay along a large portion of the Shean shoreline.

What he could determine was that there was little to prevent the expropriation of land by this or any provincial government if it was in the public interest. The *Act* identified among the circumstances under which the power to expropriate could be enacted the simple, deceptive and dangerous phrase, "for any purpose that is a public purpose."

In an era of heightened environmental concern the rehabilitation of a hazardous waste site could be spun into a tale of a vigilant government acting in the interests of the province's environment and the people's health. Couple that with the fact that the land in question now belonged to a woman who had generally terrorized a small town, who had few if any defenders, and the public perception would be that the government was wearing a white hat. While he imagined that anyone would have a hard time getting close to Mrs. Big Sandy, she did seem to have Rita MacDonald on her side. Not a bad ally since David acknowledged that it was Rita's concern for the old lady and not his own that made him sit patiently through the unfolding of documents. As they were presented to him by Rita, it became evident that regardless of his personal feelings, no one, not even Mrs. Big Sandy, deserved to lose her home at the flick of a pen. It was a story reeking of injustice no matter how justified was the Attorney General, now the de facto owner of the expropriated land.

David Cameron's complicity in this expropriation was well documented. How many editorials had he written over the past few years as *Witness* editor calling for a detailed investigation by the Department of Environment into the Shean tailings? So many rumours, half-truths and myths had surfaced from out of that contaminated soil over the years – an unnerving number of cancer cases primarily, but everything else from birth defects to blindness – that the newspaper called for an environmental assessment to dispel or confirm people's fears.

That the Shean tailings had been on a list of the top ten most hazardous sites in Nova Scotia was a fact. But environment department experts had argued that the listing was based on visual evidence only – the pooling of rust-coloured water indicating the presence of minerals in the mine waste, the oily rainbows that formed a slick on those water pools, the protrusion through the grey clay of iron rails and spikes and broken mining tools such as shovel pans and pick heads all spoke of potential contamination. The grey mountains of slag had been hauled up from under the sea and dumped there, an ugly by-product of once profitable coal. What was visible on the surface really gave no indication of what other environmental horrors might lurk beneath that clay. No core samples had ever been taken, so whether contaminants such as PCBs or other cancer-causing agents actually existed in those tailings had been neither tested for nor confirmed.

One reason for not testing soil samples, David was told off the record by one department official, was because if carcinogens were discovered in the Shean tailings, then the government would be committed to a multimillion dollar clean-up with money it didn't have. The department attitude was to leave well enough alone.

So why now? David wondered, reading the ponderous documents over and over again. The terms of compensation were clearly laid out, and Mrs. Big Sandy would certainly come out of expropriation with enough money to buy herself a more manageable house or move into a seniors' apartment complex and do some travelling.

He toyed with that image for a moment: Mrs. Big Sandy playing shuffleboard aboard a luxury cruiser somewhere in the Caribbean, still wrapped in her heavy, fake fur-collared coat worn through all seasons, heaving anyone who disagreed with her overboard. Yeah, feeding people to the sharks would be right up her alley alright, he figured. So if she ever offered him a ticket, he had better refuse, unless she also offered one to Rita MacDonald ... And there she was again, in the middle of his professional thoughts about his newspaper and government injustice, turning her head away when Mrs. Big Sandy described how she slapped the mayor across the face with the cast-iron frying pan, shoulders shaking with a laughter he couldn't share because the woman responsible was staring him in the eyes.

The morning of that incident, David recalled, flipping through his own notes, was the morning Big Sandy passed away. And a couple of hours later, six o'clock in the morning according to his widow, they had come to offer to buy her house and land, just days ahead of the first notice of expropriation. Donald Mac-Naughton and Something Something Something Lord.

Something worth looking into.

| 18 |

David Cameron stared at Peter Mansbridge reporting the news on *The National*, his mind adrift on news closer to home, news that would never cross Mansbridge's desk, the expropriation of an old woman's home in a rural outpost of eastern Canada. The children were both in bed, David's own imaginary stories of fairies and ogres having lulled them into dreams.

Pacing restlessly from the livingroom to the kitchen and back, his foot got tangled in his mother's growing Afghan. He tripped, righted himself.

"What's the matter with you tonight, David?"

"Nothing. I'm going for a drive. I'll be back shortly."

"Well if it's shortly at the tavern you be sure you don't drive back here. Remember it's just a nice walk home."

David had been thinking about the tavern, a couple of beers in the company of a couple of buddies, shoot a little pool, but the appeal dissipated when he drove into the parking lot and saw Donald MacNaughton's Chrysler there. Normally, it would have lured him inside, their spirited, brutal banter entertaining their friends, but there was too much on David's mind at the moment, and somewhere within that tangled mess of information and issues was the mayor. Not a good time for baiting or being baited.

Instead, he wheeled out of the parking lot and found himself pulling into the staff lot at the Shean Manor. The dash clock read 10:40 P.M. Rita MacDonald would still be on shift and this time of night it was probably quiet inside. It wasn't like they had nothing to talk about. A guy might even score a cup of coffee.

"So do you think she's going to lose her home?" Rita asked, pouring coffee into two cups in the nurses' lounge.

"It can happen. I've talked to some very unhelpful people in environment, public works and the attorney general's office, none of whom are vaguely aware of the expropriation and who couldn't, or wouldn't, put me in contact with anyone who might know something. The *Act* itself is pretty clear. If the government can make a case for acting in the public's interest, it just needs to serve up the papers. Once the documents have been served, the Crown has control of the land even if legal title and possession don't take place until a later date. Compensation is determined by the land value. Mrs. Big Sandy can contest, of course, but she'll need a lawyer and probably a lot of money."

"Is there anything your paper can do for her?"

"It's a story, naturally. Whether or not it's a cause for the paper I haven't decided. And frankly, how deeply I want to become involved with Mrs. Big Sandy is a question I haven't asked myself yet."

"What difference does that make?" Rita snapped. "Her home is being stolen from her and I can't see how you can't think the same thing, having seen those documents. Who she is isn't the point, or shouldn't be. It wasn't when you were in Toronto. Those stories you wrote about the homeless almost made me go broke giving my money away every time I walked down Yonge Street."

"You were in Toronto then?" David asked.

"Yes, working at St. Michael's. I used to buy the *Star* just to see your name because it was somebody from home. I saw you and your wife once or twice at the Bow & Arrow on Sunday afternoons when the fiddlers were there. You may have been a big city reporter but you were homesick for the music, weren't you? But I didn't think you were this homesick," Rita added, holding her hands out in exasperation. "What ever possessed you to come back?"

"Because this is where I've always wanted to be," David explained. "When the *Witness* went up for sale, Alexandra and I were able to put together the money to buy it. A reporter can be just as good here as in Toronto. It's not how big your readership is, but the quality of journalism they're reading."

"That's what I'm counting on," Rita replied, hiding her smile behind a sip from her cup.

"Counting on?"

"You're too good a reporter to think that Mrs. Big Sandy isn't getting screwed by somebody. You need to help her. It's the least you can do for a woman you once shot in the arse."

"Oh, shit! Did she tell you that?"

"Mentioned it once in passing, I believe. But this stinks, David. This really stinks."

David looked into her eyes, saw himself reflected there and wondered for a moment if that was where he belonged. "Yes, it does," he answered. "But I don't know how far we can take her fight.

"Look, here's what we know. Shortly after Sandy died his widow was notified of the expropriation of her home and property. The Attorney General is the person who holds the deed in the name of the Crown, or the government. The reason for the expropriation, according to the documents, is to rehabilitate a piece of property that nobody can deny is a potential nightmare of carcinogenics. I don't think anybody in Shean will be opposed to the idea of cleaning up the MacArthur land. Hell, I'm not.

"What's tougher to see is an old woman evicted from her home, but if the compensation package is hefty enough, public sentiment, whatever there is of it for Mrs. Big Sandy, will side with the idea that she's getting a better house somewhere, maybe even in the seniors' complex.

"Wait! I stand corrected. If she's moved into the seniors' apartments, one of Shean's demographics won't be dancing for joy. But living in another place, a house, an apartment, she'll be warmer, healthier and financially better off. So will the town if that land of hers is capped and sealed with clay or however they plan to rehabilitate it."

"So you don't see any problems?"

"I don't. Not if I ignore the fact, and I suspect it is a fact, that the morning Sandy died Donald MacNaughton and an unknown stranger showed up at Mrs. Big Sandy's door offering to buy her house and land. And if I ignore the fact that she received her expropriation notice shortly after Sandy's death. Just too timely."

"Sandy was sick for a long time, maybe a year, before he died," Rita joined in. "That's how long we know about because that's when he finally went to the doctor. But if somebody knew Sandy was dying, and everybody in town did, and that it might be possible to expropriate his property, they may have been preparing this for months, is that what you think?"

David smiled at her subtle manoeuvring. "That's what I'm beginning to think about now."

"So what's going on, David?"

| 19 |

"So what's going on, Donald?" David asked, taking a stool beside the mayor and signalling the waitress for a cup of coffee. Word of the expropriation of the MacArthur property, information he thought was held in confidence by the widow, Rita MacDonald and himself, was all over Shean a day before the next issue of the *Witness* was due to hit its streets with the breaking news.

MacNaughton sipped from his coffee and smiled at David in the mirror behind the counter, neither one turning his head sideways to look at the other. "Don't tell me the award-winning newsman has missed the big story. They tell me Mrs. Big Sandy's property is going to be expropriated. Thought you would have heard about that by now."

"When did you hear about it, Mr. Mayor?"

"Maybe it was on the CBC this morning that I heard it. Or did I hear it later, right here in the Gulf Grill during breakfast? Or was it when I took a walk through the park after breakfast? God, come to think about it, I think my wife heard about it in the Co-op last night, or maybe when she was at bingo. You know how hard it is to keep a secret in this town, David."

"Yes, I do, Donald. So many secrets in fact that I don't know which secret to lead with this week, the secret about the expropriation or the rumour I heard of somebody filing a false accident report, telling the RCMP that he had gone into a ditch when it was actually a cast-iron frying pan that he had run into. So what's going on, Donald?"

MacNaughton reddened but didn't lose a beat. "Look, can we go off the record here," he asked, looking over his shoulder, gauging their privacy.

David gave the suggestion a moment's thought. "Go ahead, Donald, nothing you tell me here will be on the record, because I'd like you to fill in the background. And because you know that you can count on me finding another way to get the same information for my story, so go ahead."

"Okay, I've known for some time now that the property was going to be expropriated. I may even be responsible for it. As mayor I've been concerned for a long time about having a potential toxic waste site practically in the middle of town. Practically? Hell, we both know that place is full of poison. I've raised it a few times with the Minister of Environment at meetings in Halifax, naming the MacArthur property itself, but I never miss an opportunity to remind one of the heavyweights that we've got some serious toxic concerns here. So a few weeks ago I was given a heads up that the expropriation was going ahead, part of the government's new green plan. Pre-election green plan, of course, but if we can benefit as a community, great. Even you and I can see eye to eye on this issue, David."

"About the rehabilitation of the MacArthur property? Of course I can, but I don't see why the land needs to be expropriated. Why couldn't the province just cap it with clay to contain whatever's in there, and let Mrs. Big Sandy keep her place? Same benefit to the community."

"Liability questions. You know the government's not going to contract out an environmental rehab program without having control over the property. So the property needs to be expropriated. No big secret there."

"No big secret? I have a friend who still works for the *Toronto Star* – business reporter – and I'm sure that if he was looking at this story, especially the part you left out about yourself and Mr. Lord offering to buy the MacArthur property just days before the expropriation notice, he'd have some questions. Especially if the price you offered was lower than the province's compensation. I'm pretty sure he'd call it insider trading."

"Jesus, David. We're off the record here, but it's not what you're thinking. I wasn't trying to steal the woman's property. Christ, I'm not that stupid." Donald MacNaughton paused, breathing deeply, bringing his voice down. He rubbed his freshly unwired jaw thoughtfully. "Maybe almost that stupid but not quite. If you know about C.J.M. Lord, then you know he's an investor, and he's been making some inquiries about opportunities here. He likes the area, plans to build a house here, a summer place at least, and wouldn't mind helping the town out, if there's a profit in it for him, of course."

"Of course, but why the MacArthur property?"

"Socialists like you don't get it, David, but capitalists like C.J.M. Lord can't stand government interference in people's lives. Expropriating private property is even worse than forcing them to pay taxes. The expropriation came up in a conversation late one night and he got this idea that he was going to save a fair maiden in distress. What'd he know? What'd I know? At least he got out of there with his head intact which is more than I can say for myself. And that's all there was to it. And we're still off the record, right?"

———

"If they think they're going to take my god damned house, if they think that I'm just going to sit here waiting for some bastard of a policeman to tell me to leave, well let me tell you I got one more good fight in me. Yes siree, girlee, I have one more fight in me and I'll die right here at this table before I let some son of a bitch of a policeman put me out on the street. Do those people think we lived like wolves in a cave all these years? That me and Sandy didn't have a house of our own, a home of our own? That's all we had! And that's all that's left for me out of this whole terrible mess of a world. That's what Sandy left me. That's what this is, our home. My home now."

Mrs. Big Sandy reached across the table and grabbed the letter that informed her that she had not much more than a week to find other accommodations, offering help in finding those accommodations if she wished. She crumbled it to garbage in her white-knuckled hand and threw it back toward Rita. The nurse let it fall to the floor.

"Mrs. MacArthur, I don't know what you can do. I can't believe that this is happening to someone I know. It's terrible to say but with all these documents and lawyers involved you may have to leave here."

"I will never–"

Rita put up her hand, surprised that it succeeded in silencing the woman. "You may need to leave here. I know you don't want to hear that and I know you're going to fight it but even if you do, you could lose and then what will you do? Planning for the possibility of a different future doesn't mean surrendering. Sometimes your plans for yourself and what life has planned for you go in different directions. I know a little about that myself. Where would you like to go? You should decide that, not somebody else."

Mrs. Big Sandy bristled at the words but asked, "You're a bit young to be lecturing me on what life can and cannot do, young lady! Besides, what choice do I have?"

"There's the Shean Manor…"

"Where Sandy was?"

"Yes, it's a seniors' care facility…"

"There's nothing up there but a bunch of carcasses waiting to be buried. Do you expect me to sit around for the rest of my life with my mouth hanging open like this? And be housebroken all over again just like I was a baby in diapers? Well it doesn't matter anyway because I'm not leaving here. Not now, not ever."

"There are also the seniors' apartments, you know the buildings. You've probably visited them already."

"Visited them! And why would I do that? A bunch of old women in bridge clubs who can't even play bridge. That's what Sandy used to say, they can't even play bridge but it sounds ritzier than having an Auction 45 Club or a Crib Club or a club-sandwich-to-go club. Imagine me having to live in the middle of them. But thinking about it, it sure could be fun, couldn't it, if I put my mind to it. I could corner them all in that clubroom of theirs where's there no escape, and half of them in walkers. I don't even know what I'd do with all that power but that's the stuff for daydreams and this is a real nightmare I'm in. I won't leave my house! Tell them that, Rita. Please for the love of God tell somebody that for me."

| 20 |

David Cameron sat at his desk trying to decide on an editorial, feeling the stress of the day, of the week, gnaw at his stomach and nerves. Mrs. Big Sandy's pending eviction and the apparent reclamation of the old mine tailings was a big story in the context of Shean's day-to-day life but he was publishing what he knew to be a half-arsed job of the story.

It was the kind of a story that required full-time attention for at least a week or two but the reality of a weekly newspaper with two reporters was that the rest of life in Shean or the surrounding county didn't stop just because something larger than usual was elbowing its way onto the front page. The week that should have been devoured by Mrs. Big Sandy's eviction and the plans for reclamation of the mine tailings was also shared by the obligatory coverage of Friday night's volunteer fire department's annual banquet and dance, a school bus accident on Main Street that scared but didn't injure any children, the Salmon Association's concern with erosion along the river banks threatening pools where salmon gather and grim predictions for the season ahead regarding tourism.

Tim Donovan was lost for the weekend covering a minor league baseball tournament and a year-end dart tournament, chasing down the RCMP about a series of break-ins at a number of summer homes outside the town and then needing to cover a Saturday night concert kicking off a summer of fiddles and pianos and dancers and Gaelic singing.

The whole of production day David normally devoted to the writing of his stories, which he preferred to write in his home office where it was more peaceful, less interrupted than the newspaper's office. When he finished he would go to the office to take part in the layout, and as a final duty, pen the *Witness*'s weekly editorial.

With the completion of his home writing, his stories emailed in for proofreading, David recalled something he had meant to do. He leafed through his notebook and found the name Donald MacNaughton had inadvertently provided, C.J. M. Lord. He was typing the name into Google to search out the background of Shean's mysterious benefactor when the sound of a child's scream froze him at his desk. What he heard next was Mary's tumbling down the stairway. Seconds later he found his daughter at the bottom of the stairs unconscious and alarmingly white. His mother covered her granddaughter with an afghan from the couch while David dialled 9-1-1. The ambulance arrived within five minutes and he followed the stretcher into it.

At the hospital, Dr. Andrea Wallace took cool, efficient stock of the emergency, gesturing to keep David back a distance but not banishing him from the room while she and the emergency room nurse took the girl's vitals. Mary's eyes slowly opened, and Dr. Andrea asked questions that the crying girl answered. Mary occasionally touched her left arm with a timid right hand, exploring the first really horrible thing that had happened to the child in the physical world. Her answers seemed to relieve the doctor, who sent Mary for X-rays that confirmed the physician's suspicion that a broken arm comprised the total damage from the nasty fall. She set about putting the arm in a cast.

Watching the procedure, David felt an upswell of gratitude on behalf of himself and all of Shean. Andrea Wallace had graduated from Shean High School at the top of her class, a position she continued to occupy throughout university and medical school. Three years ago, a newly minted MD, she returned to Shean to practise medicine. Health care in Nova Scotia, throughout all rural Canada for that matter, was a system in trouble according to the relentless reports of weekend emergency room closures because of doctor shortages in small- and medium-size communities. *The Witness* had never had to carry that message, thanks to the fact that the town's aging squad of doctors was being shored up by Andrea Wallace's coming home. That terrifying message of emergency closures was, for the time being, a distant threat.

Few people saw up close on a weekly basis the effects of population loss the way David did. It was present either overtly as or as sub-text in just about every story he wrote: a primary class enrolment last September that was half what the school would graduate at the end of the month; the migration to Alberta's mega projects which swallowed the young and unemployed in Shean, leaving virtually no one between the ages of twenty and forty at home, and most would eventually opt for not coming back at all. Professional opportunities for the best educated of Shean's children were few and even when available the will to return was usually lacking. Dr. Andrea Wallace was one of the exceptions, and exceptional, David thought as he listened to her instruct his daughter on what she could and could not do with the arm in the cast.

"...and I want you to make me a promise," the doctor told her patient. Mary's eyes opened large in silent promise to do the doctor's bidding. "I want you to promise me that you won't break this arm until the other one is better."

The attention she had given to his daughter's health gratified David as he reviewed the day, what had and what had not gotten done. During his time in the hospital he had not turned a single thought toward the *Witness* until Mary was safe and no longer in pain. It was assuring to know that the newspaper wasn't the most important thing in his life. There had been and would be times when the business or the content of the paper consumed him so that days or a week would pass before he became conscious of the children beyond going through the motions of his duty to them and it worried him that the paper may be supplanting Mary and Tony in importance. It wasn't. It wouldn't.

———

What he had to tell people about Mrs. Big Sandy MacArthur's loss of land and forthcoming eviction was a watered-down, distracted version of the truth. In his talking to people, officials or the general public, it was evident that most favoured the expropriation. No one was taking delight in Mrs. Big Sandy's eviction, or not many people were, but most people seemed to see the big picture. The idea of an industrial scar being cosmetically covered with thick, red clay and sprayed with grass seed, and the improvement it would make in the town's appearance, trumped, not always without sympathy, but trumped Mrs. Big Sandy's claim on the land. Knowing that she would be compensated made it easier to support the expropriation. A win-win situation, as the biggest winners in situations such as these liked to say.

Councillor James Jamison, David's story related, was happy with the prospect of reclamation. Jamison, chair of the Shean Development Commission, saw the idea of capping the old mine tailings as a step toward his vision of a golf course to anchor a development strategy that had tourists as its primary focus. Once the Jamison-led strategy left that solid theme, its plans for Shean grew vague and hopeful and full of platitudes. David could appreciate how animated Jamison became, development ideas growing in his mind as he spoke with the reporter, the councillor finding it amusing that he and Donald MacNaughton were in agreement about something.

With just one assignment left, David Cameron began scribbling notes on his laptop, outlining his choices for an editorial. They included editorial empathy with Mrs. Big Sandy and the celebration of James Jamison's renewed vision for Shean. Consumed by Mary's accident, his thoughts on either of those other topics faltered and finally failed. Instead, he wrote a fluid appreciation for the professionals in medicine, education and business who chose to return home to Shean or, originating from elsewhere, chose Shean as their home. Many others might consider Shean, he wrote, if the option existed for them. But most people, former Sheaners from the young to the middle aged, do not have the choice of deciding if this is where they want to be. People can't be forced to live where they don't want to be, the editor argued, but it is the town's responsibility, through leadership from the mayor, to create an environment where young people at least have that choice of staying in Shean. Like Jamison's strategic plan, the editorial was vague and hopeful and full of platitudes.

| 21 |

"A stiff little prick with no hair and a necktie as tight as a noose."

Rita suppressed a smile at the accuracy of Mrs. Big Sandy's description of the man who had accompanied Mayor Mac-Naughton the morning of the frying pan incident. Both men were now standing in the main entrance of the town hall while Rita waited her turn with the mayor. MacNaughton was an unlikely place to begin but her campaign on behalf of the widow needed to begin somewhere.

"Rita," MacNaughton called, signalling that he could see her now. They walked into his office, the same office from which the mayors of Shean had managed the town's affairs for more than a century, some ineptly, some adequately, none full time. Like his predecessors, Donald MacNaughton was mayor on a part-time basis in exchange for a modest stipend. His income, like that of most of the councillors, came from independent sources. MacNaughton's family business in home hardware was started by his grandfather, and three generations later was still thriving despite the economic challenges facing the small town. Despite the part-time job description, the role of mayor could consume a person full time if he allowed it – and Donald MacNaughton seemed to have let that happen, leaving his brother Sylvester to manage the family business.

"I know I should have made an appointment," Rita started by way of apology but it was dismissed with a wave of Mac-Naughton's hand.

"If I was the mayor of Toronto it might be necessary but here it's catch as catch can and you caught me. What can I do for you, Rita? Is this about your father?"

"No. Dad and your brother can sort out their own problems. And I'm not proud of my scene in the park. I've come about Mrs. MacArthur, about the expropriation, the eviction really. I'm asking if there is anything you can do to slow this down, to give her time to breathe, to get used to the idea. I don't understand the rush."

Donald MacNaughton seemed to be giving Rita's request serious thought except that in his reflective silence he vigorously massaged his healed jaw, giving her a peek into where his thoughts might really be.

"Rita, this isn't really a municipal matter. It's provincial. It's the attorney general's action but even if there was something I could do I'd need to think long and hard about it. I, and council of course, have to act in the community's best interests and in this case I believe the rehabilitation of that property is in everyone's best interest, Rita. Even Mrs. Big Sandy's. She's alone in that huge house that's practically falling down. She has no family. None that will claim her anyway," the mayor said with a wide smile that shrank and vanished with Rita's refusal to respond. "Look, Rita, the attorney general acts for the province in these matters, and the province rarely consults with municipalities about its intentions unless there's political gain in it. He's the person you would need to talk to, Rita, but he's acting at the insistence of the Minister of Environment, and from what I understand even the premier, and I don't need to tell you that anybody trying to clean up the environment is on the side of the angels these days. Do you follow me, Rita?"

Rita nodded what she imagined he saw as her "pretty little head" in assurance, and tried to count the number of times he had used her name in their short conversation, wondering if it was the remote beginnings of flattery or just a politician's annoying habit.

"So you see, Rita, the A.G. is the person you would need to speak with. You can call him, and I can get you his direct number, but what it comes down to is a stubborn old woman's wishes against the health of a whole lot of people."

"And what about the wealth of a lot of people, Donald? Or a few?"

"Meaning what?"

"Meaning that the reclamation could mean a golf course on that land, according to what James Jamison had to say in the *Witness* this morning. That would mean money in somebody's pocket eventually, wouldn't it? Is that why the rush is on?"

"Rita, it's quite possible that James Jamison is a bit premature with his speculation. A golf course is not off the table but who's to say what options might present themselves for Shean as a result of the rehabilitation. Regardless of who invests, the coffers of this town are sorely in need of a broader tax base. I don't know who benefits directly or indirectly in the end, but I do know that Shean itself benefits regardless of who it is. I'll get that number for you now, then I need to meet with some other people."

Rita had never paid much attention to politics but she felt she was getting educated in a hurry. The Attorney General had taken her call and it obviously took him off guard – his first question was to ask her where she got his number. Maybe it was a mistake to try to lighten the question by telling him she found it on the wall of the women's washroom in the Five Bucks Beverage Room, but her instinct had been to protect Donald MacNaughton, although she couldn't imagine why. The Attorney General had been brief and to the point; nothing she could say would alter his decision regarding the expropriation of the MacArthur property.

Attempts to speak with the Minister of Environment were even more futile since she couldn't get past the department's information officer, whose sole mandate, it was clear, was to divulge as little information as possible.

There was no help for Mrs. Big Sandy, and that was the stomach-churning message that Rita was forced to deliver later that day.

"I'm sorry, Mrs. MacArthur, but I don't know whom to turn to now." Her thoughts turned to David Cameron and the *Witness*, which Rita had felt at one time was their only hope. David Cameron had let them down, she thought, reporting objectively on the eviction but avoiding any defence of the victim in his wishy-washy editorial, where he never touched the issue at all.

"Nothing to be sorry for since there's nothing you'd have been able to do anyway. It's what Sandy always said, that politicians are the worst kind of slaves because they sell their souls to the highest bidder and people like us, the people who vote, don't bid very high. But some bastard bid high enough to steal Sandy's land, didn't they? There's nothing to be done for it now. Some things can be changed and some things can't. " She reached across the table to pick up Rita's empty cup.

"I don't want a reading," Rita said, trying to draw it back.

The old woman let the cup go, looking hard into Rita's eyes. "There's nothing to be scared of, not in that there cup and not in your own life, not unless you let people make you scared. That's what Sandy learned me and that's what I'd like to learn you, that all the Donald the Bastards in the world aren't worth getting scared of, no matter what they think they can do. You remember that, okay? That there's nothing to be scared of."

"Maybe you already taught me that, Mrs. MacArthur. I'm not one bit scared of you any more." Rita smiled through a nameless discomfort, a discomfort that followed her up the driveway to work, as if she could feel Mrs. Big Sandy's eyes still watching her.

| 22 |

David walked back to the *Witness* van to change the batteries in his camera, ducking under the stretch of police tape. The large, forlorn house looked under siege: Sheriff John Thurber's SUV, Corporal Harry Noseworthy's RCMP four-wheeler along with two other RCMP vehicles used by the three constables under his command, Shean's volunteer fire brigade in full force and uniform and, beyond the yellow tape, scores of onlookers piecing together fragments of gossip, trying to create a version of events upon which they could all agree.

Among the firefighters David recognized Donald Mac-Naughton readying the hoses beside the truck. He ducked back under the tape and wandered over to the mayor. While he was naturally suspicious of most of MacNaughton's motives, David knew that his volunteering for the fire department wasn't just about public image. A long time ago, when they shared their boyhood dreams, being a fireman was first among Donald's heroic choices. Besides, since buying the *Witness* there had been enough fires, grass fires, midsummer forest fires, midwinter chimney fires and serious house fires for David to reaffirm that knowledge.

Donald loved being a fireman. In his role with the department he never involved himself in the power structure of the brigade. He simply went out for every training opportunity, turned up for fires and fought them with passion.

"So what's going on, Donald?"

"Seems to be your favourite question, David."

"So what's going on? Your take on the situation, Mr. Mayor?"

"Well the crazy old bitch in there fired both barrels of a shotgun over the sheriff's head when he tried to deliver the eviction notice, then threatened to set the place on fire if anybody tried to come in and take her out. We're here just in case. Good news for your paper, I suppose."

Inside the large house Mrs. Big Sandy poured a cup from a roiling pot of tea and sat herself at the kitchen table, deep breathing to calm herself. She drank from the cup and looked at the pile of papers and lighter fluid–soaked pieces of kindling in the pile she had made in the middle of the floor. This she showed to the sheriff when he knocked on the door with his silly piece of paper, her eviction notice, but all she could really remember was the look on the sheriff's face when she fired that first shot over his head. Funniest thing she'd ever seen. Oh, if only Sandy could have been here. Were you, you bastard? she asked, her eyes drawn toward a spot in an upper corner of the room. A second later the second shot caused a huge wet stain to spread down the front of the sheriff's light khaki pants, and then he was running.

She had watched her husband's life shrivel to nothing in a hospital bed so nothing about what she was planning was one bit frightening. The only thing she feared was that she would scream when the burning reached her, and the embarrassment of all those sons of bitches out there in her yard hearing her, thinking she was hollering for help, but pity the poor bastard that dared come through the door to save her. The shotgun in her lap was double loaded again, cocked.

She was prepared to sit there until they all left and left her alone.

She had given up trying to understand what was happening, how anybody, government or anyone else, could just decide to take away her home, send some geek in a uniform with a piece of paper she wouldn't use to wipe her arse and send that weasel to throw her out on the street and tell her that there was nothing she could do about it, nothing anybody would do about it. Who picked her out anyway? Who was picking on her anyway? A widow who doesn't even know how old she is? Oh, she used to know and it's written down somewhere in the attic but what does it matter? She's old, that's all she knows, but she didn't grow old fainting every time someone hollered at her. In fact, she'd racked up the occasional faint herself because she could always holler back, louder and more ruthless. It seemed to work on everybody except Sandy, who could holler out some of the funniest and nastiest things she ever heard when they were fighting. But they never went to bed mad, not once in more than sixty years. Those people out there had always been laughing at her and Sandy, telling stories about them for as long as they'd been together as man and wife. There wasn't one of them had the goddamned guts to laugh at them to their faces. She missed Sandy, didn't care what happened next. If those fools out there didn't know that then they were stupider than she or Sandy ever gave them credit for. Let them try to evict her, just let them!

"So what's going on, David?" Ronald MacDonald was leaning over the yellow tape trying to get David's attention, Don Alex beside him. "Is it true she took a shot at the sheriff? Better hope she doesn't get you in her sights, boy. She owes you one."

David nodded without answering, sensing that Ronald was less interested in listening than reporting what he knew about the incident unfolding before them. "Do you know that she might have an old box of dynamite in there that Sandy stole from the mines when they were still working? If she does, there'll be nothing left here but an open-pit mine. I remembered about that when I heard what she's up to, that time the dynamite was stolen from the old powder room. There were a lot of people worried that it was kids and that they'd blow themselves up, but there were people, myself included, that thought Big Sandy stole it. The man wasn't a thief, now I'm not saying that because to be a thief you have to be sneaky and Sandy, well, Sandy was a lot of things, but he wasn't sneaky. But the way he saw it, he told me this himself once, was that if people were stupid enough to leave their things just lying around, in the yard say, then they deserved to lose it. So he'd just pick it up – a shovel, a pick, a wheelbarrow. He didn't consider it stealing, just taking advantage of an opportunity."

Ronald nodded his head in agreement with his own words and Big Sandy's impeccable logic. Having caught David's attention – the reporter prodded him with an impatient, "And!" – Ronald returned to his subject. "Oh yes. Well, somebody broke into that powder room and walked away with a box of dynamite. What made me think it was Sandy at the time was that it came out that the person who was responsible for locking the door had left it unlocked. An invitation to Big Sandy if ever there was one. I didn't ask him outright, but we'd be having a few, you know, and once the subject came up and I asked him if he knew what happened to it. He told me nobody better ever come around looking into his attic. Perhaps it was bullshit because Sandy was prone to that too, but the attic was where he kept his stash of booze when he was selling it and it wouldn't surprise me if he booby-trapped the place in case the Mounties ever came. So I'm guessing Mrs. Big Sandy is sitting on top of that case right this minute waiting for us all to come closer. That's what I think. So what've you been hearing?"

David looked around at the crowd, wondering what the range of an exploded box of dynamite would be, but played down these thoughts. "Nothing about dynamite, Ronald, and I'd be careful about spreading that rumour around. From what I know she's in there with a shotgun and the makings of a bonfire drenched with some kind of gas. Shot at the sheriff but it's Noseworthy's case now. The sheriff's just a bailiff really, delivering things like eviction notices, but when shots are fired it's the RCMP's problem then. Personally I don't think Noseworthy knows how to go about defusing the situation."

"Defusing the situation? Is that what he calls it, a 'situation'?" Ronald said. "Hell, he's been here long enough to know that Mrs. Big Sandy's not exactly what you'd call a sit-u-a-tion, David. She's what you'd call shithouse full of trouble. Still I suppose it helps that's he a Newfoundlander. From what I hear they got their own share of characters over there too, so he probably won't screw this up as bad as one of those new recruits that they send here from Toronto or Ottawa, kids fresh out of Regina in their spiffy new uniforms and no more sense than that one in there with her gun and her bonfire and her dynamite. She's not my favourite person, David, but she's my favourite character and this town is running out of characters in a hurry. All the old ones, and none of the younger people are showing much promise. Too much education or something. If she blows up that house it'll be the biggest story she was ever involved in, but it will be the last of her and that's kind of sad because there's no more Mrs. Big Sandys on the horizon. The town's changing, and just because there'll be no more Mrs. Big Sandy to terrorize us all into pools of our own diarrhoea it doesn't mean that it's changing for the better. Just getting more common's all."

David drew himself away from the yellow line of tape, replaying Ronald MacDonald's hopefully premature obituary through his mind. He was saddened by the older man's accuracy, but noted that Ronald MacDonald, who had taken to wearing his clan kilt daily and was at war with a corporation that didn't know he existed, was himself one of the town's feature characters. David wondered how Ronald's vow to never again don anything but a kilt in honour of his ancestors and to war against corporate giants would work out for him when winter came.

But the old man was right. Shean was changing. Some of that change was in the shape of improvements such as the park, and perhaps even the eventual rehabilitation of the mine tailings, but those grey and black tailings, ugly as they must appear to strangers in Shean, had always been so deeply ingrained in the character of the town that David had never seen them as ugly. Shean had never been able to lay claim to being a beautiful town, not from the moment that first mine opened and the smokestacks began belching black smoke and mountains of grey slag and red ash began to take form. But he had always felt that the town made up for in character what it lacked in touristy beauty, and the slag heaps were part of that character the way a scar can sometimes bring a compelling aura to an otherwise plain or unattractive face.

The capping and greening of the mine tailings was necessary, David knew that. Health, the environment, even the proposed tourism-based economy of Shean's development plan required it, but there was an emotional price to be paid by those who felt as he did. More disturbing, though, was Ronald's lament for the town's once-vibrant cast of characters. Mrs. Big Sandy may have been queen of the misfits who fit so well into the temperament and culture of the town, but she was just one of many quotable and colourful characters whose actions and antics had become stories passed down through the years. They were a democratic demographic, those characters that had been spawned by Shean: doctors, politicians, bootleggers, priests, the occasional Mountie and a myriad of others, but they were an endangered species.

He looked toward the large, grey house again, imagined the looming tragedy that threatened from within, and wondered what he or anyone could do to resolve it without loss. He could think of only one possible resolution and reached for his cellphone.

| 23 |

David watched Corporal Harry Noseworthy's face drain from robust to corpse white as the reporter's words sank in.

"I just thought you should know, Harry. It's strictly rumour but a few old memories in the crowd recall a case of dynamite being stolen from the mine forty, fifty years ago, and it never turned up. The gossip, and that's all it is, I won't even be reporting it unless it turns out to be true, is that Sandy MacArthur stole it. It's a long shot, but it's possible that it's in that house."

The corporal contacted his constables on a secure transmission line on his Blackberry. David could see each of them from where he stood, watched their body language as they read the message, the involuntary backward steps, almost Keystone comic but for the circumstances, their eyes flickering from their mobiles to the house, waiting for further orders. Noseworthy wasted no time sending them. Begin moving people back. Push the yellow tape another quarter mile if possible. Explain nothing. Ignore the insults. Do it now!

"Do you honestly think she'll do it, David?"

"She's old, alone, angry, bitter. She might do anything."

"I've been on speed dial to her phone but she's not answering. I can't make contact and every time I turn around this thing grows bigger and scarier. She's crazy, but there's nothing we can do except watch and hope and keep people away until the provincial command can get somebody here – a hostage negotiator – to talk this woman down."

"What's he going to do, talk her into letting herself go?"

"Something like that. There's nothing in the manual about how to deal with an eighty-something-year-old woman with a loaded double barrel sitting on a keg of dynamite beside a bonfire. I know. I tried to look it up in my Mountie manual. Nothing. This is a first for me. This may be a first for the force. How are we going to get her out of there?"

"I called Rita MacDonald. She's arranging to come down once she knows she's covered at work. I hope you'll let her try to talk to the woman who's holding herself hostage in there."

"Let a civilian try to walk into that house? I would be posted to Resolute Bay for the rest of my life. That's a bad idea, David."

"Maybe. But I think Rita may be the only person in this town able to reach Mrs. Big Sandy. They have a relationship. The old woman talks to her. I've seen them together. Mrs. Big Sandy would never admit this, but she was deferring to her. Talk to her anyway, Rita that is, and I promise you a free subscription to the *Witness* for however long you're in Resolute Bay."

Both men watched Rita talk her way past the sparse security and walk toward them. Her face was drawn as she stopped before reaching them and leaned against Noseworthy's police vehicle and stared at the house, unpainted and weathered from years of wind and rain, but at the moment flashing its windows in the glow of the summer sun. Rita had never studied it closely before or imagined it in anything but fog and rain and darkness, haunted by the town's tall tales.

In sunlight the house was really quite something else. It hadn't been built to be sinister: a design of fine lines and pitches must have made the place elegant before a century of soot and cinders had fallen upon it. Over the years, the house had fallen into the hands of generations from fathers to sons, each of whom understood less and less about themselves and where they came from and what their bloodline was capable of accomplishing. The house had become as lost as the family, and it was doomed.

"Let me try to talk to her," Rita said, turning to Corporal Noseworthy. "I think I can reach her. Someone needs to try. She may let me in, so please don't go all Mountie on me."

Corporal Noseworthy stopped worrying about superiors and professional negotiators and took charge of the situation he was in.

"How do you propose to get in the house?"

"I'm going to walk up and knock on the door and ask if I can come in."

"You may not have heard but she took shots at the last person who knocked on her door."

"I know, and she'll want to tell me all about it.

———

"Knock any louder and I'll shoot this thing right through the door, whoever you are!"

"Mrs. MacArthur, it's me, Rita. Can I come in?"

"Go away! I'm not reading any cups today."

Rita turned the doorknob but the door was locked from the inside. "Mrs. MacArthur, please let me in. We need to talk. I don't want you to hurt yourself or anyone else. I'm not going to go away so if you try to shoot at anybody or set the house on fire you could hurt me. I don't think you want that, if not for my own sake then for the sake of my great grandfather."

A long silence was finally broken by the shuffling of a chair and a sense that the large woman had moved closer to the door.

"Is the police out there waiting to break in as soon as I open this door for you?"

"No one is here but me, Mrs. MacArthur, I swear."

"Well then, when I open this door you step in fast because if I see any of the clowns in that circus out there I'll blow their damned heads off, do you understand?"

The door swung open quickly and Rita hurried through as it slammed behind her, the bolt clicking in place. As she turned she saw Mrs. Big Sandy drive half a dozen kitchen knives behind the door frame, knife handles resting against the door itself. She turned to Rita, still holding the shotgun. The nurse pretended not to notice and walked to the stove where the teapot was roiling in the heat, and through the clear Pyrex glass she could see the loose leaves tumbling in the boiling water like a brown Christmas snow globe. She poured herself a cup and turned to her host who had seated herself again at the table. A large box of wooden matches lay beside her own teacup, the smell of lighter fluid from the pile of rubble beside the table strong in the warm air. Rita sat on what had out of habit become *her* chair, trying to comprehend the still life of violence across from her, the shotgun, the matches, the makings of a bonfire, the uncompromising commitment in Mrs. Big Sandy's eyes, and wondered what she thought she was going to be able to do about it.

"I'm not leaving here," Mrs. Big Sandy said as though reading her thoughts. "I know why you're here but I'm not leaving this house. Whether they tear it down around me or I burn it up in front of them I'm not leaving. I'm not letting them stick me in one of those goddamned living coffins that the government builds to get rid of its old people. I'm not! Besides, now that I shot at the son of a bitch of a sheriff I suppose I'll be going to jail. I'm not going to jail! I'm not!"

Rita could see that Mrs. Big Sandy was re-stoking her infamous rage, but felt her own anger rising over the old woman's constant trashing of the Shean Manor. "Mrs. MacArthur, I work at the Shean Manor and I'm proud of the work I do there. The whole staff is. And the residents who live there are not living in an open coffin. That said, is this what Sandy would want you to do?" she asked. "Hurt yourself like this?"

"What do you know about Sandy but the gossip that the creatures in this town made up about him? Nothing, that's what you know. Nobody knows nothing about the life we had here in this house and they can't know what that meant to us, the way we looked out the window every morning to see the coal mines pouring smoke out of their stacks and the mine train taking their garbage, their shale and their ashes and pouring them all over Sandy's land. And if people thought Sandy didn't care, well they're wrong because he did. He used to say to me sometimes that something went wrong with his family and the way things turned out, that was plain to see as the nose on his face. But he used to say that, that this wasn't what his great grandfather meant when he brought his family over here. And when they got here his sons helped him cutting trees and making the first house they lived in and clearing the fields and making fences with the stones or piling them in tall piles and burying their dead in those there sand dunes down there.

"And then the coalmines came. That's what killed this place, Sandy said. The coalmines killed this place! It used to be beautiful, that's what he said. People'd be surprised to hear Sandy talking like that and nobody ever did or they would have gotten their faces broken if he heard them listening to him when he talked like that. But that's what he used to say, that this place where his great grandfather lived – not this house, the other one – was beautiful, like the sunsets out there in the ocean that he'd watch and nobody, not even me, not even God, could get a glimpse of what he was thinking but he'd watch and say nothing and then come downstairs from up there on the widow's walk and pour himself a big drink and one for me if I wanted it, then another one for himself and another one and sometimes after two or three or four or five he'd sit there with this look on his face and crush the empty glass in his hand, just crush it and I'd be bandaging his hand and he'd hardly notice. Good thing his hands were hard as bark because the cuts would have been gashes if they weren't but he'd sit there and mumble about how beautiful things used to be but he never saw it that way, not ever, just what his grandmother told him it was like before the coal mines came and then his grandfather began giving permission to the mine to put their junk on his property. Oh, he was well paid for it, but in the end what good did it do the family. They built this place, Sandy said, and left it to him and he hated it, not the land under it but the house and what it cost them all, the MacArthurs."

Mrs. Big Sandy began the deep, angry breathing that Rita had come to recognize as an effort to get a grip on her temper, to cool herself down. Rita sipped from her cup of tea made bitter by hours of boiling with Mrs. MacArthur just pouring more water and throwing more leaves into the pot to keep herself fuelled.

"Strong," Rita said diplomatically. "Mrs. MacArthur, if Sandy hated the house so much would he really want you to end your life in it like this? I'm not saying that you'd have to go to the senior citizens' units or the Shean Manor but there must be somewhere else you can go."

"Hell! That's where people would like to see me go, isn't it? And I'm thinking about obliging the bastards."

"Think of some of the other things you could do to upset them, though. Like renting yourself a nice new apartment with the compensation money from the government or even building yourself a new home. You don't need to do this, Mrs. MacArthur. You're still healthy and have years of living ahead of you. Ask yourself what Sandy would really want. Please."

Mrs. Big Sandy lifted her cup to her face and drained it, making Rita shudder at the thought of the bitter fluid, but when she slammed the cup back down on the table Rita leaned across, took it in her hands and began studying the cup's interior.

"What are you looking at?" Mrs. Big Sandy asked.

"The future. I'm looking in this cup and what I see is a lot of tea leaves, a lot. That means that there's a lot of future in this cup. Your future."

Mrs. Big Sandy snatched the cup away from her, glanced into it and hoisted herself to her feet and walked to the stove for a refill, showing the pot to Rita, who signalled that her own cup was still full.

"Mrs. MacArthur, you told me one time that I could look through the house whenever I wanted. Do you mind if I do it now? It doesn't look like there's going to be another time. I don't want this house to be gone, never having known anything about it."

Mrs. Big Sandy spent a moment absorbing the request, but she did tell the woman, "Just get back here before the fireworks. And if you see anything you think is worth something, go ahead and take it."

| 24 |

When he saw Rita MacDonald entering the MacArthur house, Donald MacNaughton left his post beside the truck and joined the knot of men gathered at Corporal Noseworthy's vehicle. The Mountie, the sheriff and the newspaper editor – not a group any politician would willingly allow to linger within earshot. The story they were concocting might need some polish and spin if Shean was going to come out of this looking good, or at least not looking as stupid as it sounded in a thirty-second sound bite about an old woman with a shotgun and a gas-soaked bonfire who had already fired shots at the sheriff and who wouldn't leave her house because the government was taking it away from her. It was easy to see where the sympathy in this story would go. MacNaughton knew he needed to find a way to stand beside the poor woman without getting shot.

The drama unfolding at the MacArthur house had drawn the attention of the entire town and beyond. CBC radio in Sydney had picked up the story from a listener, and the *Mainstreet* host was trying on air to reach Mayor MacNaughton for an update. Meanwhile, reporters from the daily papers arrived from the island's only city, where the important news action usually happened. The CTV television reporter searched for local sources, finding Ronald MacDonald both easy to engage and, with his kilt, a cameraman's dream. The situation had all the makings of a damage control nightmare, MacNaughton knew.

"So what's going on? Did I just see Rita MacDonald walk through that door and into the arms of that madwoman? If anything goes wrong you're going to have a lot to answer for, Noseworthy. As mayor I should have been consulted about a decision like this, and don't tell me that I have no input because I'm a civilian civil servant. I'm the one who collects the taxes that pay your wages and it's my town you're being paid to protect and I have a responsibility to my people to see that everybody is safe. Letting that woman go in there is not safe!"

"Do your campaigning somewhere else, Mayor, because I haven't got time to care about your problems. Drop the attitude and perhaps I'll tell you what's happening here," Noseworthy said, spelling the words out with his finger on MacNaughton's chest.

The mayor retreated, and softened his offensive. "That's all I'm asking, Corporal, to be informed. I was just being stupid a moment ago. Tell me, what is going on?" He tried to keep his back to the others, isolate them from his conversation with the corporal, but the sheriff and the newspaper editor simply crowded closer to hear, the Mountie indifferent to whether or not they heard.

Corporal Harry Noseworthy told Mayor Donald Mac-Naughton what had transpired over the last few hours, including the possibility that there was dynamite in the house, a fact that no one, officially or through gossip, had reported to the mayor. "Dear Jesus. This thing is starting to turn awfully real. What are her chances?"

"I don't think Mrs. Big Sandy will hurt Rita," David Cameron answered. "I'm not so sure what else she is capable of any more than yourself. We've been living with the same time bomb all our lives, but she won't hurt Rita. I'm sure of it."

"She came to see me a few days ago," MacNaughton answered. "Rita that is, but she came because she wanted me to stop the eviction."

"Why didn't you?" David asked.

"Why didn't I what?"

"Stop the eviction."

"It's out of my hand..."

"Bullshit. You've got as big a collection of political favours out there as anybody in this province. One phone call. Maybe two."

"You're giving me too much credit, something you've always neglected to do in your editorials. I can't order any minister in the province to do anything. And I didn't do anything this time because I didn't think I should. That old woman's not safe in that house. The town's not safe as long as that house is there stopping the environmental reclamation. So no, I wouldn't have called, but that's got nothing to do with this. We've got to get those women out of there. Alive."

Although he barely noticed it, MacNaughton's own thoughts about damage control vanished into the very real, potentially tragic damage facing everyone, especially Mrs. MacArthur and Rita MacDonald. He walked a little distance away to dwell on what he could do. Nothing, he knew. It was all in the hands of Rita MacDonald. Donald MacNaughton was a praying man, although normally the subject of his prayers was himself.

Rita MacDonald left Mrs. Big Sandy sitting at the table amid her plans for destruction, certain the old woman would do nothing while Rita was still in the house and still in danger. It grew quickly clear to her that Mrs. Big Sandy had abandoned most of the large house, having drawn it down to the size of a small apartment on the first floor. Beyond the kitchen was a bathroom, and across the hall from the bathroom was a room that had once been a large livingroom but was now a bedroom, the room's original furniture pushed aside to make room for a double bed. From the men's clothes hanging on a free-standing clothes rack it was evident that the move had been made before Sandy's hospitalization, maybe when he became sick, or perhaps much earlier; the economics of heating and lighting such a large house having undoubtedly driven the elderly couple into a small corner of the mansion.

Mounting the stairs to the second story, Rita roamed through the rooms, mostly bedrooms but there was one that had been used as a sewing room by one or two generations of the MacArthur women, although she doubted that Mrs. Big Sandy ever made much use of it. It was a dust-laden level of the house whose furnishings were an amalgam of no-down-payment-for-two-years junk and exquisite expensive pieces. The second floor hall was lined with heavily framed black and white photographs yellowing with age behind ovals of glass from which the local lineage of MacArthurs stared out.

More MacArthur photographs marched their way up the stairs wall leading to the third floor where more bedrooms were found, as if planned for ever-expanding generations of a family that had already petered out, its last son recently laid to rest without an heir.

If she didn't look out any of the windows that boasted a view of unrelenting heaps of slag and ash and decades of the town's garbage and junk, Rita could easily imagine what the house had once been, and could see in its still solid, square structure how easy it would be to return it to its original intention. But its only future was rubble. She could imagine nothing that would change that.

In the ceiling of the third floor a short rope hung down from a trapdoor and Rita tugged gently upon it. The ceiling door drew down slowly, soundlessly, toward her, delivering the stairway to the attic. She ascended quietly, feeling nervous for the first time in her exploration, sensing her violation of whatever secrets had been hidden or discarded up here. Her arm swept through the dark air as she searched for a dangling chain, an educated guess since that was how the attic of their own home was lit.

Her hand came in contact with a cord and she pulled, shying away from the sudden glare of unshaded light, the naked bulb swinging so that a crowd of shadows swayed wildly against the walls, becoming still when her hand steadied the hanging bulb. Oh, she and her childhood friends could have spent weeks here exploring the horrors of their imaginations. Old dresses and coats hung from the walls, trunks and baskets were filled with whatever was not worth keeping but too good to throw away, broken furniture and toys and tools someone had stored with the intention of eventually fixing whatever was fractured or amputated. The space was dimly lit through the years by a meagre ration of sunlight filtered through two small portholes at the east and west ends of the house, which were shaded by curtains of cobwebs.

She moved carefully among the chaos collected here, conducting a surface examination of the clothes, lifting lids of unlocked trunks, shifting their contents hurriedly for a sense of what they contained, becoming overwhelmed by a nostalgia that was not her own, that had belonged to someone, some woman, who once lived in this house, whom she sensed had moved through this attic quietly reliving something long lost, a child or a dream or a hope for the future. It was a feeling that stubbornly refused to leave her. She found herself wishing she had weeks to walk through these rooms, this attic. It was a house constructed out of someone's vision for his or her family. She longed to know what went so desperately wrong between the vision that constructed the house and the present moment that had sentenced its still-strong walls to destruction.

Lifting another trunk lid, she removed a layer of clothes to reveal a box covered by a large piece of felt. She lifted the felt cloth and her breath caught at the sight of the dynamite. She thought Corporal Noseworthy had been mad when he asked her to keep an eye open for the missing explosives if she got inside and had an opportunity to look around. Knees weakening, she sat back on a one-runner rocking chair and stared into the open trunk.

Slowly Rita's mind returned from its flight into fear and she began to wonder what to do with this knowledge thrust upon her, and what was to be done came in a flash of heat and perspiration. She lifted the felt to rub her forehead when a cloth arm dropped down, grazing her face. She made a whimpering scream. She drew the felt further away from her and studied it more closely. It was not a cloth but a coat, a child's coat. It was not felt, she realized, but a once lovely child's coat that had been washed and shrunken and ruined and still the child was made to wear it. She knew the story. She had heard it not so very long ago in the middle of the night during a shift at the Shean Manor. She lifted the coat to her nose and sniffed deeply of the musk and dust and felt that she could inhale the scent from three quarters of a century ago, the scent of her own great grandfather trying to wipe the tears and mud from a small girl that no one would ever be that kind to again, and Rita knew what she needed to do.

Having given the television reporter his off-the-cuff take on the events unfolding in Shean, Ronald MacDonald was busy trying to interest her in his own investigation of a certain fast food company that was making life difficult for MacDonalds who wanted to go into business using their own name. But the reporter was already moving on in search of another colourful source when Don Alex tapped his friend on the shoulder.

"Ronald, they're saying that your girl's gone into the house to talk to herself!"

"Rita?"

"That's what they're saying everywhere. I didn't see her go in myself, but I saw her coming here in her car, it's over there, but I can't see her anywhere now."

Ronald, without another word, ducked under the police tape and brushed past one of the firemen on guard and walked quickly toward the group gathered at the police vehicle.

"Is Rita in there!" he demanded. Nods of awkward acknowledgement made him turn purple with rage.

"She volunteered to go in, Mr. MacDonald," Corporal Noseworthy tried to explain. "She was determined, and to tell you the truth she may be our only hope to end this thing peacefully."

"A fine bunch of men you are, a Mountie, our fearless newspaper editor, our heroic sheriff in his clean new pants, and Mr. Mayor Himself, our very own laird and leader, and not one of you with the sense of a donkey. You let my daughter walk in there with that crazy bitch. She's already shot at the sheriff here and you let her go in there. If anything happens to her you'll all have a price to pay, believe you me, a price to pay, and it won't be money.

"Why did you let her do that? Why? Oh, God, if she's hurt I'll– I'll–" His voice broke.

"Why don't you sit in my car here, I'll turn on the air conditioning," Corporal Noseworthy said, guiding an unresisting Ronald into the cab and turning on the cool air. David Cameron watched his fiery old friend slump and age before his eyes, staring out the windshield at the large house, making no effort to hide his tears.

| 25 |

David Cameron noticed Tim Donovan moving through the crowd jotting notes, snapping pictures, reminding him that he wasn't a local spectator either. He had a job to do. Lifting the camera dangling from a strap around his neck, David began taking more pictures, this time focussing on the house, conscious that at any moment something newsworthy might happen: a shooting, a fire, an explosion.

The Witness's front page didn't need any more than it already had but with reporters from television and the dailies in Shean searching for a justification for their time and travel, he wasn't about to be scooped. David was aware of a perception among reporters and editors of television and the large dailies that their provincial or national stories mattered more than stories reported in small-town weekly newspapers. David knew different.

He knew people would tune into the television news and pick up the daily newspapers to read about themselves. Some would be offended and some would be defensive of the portrait of the town as seen through the eyes of people who had never been here before. But it would be the stories David and Tim told that would become the town's permanent record, and if corrections were required – even if those corrections were for errors in reporting by other forms of media – the Letters to the Editor would set the record straight.

It wasn't a competition for David, so he stepped aside and let other media go about their business, being as helpful as he could. For the most part he stood among the very people the press wanted most to interview, discussing the possibilities, the problems, their silent faith resting on Rita's shoulders. No one wanted to jinx that slim hope by pissing off some touchy god so her name went unmentioned among them.

He thought, too, as he scanned the scene with his camera, about how Rita MacDonald seemed to be materializing in front of him over the past few weeks, feature by feature, trait by trait. He was stricken with an inexplicable longing to know her.

A slight movement re-focused his attention on the house. Lowering the camera, he confirmed with his naked eye what he was seeing then raised the camera again, zooming the telephoto lens out to its maximum. There was movement on the roof of the house. What he was seeing was the very slow raising of a hatch, the means through which the house's occupants accessed the widow's walk, the large, flat, railed platform on the roof from where occupants could look far, far beyond what a century of industry had done to their land.

A head and then shoulders emerged and David hesitated before clicking the camera, knowing who it was and what he would probably need to do with this photo or another like it. She probably wouldn't be happy, but his ethical questions subsided as she lifted herself to a sitting position on the roof and began pulling something up toward her. Soon a box-shaped package covered in cloth came onto the roof at the end of a length of rope. By then the activity on the roof had attracted universal attention. Only when the package was safely beside her did she look around and begin to stand up, signalling with one hand that she was well and with the other for silence. Not a murmur followed as she moved to the end of the roof deck, looked over the side, went back and retrieved the box, balanced it on the rail and checked the knots in the roll of fishing rope she had found in the attic (another of Big Sandy MacArthur's unofficial finds) and slowly began to lower it over the side.

Corporal Noseworthy broke away from the cluster around him and was ordering everyone else to stay put while issuing a Blackberry alert to his constables at the very moment the special detachment of RCMP officers arrived. He didn't have time for them, he said, insisting that they wait until he was ready to brief them because at the moment this new development was more important than any chain of command.

Just as the new commanding officer was about to say something, Corporal Noseworthy turned and ran toward the house and stood under the lowering box, aware of what it probably contained. Looking up at the strain on Rita's face dispelled any doubts. She wasn't rescuing family photographs.

Once Noseworthy had a secure hold on the container, Rita threw the rest of the rope after it, and before the police officer could ask anything of her, she stepped back. What the RCMP officer couldn't see then, but that was visible to the rest of the anxious audience – including Ronald MacDonald who was now out of the truck and being restrained by members of the tactical police from rushing toward his daughter and the house – was Rita disappearing from the widow's walk back down the hatch and into circumstances no one could any longer imagine.

"Whew! That's one gutsy girl," Donald MacNaughton said from one side of the tape to David on the other side. As a fireman he had been recruited to keep the crowd safely on the other side, including David, Ronald and the sheriff.

They had all been ordered back beyond the police tape by the newly arrived commanding officer, who had ordered the firefighters to move people back even further. Having cautiously removed the box from Noseworthy's arms and carefully unwrapped Rita's gift, the policemen found themselves facing five layers of dynamite sticks. The commander pointed out to the local corporal that the aged explosives had sweated their nitroglycerin, which then crystalized on the outer wrappings of the sticks. The woman had been foolish to move the box, and Noseworthy had been doubly foolish to catch and carry it.

They'd been pushed back for their own safety, David recognized, but they had also been pushed back to provide privacy because it was clear that Corporal Noseworthy was undergoing a dressing down from superiors that could well end with the predicted stationing in Resolute Bay. It was also clear to both David and Donald that the corporal wasn't making any apologies for his handling of the situation and David made a note to remind himself to mention it in his article.

"She always was a wild one," Ronald MacDonald said in answer to Donald's observation about Rita. He was still worried but immensely relieved that the explosives had been removed from the house and quietly grateful that he was the one who remembered the long ago rumour about the dynamite and Big Sandy's cryptic allusion that it had been him who stole the box. "But Jesus, what's she doing in that house to begin with? That old quiff in there is capable of anything."

"She won't hurt Rita, Ronald," David said, an assuring hand on Ronald's shoulder. "I believe they're friends."

"Friends? Jesus Lord in Heaven, why can't she have friends her own age? Or a boyfriend? But do you think she has time for the men around here? No. Scared of settling down's what she is. Came home to look after me but this's not where she wants to be, never was. Never said it to me, of course, but if it wasn't for my stroke she'd be somewhere else. Came home to take care of the old man and not a word said about it, but I know. I know. That's the nurse in her, don't you see.

"Always used to say she became a nurse so she could travel wherever she wanted because there's always a need for nurses, but what she really always wanted was to be taking care of things. The same as when she was small, bringing home hurt gulls, stray cats. Couldn't tell you how many lambs and calves she wouldn't quit on when I was ready to give up, and just about all of them turned out okay. Just like me when it was my turn to be her lamb or calf. Oh, Christ, she doesn't need the likes of that one for a friend, not Mrs. Big Sandy."

"Like you said, Ronald: taking care of things when nobody else would," Donald MacNaughton said.

"Donald," David asked, "would you have done things different when she asked you, knowing what was coming?"

"Off the record," MacNaughton said, pausing until David nodded, "probably not. The town doesn't need this kind of negative publicity but it does need development and that woman and that house are standing in the way. And there's nothing personal in it, David," he added, rubbing his jaw to make his point.

| 26 |

The door of the large house opened and as Rita stepped outside she heard the lock snap into place behind her. She stood on the steps as if deciding her direction then walked toward the cluster of RCMP officers, her only interest among them being Corporal Harry Noseworthy.

When she reached the group a different officer stepped forward and introduced himself as Superintendent Daniel Ranger. He began to chide her about the foolishness of her behaviour but Rita brushed past him and stood in front of Noseworthy.

"I think I can get Mrs. MacArthur to come out of the house but only if you promise not to arrest her," she told him, then turning toward the crowd signalled for someone to come forward.

"No civilians are permitted within this parameter, Ms. Mac-Donald," the superintendent said, stepping back into the centre of the discussion as Ronald MacDonald, Donald MacNaughton, Sheriff Thurber and David Cameron approached, each responding to her beckoning. "And as for arresting her, she's left us no choice."

Ronald MacDonald stepped in front of the police officer and threw his arms around his daughter, who briefly returned the hug then freed herself to continue the negotiations. "I think I can convince her to leave the house if she isn't arrested," she repeated for the benefit of the newcomers. "This can all end peacefully...."

"Peacefully means she surrenders her weapons and herself to police custody, Miss," the superintendent said.

"...and nobody needs to get hurt," Rita continued, talking through the superintendent's authority and kept addressing Corporal Noseworthy. "For the love of God, she's an old woman who doesn't know what's happening to her, doesn't know who's doing this to her, doesn't understand anything about it and frankly neither do I. What's to be gained by putting her in jail, Corporal?"

"Nothing really," Corporal Noseworthy agreed, wilfully ignoring the glare from Superintendent Ranger. "But she did shoot at the sheriff."

"But what if no charges are laid? Would she be free to go then?"

"Free to go! Free to go! I want that woman arrested," Sheriff Thurber said. "She took a shot at me. Two shots in fact. I intend to lay charges if the police don't."

"Wait a minute, Sheriff. Let's think about this," Donald MacNaughton reasoned. "The town looks bad enough as it is. The trial of an old woman who'll probably be found crazy anyway isn't going to do you or the town any good. It's best if this thing is just made to go away. Can we do that, Superintendent, make the whole mess go away?"

"You're surrounded by television, newspapers and who knows what Internet gossipers so I doubt if anything can make this go away, and I certainly have no intention of making it go away," the officer answered.

"But that's just for a day a two, that Internet business. A trial could mean people writing about it and talking about it for weeks before it ever gets inside a courtroom. It'll make Shean a joke all over the province just when something good for the town is on the verge of happening," MacNaughton argued.

"That's your problem, Mayor," Sheriff Thurber replied. "The woman shot at me. If she hadn't missed me I might have been killed for carrying out the Queen's orders."

"I doubt that she missed you, John," David Cameron interjected. "If you were standing in her doorway threatening to evict her, which you said is what happened, then Mrs. Big Sandy had you point blank. She's old but she's not blind."

"Save it for your newspaper, David. All you people are bleeding hearts but I'll have my pound of flesh, yes I will," the sheriff said.

"Quoting Shakespeare, Sheriff?" David asked, certain that the sheriff had no idea what or who he was talking about. Meanwhile his gaze fell to the display screen on his digital camera. "I'm in the business of quoting people myself, and if Mrs. Big Sandy is arrested for shooting at you then it's my duty as a journalist to report exactly what happened right down to running this picture since that seems to be the greatest damage done to you by her shotgun." David showed the sheriff a chosen frame.

Sheriff John Thurber tried to see the tiny photograph by squinting at it but finally pulled his glasses from his pocket and hung them on his ears then took a closer look. It still took a moment for the image to register. "You can't print that picture! I'll sue you for every cent you have if you do!"

"It's what I do, Sheriff. This picture blown up ten or fifteen times and run in full colour on the front page will inform readers of the damage that Mrs. Big Sandy's shooting spree has caused. The stain in your pants shows up quite sharply against the rest of your uniform, don't you think?"

"Aw, Jesus, Cameron, you can't run that. I'll be a laughing-stock. Promise me you won't print that and I won't press any charges, please. But even if I don't the police still can so promise me you won't run it as long as I keep my part of the bargain."

"Well that's going to depend on the RCMP and how far they want to go with this, John."

"What the hell is going on here?" Superintendent Ranger hollered, shaking his head, trying to get back to logical police work. "There are five policemen standing here witnessing what is clearly blackmail, there's a box of unstable dynamite right over there, an old broad with a shotgun in that house threatening to burn it and herself down and you're all talking as if it's a picnic." No one disagreed, they just stood there waiting for whatever was coming, the superintendent the least interesting part of whatever that was going to be. Purple faced, Ranger turned to Noseworthy. "Corporal, can you make sense of this?"

"I think I can. It's a local issue that's gotten out of hand but Rita here has defused it, really she has. The dynamite's safe, sort of, and I believe she can walk Mrs. MacArthur out of there unarmed, but only if there's no arrest. Mrs. Big Sandy, that's the local handle for Mrs. MacArthur, is a formidable legend in this town and she got that way by saying and doing exactly what she means to say or do. I have no doubt that she will burn the place down around herself unless she gets her way and it's my opinion, Superintendent, that in this case we should let her have it. As long as the shotgun is left in the house and Rita is in no danger then no real damage has been done."

"Damn it, Corporal! A crime has been committed here. We can't just turn a blind eye to that, not when we are in the public eye. Or haven't you noticed?" The superintendent took in the entire audience with an angry sweep of his arm.

"Isn't there something called a peace bond?" Rita asked, exasperating the superintendent by continuing to direct her questions to Noseworthy.

"A peace bond won't – "

The corporal cut off the superintendent's words. "Yes, courts can place someone under a peace bond if they promise to keep the peace," the police officer offered.

"We have a magistrate here in Shean. He's probably up in the crowd. He can draft a quick peace bond," Mayor Mac-Naughton suggested.

Superintendent Ranger shook his head. "A peace bond!"

"What do you think?" Noseworthy asked his superior politely.

"What do I think? What do I think? I think this is something new in all of law enforcement. Vigilantism by peace bond. But I suppose a bond will have to do considering ... I don't know what the hell I'm considering, but I have another question. If she's not going to jail, where is she going?"

"Home with me, officer," Rita MacDonald answered.

A gargling sound came from their midst and an alarmed Rita turned to her father, who was making sounds but no sense. Fearing another stroke, she began to examine him for the signs when he found his voice. "Are you daft, girl. Home with you? You're taking that creature home to our house without asking me? I won't allow it!"

"I was afraid you'd feel that way, Dad, so if we can't come home then I'll get us a motel room tonight and tomorrow we'll find our own place to rent. It will only be for a little while, Dad."

Ronald sagged into surrender. "Okay, but from tonight on it's me that sleeps with the shotgun in his arms, girlie, not her."

"We talked about it together inside. There's a compensation check coming for the expropriation so she can buy a lot of land and a new mobile home and get settled on her own. But that reminds me, I was through the house and I wonder if there can be a delay on tearing it down. I believe there are some valuable antiques in there. I'd like to ask an expert from Sydney or Halifax to come and have a look. If I'm right, then between the compensation money and the money for the old furniture Mrs. Big Sandy could live very comfortably. Can I tell her?"

Superintendent Ranger looked into a thoughtful distance and cleared his throat before replying.

"First, we get a peace bond for her to sign. You take it to the house with you. No formal charges will be laid but the incident and the evidence, including the dynamite, will be kept against anything if this plan of yours goes awry. Corporal Noseworthy, I don't know what kind of detachment you run here but don't expect to be moved from it or promoted in the next few years."

"No Resolute Bay?" David queried. His question was ignored by both police officers.

"When I see that woman safely in whoever's custody it is, yours or Ms. MacDonald's, then my men and I are securing the dynamite and getting into our vehicles and leaving town, and we are leaving explanations to the press to you, is that clear?"

Noseworthy nodded in the affirmative.

Rita MacDonald sat across from Mrs. Big Sandy, both of them drinking strong boiled tea while the nurse explained the necessity of the old woman signing the peace bond as a guarantee that she would behave peacefully once they left the house. Mrs. Big Sandy laughed.

"That paper's not worth the words printed on it, whatever they are. Sandy must have signed a hundred of them there things. His "get out of jail free" cards he called them, then he'd go out and break somebody's nose just to break the peace, but I'll put my squiggle on it if that's what you want."

Rita folded the paper and placed it in her pocket. "Perhaps we better go now."

The old lady looked around her kitchen for the last time. Without a word she stood up, walked to the stove and picked up the cast-iron frying pan. Turning to Rita, she explained, "Just in case some bastard cop tries to put the handcuffs on me once they get me out there."

"Nobody's going to do that, Mrs. MacArthur," Rita said, opening the lock and swinging the door wide. The RCMP officers and constables were arrayed in a way that assured they would have cover, and have the suspect covered, if something did go wrong, but no arms were drawn. Mrs. Big Sandy stood in the doorway beside Rita then turned back toward the kitchen.

"What is it?" Rita asked.

"Oh, nothing dear," she said, and with a flick of her hand scratched a wooden match across the bottom of the frying pan and threw the lit stick into the oil-soaked pile on the floor. "Just lighting a candle for Sandy, that's all."

| 27 |

"Your story about Mrs. MacArthur's standoff was a good one, David. For someone who doesn't seem to care one way or another, she certainly knows how to get headlines," Rita said.

"And how to nearly get herself jailed in the end," David Cameron added.

"I was afraid that was going to happen when the house went up in flames, and so did the superintendent. At least, I saw smoke coming out his ears. He wanted Noseworthy to arrest her on the spot for arson. Harry was pointing out that they would look foolish charging a woman with arson for burning down her own house, the same house the government was kicking her out of so they could tear it down. The superintendent was furious but he could see how stupid they would all look so he went aboard Noseworthy, screaming at him that if there was any negative fallout from the incident, any at all, it was coming down on the corporal's head and his alone. "I accept that, sir," was what Noseworthy answered. I like him.

"Donald MacNaughton wasn't very happy with the superintendent either. Once the fire broke out he thought it was a great opportunity for the department to get some on-the-job training but the superintendent nixed that because he was afraid of more explosives in the house. Turns out there weren't any, but I guess he made the right decision. Too bad, though, because the brigade doesn't often get the chance to practice the way they could have; MacNaughton loves a fire. Always did."

David and Rita had run into each other in the Co-op for the first time since the MacArthur house drama. The *Witness* had told its story. Rita had gone back to work. With more to say to each other than they could convey across shopping carts, David suggested coffee at the Gulf Grill. They put their groceries in their cars and walked the two blocks in a warm afternoon sun. The grill was empty. David guided Rita toward one of the booths.

"So how are Ronald and his new boarder getting along?" David asked.

"Did you ever bring a new cat home when there's already one who thinks it owns the house? That's how it is, giving each other a wide berth and hissing a lot under their breath, but they haven't attacked each other yet. I'm just glad he didn't take a stroke."

"That's what brought you back here, isn't it – Ronald's stroke?"

Rita swirled the coffee in her cup, thinking about her answer.

David waited, brushing a few crumbs of toast off the table. The Arborite tabletops were part of a recent renovation of the town's favourite hangout, cheaper than replacing the booths outright just to get rid of the wooden tabletops that had been carved with more initials than most school desks.

"Yes," she replied. "Dad took a stroke and someone had to come back to look after him. Who else would that be but the unmarried sister. She has no children so she has no life, although I must say I've found my life pretty interesting these past few weeks. But to answer your question, I would have come anyway. This is just not the place I wanted to be at this time, or ever for that matter. But Dad matters more than that, although I think there may be some subconscious resentment buried inside me, bringing Mrs. Big Sandy home to him. Some Freudian revenge perhaps. He may never forgive me. So now you know how I got trapped here in Shean, but what are you doing back here, David? I don't get it. I told you once before that I was working at Women's Hospital in Toronto when you were working for the *Star,* when you wrote those stories about the homeless.

"I wasn't long in Toronto, and I think those homeless articles began just after I arrived. The last one, the one about the homeless man's death, was in the paper a week or two before I left. He was from home, wasn't he, that man?"

"Yes he was, and the further you are away from Cape Breton the smaller an island it becomes. But he didn't want people back home knowing what happened to him. Pride, I suppose. He was that easy to recognize, was he? I was trying to make him anonymous. Didn't do such a great job, did I?"

"Oh no, it's the great job you did that made him come alive for me, and not just me. I was caught up in the articles myself, but I knew from reading them that this man was special to you because he was from home and he was helping you get your job done. Most people in Toronto or out west who read those stories wouldn't have been able to tell if he was a Cape Bretoner or a Mexican, but anybody from here could see right through him. You won an award for that, didn't you?"

David nodded. The tinkle of a wind chime sang softly of the arrival of more customers, nods all around as one of them signalled an order with three raised fingers, a round of coffee, as they slid into a booth.

"So why did you leave it all there and come back here? I don't get it. It seemed like you were going someplace as a journalist."

David paused before answering, wishing that the simple gesture he just witnessed, the ordering of three cups of coffee, could speak for him. There was something in the gesture that explained a place so familiar that nowhere else could ever be called home. "It's simple. This is where I want to be, where I've always wanted to be. I've known that since I was six years old but it isn't always easy for anybody who wants to be here to find a way to stay. I couldn't. The *Witness* couldn't hire another reporter when I finished my journalism degree, but that's what I wanted to do with my life, journalism, so I went to Toronto. Got a lucky break there with the *Star*, earned my own byline, an award or two, so yes, things were moving nicely. Then I had an opportunity to buy the *Witness* and, for me, that was the best of both worlds, doing what I wanted to do in the place where I wanted to be. I'll never regret going to Toronto but nothing could pull me back there. You don't feel the same, I take it."

"Not exactly. Do you know that I was only hours away from setting foot on a luxury liner sailing to the Caribbean and then on to the Mediterranean? I was hired as the ship's nurse. Aspirin and Band-Aids for the seasick and the rum sick – seeing the world in the process. It's what I left Toronto for, to go to Florida where the ships are. Then word came about Dad."

"So what do you do with your time now?"

"All my spare time is taken up with shotguns, bonfires and dynamite, the usual Barbie Doll distractions," she said, a smile punctuating her words.

"And when you aren't being a comic book heroine?"

"I work, I read, I go for walks, I email friends who are working aboard cruise ships just to make myself bleed. I don't date, if that's what you're getting at. Oh, I put that wrong, didn't I? What I mean is that I haven't dated anyone even semi-regularly since I came home. I guess I'm too suspicious of single Cape Breton men of my age range to trust trying out a relationship with anyone. It's that Cape Breton lottery thing, you know?"

"Cape Breton lottery?" David asked, mystified.

"Come on now, don't tell me you never heard of the Cape Breton lottery. A man wins it when he marries a nurse or a teacher. I'm not ready for that kind of surrender yet, just so some man can stop living with his mother and start living with me." Rita blanched. "Oh, I didn't mean you living with your mother. I ... I'm not doing this very well, am I?"

"For the record and for my own embarrassment, I do live with my mother. Moved in with her when Alexandra left, for the children's sake. But I still do my own laundry," he added.

"Aw, poor boy! Walks down to the river with a rock and pounds the shit out of his own underwear. I can't imagine why I long to be elsewhere." That was the last thing said between them for several minutes because every effort to resume seriousness disintegrated into another bout of laughter.

But even amid the laughter Rita hoped she had made it clear that she did not include David in her cliché of the Cape Breton male, while amid his own laughter David absorbed the message that coffee was as far as they were going together.

| 28 |

The sun poured its early promise of summer down on Shean and all those who were free of obligations, and many who weren't, poured down to the beach to bask in the golden sand or courageously dip in the water of the Gulf of St. Lawrence, which still held within its blue allure memories of recently departed ices floes, a chill that would vanish in a week or so, leaving a marvellous warmth of water behind.

David Cameron was among them, having left the office and driven home to pile Tony and Mary into the car and take them to their assignment: to photograph a summer day at the Shean beach. It was time to run on the front page something with a sense of fun and a sense of the summer to come.

David never tired of the awesome transformation that took place with the changing of the seasons in western Cape Breton Island. Eight months ago, enraged autumn tides, driven mad by relentless grey winds, had unleashed their fury against the coast-line, pounding powerful, frightening breakers against the dunes that in their retreat dragged the golden sand into the depths of the sea, leaving in their wake a rough beach of boulders and rocks and hard-to-walk-on gravel. Three months ago the entire Gulf of St. Lawrence coastline was besieged by an armada of polar ice floes that had drifted down from northern regions to lay claim to this more southern empire. Cold winds whipped across the seal-populated ice, transporting northern clouds that dumped almost daily cargos of snow.

Occasionally, small lost colonies of the seals came ashore to whelp their young when the ice was so packed that breaches in the ice that normally allowed seals access to and from the water could not be found. These were emotional occasions for everyone, from those who thought the young seal pups were beautiful expressions of life amid the relentless lifelessness of winter to those who thought that seals were water rats to be destroyed.

The past February, when David heard that there were whelping seals on the Shean shore, he drove to the school to parole Tony from grade three and Mary from primary, believing that this opportunity to see Nature giving birth was worth an afternoon of missed geography lessons. When they got there, unfortunately, a bloody massacre awaited them. More than a few people had also heard about the whelping and raced to the shore, shooting and clubbing and killing, then vanishing, leaving in their wake two heart-broken children who needed to sleep on either side of their father that night while he tried to soothe them with meaningless explanations.

With the withdrawal of winter, the stony coastline remained for many weeks while lobster fishermen prepared their traps, loaded their boats, tracked the moving ice to ensure it was far enough offshore for them to safely set their gear as the season's opening day, the first of May, approached. The season would last until the first of July.

Softer tides ebbed and flowed ashore and slowly unloaded countless tons of the sparkling golden sand that it had stored safely away for the winter, so that by early June the rocky shoreline was once again the beach of everyone's memory. It was on this miraculous, ever-returning sand that David relaxed on a large beach towel while his children went about their duties.

Mary's interest in her assignment flagged quickly when she came across several of her friends laying the foundation for a sand castle and soon her small digital camera was stuck inside one of her sandals and she was merrily, one-handedly, involved in the construction of a royal residence.

His son took his assignment far more seriously, almost too seriously, felt David as he watched the boy move among families setting up their day camps, clusters of young people flirting, dripping swimmers emerging from the still cool waters. But when he brought the camera to his father, David was impressed. Tilting the camera to get a half decent view on the digital screen David could see that the boy's eye was that of a natural. The frames, as well as he could see in the glare of the sun, were already well cropped to capture exactly what his son had intended. This was a talent to encourage, he thought, as a shadow fell across him.

He looked up into the backlit silhouette of Rita MacDonald, a jolt not unlike joy passing through him. With a hello, she sat beside him. "Let me see," she asked, reaching for the camera. "You're down here working, or is this camera just an excuse to be down here at all," she teased. Tilting the camera as he had to get a sense of the pictures it contained, she said, "They look nice."

"They're not mine, they're Tony's. I've hired my two children as photographers so we're all working down here today, although Mary seems to have found other interests," he said nodding toward the already towering castle. "What is it about children and castles anyway?"

"Romance. When I was that age, and for a good many years after that, I suppose, there was always a brave knight who would rescue me from the horrors of Shean and spirit me away to a castle in Spain. Still waiting but I'm a patient girl. You know what you should do with one of these pictures?" she asked. "I don't mean that, what you *should do*, but what I would do if it was my newspaper. I'd make one of these pictures huge and then right under it I would put a picture from last February, one of those storms we had when the snow was banked God knows how high. I'm already hearing people complaining about the heat and it isn't even July yet! Maybe that would remind them to take advantage of it instead of bitching about it."

David filed Rita's suggestion away. It was a good idea but it was also a way to say in not so many words that he was listening to what she had to say. Otherwise, the two-piece distraction of her swimsuit left him with little to say, forcing him to turn his gaze toward an uninteresting part of ocean as he asked about the state of affairs at her house.

"When the weather is this good I usually come into work early just for this reason, to take a dip before my shift starts. I've been leaving the house a bit earlier most days now. Since that afternoon when we had coffee it's been getting a bit better there. In fact, last night when I came home from work Mrs. Big Sandy was waiting up for me with a cup of tea, which she usually does, but instead of unleashing one of her tirades against governments or Donald MacNaughton or one of her other favourite festering sores she started on me about Dad's fear of McDonald's coming to Shean. In her mind she thinks they named the clown after my father, and that he should sue McDonald's because of it. Who knows what facts and fictions Dad's filled her head with, but she's clearly on his side in this fight, and it's not just the thought of a fast food restaurant coming to Shean. From what she said, four generations, five generations back, she's a MacDonald as well, and from dad's own silence when I asked him about it this morning, I suspect that it may be the same MacDonalds, that Dad and Mrs. Big Sandy have a common ancestor right here in Cape Breton. It's certainly not uncommon but I don't think Dad, who loves to explore our family's genealogy, wants to confirm this suspicion that's she's planted in his mind. If he wasn't afraid she's right he could check it on the Internet in five minutes, the way he checks out everything now. Instead he just shrugs at the suggestion. Don't be surprised if she lands at your office demanding a front-page article warning people about the possible coming of McDonald's. Anyway, today I had to get out of there before I gained weight from all the hamburgers that will be eaten by the clown if that restaurant comes here."

David enjoyed Rita's telling of her plight, adding, "It would make a great story, how Ronald MacDonald, that's our Ronald MacDonald, is conspiring with his second worse nightmare to prevent the arrival in Shean of his very worst nightmare. Jesus, Rita, the stories I can't tell in the *Witness*!"

"I bet that's what makes your paper so popular, you tell the town's stories but you don't embarrass people with gossip. But I bet your notebooks are full of this kind of stuff," Rita guessed.

"Yeah. I'm keeping them in case the paper ever goes out of business, then I can publish them all in the last edition and blow the lid off this town with all the gossip I've hoarded over the years," David quipped. In fact David did keep a journal of things he'd heard, town stories that belonged solely in the oral tradition. The day might come, he felt, when he would have time to indulge in every reporter's fantasy: the bestselling novel.

Mary ran up to her father, grabbed his hand and began urging him to come help with the castle. David reached out and grabbed Rita's hand, dragging her into his daughter's plans. More than a dozen children had trenched the sand into a large moat within which stood a gravity-defying architecture of sand pail turrets, carved windows and scraps of cloth flying their colours from small pieces of driftwood.

"Daddy, we can't reach up there any more," Mary explained. "You have to do it."

With the children acting as onsite engineers they directed David and Rita, both tall enough to reach where the pails of sand needed to be placed. "If this thing collapses like it should have done an hour ago we could be buried alive in an avalanche of wet sand," David mused as he carefully upended another pail.

"Buried in my own castle just like a proper queen," Rita answered. "David, this is the largest structure I've ever seen on this beach, the largest we'll probably ever see. How did they do it?

It's got to be ten feet by ten feet and more than five high where you're standing. Oh dear, did you feel that?"

"Feel what?" David asked, fully concentrated on lifting the pail away without causing mishap.

"The moat, David. I'm standing in the moat and my feet are wet. The tide's coming in. The children are going to be so disappointed. What's that about time and tide waiting for no man? Well the tide is here and the time has arrived for me to get to work so I'm leaving it to you to deal with the trauma. Perhaps if you phone the hospital they can dispatch a team to deal with the post traumatic stress disorder these children will feel when they see their hard work coming to nothing."

Stepping away from the castle and across the moat to admire his own handiwork crowning the castle, David watched the first advancing wavelets lap at the base of the castle like a kitten at a milk saucer. "I don't think PTSD will be a factor. If there's something children love more than building, it is watching something being demolished," David said, nodding toward the clutch of children standing together already anticipating the worst. Or the best. And just beyond them Tony was snapping pictures, positioning himself to record, frame by frame, grain by grain, the demise of the short-lived castle.

| 29 |

The front page of *The Shean Witness* looked nothing like the summer fun issue David had in mind a few days earlier. Its two-inch-high morbidly black headline chronicled a much darker report. As the editor sat before his monitor writing and rewriting the headline as well as the main story's lead, a deep-seated fear gnawed at his stomach.

The story of Mrs. Big Sandy's eviction had abated, vanishing wholly from the provincial media, and relegated to barely breathing updates in the *Witness,* updates assuring readers that neither the RCMP, government agencies nor the municipal council were laying charges against the old woman. David turned his attention to the reclamation plans behind the eviction.

Those tailings on the old mine site and beyond to the hundreds of acres of land where Mrs. Big Sandy's house had sat had long been on the province's hit parade of toxic sites, which for David bore repeating in the *Witness*. Since no core samples had ever been taken, the Department of Environment's own assessment of the site was based solely on visual evidence. The *Witness* had advocated for years for the department to probe deeper into the potential dangers posed by a half century of mine waste and decades of municipal garbage. Taking core samples was the most obvious way of measuring what lurked within the hazardous site. The government's reluctance could be described in three words: Sydney Tar Ponds.

The tar ponds, a toxic waste site in the middle of Cape Breton Island's only city was caused by a century of steel mill residue. It was considered Canada's most dangerous environmental problem. A death sentence that had carried off uncounted numbers of residents through various forms of cancer, according to critics. Every effort to reclaim and rehabilitate the tar ponds met with opposition from one community sector or another so that hundreds of millions of dollars and several abandoned plans later, work was barely beginning on the cleanup. By avoiding a deeper examination of the Shean mine tailings the provincial government could avoid the discovery of alarming carcinogenics and decades of lawsuits.

Despite the *Witness*'s argument that people needed to know what health threats lurked within their midst, David discovered that for the most part people weren't all that anxious to be enlightened. They were like patients who prefer their doctor treat a disease without describing in detail exactly what is being treated, or hopelessly treated. They did not want to hear about cancer or radiation burns or chemotherapy. And their preferred alternative to hearing about clay and ash filled with carcinogens was to simply seal the tailings, with all their untold secrets, under a thick mat of heavy clay, frosted with another thick layer of top soil, then seeded to provide a large green space. Capping the site with clay was the least expensive and most publicly popular alternative, and would, according to theory, keep whatever health dangers lurked beneath the clay concealed and inactive.

The possibility of a green space raised many suggestions about how it could be put to use by the town. There was the perennial topic of a golf course, of course, while others would be happy with a series of walking trails or some other recreational outdoors concept.

Details of the currently proposed reclamation plans remained elusive, however. Requests from the *Witness* to the Department of Environment and the Department of Mines and Minerals brought vague replies if replies came at all. Freedom of information requests were stalled behind hundreds of other requests for information on other government files, plans, programs and projects. The Nova Scotia government had made its freedom of information legislation its own best friend, taxing inquiries at discouragingly high prices for research, and giving deputy ministers the power to delay or refuse any request deemed not in the public interest. The province's *Freedom of Information Act* had, in fact, become the most anti-democratic weapon in the current government's arsenal of self-protection.

When a couple of construction trailers appeared on the old mine site with still no information released by any government departments or forthcoming from a company called Resource Reclamations Limited, David drafted Tim Donovan away from his standard summer assignments to work with him on getting information.

Government legislation called for an environmental impact study before projects posing a change to the environment or to a community could move forward. Tim pursued that avenue, trying to coax, seduce or bribe information from many Halifax bureaucrats. He was passed along from one public relations person to another until, frustrated, he reported to David that he couldn't get any further than the army of communications officers that form the frontline of the provincial bureaucracy.

"David, the government's hired an army of these meaningless little drones whose job is to smile sweetly and sound foolish as they read their silly little scripts and keep people away from the Cabinet minister and the truth, whatever that is in politics."

Tim Donovan had gotten nowhere with his inquiries and David Cameron had fared no better. He had contacted anyone and everyone he knew in provincial departments that might have any inkling, insight or direction to offer. Yet two construction trailers, most likely to be used as offices, were on site at the MacArthur land. A crew from Nova Scotia Power had erected a couple of additional poles, extending the power line from the rubble of the burnt house to the trailers, which remained empty, divulging nothing of their purpose. Clearly, the first steps in the reclamation process had been taken.

People would be expecting an explanation and they would be expecting the *Witness* to provide it. Two days of inquiries, interspersed with the necessary business of the paper – taking pictures and writing stories – that would fill the coming week's paper, left David feeling impotent. He found himself immersed in the rare longing to be back at the *Toronto Star* with its specific assignments and extensive resources.

Ronald MacDonald rarely came into the *Witness* office, preferring to banter with David on a park bench or in the Gulf Grill, but his timing couldn't have been worse, David thought, as Ronald approached his desk accompanied by Don Alex.

"Any idea what they're planning down there on those old mine tailings?" Ronald asked.

"Looking into it right now, Ronald, and to tell you the truth I'm pretty busy with exactly that issue. Is there anything I can do for you?"

"It was Rita who said I should come see you this morning," Ronald explained, David's coolness thawing noticeably upon learning that Ronald was an emissary from Rita.

"What does Rita want?" David asked.

"Nothing for herself, but when Rita came home from work last night myself and herself, not Rita but HERSELF, were having a cup of tea. She, Herself that is, was telling me about breaking Donald MacNaughton's jaw with a frying pan. You must be slipping, David. Never saw that story in your paper. Anyway she remembered the character that was with him that morning, this Lord guy. And what was he doing with the mayor? I asked her, but she said she didn't know. He never said a word, just ran like a jackrabbit when Herself started swinging that cast-iron tennis racket of hers so I said let's see if we can find him and into the Google I go, searching for our Lord by trying three initials over and over, different ones every time, and..."

David paled with early recognition of where Ronald's story's was going and swung his chair around and punched in the name as Ronald took up a post over his left shoulder while Don Alex squatted over his right. The morning Mary had fallen down the stairs and broken her arm David had been in the process of entering that name – C.J.M. Lord – into his home office computer for a search. Since then it slipped his mind altogether. Ronald's right, he thought, I must be slipping. He called Tim Donovan over to join them at his desk.

"Well he's a character of ill-repute as they say in the stories," Ronald commented. "Not exactly a member in good standing with the Green Party, I'd say, not that I'd ever vote for them myself..."

But David wasn't listening. Clicking the search button, almost immediately the first page of several thousand websites where the name of C.J.M. Lord or variations of it could be found appeared on the screen.

"Start with that one there," Ronald directed. David clicked on the link. A half hour and a dozen links later a profile of the man was taking shape.

Perhaps C.J.M. Lord was a stranger in Shean but he had attracted considerable attention elsewhere, earning testimonials in the business sections and front pages of papers in Virginia and West Virginia. The fossil energy industry lauded Lord as one of the early innovators who transformed coal mining in the Appalachian Mountains. For two centuries coal was mined in those mountains in the traditional manner of men going underground to carve their way through black seams, but no more.

Lord, CEO of Knight Seam Holdings, which managed the interests of a number of separately incorporated coal companies, had gotten state permission to begin a more efficient means of mining: mountaintop removal coal mining. The millions of tons of coal trapped under these mountains could be liberated at less cost and with more speed if the mountaintops could be clearcut, and then the mountaintops themselves blown off with explosives. Large machines pushed the rubble over the edge and down into the valleys below. It took on average about a year to explode away a third of the height of a mountain, and that's where the prize was found. Acres of black coal that could be ripped out of open pits and sent off to market in moments compared to underground mining that took years to develop, and many, many years more to mine the same amount that could be extracted via an open pit in days or weeks or months.

The first profits the company realized in its venture when it began strip mining mountain coal came from the wages that would normally be paid to hundreds of underground miners. A mine that once needed two thousand miners now operated with less than one hundred. The per ton cost of production was lowered to near pennies but the price of a ton of coal in the marketplace crept steadily upward, as did the profits. C.J.M. Lord was a new breed of CEO, imaginative and innovative, one paper wrote.

Now just about every mining corporation in those coal-rich states was tearing the tops off mountains.

C.J.M. Lord was also under relentless criticism from friends of the environment, vilified for being another carbon-based corporate leader. Calculations published online showed the generous contribution Knight Seams's annual tonnage of coal made to global warming. His companies had been sued for perceived crimes against the environment but never successfully, and he had frequently sued back for libel, always successfully.

Lord left his position with Knight Seams amid the investigation of claims that industrial deaths from accidents among the company's non-unionized employees were disproportionately high. In his latest venture, according to a recent newspaper report, Lord was CEO for a new corporate concept, Resource Reclamations Limited, described as taking an environmentally friendly approach to mining.

"The man must have been struck by lightning on the road to Damascus," David said aloud as they sifted through various Internet articles that revealed to them a portrait of someone who was soon coming into their lives and into the future of their town.

His remark caught the attention of Ronald, who had wandered over to the coffee machine while Don Alex wandered outside and away. Ronald was drawn back to the editor's desk, where David was writing information into his notebook, still a pen and paper reporter in what was becoming a cut and paste industry.

C.J.M. Lord was a much different person today, according to reports. A revelation he refused to share publicly had made Lord "conscious," his own word, of the damage being inflicted on the planet by the search for resources. He did not condemn the search nor the resources, but explained that someone would be needed to minister to the land, to repair it, restore it, to heal it, following along behind the mining industry like gleaners following harvesters in a famous painting, salvaging whatever was left behind in the tailings and rehabilitating landscapes that had been traumatized.

"What do you think, David?" Ronald asked once they had exhausted themselves with information.

"He's a coal baron. Those guys don't get religion," David said. Tim Donovan spoke his next question for him. "What's he doing here? Shean's mines are long gone."

"Unless there's coal right under our feet, Tim," David said thoughtfully. "What if Resource Reclamations Limited isn't planning on making a green patch for the town." David began flipping through his notebook. "The company has been formed, but there's nothing on where it has operated in the past. It looks like the Shean reclamation is its very first project. That last article we looked at said something about salvaging and rehabilitating. Salvaging what? There's more going on here than we know and my sick gut tells me that this guy's here to dig an open pit."

Excusing Ronald and walking them to the door thanking him for their help, David came back to huddle with Tim. "We have about four hours before we have to get this baby to bed Tim, and so this story is all that exists for us. Let's go back and bombard the Department of Mines and Minerals, environment, the mayor, C.J.M Lord himself if we can find a number, and use the words 'open pit' and 'strip mining' like we already have confirmation. See if we can force someone into springing a leak. On the record or off the record, with or without confirmations, my gut tells me that the open pit is our headline."

Four hours later, the newspaper's printer received the digital pages with the tabloid's weekly front page carrying two-inch-high lettering asking: *RECLAMATION*: Green or greed? Fears grow over strip mine instead of public space.

| 30 |

Normally David wouldn't have answered the newspaper's phone at that hour. It was customary for him to linger in the office once the paper had been put to bed and the staff had gone home. It was a time to reflect, to meditate, to feed his addiction to FreeCell, but tonight he was deeply distracted by the story he had just written. Circumstantial evidence might work in criminal court but it didn't carry much weight in libel hearings, and that was all he had really, circumstantial evidence based on his and Tim's speculations. He was wide open to a libel suit and vividly aware from news reports he had found online that C.J.M. Lord used them often to silence the media. He had never lost a suit. But not going with the story would have cost him a lot more, David told himself. The information needed to be put out there because he felt the truth of it, and the people of Shean needed to be aware that all was not necessarily well with the town. The damned nobility of his decision, now that it was irretrievable, had him scared shitless, so when the phone rang reflex lifted the receiver.

"David? I was hoping you'd still be there. It's Rita. This may sound stupid but do you go to bed early?"

"As early as you'd like," was what he wanted to say but he had mired himself in enough trouble for one day. "No, around midnight. Why?"

"On my way into work today I dropped my car off at the Ian's Esso for its annual checkup. I was supposed to pick it up during my break but completely forgot and I need a drive home after work. I get off at eleven."

"I'll be there."

"I'll spare you all the 'Are you sures?' and 'Am I imposing?' and just say thank you. Thank you."

Rita put down the phone and hoped she had been convincing when she said she had forgotten to go after her car. Well, she had almost forgotten and even asked herself how she would have gotten home if she hadn't remembered that she had to get her car. She would have to ask someone who wouldn't want her walking seven miles at midnight. Who would that be? And then she let herself forget.

David put down the phone, pleased with the pending company of Rita MacDonald, if only for the few minutes it would take to drive her to Ronald's farm. He couldn't imagine anyone he would have preferred to see right now. Checking the wall clock he saw that he still had two hours to wait for that moment so he reheated a cup of old coffee in the microwave and went back to his desk. The image of the front page with its dire headline above a large photograph taken by Tony at the beach earlier that week filled the screen. The back page, he was happy to remind himself, was taken up by two large photographs, another of Tony's beach shots, and above it another photograph, one of Tim's, taken in a February blizzard that had paralyzed the whole town for two days. Above both photos a headline asked, "Complaining about the Heat?" The disturbing front page vanished as he clicked online and continued his search into the corporate history of C.J.M. Lord, assembling evidence for his own defence.

"Thank you for picking me up," Rita said, sliding into David's Toyota.

"Thank you for sending your father to the office today."

"Was it important?"

"More important than you know. More important than I know."

"What don't you know?"

"Why C.J.M. Lord is here is the first thing I don't know. My gut tells me we're going to be fighting an open-pit mine in Shean. According to Lord in a U.S. newspaper article, the 'reclamation' in Resource Reclamations is the reclaiming of residual resources. They sift through the waste, here that means the slag dumped at the old mine sites, recovering coal that escaped the first processing. Perhaps they restore the land in the process but the company's first interest is the coal. If I'm right and it goes ahead we're in for an awful mess right in the middle of town."

"Down there between the town and sea?"

"Between the town and the sea, yes, but considering the size of the coal corporations Lord has headed it doesn't make a lot of sense. There's not that much coal to be recovered. I can't imagine there's enough coal there to earn a small operation a decent profit, so what is Resource Reclamations doing here? It's a new company and it's looking for a place to begin, and it may have set its goal on all the coal in and under Cape Breton. The island is sitting on top of five billion tons of coal and not an ounce of it is being mined."

"But most of it is under the ocean like the Beaton Seam. You can't get at that with an open pit, can you?"

"No, but there's money in coal. Despite society's reliance on oil, coal still plays a major role. They still burn over a billion tons of coal in the United States alone every year, so environmentalists are daydreaming if they think that the energy industry is just going to let half a trillion tons of coal just lie there while the world converts to wind or solar or whatever.

"In Canada," David continued with the authority of one only recently versed in a subject, "Nova Scotia is the friendliest place for getting energy from coal. Most of our power generators burn coal and all of it, every single ounce, is imported from the United States or South America despite Cape Breton's wealth of it. With the kind of mining techniques they're using today, underground mining became non-competitive and so the last mine on this island closed back in the 1990s. But the coal is still sitting there, tempting somebody."

Too soon David was at the foot of Rita's driveway and as he slowed to turn in he cursed himself for going on about coal instead of talking about something she might be interested in.

"Won't you come in for a cup of tea?" she asked when he stopped in front of the old farmhouse. "Somebody's still up by the sound of it." They could hear a fiddle tune as they stepped out of the car. "Dad's playing. I think it was that fiddle that brought him back so quickly from his stroke, using his left hand for holding it under his chin and the fingering, of course, but God you should have heard it when he was learning all over again. Just like any beginner and it near drove me crazy but now he has a bit of command of it again."

The scene in the kitchen was one David wished he could photograph. Ronald was sitting on one of the kitchen chairs playing a series of tunes surrounded by a home that had barely changed in the hundred years since it was constructed. The painted wood walls had never been blemished by wallpaper. Though it had been partly converted to an oil burner, the massive Enterprise stove, older than anyone in the kitchen, was burning wood from a stack beside the stove. The now rare sight of a kitchen couch tucked along one wall was covered with a worn patchwork quilt. In the rocking chair on the other side of the Enterprise, listening with a critical ear sat Herself, as Ronald had dubbed her, with a cup of tea in her hand, chair rocking in rhythm to the music.

Ronald brought his tune to a flourishing end with their entrance. Mrs. Big Sandy eyed David with suspicion.

"And how long has this been going on?" she asked, having paused before the question just long enough to confirm that Ronald wasn't going to perform his fatherly duty.

"There's nothing going on," Rita and David answered in unison, feeling in that moment like awkward teenagers.

"Sounds rehearsed to me," Mrs. Big Sandy accused, and while the embarrassed pair explained about Rita's car to Ronald, the old woman went about making a cup of tea for each of them, mumbling to herself – an uneasy sound that intimidated David as she moved about the kitchen, entering the pantry to retrieve something to serve with the tea, biscuits.

"Made them herself," Ronald's whispered warning informed David, adding, "I've got a pocketful of the things."

The task seemed to settle her and the two men relaxed into their chairs, rested their elbows on the table, and began to talk.

"So what's happening, David?"

Ronald's question was as broad and meaningless as any social inquiry and as intense and direct as an inquisition. David briefly weighed what was happening: his thoughts as he put the paper together, the vague evidence leading Tim and him to the conclusion that Resource Reclamations Limited was planning an open-pit mine in Shean, his feared vulnerability to a lawsuit.

As he watched Rita, still in her printed-flowers uniform, he remembered too the *Witness's* back page, how he had placed a large photo of Main Street buried in a February blizzard above one of Tony's warm summer scenes from this week's beach. He wondered what Rita would think when she saw it, thinking too that he may well have gone too far. He may as well have gone out and carved their initials in a tree or engraved them in a stone at the breakwater. He felt suddenly foolish and steered himself away from all those thoughts with a, "Not much, Ronald. Yourself?"

"Not much."

"Nice to hear you playing again." Ronald was a kitchen fiddler who rarely appeared in public except at the annual gathering of the Cape Breton Fiddlers Association at the Gaelic College in St. Ann's.

"Thank you," Ronald answered, watching Mrs. Big Sandy disappear back into the pantry before adding, "I find it best to do those things I can do that keep my mouth shut and out of trouble in the process, like fiddling, if you know what I mean."

"It's not polite to whisper because it usually means you're talking about the other person in the room," Mrs. Big Sandy scolded from the pantry doorway, carrying butter and a jar of molasses, which she placed beside the biscuit. "Eat!" she ordered.

David was going to make some sound about not being able to sleep if he ate so late at night but her waiting stare was withering and he reached for the biscuits despite Ronald's warning, broke one, buttered it, drizzled a spoon of molasses over it and took a bite. As he chewed, the old woman stood waiting with the arrogant assurance of a chef awaiting a five star review. David washed the bite down with a mouthful of hot tea while nodding toward Mrs. Big Sandy with sincere approval and took a second bite, feeling Ronald eying him intensely, as if expecting David to pitch forward across the table clutching his stomach as if in the last seconds of his life.

Rita buttered one of the biscuits, passed on the molasses and ate. "God, Dad, I'm surprised you left any for us the way you like fresh biscuits."

Ronald's curious hand then ventured forward while Mrs. Big Sandy eased herself back into the rocking chair. "What's that stiff little prick going to do with my land, Mr. Newspaperman?" she asked David. "Oh, I should have swatted that bug with my frying pan when I had the chance, that's what I should have done. Flattened him as thin as the holy host itself's what I should have done. Stealing Sandy's land but if you think Sandy's going to let him get away with this you got another thought coming," she said, swelling with rage.

"She's stoking the boiler, David," Ronald whispered out the side of his mouth, never taking his eyes off Mrs. Big Sandy.

"I don't care if you think I'm crazy but Sandy won't put up with it, not with that creep stealing his land and driving me off it. Sandy's still around you know. I feel him and don't you dare laugh at me when I say that because I'll– I'll–"

"Thar she blows!" Ronald whispered into his teacup.

"I'll..."

"Mrs. MacArthur, would you like another cup of tea?" Rita asked quietly, distracting the woman rather masterfully David thought with a great deal of relief as Mrs. Big Sandy turned to her, slightly confused by the interruption, then nodded as she sat in the rocking chair.

"He is you know," she continued conversationally. "I mean it, what I said. I feel him. You can't be around somebody for most of your life and not know what it feels like when that person is around you. He speaks to me through the teacups, you know."

Ronald MacDonald tried to hide inside his cup, drinking deeply, smothering laughter, sneaking a panicky look at David, who was only looking for an excuse to get out of there.

"What Mrs. MacArthur means is that she can read the tea leaves. Is that how you talk to your husband, through the leaves?" Rita asked.

"Do you think I'm crazy, dearie? I certainly don't talk to Sandy through the tea leaves. That's how he talks to me, through the leaves. I just talk to him the normal way I talk to you. I say, 'Sandy you old bastard the world's falling apart without you here holding it together.' That's what I say, that and other stuff's that none of your goddamned business so don't go asking because that's what I'll do, tell you it's none of your goddamned business! And it isn't!"

Mrs. Big Sandy sat back firmly, the bulldog features long ago hardened to a permanent mask, dared any one of them to challenge what she had just said. The non-challenging silence of everyone else's eyes lowered, illiterately examining their own tea leaves, prevailed, a silence she could not allow to linger long before she was consumed by it and began again to fill it with the sound of her own voice.

"Whatever they're planning down there in Sandy's land is never going to happen, I'll tell you that! Sandy won't allow it. He won't! He told me! He told me to curse the land. You don't believe that, do you? I see your heads lifting like the skeptics you are but Sandy's ghost is down there, I know because I put him there myself. He asked me to help him and I did and he told me that nothing is going to happen to his land and whatever does happen down there won't happen for those who stole his land and threw me upon the mercy of strangers! No sireee! He's there now and he's not going anywhere, not to heaven or hell or anywhere else until what happens to his land makes me happy. And do you know what will make me happy? Nothing. Nothing at all! So there. Put that in your newspaper and smoke it, Mr. Newspaperman!"

David didn't allow another silence to refuel Mrs. Big Sandy's rage. He made his apologies and took his departure from the MacDonald farmhouse. Rita accompanied him to his car, and once they were safely beyond the closed kitchen door, she made an amused apology for her houseguest's outbursts.

"What can you do about it?" David asked, shrugging helplessly. "But tell me, is that frying pan on the stove the one she took out of her house?"

"Yes. As soon as she moved in she took our frying pan off the stove and shoved it in a cupboard and put her own on the stove. I was afraid she was going to begin moving everything but that's all she did. I think it's like a security blanket. She clings to it whenever she can. Defends herself against the world with it, I guess. What do you make about her relationship with Sandy?"

"Make of it? Can't say I gave it much thought. Do you make something of it?"

"I'm not sure, but some of the things she says ... I guess I always assumed that they were just two miserable people who lived together and between them frightened half the town, but now I don't know. I hear her say such tender things sometimes. Not that she means for anyone to hear them but they slip out in the middle of those rants of hers. She misses him something terrible, and that makes me wonder what more they had between them than the stories we tell about them."

David stopped at the door of his car, turned his back and leaned against the vehicle. There was no chill in the air, a sign that the good weather had arrived for an extended stay. Rita had struck upon a point he had often pondered himself. He had given it a lot of thought following the incident at the paper when the *Witness* had published Johnny Petticoat's nickname, and the hurt the man clearly felt about how he had been characterized when he thought he was doing something good for the community. Never mind that the man, with or without a nickname, was generally a fool.

"We make them, don't we, those characters like Mrs. Big Sandy? Shean has a rich seam of them running through who-knows-how-many generations. What I think I've learned since coming back to the paper is that characters don't see themselves as characters. They're just people trying to get through their lives like you and me but for whatever reason they become trapped inside the stories we tell about them. No idiosyncrasy goes un-characterized, and thank God for that, but you're right. We have no idea how Mrs. Big Sandy feels, or what she and Sandy shared."

"They may have been Shean's great love story for all we know," Rita added, "but when I try to imagine that, I think of her up on the widow's walk of their old house and Sandy down in the yard calling, 'Hark! What light from yonder window breaks?'"

"That's some imagining," David said, laughing as he opened the car door, slid behind the wheel and rolled down the window.

"Thanks for the tea and the company. I needed a distraction."

"Is that what you call me then, a distraction?"

"I'm going to start my car now and get out of here before you go back for Mrs. Big Sandy's frying pan," David said, the engine roaring to life.

"Thanks for the drive home, David."

"Anytime. I mean that, Rita," he added, easing away from the house.

Rita MacDonald watched the car's taillights redden the darkness and disappear. She remained there for another few minutes listening to the roar of the ocean lapping at the edge of their farmland where it dropped off into the Gulf of St. Lawrence. The night was still, not a breath of a breeze, yet if she walked to the shore, she would find the sea coming onto the land in a tiny, gentle lap of wavelets. So where did that ocean roar she was hearing come from? A light went on in the bedroom Mrs. Big Sandy occupied and Rita stood there a few moments longer with her thoughts.

| 31 |

The *Witness* reached readers the following day with a front-page story so disorienting for some that they searched for the paper's date to be sure it wasn't an April's Fool issue that had gotten lost in the mail. Appalled was what some felt, and fear filled others, and still others filled with hope and others with doubt. Throughout the day the discussion of the possibility of an open-pit mine in Shean outshone the weather as a topic, and for a full day in Shean no one asked, "So what's new?" because all knew.

Having overseen the distribution of the paper, David left the office, walking through the cloud-covered day past the empty, rain-threatened park to the Gulf Grill, which this afternoon was loud with remarks, arguments and head-shaking silence. Every head turned as he entered, some staring with accusations, as if the *Witness* had conjured this story out of whole cloth (which to some extent, David knew, was true). Others, misreading the paper's report and crediting David with offering Shean an economic proposal, nodded their approval of his idea of bringing a coalmine back to Shean, something somebody should have thought of long ago.

Ronald MacDonald and Don Alex were poring over a single copy of the paper at the counter, it being Don Alex's habitual manner to read the weekly news over someone else's shoulder. David doubted if Don Alex had ever purchased a copy. Both men acknowledged David with a nod and returned to their reading while Theresa delivered a cup of coffee, distracted by thoughts of whether a coalmine was good news or bad news for the Gulf Grill. Ronald MacDonald had long ago planted in her mind his fears of a McDonald's opening in Shean, which he assured her would mean the demise of smaller, locally owned businesses. That's how corporations operate, he explained – they crush the competition.

David was grateful for the relief of the silence that greeted him, a silence that was shattered a moment later when the grill's door opened, then slammed. "Cameron, you bastard!"

David turned toward the door and Donald MacNaughton's flushed rage. "Didn't realize we were related, Mr. Mayor."

MacNaughton's face collapsed momentarily at the insult then flared again as he waved the newspaper like a weapon, walking toward its editor while some patrons raised their cups toward Theresa signalling for a ringside refill.

"What do you think you're doing, printing this bullshit? This is nothing but scare tactics to try to stop this town from progressing. This is the worst kind of reporting, that's what this is, but that's your style, isn't it, printing garbage."

"Is it true?" David asked.

"What's truth? Slandering the name of someone who has a plan to help this town, or writing garbage about environmental destruction when you've never seen the whole picture? This is nothing but more of the same left-wing distortions that fill this newspaper every week. A real journalist would have gotten the whole story before he printed it, but half a story that tells just your side of the story is all you wanted, right? That way you get to poison people's minds with this crap!" MacNaughton's raised hand crushed the paper into a threatening fist that brought David off his seat and into a quietly defensive position in case Donald's anger turned to blows.

"You still haven't answered my question. You wouldn't answer your phone yesterday because you didn't want to answer the question then and you won't answer it now," David fired back, raising his own hands, palms open, to emphasize his own frustration. "Is it true? Is Resources Reclamations Limited opening a strip mine in Shean?"

MacNaughton grew suddenly still, thoughtful.

"You know something, David, it's not you I'm going to talk to about this. The only thing I'm going to talk to you about can be said through the town's lawyer. As for myself, I'm going to talk to people one on one about this article of yours. Let them know what's at stake and what's at risk because of you and that damned rag of yours."

A rumble like thunder froze the confrontation as all heads turned toward the cafe's large windows, which filled with shadow as a tractor trailer carrying a massive yellow machine crawled over Main Street, followed by a second carrying the large arm and shovel of an excavator, like a monster Meccano set in need of assembly. The shadowy moment vanished, leaving in its wake the fading rumble of large trucks.

"I guess that answers my question." David's calm voice camouflaged the emotional cocktail of one part grateful self-preservation in knowing now there would be no lawsuit despite the mayor's threat, and one part terrible sense of foreboding that Tim Donovan and he had stumbled upon a force neither the paper nor the people of the town would be able to fight.

The mayor watched the machinery pass and without another word left the newspaper editor standing there. As he closed the door behind him, David knew that Donald MacNaughton had not retreated in defeat.

David Cameron stood on a hill overlooking the abandoned mine site. Power lines ran to the two construction site trailers that had already been hauled onto the property. The two tractor trailers had been unhitched from the trucks, the trucks themselves deadheading back from where they came. A handful of men walked around the site, busy at nothing by the look of it. David snapped his camera, scribbled observations and thoughts into his notebook and was taking more pictures when one of the people in the frame waved and called his name.

Old hockey teammate and high school friend Victor Mason joined David on his perch. Victor was popularly known as the Gentle Giant because of his size. Outside the arena, his intimidating size was softened by a natural kindness. Inside any arena, nobody wanted to get between him and the boards. They rarely saw each other now, Victor having followed the country's construction booms from southern Ontario to Calgary to the diamond mines in the Northwest Territories and most recently the tar sands of Fort McMurray. David was able to track Victor's travels because Victor had always been a devoted subscriber to the *Witness*. In fact, twenty five percent of the *Witness*'s subscriptions came from people from Shean who were either working or settled elsewhere, people who had left home but never moved away, was the way office manager Cheryl Horne put it.

"When did you get back?" David asked, learning that Victor had been home now a couple of weeks, and that he would try to stretch those weeks all the way through the summer before heading back to Fort Mac. "Learn anything down there?" David asked him.

"They hired a half dozen people so far, labourers, Mac-Naughton's buddies, so it's clear whose arse you're going to have to kiss to get a job around here. But they'll need more than those tits on a bull if they're going to operate that machine down there," Victor said. "They're going to need to bring in two or three cranes just to put the excavator together. They'll need someone to operate it."

"Is that what you were doing down there, looking for a job operating that machine?"

"Just curious. Just thinking it would be nice not to have to go away again."

"Look Victor, I'm done here. Do you have time for a beer, shoot the shit?"

"I don't think this place has even changed its dust since the pope was an altar boy," Victor noted, looking around the dim interior of the Five Bucks Tavern, named for a decor that featured five buck heads mounted high on the walls. From their antlers still dangled strings of tinsel from the tavern's annual seasonal efforts. The suspicion was that the tinsel had hung there ever since the tavern's first New Year's Eve party some time long before David or Victor were old enough to buy a beer in the place. The glassy-eyed deer surveyed the near empty room while the two patrons decided where they would sit.

"I've been to a lot of taverns, but nothing feels more like home than this herd of Bambis gawking at me," Victor said, tipping his beer glass to the five silent observers on the tavern wall. "But the *Witness* makes up for them when I'm away. I gotta tell you, David, that paper of yours is a lifesaver. It always gets to me two or three weeks late but what the hell, it's still news from home. Know what the wife did the last time I left for out west? I opened my gear in the bunkhouse and what do you think's the first thing facing me?"

David shrugged. "The *Witness*."

"Nope, the telephone book. When I get the paper I go through it from arsehole to appetite and when I get to the classifieds I'd be calling home, telling the wife there's a house for sale on Munro Street and I'd be asking her who's selling it. There'd just be the phone number, right? So I'd ask her to look it up. She found that a real pain in the butt, going through all those numbers until she found out whose number it was, so I guess what that phonebook was saying to me was look it up yourself, buster. And I do.

"I read your paper today. Didn't have to wait two or three weeks this time. You're not too happy about this mine business, are you? It's jobs."

"At what price, Victor? I don't suppose anybody here's got a better idea than you what strip mining does to a place."

"You mean because I've done it? You're right, though. It's a mess. Messing up the whole world, according to you people. But you know what I do? I go through my job just like a guy in a slaughterhouse or a seal hunter goes through his, just go to work and fuck the world. You're probably right about this global warming, though. Christ, I'm not stupid. Of course we're killing the planet but they're paying us a shitload of money to do it. I built a new house on the old man's old lot. You've seen it. It's paid for, built and paid for in five years. Sandra and the kids love it and so do I when I get home. But you know what happened to me today? This is really funny. The wife was walking me through the garden, pointing out all these names of flowers that women pay attention to and who comes along but the paperboy. So I'm standing there in my garden in the middle of my hometown where I escape to whenever I can because it's so far from the mud holes where I work and what do you know, there's my old buddy David Cameron telling me that Shean's going to become another one of the world's open sores. Well I laughed. That's gotta be what they mean about karma, eh. Ah shit, David, I don't want to see it happen here."

"I don't get it. You were there looking for a job today, Vic," David said, signalling for a couple of more drafts.

"I hope it doesn't happen, I mean that, but it's going to. You've seen it with your own eyes, so if I get a chance to stay home with the family and make good bucks, I'm going to do it. That's what all this economic development shit's all about, anyway – getting people like me back here, people who want to be here, but can't. How many times did you write about that?"

David and Victor had gone through enough old times and glasses of draft that the newspaper editor knew better than to get into his car when he came back out into the sunlight, opting instead to walk home for supper, passing along the way something that took a while to register on his beery thoughts. Posters. The town was plastered with posters – telephone poles and store windows filled with an announcement of a public meeting called by the mayor and council to be held in the fire hall the following night.

| 32 |

"Going to the meeting tonight?" Ronald asked as the newspaperman approached his bench. David had stopped his car when he noted his kilted friend sitting in the park, head tilted back to inhale what was becoming a rare burst of summer sunshine. Curiously, Don Alex was seated at a separate bench. Assuming Ronald's question was rhetorical, he didn't bother to answer, having just moments before assigned Tim Donovan to cover the meeting because David wanted to become part of the discussion, not some semi-objective bystander.

"What's with Don Alex?" he asked, taking a seat beside Ronald.

"Stupid bastard wants the mine. Thinks it'll be good for the economy. The economy! Ha! A lot he knows about it. Wouldn't be in favour of it if he was still young enough to be hired on, I bet, the lazy thing that he is. Always was, and I told him so. I was just thinking about him and it makes me interested to see who'll be in favour and who'll be against."

"And where did your thinking take you?"

"For it, the mine that is, will be the mayor and all his cronies, and some business people, and who knows all else. And against it'll be the tree huggers and yourself, the paper that is, and myself, and Herself, of course, who told me she wants to go to the meeting. Rita's working so you know what that means, getting someone to drive us, then me walking into the hall with her. I hope people got enough sense not to start thinking … burrr! For God's sake, David, don't you dare point your camera my way. There's no need of something like that going in the paper."

"So do you think more will be for it than against it?"

"Doesn't matter. Politics always gets its way. That newspaper of yours is a good thing to have, good for telling us what's going on, like this mine which we wouldn't know a thing about yet except you telling us in the *Witness*. But, and no offence meant by this, David, but when has it really mattered – your paper, I mean – whenever there's a political decision involved? Never, I bet. Politics!" Ronald said, spitting the word. "The meeting will be fun, though, which is the least we can hope for in all this, to have a little fun along the way. I hope Herself goes aboard Mac-Naughton. I'll have to remind her to bring along her frying pan."

"You two are getting along okay? Even when Rita's not there to referee?" David asked, finding an opportunity to say a name that had been teasing his mind more and more in recent days.

"Aside from having to keep my silence when she goes on about Sandy's sainted memory, we're managing. There's things I never thought, though. That the woman could bake biscuits. Thanks to you, I know that now, and a pan of them for break-fast's no hardship except for Rita sticking that damn bucket of margarine in front of me and disallowing the butter. They beg for butter those biscuits do. And the rosary! When she's not ranting on about something like yourself or MacNaughton, she's on those beads like she's a nun or something. Never figured her for a woman of faith, I didn't, but I guess you get to be her age you start grovelling.

"Did a bit of it myself when I had the stroke. But you're right there when you mention Rita the referee. She has a way with Herself that's like Jesus calming the seas when he was in that boat in that storm. But Herself can get to Rita, too. My daughter's not all business the way she likes to pretend, I'm noticing. Mrs Big Sandy gets under her skin teasing her – hell, tormenting her – like with the night you drove her home from work. I haven't seen my little girl blush since she was in high school. Which means as a father I have to ask. You and Rita...?"

David felt himself redden and hoped the old man would put it down to too much sun.

"Believe me, Ronald. Rita's not interested in me or any other men in Shean and she's got good reasons. She's a lovely girl, woman, I mean, but I'm a man with two children."

"Who lives with his mother, I might add," Ronald interjected.

"Who lives with his mother," David sighed.

"I know Rita wants to go away again which is probably why she doesn't want to get tied down," Ronald explained. "She doesn't say it, about going away that is, and I pretend I don't know because it's not easy to know your youngest child, your baby, is sacrificing her life for you, but that's what she's doing and I don't know what to do about it because she did save my life, David. Saved it with her nursing and she saved it for real when she stuck that fiddle back in my hand and made me play. And I don't mind admitting to you that I'm afraid to have her go away again. What if I– What if it happens to me again? I don't know what to say about what I know about her, so I just keep my mouth shut."

"Perhaps you could just say thank you. That might go a long way, for her to know you appreciate what's she's done, what she's doing," David advised.

"Do you think? I hadn't thought of saying anything like that. Perhaps I will. Perhaps I will."

"What scheme are you two cooking up to keep this town from getting its fair share of money and jobs?" Don Alex passed in front of them, stopping for a moment to address himself to Ronald. "I hope that mine comes here soon and you know what else I hope, Mr. MacDonald? I hope they open the biggest Mc-Donald's in the world right there where you're sitting in that silly dress. Think of you looking like that and calling that other Ronald a clown."

The two men watched in silence as Don Alex walked away.

There were other places David could have gone to do his research but he reasoned that among those who remained lucid in the Shean Manor there were memories who could evoke for him the worst aspects of living in a coal mining town. Old miners resided here, but more important were the women. He wanted to interview those who had to handle the daily fact of coal dust, needing to test which way the wind was blowing before a wash could be put out on the clothesline and meet the endless demand for dusting windows and furniture and dishes. The coal mines, he had heard often enough, put nearly as much coal into the lungs of miners' families as into the miners themselves.

He found Rita in the palliative care ward where exonerated killer John Dan MacLean was breathing the last of his life through lungs ravaged by cigarettes. Rita's duty was to make him as comfortable as possible, and considering the state of John Dan's deteriorated mind, he was not someone David would be talking with anyway.

"You need to talk to the members of our Bridge Club. They're all experts at Auction, naturally. According to Mrs. Big Sandy they call themselves a Bridge Club because it sounds more prestigious," Rita explained when David told her his mission.

After making John Dan comfortable with enough morphine to help him sleep for at least two hours, Rita brought David to the recreation room. In this confined room, some residents sat watching "their show" on afternoon television, while others gazed out the window in boredom. Around a small round table sat four women in a fevered game of Auction 125.

"If I can interrupt you ladies for a moment, I believe you all know David Cameron? This is Gloria MacKie, Marie Jeanne

Doucet, Catherine Allison and Joan Mason. He'd like to talk to you, if he could, about the old coal mining days, I believe. Would that be okay?"

The women agreed but not before they played out the hands they had been dealt, and Rita signalled for David to follow her to the nursing station, where she filled a tea pot and piled oat-cakes on a plate. "They'll be delighted if you actually pour and serve them," she advised. "If you have time when you're finished, want to stop for a cup with me?"

There will be time, David thought as he wheeled a table of tea and cakes back toward the women in the recreation room.

| 33 |

"I don't know why you'd play the Jack of Spades and kill my ace of hearts," Gloria MacKie scolded her partner, Catherine Allison, as David returned with the tea trolley. "You should have reneged it and we'd have made our bid."

"Oh, shut up! Twenty five was a stupid bid to make anyway when you didn't even have a Jack..."

"Milk for everyone?" he asked, getting nods from Catherine, Marie Jeanne Doucet and Joan Mason, with Gloria adding half a teaspoon of sugar, explaining that "at my age I like things to be sweet, especially when you have to play with a sour partner."

"Oh Gloria, shut up!"

"Girls! Ladies! What should I call you anyway?"

"You can call me anything but what you called me in that paper of yours last month. '91 years young.' That's so stupid."

"It won't happen again, Mrs. MacKie," David promised, realizing with the woman's words just how patronizing and foolish the overworked cliché was. It would never be used again in the *Witness* unless it came as part of a paid-for birthday wish or some other revenue-earning milestone.

David was familiar with all four women. Gloria was the oldest. Joan Mason, whose only son Victor had been a late-in-life ambush, was the youngest at seventy-three, still sharp minded but restricted to a wheelchair and the full-time care she could only get in the Shean Manor. The other women, Marie Jeanne and Catherine Allison, were somewhere in their eighties.

David pulled a chair up to the table upon which he placed a notebook. He checked the battery power in his digital tape recorder and inserted it in his shirt pocket and explained himself.

"I'd like to write a piece for next week's *Witness* on what it was like living in Shean when the coal mines were booming here. I know toward the end, from the late 1930s until they ended in the late '50s, that there wasn't a lot of production, but what about earlier, when all four mines were operating and hundreds of miners were working? What was the town like? I don't mean the fact that there were twenty-seven places along Main Street selling booze, or the weekend brawls between the Scots and Belgians and whoever else wanted to fight. I'd like to know what it was like raising a family then. You've all been housewives, parents. I get the impression it was an ugly town. How did you see it at that time?"

There was a silent pause that David's experience told him was not reluctance but indecision as to who should start, one of those moments when patience is a journalist's best friend.

"Well, I was alive for almost it all, from the end of the First World War anyway, so I may as well start," Gloria MacKie said. "I'm glad you're asking about this and not what I had for breakfast this morning or I'd have to look it up in my diary," she chuckled, settling her wiry body into the chair. "Is this for one of those stories about the world's temperature going up? Is that what you're asking, about the smoke and soot and coal dust that they blame everything on these days?"

"In a way, I suppose it is," David conceded. "But there's talk of another coal mine for Shean, not underground but on the surface, a strip mine, so I guess what I'm looking for is what people have to look forward to if there is another mine. You've all lived through it."

"And I'd live through it all again if the Lord would let me, but to tell you the truth I prefer to live through something else instead," Gloria said. "To tell you the Lord's truth, though, I didn't know how bad it was until it ended, the mining I mean. Those words came so easy to me when I said them before, the smoke and soot and the coal dust, because that's what it was, a dirty town. Dirty day and night. You were forever scrubbing the smoke or the soot or the coal dust, out of the kitchen counter or the kids' ears. When you did do a wash and hung it on the line you had to do it when the wind was blowing that awful stuff the other way, and then you were practically living in the kitchen window watching the clothesline in case the wind shifted and if it did you had to rush outside and rescue the sheets and the tablecloth and children's clothes and the unmentionables and get them back inside before they blackened right there on the line. Then, even if it was summertime, you had to start the kitchen stove and hang the clothes from everywhere so they could go on drying. It was terrible trying to keep a clean house. Some women just gave up, you know. Just stopped scrubbing or washing, but not me."

"Just as bad as that was the outside itself," Marie Jeanne Doucet added. "Pierre and me, we came to Shean from up north where there's no coal mines, so he could get steady work. Up north we had a garden I loved to be in, growing vegetables for preserves, but when we came to Shean it was like those pictures you see of the moon, a black moon. Nothing was growing in the whole town. Nothing at all. It was like a dead place."

"But something did grow after a while, didn't it, Marie?" Catherine Allison reminded her friend. "Do you know what grew?" she asked David, going on to answer, "poplars and buckwheat! Ha! There was a man from over Richmond County who came here one summer selling plants and saplings he guaranteed everybody would grow in their yards, even though there was nothing but ashes and coal dust in them. He sold them for one dollar a tree and one dollar a bush and they did grow. Oh how they grew! We thought they were the most beautiful things in the world and now when you look at Shean today, what do you see? Poplars and buckwheat."

"Oh the trees!" recalled Marie Jeanne. "I remember the trees. He called them silver oaks, that man from Richmond County, such a pretty name, and the buckwheat, it was really something called Chinese lace, and they grew, both of them. Oh did they ever grow. I think I wore myself out and put myself in the Manor here just fighting those goddamned weeds! Pardon my English but that's what they were, weeds, and now it's how long, fifty years? seventy five? and every yard in town is fighting the same plague. A dollar each. Do you know how much a dollar was back then? Sometimes it was half what was in the pay envelope when the mines began to slow down. We paid good money for weeds that would grow on the moon. My God, weren't we foolish?"

"We were not foolish at all, Marie," Gloria MacKie countered. "Stop cursing them and remember what they looked like the first year we planted them. We thought they were beautiful, the buckwheat or Chinese whatever you called them, and the trees, silver maple or balsam poplar or whatever you want to call them now, grew faster than any of my children. They were just like the coal miners themselves, those two things, the way they ate smoke and soot and coal dust and just grew. But I never heard one of them cough," she said, her voice suddenly less animated. "Not the way I heard my husband and my oldest boy cough. And then they died. The mine people said it wasn't the mine that killed them, but I kept my other boys, three of them, out of the mines after that. Made two of them quit and the other I wouldn't let even begin, and sent them away to find work fit for a human being, that's what I did. They all died somewhere away, different place each one of them, but not from the black lung."

The women's stories had come to a quiet end, and just as quietly David turned off his recorder and shut the notebook into which he had very early stopped scribbling notes. He felt the tea urn and found it still hot so he poured another round of tea for the women, who appeared to have turned away from remembering and resumed their card playing positions. As quietly as he had done his other chores, David Cameron took his camera from his case and without using the flash snapped a single picture from an angle that caught all four faces beginning to smile as they studied their hands, made their bids.

David rolled the tea trolley back to the station where Rita was working and waited for her to come back from the palliative care room. In the kitchenette he boiled water and poured it over teaspoons of instant coffee, thinking that John Dan MacLean's death, too, would be a small story when the dementia patient did pass away, raising once again the dust of the past and no doubt Mrs. Big Sandy's ire if anyone mentioned to her about having read it in the *Witness*.

"How is John Dan?" David asked.

"He'll be out of it soon. For his sake it can't be soon enough." Rita's thoughts turned to her talk with Mrs. Big Sandy that morning. Between bouts of appal and laughter, she relived it for David:

"What's on your mind?" Mrs. Big Sandy asked, studying Rita as she swished the tea in her cup. The nurse allowed her thoughts to surface.

"John Dan MacLean is in palliative care. He'll probably pass today."

"Pass what? A big turd?"

"No, I mean..."

"Oh, I know what you mean. He's going to die. What's wrong with just saying it? The way people are afraid of saying what they mean when then mean somebody's dying or died. 'He passed away,' or even worse, that silly, 'He passed.' They think that's going to make the worms not notice him down there, because he passed instead of died? Stupid people."

"Do you think about it?" Rita asked.

Mrs. Big Sandy's eyes grew into their own question. "My own dying, do you mean?"

"No, about John Dan MacLean and what happened to him."

"What happened to him was he lost his mind and went to that godforsaken place where you work so he could die."

"I mean what happened to him when he was a young man. Being sent to prison for something he didn't do. You and Sandy knew he was innocent. Did the two of you ever talk about telling people the truth? Of clearing his name, his and Bennie Ryan's? Maybe even telling it now. The story of what happened, the story you told me the night Sandy ... died."

"Jesus, Mary and Joseph, will you listen to yourself. You sound like one of those television lawyers. And do you think for one minute that if it was Sandy they convicted and it was John Dan and Bennie who did it that those two creatures would pop up in the courtroom between a Kotex commercial and men's aftershave to tell the judge the truth? Oh, me and Sandy talked about it. For about as long as it takes to tell a good joke, we did. Nobody was guilty, that's what Sandy said, but somebody had to go to jail because that's the way it is with the police and them there judges, so it might as well have been John Dan and Bennie. Sandy had better things to do."

"But what about justice?"

"Justice! Ha! Sandy had a saying: there is no justice, just us, and that's how we kept it, between just us. Besides, Sandy did tell them your precious truth once and that was once too often if you ask me. Now stop this foolishness and finish your breakfast and get to work so you can be there to hold John Dan's hand because that's the kind of nurse you are."

A short, amused and meditative silence hung between Rita and David before David spoke.

"Does it get to you, all this suffering? It's not like the hospital," he said, gesturing to the structure across the courtyard and to which the Manor was connected. "Most people in there hope to heal and go home. Does anyone ever leave here?"

"Not many. No one, really, but that's a discussion for another time. How was your visit with the bridge club?"

"Great. If I make it to ninety-one I hope it's in the same shape as Gloria MacKie. Drink your coffee. I'll have mine with you then pick up the children."

"Will you have them all summer?"

"As it turns out. They were supposed to have six weeks with their mother, along with Christmas, but something came up and she isn't able to take them. So they stay. It's no penance."

"I'm sorry about you and your wife. I didn't know her but ... well, I'm sorry it didn't work out, the children and all," Rita said, getting lost in her own uncertainty.

"Oh, we knew after the first couple of years we were back here that it wasn't going to work out. It could have become the same angry story you hear about all the time except an opportunity came along for her to go back to her old position in Toronto. She's a whiz of a policy wonk for the insurance firm where she works. We both realized early that Shean wasn't what she had imagined when we came here. She had a very romantic image of the place, and I guess I didn't try to modify it with doses of reality. That came later of its own accord."

"I know it's none of my business but what does 'doses of reality' mean?"

"We met one summer when I was home from university. She was studying in Toronto, that's where she grew up, and that same summer she and a couple of friends rented a car and drove east. And one night they arrived at the Glen Ian Hall, Buddy MacMaster on the stage. The hall was always full on Fridays all summer long but when Buddy was playing it added another hundred or two more to the usual crowd. Do you go there? I saw her standing against the wall close to the coatrack looking a bit rattled by it all so I took her for a square set, and she took to it like she was born to it, picking up an actual step by the second figure, hair flying, face laughing in delight, you know. We spent the rest of the dance together, and then the rest of the summer. She stayed until Labour Day.

"And then she came back the next summer. Not because of me but because she had fallen in love with this place and the music and the dances and we did spend that summer together too. I had graduated that spring and was squandering the summer before looking for work. Then I had an offer from the *Toronto Star*. I had applied in the spring when I was wrapping up journalism school, and that's what journalism's all about in Canada, playing in the major leagues: the *Star*, the *Globe and Mail*, the CBC, Global, CTV. I thought it was what I wanted, and for a while it was. We got together again when I went to Toronto, moved in together, Tony was born, we got married, then along came Mary, and a couple of years later I was given first option to buy the *Witness*. If we pooled everything we had, and convinced a bank to loan us the rest, we could buy the paper. It was going to be a partnership, a means to bring the two of us home.

"She didn't get along well as a part of the *Witness* staff. What you might call corporate cultural differences. An insurance executive workaholic from Toronto trying to remain sane amid co-workers for whom the office was a sanctuary, where last night's great domestic dramas took place every morning with somebody's husband getting verbally battered, *Canadian Idol* contestants being debated, or more serious talk about all those stories that would never appear in the paper, some for lack of proof, some because they were the stuff of tabloid gossip. But the staff was as serious and professional about their responsibilities as Alexandra was about hers. She just couldn't see it. I put it down to a cultural impasse. The staff wasn't any unhappier about her leaving than she was.

"She didn't understand why we were paying the staff for a full day when they spent at least half of it minding everybody else's business but their own. She didn't really appreciate the fact that when the paper hits the streets every week, everything that has been asked of the staff has been done, and done well. All the ads got sold and designed, the subscription list was brought up to date in time for the week's mailing, the weekly billing had gone out, Revenue Canada's share of the payroll was dispatched in a timely fashion, and whatever else needed doing got done as well.

"I couldn't tell you myself when or how most of it gets done – sometime during the lulls in conversation I suppose – but she was wrong to think we could or should get more work out of the staff by insisting on office discipline. Get more work for what? Why? Like I said, the staff was already getting all the work done.

"It worked for me. It still does, but it was so frustrating for her that she decided to stay home with the children. She was still a partner and, besides, it wasn't for work that she came to Shean. It was to dance, to listen to the local stories, to tell the local stories she was learning to tell. Eat out somewhere nice a couple of times a month. She had never experienced Cape Breton in November or February, when the dance halls are closed because there's no one to attend them, or too few anyway. And of course most of the dance crowd that she had enjoyed hanging around with had come to the end of summer and it was time for them to pack up the car and kids and drive back to Ontario or wherever, until next summer. She wasn't familiar or friendly with many other people here, at least not comfortably enough to become a casual drop-in visitor.

"I'm sorry for that, for not trying harder to help her meet other people. There are plenty of people and homes in Shean where she would have been welcome if they knew her, and where stories do get told and songs do get sung or somebody recites the litany of six generations of his family bringing it all the way from the other side of the Atlantic right into the kitchen where he is sitting, ending with, 'And that would be how I'd be related to David, through our grandparents back about the 1880s, making us what, seventh? eighth? cousins?'

"She got through the first few winters but we knew. Besides her own isolation from all she expected the place to be, there was myself and the unpredictable demands of the newspaper that kept me away too many evenings, so she was seeing very little of me at home. And we were barely able to make weekend plans because it wouldn't have been fair to force Tim Donovan to cover all weekend events. He'd quit.

"With the better seasonal restaurants closed, when we could or did go out, the choices were the Gulf Grill or the Five Bucks and the romance can wear thin in either of those places in about thirty minutes. Then her job offer came along. We didn't even need a lawyer to settle custody. It worked best for both of us, and for both children we believed, being schooled here instead of a large city school, experiencing the city with their mother when there was lots going on, Christmas celebrations, summertime. They were there for Christmas, but she had to break their first summer date with Toronto and I'm delighted."

"You're lucky, David. I don't think it happens that way very often. When I was working at Women's Hospital in Toronto I saw a lot of domestic brutality and traumatized children and separated and divorced couples capable of killing one another. Your situation is almost ideal, if there's such a thing. Have you divorced?"

"Final last month. We weren't in any hurry but it happened sooner than either of us expected. Just as well. She's a workaholic but I imagine she'll pick her head up out of her workload one day and notice someone, and she'll be free to..."

"Or it could happen to you."

"Nothing on the horizon to make me think that. Besides the kids are a handful and fun to be with. Alexandra had an insight into our relationship that I accepted and that helped us work our way out of it relatively intact. What she described to me was two people who fell in love with our circumstances. We both loved to dance, loved the music, the stories, the pace of the place, and we had each other to do it with. Even in Toronto she was eager to go to any event that was rooted in the island, the Bow and Arrow Club on Sunday afternoons, where you've apparently seen us, or anywhere where Cape Breton fiddlers and music lovers gather.

"But back here, when the place began to lose its enchantment for her, so did I. She realized that what we shared wasn't each other but what each other loved to do. I believe she's right. Either way, she's gone, and I can't believe how long I've gone on talking about myself. Will you be sending me a bill?" David asked, looking at his watch. "I need to get home and grab the children for an hour at the beach, back for supper and then the meeting. Thanks for the coffee, Rita, and I apologize if I've bored you. And I'm sorry about what's happened between your father and Don Alex."

"Their falling out, you mean. Oh, don't worry about that. They do that every time there's an election or a Stanley Cup playoff. They're like an old married couple that needs to take separate vacations every once in a while. Thank you for coming, but I need to get back to John Dan's room now."

| 34 |

By the time David reached the fire hall and made his way inside, the place was fuller than for any meeting he had ever attended in the town. Tim Donovan was already there, seated at the media table beside a reporter from CBC radio in Sydney. Ever since Mrs. Big Sandy's holding of herself hostage and torching her own home, the town had become a bit of a media sensation in the province, so the normally faraway radio station wasn't taking a chance on missing the next chapter in what could well become a Shean saga.

David worked his way to the table to talk with Tim. Just as he got there he was aware of a commotion behind him and saw Tim reaching for his camera. David turned to see a group of men walk through the parting crowd to the long table set at the end of the hall. He let out a low whistle. Donald MacNaughton's entourage included C.J.M. Lord, Mines Minister Ted Singer and Environment Minister Elmer Monke, each of the ministers accompanied by the ever-present whispering aides who serve as politicians' encyclopedic memories.

"MacNaughton's rolling out the big guns, David," Donovan said, clicking his camera. "There's some serious shit happening here."

"Yes, but what?" David wondered aloud. "Did you find anything out at the museum?"

"Nothing," Tim answered. "I went through all the charts they have about the coal, underground blueprints going back to the beginning of time like you suggested. With the exception of the Beaton Seam there's no unmined coal anybody around here knows about. And what Joseph Collins doesn't know about mining in Shean isn't worth knowing. He dug up every document I could think of. I bet he's got better files in that miners museum of his than the Department of Mines and Minerals itself. But he did make a good point, I thought. He said that in the past few years there's been so much test drilling and seismic testing going on all around Cape Breton Island, the whole of Atlantic Canada for that matter, looking for gas and oil, that there's no telling what they might have stumbled on."

David nodded thoughtfully and left the media table to place himself at a greater distance from his role as newsman.

The crowd was gathering in clusters of like-mindedness. The only obvious absence was Grady Snow, Shean's listless member of the provincial legislature for the past fifteen years. Snow probably went AWOL for fear of being asked which side he supported in the open-pit mine issue. He was just being true to his nature, which was to sit in impotent opposition asking no questions and hoping that enough relatives lived long enough to re-elect him.

Standing amid those in opposition to a mine was Carmen Langille, the young physics and chemistry teacher at the high school, surrounded by several of her students, members of the school's Green Club. The club had made the pages of the *Witness* a number of times for its initiatives within the school and for heading up street sweeps and beach sweeps and other efforts to clean up and improve the environment. An open-pit mine wouldn't sit well with them, David imagined.

Looking elsewhere in the hall, he had to wonder how long the Langille-inspired idealism would last for some of her students whose fathers or mothers were clearly hoping that the mayor's news brought some hope of a steady income to feed their children. Would parents hoping for work of any kind wean their children away from the Green Club out of contempt or guilt? It happened in politics all the time in rural places like this, the will of the parent governing the 'X' a young person marks on his first ballot.

Not surprisingly, many of those people concerned about the implications of an open-pit mine appeared to be gravitating toward David where he stood against a far wall. It had been his words that told them the story of the mine, and his words that editorialized about the risks to the town, the dunes, the beach, the very fabric of the place where they lived. He may have tried to appear objective and thoughtful but they had read through him as accurately as did Donald MacNaughton. This was not something David Cameron wanted to see happen to the town. They expected him to become their spokesman whether he wanted to be or not. Journalism ethics were fine as long as there was nothing at stake, but MacNaughton had a plan and David Cameron was the knight they were sending out to foil those plans, no matter how miscast he may feel in the role. It had been one thing to wage his own private war against MacNaughton in his weekly editorials, but David understood that this time they weren't sparring for the amusement of readers. This time something as serious as the future of Shean was at stake and he felt ill-prepared for a battle to which MacNaughton had come fully armed.

It didn't help that along with those people like Carmen Langille who looked to him and the *Witness* for leadership, there were those who were clearly shunning David Cameron, barely offering a nod of acknowledgement if they made accidental eye contact, including Don Alex, who stood among those men who curried favours from MacNaughton.

David's confidence was further eroded by the sheer force of MacNaughton's entry into the hall. A corporate CEO and two Cabinet ministers. The issue they were all gathering to discuss, and hopefully oppose, was clearly much further along than the mere proposal stage. Backroom manoeuvring had obviously been going on for some time. David's gut feeling was that they were all here to hear about a done deal.

Spotting one of the few empty seats, David sat himself beside Victor Mason, whose general indifference to the issue was a bit of a relief. Victor had said he didn't want the mine to happen but if it did he would be looking for work there. David suspected there was a great deal of that kind of pragmatism present in the hall.

"You were talking with the old lady today, were you?" Victor asked.

"I interviewed a number of people in the Manor about the mining days. A piece for next week's *Witness*."

"She was telling me, and she was telling me that she never said a word. Is that right?"

"Actually when I think about it, Victor, that's true. She was very talkative until the interview started but then she went quiet. You're mother's not an old woman, not by Gloria MacKie's standards anyway – she would have just caught the last days of the last mine, I suppose, not when they were going full blast. That's probably why she was quiet," David reasoned.

"Maybe, but I think she was protecting me, too. I had been to see her in the morning. Most mornings I usually rush into the Manor with a feed of something she likes, smelts, lobster, eel, something edible before they feed her breakfast. Probably against the rules but she and I have this don't ask–don't tell understanding. This morning I was telling her about the possibility of the mine and my going to work there. She reads the paper anyway. She knew you were sniffing around for something more than history so she kept her mouth shut. Wants the mine to happen so I can stay home. If I could stay home, you see, maybe we could take her out of there, back to our new home. We built a suite at the back of the house that's designed for getting around in a wheelchair. Just in case. But it's too much for the wife to take on along with the kids, being alone and all. It's not easy deciding what's best for everybody, is it?"

"Is that what you think I'm doing?" David asked.

"Oh hell no. I wasn't talking about you, your editorials, if that's how it sounded. But when you think about it, it's easier to solve the world's problems when there's nobody real in the world, when the world's just full of words. We did a pretty good job of doing that ourselves over a few beers the other day, solving everybody's problems from here to Afghanistan, didn't we, so don't take it personal because I didn't mean you, or just you. Besides, I still don't know what I want to see happen here."

But David's thoughts were locked on the perception, Victor's and however many others', that David believed that all the answers anyone needed were to be found in the weekly scriptures of the *Witness*'s editorials, but it was a dark self-indulgence from which he was quickly distracted by the shadows that fell over him, cast by Ronald MacDonald and Mrs. Big Sandy.

"That little twerp that works for you snapped our picture when we came in. You tell him if he puts that in the newspaper I'll shake the shit out of him and he can use that same newspaper to wipe his dirty arse."

"He won't do that, I promise you, Mrs. MacArthur," said David, but the woman didn't seem appeased. Under her glare David remembered his manners and stood up, offering her his seat, which she took as her right.

Victor, with suppressed panic, wiggled his chair the few pathetic inches he could away from his new neighbour.

| 35 |

Donald MacNaughton tapped at the microphone, sending a crackle through the audience, then called for attention. His efforts were passed along group to noisy group until a quiet fell over the fire hall. The mayor opened the meeting by introducing the people at the front of the hall, apologizing for the suddenness with which the meeting had been called. "*This* made it necessary," he explained, holding up the most recent copy of the *Witness* with its bold headline predicting plans to open a strip mine in Shean.

"This is just the kind of irresponsible journalism that keeps this town from making economic progress and we all know how desperately this place needs economic changes, positive changes that can produce jobs, business opportunities, investment. I've already introduced C.J.M. Lord around town, whose company is prepared to make that very substantial investment, and that investment comes with its own commitment. I can tell you, and I hope I'm not speaking out of turn here, Mr. Lord, but I can tell you people that this gentleman is not only investing in our town. He is currently looking at properties with the intention of building a new home here. That's the kind of commitment that's needed, and that we should welcome, not slander like this," he added, raising the newspaper's front page again.

MacNaughton's words were met with a solid round of applause although David could see that the mayor's buddies and hangers-on were dispersed through the hall, encouraging others to clap with their applause. He remained silent, leaning against the wall beside Ronald MacDonald.

"David Cameron," MacNaughton continued, still waving the paper, "would have you believe in this article that the worst thing that could happen to this town would be a return to mining. Mining built this town. People my age know that, have always known that, but there are others here, the town elders I would call them, who know that truth first hand because they worked in those mines, made this town thrive and come alive. Made it a good place to raise a family. It's still a good place to raise a family. If it wasn't, if I didn't believe that, if you didn't believe that, would any of us still be here having families, having children? The worst part of raising children here is watching them leave. It's happened to most of you who have raised families here, and it will happen to me when my own children are older. It will happen to David Cameron when his children are grown. Unless something can be done about it, and as you can see here beside me, it's not just a major investor that is prepared to bring about the change we need, but the full force of the provincial government itself is standing with us."

Applause came again and this time David detected more spontaneity, and no signs of questions. He raised his hand and MacNaughton acknowledged him.

"I'll say up front that I don't think a strip mine or open pit or however you want to characterize it is a good thing for this town," David said, raising a spattering of heckles, "but what I want to ask is why the council is moving ahead with this plan which has been sprung on the town without warning or discussion while shelving its own economic development piece brought before council by its economic subcommittee this spring?" David heard mutterings that suggested that the fate of the suspended development plan wasn't his concern alone.

With the suddenness of his response, MacNaughton was clearly ready for the issue to be raised.

"Council has been exploring numerous ways that we can get ideas and people to work in this town, and I want to say up front that the development plan hasn't been 'shelved,' as you characterize it, David, it has been tabled. Some of our councillors and volunteers have worked long and hard on the plan and it will receive the dialogue and respect it deserves, but in the meantime something came along that may supercede that plan, and that's what we're here to discuss."

David spoke again. "That something that came along, by which you mean the mine, didn't come along overnight, Donald. There had to have been talks with the company, clearly with the provincial government, with everyone but the people who live here and who will have to live with whatever consequences there are, and if you check with other communities that have been subjected to open-pit mining, in most cases you will find that there have been consequences, bad consequences. So why can't we discuss the subcommittee's business plan along with the mining proposal tonight? Provide people a choice to consider."

Murmurs and scattered applause, but the mood of the room, David suspected, was really irrelevant. The outcome was predetermined, and he needed to make people aware of that if he could, but Donald MacNaughton was already responding.

"The main thrust of the subcommittee's plan, and I apologize if I sound as if I am slighting the committee's hard work, but the main thrust focuses primarily on tourism development. Let's examine that avenue of development for a moment. It's not as if Shean is some ideal tourist attraction. We have a beautiful beach for two, maybe three months of the year. There's talk of a golf course to draw people here, but again we're talking only three or four months of the year. Beaches and golf courses do us no good in February when people can barely afford to heat their homes. This is a town that is run down and running out of options.

"Shean was built on coal but there hasn't been an ounce of coal mined here since the middle of the last century. Just take a look at the place, a quarter of the houses people live in are company houses built by the original coal company. We have a coal miners museum. We know coal. It's been a long time since we mined coal but it's still in our blood. People here still sing coal mining songs, hell they still *write* coal mining songs. How many times has that newspaper of yours evoked Shean's proud coal past? As I said, there hasn't been coal mined here in more than half a century and in all that time there hasn't been any other economic solution, no job base, no serious business tax base. It's a miracle this town survived at all, and now the opportunity for it to survive into the future is present right here, right now, and that future, just like the past, is coal."

"What's made this town survive against the odds is the fact that it's home, Donald, our home," David Cameron offered in challenge to the mayor's rationale. "Yes, when the mines were working Shean was prosperous and miners came here from Scotland, from Ireland, from Belgium, from Acadian villages close by and from far off mining towns. But there were families, like Ronald MacDonald's people here, who had already been farming this place a hundred years before the mines. There was a commerce here that made it possible for people to live in Shean long before the mines opened.

"The mines opened and then they closed, but something good happened to this town during that time that had nothing to do with economics. Mining is a migrant job, and most of the miners who came here expected to move on to the next boomtown when Shean's mines were exhausted, and many did, but many more of them had married into the mostly rural Highland Scot population that was here. By doing that, by marrying people who lived here they sunk more than underground tunnels into this town, they sunk roots into it, their own and their children's. In Shean they had found a home that welcomed them. That sense of home has been passed down generation to generation ever since. People are still leaving here to look for work elsewhere, but what maintains this town is not political leadership, and certainly not the kind of leadership you're offering people here tonight. What maintains this town is the fact that families have cherished this place as home for a long, long time. What you're proposing isn't moving toward the future. It's moving back into the past."

The public meeting was turning into a two-man debate about the future of Shean, but most people had become interested in listening to them. They argued the pros and cons of Shean's future quite well, most thought.

"You're the one living in the past, David," Donald accused the editor. "Let's face it, the two of us, you and I, have it pretty damned good here in Shean. Better than most, I'd say. I have a family business that's still sound and you have a newspaper that pays your bills. But most people don't enjoy that level of security. Too many people in Shean have to leave to find work. Maybe they go to Alberta or the mines in Northern Ontario or take jobs offshore, and send their paycheques back here to keep their families going, but is that enough for you? Are you content with that? You don't need to go away to feed your children. I agree with you that this is home. It's my home as well as yours, but for how long?

"Do you recognize this front page, David," Donald asked, picking up and waving another copy of the *Witness* from a small stack he had brought to the meeting with him. "The front page from a copy of your newspaper from this past spring. The headline reads, 'Teachers to be cut, elementary classes to be blended.' We all know what that means. That there aren't enough children being born here to fill one primary class, and the per capita education funding from the province means that the local school board's budget is cut again as it was cut the year before and the year before, and with each cut we lose a teacher or two."

Donald MacNaughton picked up a second issue of the *Witness*. "This paper has an editorial lambasting the provincial government for not taking action to prevent or repair damage to our roads. It's easy for us all to agree with Cameron's arguments, after all they're the same things we all talk about every morning in the Gulf Grill, but what David Cameron doesn't address in this or any other issue of his paper is the larger reality of living in rural Canada."

Donald MacNaughton waited a beat for someone to ask the obvious question regarding that larger reality. No one did, but the silence was attentive enough to urge him on.

"Canada is now an urban country, people. Whether we like it or not, the fact is that eighty per cent of the population of this country now lives in urban areas, in cities. When people living in rural communities like ours look around, what they see are roads crumbling, infrastructure collapsing, schools in need of repair, hospitals that are losing beds every time there's a new provincial budget. Shean, like every town its size, needs a massive investment. How long will we go on thinking that we have some inherent right to demand new roads, new schools? That we keep our hospital and whatever other services we've grown accustomed to? Soon in this province alone it is going to be possible for a political party to govern from the population centres, Halifax, Pictou-Cumberland and Sydney.

"When that happens, and it will happen, it will happen federally and it will happen provincially, but when it does happen and we go hat in hand to the capital demanding our fair share, what those politicians in power will do is ask the people of Halifax, of Pictou, of eastern Cape Breton if they are willing to pay higher taxes so people in Shean can have better roads or a new school.

"I think you know what the answer will be. People in this province feel they are already paying too much taxes. So it is up to us here, the people of Shean and rural people in every other nook and cranny of this country, to come up with ways to generate our own revenue, to generate our own tax base. To put it bluntly, people, to find a way of paying our own way, or at least a large part of our own way so that when we do go to Halifax or to Ottawa, we can demonstrate that we are prepared to be full partners in the rebuilding of our town. The presence of Resource Reclamations Limited gives us that chance."

Carmen Langille stepped to the public microphone to question MacNaughton.

"What Resource Reclamations is proposing is to destroy the most sensitive part of the environment we live in, the dunes and, who knows, maybe even the shoreline in the process. This mine everybody's talking about is awfully close to the shoreline. Can you tell me how many jobs it will create and what will be the cost to the rest of us? Your own development committee's strategic plan calls for developing the reclaimed slag heaps as a tourist attraction, to build on tourism. That may not be everyone's ideal solution. It's not yours Mr. Mayor, and it certainly isn't mine. I would also like to see year-round employment for people. But the economic plan does focus on improving what we have here in Shean, not destroying it, and what we have is beautiful."

MacNaughton acknowledged the teacher's question, answering, "Yes, it is beautiful here and I don't need lessons from anyone on the magnificence of a sunset, but the truth is that everywhere in the world is beautiful. Deserts, mountains, oceans, wherever it is people live they find something beautiful about that place, and when those places get into economic trouble the first thing they turn to for a solution is tourism. Shean has a lot to offer in the beauty department but so do a lot of other places and so we will always be competing against the rest of the world. To be truthful, I'm not anxious to have Shean's economic fate depend entirely upon the travel whims of Americans or Europeans or people from Ontario. What is being proposed right now for Shean is a solid economy, well-paying jobs and the resurrection of an industry that should be supplying fuel to Nova Scotia's power generators instead of having the stuff imported from Venezuela or the United States the way it is now. Cape Breton Island is sitting on one of the world's major supplies of coal. It's not pretty and it's dirty but it's ours and it's going to waste in the ground while coal from other countries pollutes our air. It's a sad fact that Nova Scotia's coal-fired generators are among the most environmentally damaging structures in the country but that's not going to change overnight. The least we can do is pollute the planet with our own goddamn coal!"

A wild cheer rose in the hall and MacNaughton signalled for calm. "But I know and everyone here knows that the fossil fuel industry is working around the clock to develop clean coal technology and the sooner that happens the better. I'm not in favour of contributing to gashouse emissions but I am in favour of taking advantage of our own abundant resources."

David Cameron raised his hand, and returned to the mike. "You want us to give a stamp of approval to an open-pit mine when no environmental impact study has been carried out, when all the documentation surrounding the negotiations between Resource Reclamations Limited and the province are confidential, when we know nothing about what's planned? How much coal do they think is there?"

"Enough to give this town a fighting chance," Donald answered. "But I'll ask the honourable minister to answer your question regarding environmental impact. Mr. Minister?"

Elmer Monke stood at the front of the hall to explain his department's decision. "Our choice was not to conduct an environmental impact study at this time because we weighed the benefits of the study against the benefits to the community. The impact study is important and it will take place, but an environmental impact study can take months, even years, and that's just not feasible if jobs are at stake. Cabinet's position, the premier's position, is that Resource Reclamations's corporate mission is the restoration of the environment where industrial damage occurs. Overseeing and monitoring that restoration is where the Department of Environment's primary responsibility lies. What my department will be assessing is the quality of the restoration of the residual mine tailings when the resources buried within those tailings have been extracted.

"I have permission to speak on behalf of the premier who regrets that he couldn't be with us tonight. Regarding the charges of secrecy around the government's agreement with Resource Reclamations, the premier wants to assure the people of Shean and the province of Nova Scotia that it is not uncommon when any government enters into agreements with the private sector for certain aspects of those contracts to be confidential because they contain within them sensitive information supplied by the company that could be detrimental to that company if its competitors were to become aware of the content of those corporate disclosures. There's nothing more sinister than that happening here."

David followed up his question with another, addressed this time to the minister.

"What an open-pit mine, a strip mine, means is that this company will be licensed to destroy an environment we value. There's no indication that this corporation is giving us any assurance that they won't leave behind the same level of destruction as the other corporations led by Mr. Lord have left behind. Those environmental disasters have been detailed pretty deeply in this week's issue of the *Witness* – what happened in West Virginia, in Virginia, in other states south of the border. His former corporations didn't give a damn about those towns and villages and there's no reason to believe he or his corporation will give a damn about ours. And don't tell us that ploughing the waste from the open pits back into them then spraying the whole works with fertilizer and seed is going to restore one of the most fragile ecosystems along this coast – the dunes, the wetlands, the beach itself. Corporations under this man's leadership have been very profitable disasters everywhere they've operated, but not at all profitable to the people whose rivers or reservoirs or homes have been ruined."

"One person's home in this town has already been ruined!" Mrs. Big Sandy hollered out from her seat.

"David, I think you're being an alarmist," MacNaughton said. "Your kind of people don't want anything ever to change. Fortunately it's not up to you alone or a handful of your friends. It's up to all the people of Shean and they will decide what will happen. Do we want jobs here, a tax base, improved services, a better quality of life? I think we do, and now we have an opportunity."

A burst of shouts and applause filled the hall, salted with a chorus of boos and other expressions of non-support.

"You're hypnotized by the tax base, aren't you, Mayor," David Cameron said. "Tell us this, is this development going ahead without Shean having to make any tax concessions to Resource Reclamations, none at all – no tax holiday, no preferred rate, no deferred taxes? Or is the tax base you're counting on rooted in higher assessments for our properties because of industrialization? What guarantees do you have?"

The mayor stepped back to the microphone with smug assurance. "I can tell you and other taxpayers present this much. The subject of Resource Reclamations paying taxes to the town has been raised by Mr. Lord himself with assurances that there would be no effort to avoid payment. I'm sure that he will give that same assurance to the town right here tonight. But development means jobs, David, and jobs mean more money to spend which means that there's more incentive for people to invest in larger or new businesses in Shean and that increases the commercial tax base significantly, which means that not only can we expect property taxes to remain the same, we may even see them decreased. I pay taxes, too, and the less I need to pay the better I like it."

| 36 |

Once the initial points had been made, the meeting dragged on for an hour or more past the point of boredom, with the same questions being posed and the same answers dissimilating the same information, although the dragged-out process did unearth one piece of information damning to those who opposed the open pit. C.J.M. Lord, a mute presence at the front table, broke his silence for the first time to answer questions that had already been asked and answered. Then Victor Mason raised a question about wages, benefits and unions.

The dumbfounded audience heard C.J.M. Lord tell those present that the project would not go ahead unless the workforce was protected by strong labour laws which, he pointed out, was one of Nova Scotia's legislative strengths, strong labour laws brought in following a terrible mining tragedy in Westville. Whether that included the presence of an international union or an independent organization formed by the employees themselves negotiating for themselves and not for some international union, the miners would be protected.

Lord had come late to the recognition that unorganized employees did allow some corporations to exploit labour in a way that an organized labour force would never stand for. But in his extensive, yes, even personal, experience he learned that in questions of safety and production, lax labour standards on the job site led to unacceptable corporate costs in injury or death settlements, in government investigations and in overall production and morale.

Lord acknowledged that his intentions weren't wholly benevolent. As a person who had spent his professional life in mining, he was aware that under Cape Breton Island lay massive, untapped seams of coal that could not go on being ignored forever. Resource Reclamation's position in Shean allowed the company to be poised to take advantage of new opportunities.

Reminding the audience of what the town's mayor had said earlier about clean coal technology, the reformed coal baron reaffirmed the fact that considerable research was taking place in the pursuit of clean coal and he didn't see why an arm of his own corporation shouldn't expand to become a leader right here in Shean in making this vital resource less of an environmental concern.

On that note, Donald MacNaughton adjourned the meeting and the milling about and departures from the hall began.

Flanked by Ronald MacDonald and Mrs. Big Sandy, David made his way to the media table, where Tim Donovan was packing up. The two reporters gave each other an understanding look, one that said it would be difficult to spin the story away from what had happened in the hall. David's unspoken sense was that this battle had clearly been lost, and that in the war for Shean's future, the loss may have been crucial.

"There's Rita now," Ronald said, and David turned to see the nurse swimming against the crowd toward them, coming at the end of her shift from the Manor to pick up her two other senior wards. As Rita reached the table, her arrival coinciding with the arrival of Donald MacNaughton, David realized the meeting had lasted past eleven o'clock.

Despite the tone of the evening, which had been all Mac-Naughton could have asked for, signs of tension were visible around his eyes. He was a politician doing a follow-up with the media, stepping aside with the radio reporter for a moment, then turning to David Cameron. "If there are any other questions..."

David nodded toward Tim Donovan, letting the mayor know that the story in the next issue of the *Witness* would bear Tim's byline and that it was to him the mayor should be speaking. He told the young reporter to give him a call if he had any questions then turned to the others. "That went pretty well, don't you think?"

"Pretty well for you, perhaps, but no one has adequately explained how it can go ahead without an environmental impact study."

"Would it make you happier, David, if I just went down there and lifted up all those poor little frogs in that piece of swamp you're so worried about and took them home?" Donald asked. Sarcasm smeared his smile.

"If you did that it would be just to eat their legs like a Frenchman, if you ask me," Mrs. Big Sandy answered.

"Well, no one is asking you," Donald answered.

"No one asked me when they burnt down my goddamned house either, did they, but why would they. It gets you exactly what Sandy said it would get you. Sandy always said you couldn't trust the Bastards, you or your whole clan. Your people didn't get that name for nothing, he said. And that one, he said to me, meaning you, Donald, when you became mayor, he said that one will sit in the town office selling out this town until he's invited to run as the MLA and gets into the Cabinet. That's what my Sandy always said about you."

David glanced at Donald and caught the telling shock of his expression as Mrs. Big Sandy stripped the frock of his naked ambition.

"You stupid quiff! Too bad I didn't shoot you in the heart instead of the arse." His words hissed with rage.

A profound silence enveloped the small group while MacNaughton fled from his emotional outburst before it escalated into open warfare with the elderly woman, leaving the rest to ponder his confession.

David felt Rita and Ronald's eyes on him, Tim's look of ignorant bafflement, but mostly Mrs. Big Sandy's burning glare. She finally asked the question. "What did he mean by that?"

The quarter century-old memory resurfaced in vivid freshness, a Saturday morning when Donald and David were target shooting at old liquor bottles in the dump that was Big Sandy MacArthur's massive back yard. David had set a bottle on top of a large rock and Donald aimed, fired and missed. He then passed the gun to David, who was preparing to take his shot when the nightmare figure of their boyhood tore out of her house in housecoat and a pair of bloomers covering the rollers on her head, screaming about murder. Neither boy waited to find out what had happened, they just put as much terrified distance between themselves and the old woman as they could. When they hit Main Street the boys separated, Donald going his way while Mrs. Big Sandy chased after the still-armed little creep who had tried to kill her.

When David had told them his story, Mrs. Big Sandy stared at him with all the contempt her bulldog frown could muster, finally breaking her silence with, "Well what a waste of hate you've been, Cameron! You should be ashamed of yourself, making an old woman have those thoughts when I should have been hating somebody else!"

She turned in time to see MacNaughton going out the door in the company of Lord and the Cabinet ministers. "I'm not done with that coward yet, believe you me! That little swat with the frying pan doesn't even count because I didn't know then what I know now, but if I get another chance I'll flatten him like a fly on the wall! And I should do the same to you. You were probably laughing at me all these years, the two of you, making me think that it was you who shot me when all the time it was that bastard, and I don't mean his name when I say that! Laughing at me, the two of you." Mrs. Big Sandy's breathing began the dangerous heaving that preceded the best of her outbursts.

David knew it was pointless to try to explain that ever since that day Donald and he had never laughed at anything together again, so his eyes pleaded with a near-hysterical Rita MacDonald to come out from behind Mrs. Big Sandy's back where she was hiding her delight and rescue him.

"Mrs. MacArthur, we have to leave now. I've had a hard day. I'll drive you and Dad home." To David she added, "John Dan MacLean died about an hour after you left today."

"Did he indeed?" asked Mrs. Big Sandy, "Well won't he and Sandy have a lot to talk about tonight? They were always friends, you know."

"Considering where Big Sandy probably is, John Dan will have to talk awfully loud, eh, David," Ronald whispered out the side of his mouth as he followed his daughter and his houseguest out of the hall.

"There's a couple here to see you, David," Cheryl Horne said, leaning into the editor's office. David walked to the front desk, a smile forming around the words, "Bethany. Jim."

Bethany Burke and Jim Turner, co-workers from the *Star*, had been a couple since before David joined the Toronto newspaper. They had remained in touch since his departure.

"We thought for this vacation we'd come to the Far East for a dose of that Maritime wisdom you used to peddle to us gentiles in Ontario," Bethany explained as David walked them back to his office. "Or some of that good booze," Jim added.

"Lots of the latter, but I'm a bit short on wisdom these days," David said as Jim picked up a copy of the *Witness* and perused its front page. They had become friends during his years at the *Star* and nothing had changed, Bethany was an investigative reporter on the political beat and Jim was a business reporter.

"This your big story this week?" Jim asked, laying the paper back on the desk. "It looks like an obituary."

"Reads like one, too," David said, outlining for them the precipice upon which the town stood as it looked into the future. Like his editorial, there was little objectivity in his report. "But I shouldn't be airing the town's dirty laundry in front of tourists. Have you got plans, or just winging it?"

"Our plans are to wing it. We checked into the Western Sunset Motel," Bethany said, looking tentatively at David for a reaction, which was positive. "We expect to be here for a day or two, drive around the Cabot Trail, and then we want to go to Newfoundland."

"Yeah, we were only considering going to Newfoundland but now it's definitely a destination," Jim added. "This Mountie stopped us for speeding and told us that the only excuse for driving that fast in Cape Breton was if we were trying to catch the ferry to Newfoundland, which he said would be understandable."

"You've met Harry Noseworthy then?" David said.

"That's the name, a corporal. Anyway, he told us where to go when we get there, a couple of good drinking spots where the music's as good as it gets. We'll head off the day after tomorrow," Jim said.

"Newfoundland's always a good idea," David agreed, "but when I report this in next week's *Witness*, that the RCMP are poaching tourists for Newfoundland, I may be able to get Noseworthy posted to Resolute Bay."

"You're not going to do that?" Bethany's uncertainty made David laugh.

"No, Bethany, but I will try to scare the shit out of him. His superiors don't need any more attention drawn to him, but we'll get to that story a little later. Since you have just a couple of days here and I need a break from all this foolishness," David said, gesturing toward the paper on the desk, "here's what's going to happen: I'm your guide and tonight we go to the Five Bucks for some fairly edible food and some music that will make your trip to Newfoundland seem wasted, and we ourselves will get wholly wasted.

"Tomorrow morning, hungover or not, we are heading over the Cabot Trail. Normally, I would recommend taking two or three days to explore all its nooks and crannies, but I'll give you the fast forward version and we'll be back here before dark, where I'll have a load of live lobsters delivered which we will boil at the house when we get home and eat with gallons of cold beer.

"Now I suggest that you drive to the beach. You'll find the kids there with their grandmother. Spend as long as possible there while there's still sunlight. I'll clear up a few things here and join you. Then we'll get on with our adult plans to act like adolescents."

The idea of a couple of days away from the paper in the company of friends he enjoyed was exactly what David needed, showing off his town and his island, far from angry thoughts about Donald MacNaughton, open-pit coal mines and the destruction he dreaded.

He let Cheryl, Helen and Mary Agnes know that he would be unavailable for a couple of days, his announcement met by shrugs that meant it would be business as usual around the office with or without him. He left a note on Tim Donovan's desk asking him to pick up David's slack on a couple of soft stories. As he was about to leave his office, a thought occurred to him. Picking up the phone, he dialled Ronald MacDonald's house.

"Hello, Mrs. MacArthur. Has Rita left for work yet?"

"What do you want to know that for?"

"It's personal, Mrs. MacArthur."

"Personal! How can it be personal when you don't have the decency to come here to see her, just call on the telephone like one of those stupid people who call people for a living, selling God knows what, including God, I might add."

Holding the phone to his ear with one hand and holding his head in his free hand, David tried not to scream at the woman. He took a deep breath. "Some friends are visiting and we're going over the Cabot Trail tomorrow and I was wondering if Rita would like to join us."

David could hear Mrs. Big Sandy's voice turn away from the mouthpiece, yelling, "Rita! It's that David Cameron and he wants you to go over the Cabot Trail with him although I don't know why you'd bother. You can see all the trees you want right from the front doorstep..."

"Hello, David?"

"Yes. Well, I guess you've heard why I'm calling. I know it's your day off and I have friends visiting and..."

"I'd love to go. In fact I'm begging to go. Please let me go!"

"I suppose it wasn't polite for us all to pile into your kitchen like that this early in the morning," Bethany said as a sort of apology to Rita while David drove them down the driveway, "but David insisted that we meet your mother."

An instant later David's right bicep was throbbing from Rita's sharp-knuckled revenge. She went on to explain to David's friends, her humour-filled stories unreeling from the day Mrs. Big Sandy moved into the MacDonald house, back to her burning down her own home, to the deathbed confession of her husband and back through an anthology of tales that had framed the woman's legendary status, receding to the moment she had been shot in the arse by Donald MacNaughton, an action which cast David for decades as the wrongly accused. Rita's entertaining narrative carried them as far as Chéticamp and a hefty Acadian breakfast in a building housing an artisan's co-op along with a restaurant which, according to Rita's review, provided the best food in the village, pure Acadian fare. Afterwards, over coffee, they sat around an open map at the table planning their one-day assault on the Cabot Trail.

David proposed that if they were fast enough on a twisting road that discouraged speed they could still find time to visit Meat Cove, a remote hamlet of haunting land and seascapes carved through time into a rugged beauty at the edge of the world.

"But if we go to Meat Cove there won't be time to go to Gampo Abby," Rita interjected, explaining that a few miles up the Red River Road was North America's only Tibetan Buddhist monastery, an oasis of peace even on an island as generally peaceful as Cape Breton. "Peaceful when everybody isn't brawling on Saturday night," she added.

David and Rita argued merits back and forth until they realized that Bethany and Jim were exchanging looks.

"What?" David asked.

"I don't know if the subject's come up yet, but if not, it seems clear that you'd make an ideal married couple," Jim explained. "You sure have the nuts and bolts of marriage down pat."

"Oh, we're just friends," David and Rita answered in embarrassing unison, not because it was a lie but because they were fatefully aware that it was true.

"And it's absolutely none of our business, Jim. So here we are at your mercy, temples or mountains, none or both, or is there really a difference between a temple and a mountain anyway, and what else is there to see?" Bethany looked through the restaurant window at the harbour, trying to see the whales beyond.

The discussion between Rita and David continued. They debated what was reasonable, given the hurried time line David had committed them to in order to be back for the boiling of the lobsters. They took turns trashing each other's recommendation until Bethany and Jim reminded them they also needed time to see Newfoundland. Under that indictment the two guides made a quick compromise, agreeing to take their guests hiking along the Skyline Trail, a headland cliff whose thin, stony spine and alpine tundra were accessible, David noticed, by way of a boardwalk that made walking easier, but whose first duty was to protect bogs and delicate headland plants.

David had imagined a brisk walk along the groomed trail to the series of boardwalks and platforms that brought hikers to the edge of earth, ocean and sky. As they moved along he acted as host to his friends, hands sweeping toward one vista or another, canyons or mountains. He pointed to an insect trail of cars and recreational vehicles in the distance beetling along the Cabot Trail. Much of his monologue, he soon learned, was lost on all but a few dismayed birds.

Looking back, his fellow travellers had fallen far behind. Slowly making his way back to the pack he joined them hunched over a spot of mud and grass while Rita warned against poison ivy and pointed out rushes and ferns, laurel still in bloom, inedible red bunch berries, clintonia berries that hadn't yet reached their dark blue ripeness and moose tracks, a cow and calf, according to Rita. Suddenly raising her hand and head, she picked out the sound of a white-throated sparrow whose song, she claimed, echoed O Canada. Her tour group, both journalists, were absorbing it all with interest, fuelling the farm-raised woman's knowledge of the minutiae that comprised, petal by berry, shrub by tree, bug by birdsong, the larger broad brush beauty David had been content to bask in without considering its underpinnings. While the others followed Rita's fingers through the delicacy that comprised this harsh and stony place, David watched Rita, made more beautiful by her un-self-conscious absorption in the world around her.

Farm girls would know all this, he assumed, leaving his friends to their education while he walked to the platform at the end of the boardwalk. The guide books virtually promised that whatever schedule tourists were on moose would be munching nearby and pods of whales frolicking in the Gulf. He never met anyone who spoke about hiking the Skyline Trail without encountering one or both, but it must have been their lunch break. The cow and calf prints Rita had spotted were the only proof moose had been here.

How did she even know it was a cow and calf? he wondered before letting his thoughts wander away into the world around him. David felt that this place must be as unblemished a human presence as any place in this world. The narrow, rugged, rocky promontory off French Mountain, with its stony ridge and shallow-rooted flora, had emerged from a millennia-long glacial winter to withstand thousands of years more of Nature's furies, yet needed to be protected from the destructiveness of human curiosity by a network of boardwalks.

Looking out to sea and the mountains around him, David had a sense of sky-walking, of getting a god's-eye view of the world, a perspective that took his thoughts home to Shean. Its shoreline, too, was filled with fragile wonders: sunsets, the horseshoe of mountains that offered semi-protection from the worst of winter, the many moods of the ocean. But between the town and the shore there was also a structure of fragile eel grass and sand dunes, bogs and wetlands. Perhaps one day he would ask Rita to walk him through the natural garden bordering the shore of their hometown.

Shean had been blemished by the grey and black residue of nearly a century of coal mining, but he felt the mine waste, like a burl that eventually shapes the character of the pine tree, had shaped itself into the character of the town, a time-healed scar perhaps, or a birthmark. Those long-standing grey and black forms would lose whatever essence he attributed to them if men and machinery were to begin re-working those acres of mine waste. He didn't believe for a moment that a strip mine would remain confined to the blemished landscape. It would follow wherever the coal led the company. Where else could it lead but to the fragility just beyond the mounds of ash and clay? A scar or a birthmark was something a person learned to live with, but an open wound would horribly corrupt the townscape. He looked across to the bulk of French Mountain and tried to imagine a huge rock quarry formed by explosion after explosion, columns of stone dust falling for years on the vulnerable plants that Rita was so sensitively aware of. He looked to the Gulf of St. Lawrence and imagined a skyline of oil and gas derricks, comparing the moment's imagination to the impending reality facing Shean.

David grew conscious of Rita standing beside him and wondered how long she had been there.

"Wow!" was all she said, to which David mumbled an incoherent agreement that made him want to step off the boardwalk and disappear down the tree-dense canyon.

"Did I interrupt you?" she asked without the slightes.
tion of apology. The platform was more than large enough
two. "What were you thinking about?"

"Beauty," David answered. (*Jesus Christ, beauty! Why don't I
just start spouting poetry.*) "I mean I was just trying to take this
all in," David said, looking behind him. "I'm afraid I'm neglecting my guests. You've been a better host to them, so thanks, but
maybe we'd better be polite and join them again."

"I don't think that's what's going on, David. I think your
guests are neglecting *us*, trying to give us some time together,"
Rita theorized.

"Why?" asked David, instantly crushed by the stupidity of
his question. *If this keeps up my kids are going to be through adolescence before I am.*

"Well, yes, I suppose you're right. We better join them," Rita
said, then turned away and walked toward Bethany and Jim, taking the first steps toward their return along the hiking trail and
back to their journey around the Cabot Trail.

At a confectionary near the turn-off to Bay St. Lawrence,
Jim went in and returned with a collection of egg sandwiches
and chicken wraps, and two newspapers, the *Cape Breton Post*
and the *Halifax Herald*.

"The open-pit mine has made front page in both." Jim perused both papers, then passed one into the front seat for David
to read. Eating an egg sandwich, the *Witness* editor read both
stories with disappointment. Each paper reported the story
without alarm, presenting it as an opportunity for a struggling
rural town to create jobs. One openly supported the proposal for
bringing coal back in as a player in the energy game, urging its
readers and the province not to be shamed by critics. Neither
mentioned the potential devastation of the mine.

| 38 |

Approaching Shean, images of the world they had encountered on the Skyline Trail superimposed themselves in David's mind onto images of what Shean would become when Resource Reclamations Limited began its excavations of the mine tailings. Even with its grey, dead acres of mine detritus, Shean was a preferable beauty to the internationally acclaimed charm of the Cabot Trail. Perhaps that was because the town was almost wholly ringed by a much smaller mountain range, fronted by a gulf of water far less relentless and angry than the Atlantic Ocean and a far less demanding landscape to inhabit than the rugged, rocky northern island. And perhaps, he acknowledged, Shean was preferable simply because it was home.

"Look at that," Bethany Burke said, tapping David's shoulder from the backseat and pointing toward the billowing black smoke that seemed to originate in the middle of the town.

"It's late for grassfires," David said, thinking of a stack of old tires behind the Esso garage, always a temptation to children, or someone's backyard shed or a barn at the race track, each possibility underpinned by the hope that Tim Donovan was there, snapping pictures, taking notes.

The curious traffic thickened as they reached Main Street and David turned up Poplar Avenue to circumvent the jam and bring him and his guests home, where they could park the car and go see what was happening. Poplar Avenue was also lined with parked cars. The street filled with pedestrians making their way toward the smoke.

As David drove carefully to avoid hitting anyone Rita's hands went to her mouth to smother a gasp and David looked more carefully toward the source of the smoke. With an "Oh Jesus!" he slammed the car into park and jumped out, pushing people aside as he ran to the intersection where his mother's house stood, flames beginning to burst through the roof. Rita was a half moment behind and Jim and Bethany, reaching understanding, also abandoned the car.

As David raced around the street corner his worst fears were in front of him and he pushed his way through the crowd, past the fire line screaming, "Tony! Mary!" as he dashed toward the house. His effort to get there was stopped short by a tackle of firemen, it taking four of them to hold down David in his adrenalin-and-fear-fuelled strength. "No, David! No! It's too late!" a voice tried to reason as he struggled against the men holding him.

"David!"

His mother's voice loud with panic and terror reached him through the voices around him, the firefighters' shouted commands and the maddening roar from within the house itself as flames ravaged all that mattered in David's life. Still held in the straightjacket grip of several men, his eyes found his mother – paramedics were trying to administer oxygen to her but she shook the mask away. In her ruined face David saw the story, and knew.

"NOOOOO!" he screamed again, renewing his effort to break free. "Tony! Mary! I'm coming!" His voice was lost in a crash of ceilings and floors inside the house, while flames soared from a now consumed roof and a cloud of black smoke funnelled through the front door. He surged against his captors, distantly aware of physical but meaningless pain. His mother's voice kept finding him through the chaos, "David! I'm so sorry David! I'm so sorry!"

A silence descended over David like that of profound deafness and all he could see was his mother's face miming its relentless agony, and the faces around her, and around him, and the single pointed finger over his shoulder that he knew was Rita's. He followed it toward the smoke-choked door where through the blackness a figure emerged, almost invisible but for florescent yellow accents. As it staggered forward firefighters rushed to catch it, him, and to ease from under each arm the limp bodies of two children.

David was released then, released to run toward his children upon whom the paramedics were already working, asking him to stay back and let them do their work, and when he saw Rita MacDonald kneel among the paramedics he felt himself enveloped by a sense of safety. With Mary's first cough, however, David was holding her. A moment later he was reaching toward his son as he inhaled huge gulps of oxygen from a mask. Both children were on stretchers almost immediately. Walking toward the ambulance with the help of a fireman was David's mother. Her face turned to her son in desperate need of forgiveness, which she found in the sad smile he gave her.

When David tried to get into the ambulance along with his family, the paramedic stopped him. "There's no room, David," Rita explained from her seat beside Mary, "but I'll be with them until you get to the hospital. They're going to be all right. I know they are."

The ambulance drove away and David began to move, guided by Bethany and Jim, in the direction of his car, but he stopped for a moment, looked back at firemen fighting the still raging fire, and as his eyes took in the scene they fell on two firemen giving oxygen to a third seated on the back lip of a tanker. The fireman pulled the mask away and David was looking into the exhausted eyes and blackened face of Donald MacNaughton, and then David was running toward his car.

When David, Jim and Bethany got back to the car David realized he couldn't move his arm to open the door. It took Jim a minute to recognize a dislocated shoulder and get behind the wheel.

Dr. Wallace admitted all three Cameron patients overnight for observation. David checked on the children, who had been admitted to Pediatrics, and who were peacefully sleeping in neighbouring beds.

Coming back to Admitting, the throb in his shoulder had begun to assert itself now that his family was safe and accounted for. Rita, aware of the injury, told Dr. Wallace, who turned her attention to the fourth Cameron to need her help on this day.

David screamed when Andrea Wallace wrenched his dislocated shoulder back into its socket. Even in the middle of this painful distraction from the near tragedy of losing his children, he was embarrassingly conscious that he was unable to swallow the scream the way men are supposed to. And Rita MacDonald in the room. Was he ever going to run out of ways of looking or sounding stupid to her?

Feeling the pain subside, David asked about his mother, and was directed to her room, where he found her crying convulsively. Placing a hand on her shoulder, he forced her to turn and look at him. Her eyes remained closed. "I don't know what happened," she began, grimacing at the thought and the effort to put her tears aside. "I was in the kitchen getting the water in the lobster pots heated for you people when I heard something in the basement. It sounded like someone was knocking on the basement door so I opened it and the flames knocked me over. Whatever happened, I wasn't burnt but the walls were burning and I couldn't get to the ... to the door in the dining room. Mary and Tony were upstairs and I couldn't get to them. I screamed and screamed and then ran out the back door into the yard screaming for somebody to help me. Oh God, David, I'm sorry. I don't know what happened but I'm so sorry!" She began to rock the bed with her sobs. He looked at her face while she spoke and couldn't recall the last time he had looked at his mother's face, really looked at it. It was no longer the image of his mother that he carried around in his memory. The mother in front of him was old, aged more by a single day than all those lesser wrinkles combined.

"Mom, look at me." Her eyes were terrified but grew slowly more trusting under her son's gaze. He stayed until she slipped into sleep with the help Dr. Wallace had given her.

He left his mother then, returning to Pediatrics, where he stood between his children's beds, resting his arms on their raised bed rails. His main job as Dad was to keep his children safe. Would the chest-crushing love he felt for Mary and Tony from now into forever be as filled with fear as it was at this moment?

He backed quietly from the room and walked to the end of the hall, the tiny chapel lit by a single votive candle glowing within its red glass holder. There was a wall switch if he wanted to read from the Bible that lay open on a small altar, but he chose the crimson comfort of the candlelight and sat in a straight-back wooden chair and stared at the crucifix on the wall, half hidden in shadows.

He felt like praying but he had been a Christmas and Easter Catholic for too long. To come suddenly to the need for prayer while wallowing in the midst of personal crisis was a cliché he had often chided, accusing people of "suckholing to God." Well, he didn't feel that way about them or himself now. What he felt was an overwhelming need to express his gratitude to whatever presence in the universe bestows the gift of grace. Looking at the crucifix he remembered when his faith was real. Not so clear to him was when it went dormant. There had never been enough

spiritual agony involved to call it a loss of faith – it was just
general indifference. And now it was awake with questions that
had nothing to do with Christianity or Buddhism or Islam, but
that needed to be asked face to face with the blessed bestower
of grace.

How differently would he feel, he wondered, if the fire had
turned out differently, had devoured all he loved most in life?
Would his faith be just as suddenly resurrected if only for the
simple reason that it gave him a God against whom to rage,
to blame, to blaspheme? Would his mother have been as easily
forgiven, or would she have been forced to share his guilt for the
rest of her life?

But that was not the road fate or faith had taken, and he was
filled with gratitude and conscious of grace and knew where he
needed to go.

Rita MacDonald was leaning in the doorway of the pediatrics
ward when he got back and he watched her for a moment and
wished it was possible to reach out and touch her, hold her, ask
her to hold him. Instead, he coughed and she turned.

David stepped into the doorway beside her. There they kept
a quiet, joyful vigil until David began to move.

"David, Jim and Bethany went back to the motel. They said
they'd see you before they leave, or if you need them they can
stay. Anyway, you'll see them. The Grill is still open. Would you
like to go for a coffee and maybe unwind with me?"

"I can't. I have to be somewhere else," David answered, reg-
istering what looked like a hint of hurt in her eyes, and hurried
away.

David drove out of the hospital parking lot and four blocks
later stopped in front of the *Witness* office. He was inside for no
more than two minutes when he returned to his car.

| 39 |

David drove up the Highlands Road toward Seaview Place, a housing development that overlooked the town and gulf. Building lots here weren't cheap but most had already been sold and occupied by large homes, the signs of Shean's first burgeoning aristocracy. He remembered the town being more informal at one time about where people choose to live. Whether you lived on a paved street or a pothole-pocked alley, most of the houses around you belonged to friends or family. But families were smaller or vanishing from Shean and old farmland that had long been abandoned on the outskirts of town became the backbone of a thriving real estate industry. Local contractors were quick to react to Shean's new housing need, a need driven mostly by seasonal residents from the United States and Europe. It kept some people employed and was largely responsible for the success of Donald MacNaughton's hardware enterprise. Donald MacNaughton's house was among those on Seaview Place.

Indifferent to the time, David pulled into the drive and seeing a light on got out of his car. He didn't press his thumb on the doorbell but pounded harshly on the doorframe until the door opened and Donald MacNaughton was standing there.

"I'm not even going to try to say it, Donald," David said, and Donald nodded his understanding and both men continued to stand there in uncertain silence. "Is that as wide as you're going to open that door or what?" David asked at last and Donald stepped back swinging the door wide when he did. David stepped inside. "Tonight there's no newspaper, no coal mine, no politics, but there is an issue we need to get to the bottom of," David said.

"And that is?"

"This," David answered, hoisting the unopened bottle of Glen Breton Rare whiskey retrieved from his office desk. Donald's eyebrows rose to expose agreeable eyes. "It's a two-man job, for sure. I'll get the glasses."

David was standing in front of the picture window where the lights of Shean formed a small galaxy in the valley below. When Donald joined him, each man silently wondered what future the other imagined would emerge from that glittering darkness. The clink of the glasses in Donald's hand brought them back to the business at hand.

"You're not a cheap drinker?" Donald noted as David opened the bottle.

"Oh yes, I am. This was a gift I got from someone, appreciation for some story I wrote – not you obviously – and it's been in my desk drawer for a while now waiting for an occasion."

"You remember what the *Halifax Herald* wrote about the Glenora Distillery the day it opened?" Donald asked.

"I was away at the time."

"The article began, 'Cape Breton's first legal distillery opened this week...' I got a charge out of that. There used to be a lot of stills around here one time, in our fathers' time, our grandfathers', but I bet they never thought whiskey would be selling for what, seventy five, eighty bucks a bottle?"

"Steep enough, whatever it is," David said, passing one glass to Donald and taking the other himself. They tipped the glasses in a wordless toast, and sipped.

"Ahhh!" Donald said as the single malt whiskey flowed smoothly down his throat, spreading its immediate warmth all through him. He sniffed deeply from the glass. "Seventy-five bucks, eh? What I'd really like to know, David, is how can they make it so good for so little?" This sent the two men, nervous of each other's company, into giddy gales of laughter.

They were seated at the dining room table, pouring their way through the bottle, lubricating an awkward conversation that stepped carefully around trip wires in the minefield of their troubled relationship until they found their way back to the year that the Shean Miners won the provincial high school hockey title on the deadly strength of the Cameron-MacNaughton line, a line that could take chances because they knew that Victor Mason was behind them, destroying any opposition effort to break away toward the Shean goal. Back further then into pony league and little league baseball. Throughout it all was the physical finesse of their teamwork, two athletes, one coach noted, who worked together great as long they didn't need to talk to each other.

The Glen Breton helped them slide through those glory years until its sudden betrayal found them standing side by side on the mountains of grey slag the morning that Mrs. Big Sandy was shot. The two best friends had been using old pop bottles for target practice and keeping an eye out for rats when a screaming woman came charging out her back door and right at them, bloody hand raised in a murderous fist.

Oblivious to the cause, the boys took off for their lives, parted ways, each toward their own home, and never found their way back together again.

"I was never so scared in my life," Donald MacNaughton confided, gazing at the memory in his glass. "I thought I was dead."

"You were scared? Christ, Donald, it was me she was chasing. If she had caught me she'd have strangled me with her bare hands."

"Her bloody bare hands, you mean. Remember her waving them at us, bloody as hell, and hell I wished she had, you know, strangled you."

"You what! I knew you were pissed off at me but wanting her to catch me? Shit, you wanted me dead over a gun? I thought we were better friends than that back then. Strangled by Mrs. Big Sandy! Well, hell, that might be your fate now that I'm off the hook for the shooting, but if the gun meant that much to you..."

"The gun meant nothing to me. I mean I didn't really care about it. The RCMP were going to confiscate it whichever one of us had it. Once she pressed charges and they took the gun from you it was gone. I didn't care. I was just terrified of being sent to reform school in Shelburne. I kept waiting for them to come and get me, to charge me. They came twice and both times I thought it was for me. Both times they wanted a statement. I was sitting there at the kitchen table with the old man and two Mounties waiting for them to say that you had squealed on me and I was under arrest."

"I never told them it was you, Donald. I never told anybody it was you."

"I know! For fuck sakes, I know! The whole goddamned time it went on, it was thirteen days, that's how long it went on, for thirteen days I was scared shitless, couldn't sleep, waiting for the Mounties. Christ I hated you for torturing me like that. That's what it felt like, torture. You torturing me. And then somewhere in that time I realized that the Mounties weren't coming, that you weren't going to squeal, and then I really hated you."

"Why?" David asked, refilling their glasses.

"Because you were being so fucking noble, don't you see? Because I knew you were protecting me, and if it meant going to Shelburne then you would have gone, and knowing that and knowing that if the tables were turned I'd have squealed on you in a minute to save my arse from being kicked up around my ears by my old man because I was far more afraid of him than you or the Mounties or Shelburne. And by the time the issue went away, no charges, everybody turning it into a town joke, how you shot Mrs. Big Sandy in the arse and lived to tell about it, making you a kind of hero, and then everybody eventually forgetting it ever happened. All that came of it was that I couldn't stand the sight of you because every time I saw you reminded me of..." Donald let his words end there, the silence filling out the rest of the story. But it wasn't the story David was content to end with. He had one of his own to tell.

"Donald, I don't give a shit about any of that. I didn't even know what was bothering you, thought it was the gun, but you know what I missed most out of it all? That I was never able to tell you my side of the story, what happened after Mrs. Big Sandy drove us apart. It was good strategy, just like in the movies, us separating, having her chase just one of us. At least one of us would live to tell the tale.

"So there you are running down Main Street and me turning up Poplar Street, booting her for home and I was hoping Mrs. Big Sandy'd go after you because you're the guy who shot her, but she didn't know that, did she? So a few seconds after I turn up the street I hear her panting and coughing and cursing behind me. I was only twelve years old and scared, Donald, and there's nothing on this planet that can run faster than a scared twelve year old, but she was closing ground on me, so help me God, she was closing ground. I began hollering for my father and he heard me from inside the house. He thought I got hit by a car or something so he comes running out to the door, opens the big wooden storm door we had on the house back then, holding it by the inside hook, sees me, starts to come after me, then sees Mrs. Big Sandy behind me. So what does he do? He stands there in the doorway holding the door by the hook, screaming at me, 'Hurry up, for fuck sake, hurry up!' and I go running through the doorway and he slams it behind me and gets the hook on just as Mrs. Big Sandy hits the door like a linebacker. She stayed out there forever it seems before she gave up and went to get the Mounties. My father's face when he saw her..."

The two men were laughing while David continued reminiscing. "Jesus, Donald, even that night, scared as I was, and I was every bit as scared of Shelburne as you, I was in bed laughing in my mind about how much I was going to enjoy telling this to you. If you could have seen my father's face when I was running toward him screaming, 'Daddy! Daddy!'"

Donald's shoulder-shaking laughter slowly changed to convulsions of another kind.

"What is it Donald?" David asked carefully.

Donald MacNaughton lifted his tear-stained face and looked at David for a long time before he could say, "That's what your kids were calling. That's how I found them, David. They were screaming 'Daddy! Daddy!' Jesus, I'm glad I was there."

David reached across the table and placed a hand on Donald's shoulder. There was nothing he could add to the gesture and they remained that way until Donald finally got control of his emotions, saying, "Hell, I may as well put George Jones on the stereo if we're going to waste this good liquor on a crying jag."

Some time with the first glimmerings of dawn the two men found the bottom of the bottle. Donald said he needed to turn in, and pointed out that David should crash on the livingroom couch.

On his way up the stairs Donald stopped and turned toward David. "Just for the record, David, this doesn't change anything, you know. See you in the morning."

"See you in the editorial pages," David replied, collapsing to the couch.

| 40 |

David squinted against the burning sting of sunrise torturing his gummy eyes. His mouth tasted poison, and his brain couldn't quite grasp the concept of being a conscious, coherent organism, but the heat, magnified through triple panes of window, forced him to a sitting position. He had a prize-winning hangover that would never be reported in the pages of the *Witness*. The house was quiet as a tomb and he knew he needed to sneak out before he was forced to eat breakfast. He eased the door shut behind him and walked to his car.

It was an oven and he wished he could turn on the air conditioner that he refused to buy as one of the car's options. There were too few hot days to make it worth the investment, he had thought. He was having second thoughts. He rolled down the windows and went for a walk while the car's interior temperature eased its way down to the double digits. He found himself standing in front of MacNaughton's home looking down on the waking town and wondering what kind of thinking it took to believe, like Donald did, that it was more important to be overlooking the scorched scars that would be the legacy of strip mining than enjoying the priceless view of the town and harbour that his home on Seaview Place provided.

What kind of a mind indeed, he wondered when he saw the "Sold" sign pasted over the realtor's "For Sale" sign on the empty lot beside MacNaughton's, and recalled C.J.M. Lord's insistence that he planned to build a home and live in Shean. It flashed through David's mind that he too would soon be building or buying a new home. "But it won't be in this neighbourhood," he said aloud as he started the car.

It was early to be knocking on a motel door. Bethany and Jim had offered to cancel their plans if they could help David get his life resettled. There was no need for a change of plans, he told them, sincerely ordering them to continue the vacation they had in mind for themselves. They went to breakfast together but David's appetite couldn't get interested in anything but black coffee.

Jim Turner told David he was interested in pursuing David's concern for rural economies in an urban world as a story for the business section. He thought that the debate in Shean could be the face of that future. He'd be following the *Witness*'s story online and getting in touch with David when he thought he had the stuff of a decent news story.

David waved goodbye as the Ontario plates disappeared into the morning sun then he drove to his mother's home. The home his father had built and compulsively remodelled out of the sheer love of building, the home in which he grew up and where his father had died, becoming then his mother's home, and it was in that home that he had come to know his mother as someone who would be willing do whatever she could to make his own life possible. She was a grandmother who mothered his children and became his best friend, and all that she cherished, from the home itself to the memories it had absorbed into its very boards, was now smouldering before him. A fireman was leaning against a pumper, having spent the night watching that fire didn't start up again. He just nodded and left David to his thoughts.

He was going to be busy sorting through all those ashes, piecing their lives back together again, but they would. Whatever the loss, his family had escaped with their lives and so the future was something they could look forward to. He'd try to make it an exciting adventure, maybe mute some of the terror the children must have felt and that he couldn't begin to imagine. They would decide together what kind of home they wanted and build or buy it. The headache was waning and he had work to do, so he drove himself to the office.

From inside the *Witness*'s safe he pulled a package that contained all his family's important papers – birth certificates, deeds, will, insurance – and began sorting through the details of his mother's insurance before contacting the agent and opening a claim.

The staff began arriving and coffee appeared at his elbow along with a set of keys. "My sister's house on Scott Street. She uses it a couple of weeks a year for vacation. She's already been and gone so there's no rush. She says to use it until you get resettled," Lisa told him.

Telephones rang and were answered and he was left to take care of whatever personal business needed his attention, or so David thought.

"Your friends are here," Lisa informed him. David looked up to see Bethany and Jim standing behind her, tiny waves from each of them as they entered the office.

"Newfoundland's thataway," David said, pointing out the window in the general direction of the Atlantic Ocean.

"And we'll get there someday," Bethany said. "Perhaps when we do go you and Rita can join us. I think it would be a lot of fun, but that's next year's plan. This year's vacation plans have changed in the last half hour."

"We drove out as far as the Trans Canada when we changed our minds and decided that what we both really need is a working vacation. You know how stale a reporter can get when he's away from his word processor for too long," Jim explained.

"And you did say, as you moaned through your headache this morning, that you needed to take a week off to deal with family matters and insurance and such. That would leave that young reporter of yours handling the whole issue. So we're signing on," Bethany announced.

David looked from one to the other, shaking his head. "I don't think you know what you're in for. You're specialists, and this paper calls for all-purpose reporting on everything from bake sales to house fires."

"Think we're not up for it?" Bethany asked.

"No, you're not but this town is in need of a good laugh, so I'm going to walk out that door and leave you here to drown in the comings and goings of a small town. But that youngster out there is the acting editor so you'll take your orders from him. We'll see what you're worth at the end of the week, and it may be as much as I'm paying my children for their help here at the paper."

David studied his friends quietly for a moment. "Thanks."

Before leaving the office he reintroduced Tim Donovan to the two new reporters, adding that Tim was editor of the next issue, with all the powers of assigning and editing, of hiring and firing that went with the position. He himself would be out of touch for a week unless there was an emergency such as needing to rescue one of the cub reporters from the clutches of Mrs. Big Sandy. Then, with the keys to their temporary shelter in his hands, he left to get his children and mother at the hospital.

| 41 |

"The bastards!"

"What?" Rita asked.

"They went and put up a big gate on Sandy's land with a big 'No Hunting' sign on it."

"It's a 'No Trespassing' sign," Rita corrected.

"Isn't that what I said? Well, I'd just like to see them keep me out of there. I've got a good mind to go down there and trespass back and forth until my arsehole is dragging like a hen trying to lay a goose's egg! That's what I've got a good mind to do!"

Rita had noticed the gate earlier in the week, as well as the busyness of the place: equipment arriving, trucks in and out, a road being bulldozed into being across the mine tailings. It would be six or eight weeks before Resource Reclamations's work could begin in earnest, according to the *Witness.*

Rita pulled into the Co-op parking lot for her weekly grocery shopping. At the house Mrs. Big Sandy announced that she was coming: "I need to see some civilization. I can't be stuck out here in the middle of nowhere all the time so I'm coming with you."

Inside the store the two women toured the aisles while their cart filled with dietary contradictions, Mrs. Big Sandy's selection of instant, processed and frozen beside Rita's choices of fresh, low fats and sugar-free. It was in the baking supplies aisle that both women heard the name "Big Sandy" drift over from the other aisle.

Any hope Rita had that Mrs. Big Sandy hadn't heard the name shrivelled when she looked at her friend and saw her chest heaving under a heavy intake of air, precursor to one of her familiar and frightening rages.

"What I heard," said one woman, "was that Don Alex was the nightwatchman down there last night..."

"Don Alex!" exclaimed the second voice, amazed. "Don Alex working!"

"I know. Hard to believe, but I guess Ronald MacDonald called him a lazy bastard or something so he went out and found himself a job as night watchman. They're paying him cash under the table so it wouldn't affect his pension and besides, what's there to do down there? Nothing, just like Don Alex's done all his life. Nothing but walk around once in a while to see that nobody's stealing anything. And that's when he seen him, I guess. Big Sandy MacArthur big as life walking toward him."

"A ghost?"

"According to Don Alex, who swears on the Bible that that's who he saw last night down there. Big Sandy walking toward him, and Don Alex could see him and see right through him, I guess. Well Don Alex just turned around and ran through the gate and home and called in on the phone to quit this morning. Wouldn't even go back in the daytime. Wants nothing to do with the place. It's haunted, he says. Told my husband hisself this morning and anybody else in the Gulf Grill that would listen to him."

"And what do you think yourself? Do you think he saw him, Big Sandy?"

"Well I'm not a big believer in ghosts but I wouldn't go poking at one with a stick if I saw one. And they used to see ghosts all the time around here, didn't they? Remember when we were kids, going looking in haunted houses, or for that girl's ghost that was supposed to be haunting the sand dunes. So I'm not saying it was or it wasn't Big Sandy's ghost Don Alex saw, but I do know this much: if it was Big Sandy, anybody from Shean would know who it was, wouldn't they, and we'd of all done what Don Alex done. Run as fast as you can."

The conversation changed and diminished as the carts in the other aisle were rolled away. Rita had never taken her eyes off Mrs. Big Sandy, and it was like watching a volcano deciding not to erupt. By the end of the women's conversation, Mrs. Big Sandy was no longer a heaving rage but a woman with a knowing smile.

The story of Big Sandy's ghost roared through Shean like a forest fire, with Don Alex holding court in the park recounting to whatever audience was willing to listen how he had seen a dead man with his very own eyes.

With Don Alex unwilling to pursue his career in security, Resource Reclamations needed to hire two new watchmen. While most people scoffed at the ghost story, there was no clamour of applicants to replace the former night watchman if it meant walking the hills and gullies of the old mine tailings on a moonless July night. Finally the foreman at the site agreed to hire two watchmen: Mad Maddie Casey, who, according to his own long-range plans was temporarily sober, and Maddie's younger brother, Phillip.

The newly employed watchmen were kept busy because the idea of a ghost haunting the mine site pulled half the young people in Shean away from their video games and slasher movies to try to scale the chain-link fence in search of Big Sandy's ghost. There were no more sightings reported in the days immediately after Don Alex's encounter but neither Mad Maddie nor his brother could explain how a bulldozer and a backhoe had sugar poured into their gas tanks. Yes, they told the foreman and anyone else who was interested that kids or even the environmentalists from the club at the school could have gotten past them and done the damage, but neither brother thought so. They had been too alert throughout the night, less from vigilance than from fear of encountering Big Sandy's ghost. Many's the drink I had with the man, Mad Maddie reminded people, and if I'd a seen him maybe I wouldn't be sharing a drink with him but I'd be off this wagon I'm on and passed out on cheap wine by now.

More mysteriously convincing to the watchmen and those who knew Big Sandy was the disappearance of the power tools. A drill and a hammer had disappeared, they said, just vanished. One of the carpenters working on the site had left them where he was working, figuring that with two watchmen the tools would be safe enough.

"And is that all that disappeared," Ronald MacDonald asked Maddie, "just the tools that were left out in the open?"

"That's all," Maddie replied, and the men in the group gave a nodding, wordless agreement among themselves that there was little doubt who took those tools.

It was close to midnight and Rita MacDonald was seated at the kitchen table still in her uniform, having just gone off shift at the Manor. It had been three days since the sighting of Big Sandy's ghost and the news was still fresh in Shean. As she watched Mrs. Big Sandy working around the stove, Rita wondered about her elderly friend.

Whatever kind of troubled, angry marriage she and Big Sandy may have had, love was the bedrock upon which it rested, Rita was convinced, which probably wasn't true of every marriage, whatever its longevity. She had heard enough vitriolic outbursts from Manor residents directed at a husband or wife, living or dead, to learn that many men and women carried deep resentments against their spouses. In the throes of dementia, who knows what truths rise to the surface when someone's mind is freed from the boundaries of social norms.

While she suspected that an enduring, unarticulated love had existed between the couple that the town had always characterized as characters, she wondered if Mrs. Big Sandy had ever known happiness, and suspected that at this very moment the old woman was somewhere closer to joy in the news of Big Sandy's ghost than she may have ever been before.

Rita smothered a sudden laugh watching her father nearly jump out of his skin when Mrs. Big Sandy came up behind him while he was playing cribbage against someone in Israel and asked, "Ronald dear, can I get you a cup of tea?" He probably thinks she's coming on to him, Rita thought, and couldn't imagine a scarier thought running through her father's mind, especially with the ghost of Big Sandy MacArthur roaming around, revenging himself on those who had taken what he had once possessed.

That humourous thought came to rest soberly on an image of herself slouched into the comfort of the breakwater rocks, her haven against an enduring aloneness, a place she went to breathe to the rise and fall of the sea, sometimes imagining the comforting rhythm of someone sleeping beside her. Yet her star-lit, ocean-wide aloneness wasn't always steeped in solitude. Often it was shared by David Cameron, for whom the Shean shoreline also offered some sort of sanctuary. In the parking lot, their cars told of each other's presence but they had never visited the other's hermitage. Her honest thought to herself was that she had often wished otherwise, and watching Mrs. Big Sandy's humming joy over her husband's resurrection, recognized that her aloneness was well-salted with loneliness.

| 42 |

With the legal and insurance matters that had brought him to the town of Antigonish behind him, David Cameron sat in the booth of an Antigonish café sipping coffee and studying the newspaper spread out in front of him. It was the current issue of the *Witness,* and he had stopped at the office long enough to grab a copy from the front desk on his way to the mainland. He was glad to be alone.

The front page was filled with a single photograph, that of a firefighter emerging from the smoke of a burning building, a child's limp body under each arm. It was a full-colour photo but the cloudy texture of a black-clad fireman and grey smoke gave it a black-and-white quality. Tim Donovan's camera had captured the exact image that had burned itself into David's mind forever. It was an image of terrifying joy for him, of having believed for a moment that all that mattered to him had been lost, only to have it wholly restored through the courage of his least likely hero. The father in him fought back tears while the editor in him knew that this was an award-winning news photograph, and he was glad for Donovan. The reporter had brought the same precision to his telling of the story of Donald MacNaughton's heroism.

David turned the pages and his eye caught another unexpected headline, *Mine tailings haunted by former owner's ghost: watchman*. While the waitress refilled his cup David read the story of Don Alex MacLean's reported sighting of Big Sandy's ghost, smiling at the line in which Don Alex assured the reporter that he was "practically sober" when he saw the apparition. Donovan had also interviewed the replacement watchmen, who recounted their experiences, not with the ghost but with the property damage to the machinery and the theft of the power tools, both brothers underlining the fact that only the tools left out in the open were stolen. David, aware of Big Sandy's reputation for taking anything people were stupid enough to leave lying around, knew that most readers in Shean would read between the lines and see this as a confirmation of Don Alex's tale of seeing Big Sandy's ghost.

He drew a sense of comfort from the ghost story. It was the first original ghost story the *Witness* had printed under his ownership and probably for decades before that. Every Halloween, David ran a two-page section of ghost stories popularized over the years and collected by folklorists or recounted by grandparents or great grandparents, but this was the first contemporary ghost to appear in Shean in a long, long time. It was culturally significant, David thought, that in the changing nature of the world as it worked its sceptical way into all the nooks and crannies of the planet, including small towns like Shean, there still existed enough belief or imagination to sustain a new ghost story. Not an imported plot from some other time or place and tarted up to pass as a local truth, but a genuine ghost story that would be retold through one or two more generations by Shean's current children and future grandparents, and who would swear upon the popular oath, "As sure as I'm sitting here..."

"I'm almost not eight any more, you know. Next month I'll be nine. How old are you?"

"Thirty-seven," Jim answered.

"Wow, you're even older than Dad."

"So Tony, how do you like being a news photographer?"

"Is that what I am? I wondered. Dad didn't really say. Does a news pho...to...grapher make more than a dollar a day?"

"Now why do you want to know that?"

"Because if they do I'm going to tell Dad that that's what I am, a news pho...tog...rapher. Where are we going?"

"Down to the mine site. There's a man there I want to talk to, interview, and I always like to have a news photographer along to get the kind of pictures that I want with my story. So you got your camera?"

"Right here, see?" Tony said, snapping a picture of his godfather when Jim turned to look. "I put my pictures on Facebook and then Mommy can see them all the way in Toronto. Isn't that cool?"

"It certainly is. Here we are," Jim said, pulling in front of the largest trailer. "Let's see what happens." Getting out of the car they walked to the entrance, knocked, heard nothing, then Jim turned the knob. The door opened onto a dusty reception area and a desk where a receptionist would be sitting if there was a receptionist.

"Hello!" Jim yelled, then repeated it, looking at the doors on either side of the reception desk. One was labelled Cyril Bender, Engineer, and the other, C.J.M. Lord, CEO. The Bender door opened, a bespeckled head peering out, then a man asked what they wanted as he eased himself toward them.

"I'm a reporter, Jim Turner, with *The Toronto Star*."

"The *Star*! What brings you all the way down here? We're not all that much of a story."

"Actually, I'm on vacation, not assignment, visiting my godson here," he said, giving the boy's shoulder a squeeze before letting him do whatever he could to entertain his boredom with the adult conversation. "I read the local paper and it seemed to say that there's more going on here than meets the eye. Made me kind of curious. It's not often I leave my desk in Toronto to slum among the peasants, but sometimes I bump into a good story. So what can you tell me?"

"Nothing much, I afraid. I'm an engineer, not a communications officer. We've got just the one, and he's the CEO as well." Cyril Bender indicated the other door, the one Jim Turner had wished had opened to his intrusion.

"C.J.M. Lord. So the information comes from the penthouse down. Then I'd certainly like to interview the man, or at least meet him."

"Not today. Maybe on the weekend. He's here hands-on more than any CEO I've worked for, but he doesn't tell me where he goes or when he'll be back. Thinks it's really none of my business, which it isn't, and so you understand that I can't help.... Oh no, no, come out of there. You kid! He shouldn't be just walking around like that." The man pointed to the C.J.M. Lord CEO door standing wide open.

"Tony," Jim called and the boy materialized in the doorway, looking hopeful that it was time to go. "I'll be around for a few days, maybe I'll drop back some other time just in case Mr. Lord shows up. Maybe he can help me work up a story about boondocks capitalism and the opportunities that exist in Canada's emptying countryside, resources ready for the picking. Just a little imagination and money and whatever's happening here could be happening in any place like this. If I see him before I leave it might be a story, but it's not important enough to miss a day on the beach. I'll give you my card to pass along. Who knows?"

"Oh I think Lord will like to talk to you. Largest newspaper in the country and one of the things I miss most about this particular contract, the *Star*. I'm from Ontario myself, Ajax actually. And Mr. Lord knows which papers speak to Bay Street and which ones don't. He'll want to talk to you."

"So what do you think of being a photojournalist?"

"Is that like being a news photog...rapher? If it is, they're both boring."

"Then, my young friend, maybe there are more exciting opportunities for you and your camera at the beach."

"Yeaaaah! That's my favourite place but I haven't been there since the fire. I guess Dad just forgot."

"I'll only drive down there on one condition, that you let me buy you one of those famous Beach Burgers I've heard about, double patties. Think you can handle that?"

"I'm going to take a picture of it after every bite."

| 43 |

Supper had been a bucket of Kentucky Fried Chicken transported in fairly warm condition from Antigonish. With the dishes cleared out of the way, David called a family summit at the table of their temporary home. He had the *Witness* opened at the real estate section, passing it around, showing what was available for rent and which houses and building lots were for sale. His mother looked at the choices with a barely concealed sadness and David knew that there was no way for him or the children to measure the lost treasures of her life, the litany of memories she must recall now every day since the fire. She gave a shrug and pushed the paper away, conceding to whatever her son thought they should do.

"I've been thinking about it all the way back from Antigonish and my preference is for us to rebuild on the old lot. What's left of the house needs to be bulldozed and trucked away. It's a small lot but it's ours. The house is no longer there but the fire didn't burrow as deep as our family's roots in that little piece of land, Mom, so if it would be okay with you – it's your lot, after all – we could begin looking at house plans and try to get construction under way by early fall. If all goes well, which it normally doesn't with house construction, we could be in it by Christmas."

The family gathering was interrupted by the ringing of David's cellphone, the ring tone some heavy metal song the children had downloaded from the Internet and that he wasn't savvy enough to get rid of. He checked the incoming call to see if he would take it. It was Alexandra, calling from Toronto.

"David, oh God, I'm sick. When you called from the hospital and told me about the fire and everybody being safe I wasn't grasping how serious it was, or could have been. Then tonight I checked thewitness.ca and saw that photo. I threw up, David. Donald MacNaughton may be your worst enemy but..."

"I know," David interjected. "We both owe Donald more than we can ever repay him, but the children are safe. Mom too. They're here. We're in Lisa's sister's house until we figure out what to do, and that's what we were doing when you called, talking about what kind of house we want to build."

"David, I need to hold my children. I need them to be here. I can't believe I let my job get to me like that, that I told them to stay in Cape Breton this summer. Can they come now? I'll take all the time they need from me."

"You talk to them, Alex." David passed the phone to Tony. "It's your mother."

"Did you hear about the fire? ... Yes, I was a little scared but Mary was with me so I couldn't be too scared..." David could see the boy's shoulders stiffening, refusing to allow him to cry. That can come later, David thought, when they're with their mother, his mind now made up. "I don't think I can come to Toronto. Dad gave me a job. Me and Mary. My pictures are in the paper sometimes, even some of Mary's." His voice dropped to a whisper. "But hers aren't so good. Dad's just being nice. But he's paying us more than a dollar a day," he said importantly before the whisper returned, not as secretive as Tony thought because David heard him tell his mother, "I am going to tell him he doesn't have to pay me any more because we're going to build a new house and so I want him to have the money .... I don't know. I want to come but I don't. Here's Mary."

While the little girl described the events from her perspective to her mother, David asked Tony what he wanted to do. "I can't go, Dad. I have a job."

"Every job has vacation time, Tony. I'll miss you on the paper. You're a good photographer and I think that if you go to Toronto, when you come back I'll put you to work one weekend a month. You'll be Tim's helper. He's the best person to show you about taking pictures, not me. But I would like you to see your mother. She needs to see you, Tony. And Mary can't fly up there alone, not without you looking after her, just like you always do, just like you did during the fire."

Tony nodded his assent as Mary passed the phone back to her father. "I want to see mommy."

"Both children want to go, Alexandra. I won't be able to drive them up like I had planned. One option is for them to wait a week and I'm sure Bethany and Jim will be glad to bring them to you."

"No, I can't wait a week, David!"

"Then I'll book a flight now and get them to the airport tomorrow if you can be waiting for them on the other end"

"I'll be there. I'm sorry if I seemed so selfish when I asked you to keep them for the summer. That will never happen again. I think it's important that they do come to Toronto, not just to see me or so I can hold them but because the more familiar they are with a city like this the better they'll be able to adapt when they do leave Shean."

"You're sure they'll be doing that?" David asked, an edge in his voice.

"Don't you think they will? You've always said that it was inevitable, even your own leaving home. I'm glad they're growing up there but what's there for them when they're a young man and woman? You wouldn't want Tony working in that open pit mine I read about, would you? And what else is there? The paper? Is that what you really want for Tony, editing some small town paper for the rest of his life, earning a fraction of what he could earn here if he did decide to become a photographer? Is that what you want for him, David?"

"No. No, of course not," David answered, awareness mushrooming in him that that was exactly what he wanted for Tony. The old man's footsteps. He never knew that his deepest wish could be one so clichéd, so dangerous to Tony's own future. It was a thought he needed to keep in the front of his own mind as Tony continued to play a role at the *Witness*. There would be summer jobs as he grew up if he wanted them, but only if. He would need to be careful not to make Tony's life an extension of his own, to let the boy find his own way wherever he was going. The fire, it seemed to him, had opened deeper channels of thought about his life and the lives of others.

David and Alexandra parted. The house plans went on hold as the excitement grew in Tony and Mary that they were going to Toronto after all, to Canada's Wonderland with its thrill rides and water slides and sticky food.

Once the children had been finally put to bed, David told his mother that he needed to go to the office to read her insurance documents.

| 44 |

David Cameron put down the last of the insurance documents. There had been no need to rush from the house to the office to read them again. They were clear, uncomplicated, but he needed to be alone. He had lost himself in the flurry of activity following the fire, getting drunk with Donald, dealing with the practicalities through a lawyer and insurance agent, but Alexandra's phone call, her shock over what she encountered on the *Witness*'s website, made him aware that he wasn't the only person who nearly lost his family. Looking down at his hands, he saw a slight tremble and knew that the shock had finally cornered him. Or maybe it was the pot of perked coffee that had disappeared, along with the evening sun and its flaring farewell beyond the horizon. A nearly full moon had risen in its place and under its soft luminescence he studied the world beyond the office window. A soft breeze rippled the water in the sheltered harbour so that the fleet of crab boats bobbed and swayed against the wharf. The moonlight beamed a path directly down the channel that opened on to the Gulf of

St. Lawrence. On either side of the channel was the undulating silhouette of the dunes.

On this early warm nightfall a smoky red aura rose above the dunes from a teenage bonfire. Usually they weren't ablaze so soon after dark. Beach parties tended to start toward midnight, but early or late they were frequent. Always had been. Always would be. They were as much a sign of summer's arrival as they were of the courting rituals of Shean teenagers. But it was a large beach, and David doubted he or they would intrude on each other, and he felt the need to be there.

———

Rita MacDonald had been watching the moon rise behind the mountains, its ascent measuring the diminishing hours of her shift until she was standing in the parking lot of the Shean beach, needing to be there for the moment, wanting to be there for a month. David Cameron's car was there again and she had parked next to it, thinking they, at least, could keep each other company. According to their cars, they had shared the beach in winter when the weather was possible, in spring when the ice floes broke apart and drifted back north and now into the warmth of early summer without ever encountering each other. David's habit was to walk north to some enclave in the bank of sandy dunes, while she walked south to the breakwater rocks. Whenever she knew he was there her thoughts were fewer and her fantasies more frequent. She imagined that he would walk out of the night and into her presence. He never would, and she hated the danger of dreaming that he might. But tonight she stepped off the stairs that led from the parking lot onto the beach and walked along the water's edge with her shoes in her hand and her back to the breakwater.

David was disappointed to see the glow of embers breathing red in the dark, highlighting the silhouettes sitting behind it on his log. Turn back or continue? It wouldn't hurt to see who was sitting there since it was evident from the distance between them that this was not a romantic encounter. With heavy steps in the dry sand, he forged forward.

"Halt! Who goes there?" And if the voice had come to him on a midnight beach in China he would have said the same thing. "Hello, Don Alex. David here."

"Come in out of the cold and have a little something to warm you up," he said, passing him a wine bottle with a blank label, someone's homemade stash undoubtedly, though it was doubtful the owner knew it was missing.

"Yeah," said Mad Maddie. "You can have my share."

"Still on the wagon, Maddie," David said encouragingly.

"Bah, it's nothing. Been almost two weeks now so I got the bugger beat. Just keeping Don Alex company. Hate to see a man drink alone. That's where all those country and western songs, the real weepers, come from."

"I beg your pardon, sir, but we have an important man here, a newspaper man. Spells all his own words and everything. So you down here looking for Big Sandy too? Can you take a picture of a ghost, David?"

"Is that what brings you down here?" David asked in reply. "Big Sandy?"

"Not a chance. I'm not like Saint Thomas, you know. I don't need Big Sandy sticking that big fist of his in my face to make a believer out of me. I saw him once and once is enough. Here, take a swig of this here local wine, made from ingredients already mixed in a box in the Co-op. Just add water. How great is that?"

David reached across for the bottle, rubbed his hand over the lip of the bottle to rid it of Don Alex's germs, a practice shared by all boys under the age of twelve who share a bottle of pop or adults in situations such as this. David raised the bottle to his lips and plugged the mouth with his tongue, or so was the intended strategy, but he managed to miss and the red liquid came rushing into his mouth.

His face wrinkled up with the shock of it, a sugar-sweet syrup that had a substantial amount of alcohol in its recipe. It would do the job all right, but David wasn't about to go on a binge with Don Alex. Fortunately the undrinkable substance made it even easier to refuse further temptations from his already drunk buddy.

"Yeah! Big Sandy. You know I saw him, you know that don't you?"

"I know," David assured him.

"I never saw nothing," Maddie said, venturing into the conversation.

"And if you did?" David asked.

"Well maybe I'd ask him what he wants or maybe I'd piss my pants. Never had much of a handle on the things that I do. Phillip says that's because I can't tell stupid from stupider. But Don Alex here needed company. I'm getting paid for it and if Big Sandy is up there in the mine yard tearing it apart then good for him. Phillip can handle it or piss his pants or whatever. When they ask me where I was, I'll say I saw his ghost and fainted. Got it all figured out in case that happens, and if it don't happen nobody'll ever know I wasn't on the job, will they?" He tapped the side of his head as if to confirm there was content of some sort inside.

David knelt down before the two men and reached around for small pieces of driftwood to keep the embers glowing, the fire's remote heat ideal for the first cool evenings of August. The fire re-energized, he moved around and sat between the two men, occasionally fending off Don Alex's kind offers of a sip, just wanting the company.

It wasn't why he had come to the shore tonight. He usually came to be alone. But being alone could be a frightening state to find himself in. All week long the image of his children caught in the house fire replayed to an alternative and tragic ending in his mind. David was glad for the unexpected company. He looked across the carpet of moonlight reaching all the way to the horizon. His imagination used it like a spotlight, lighting the layers that lay beneath. His mind dropped through the cool stillness of the water to the lobster-inhabited floor, and below that to the Beaton Seam.

———

Under that untapped deathtrap were the miles and miles of slopes and levels that had systematically extracted the rich veins of coal that ran more than two miles out under the sea. Because mining had stopped before David and his generation were even born, they got the romantic version of it from fathers and grand-fathers, but years of reporting as much on the history of the town's industry as on its cultural forms and day-to-day life had taught him that it had been hard times even when the mines were booming because the companies were in the habit of in-creasing profits annually by reducing wages. Shean had survived one coal boom. He wondered if it could survive another.

"So what do you think of that, David?" Don Alex was ask-ing, a slight slur signalling his blood-alcohol count.

"Of what?" David asked, jarred back by the question.

"What I just said. About the new mine. That's what Maddie and me were talking about afore you interrupted us. That's what everybody talks about, isn't it? Read that newspaper of yours and you'll see. What are they up to?"

"I thought you were in favour of the mine," David said.

"What's that got to do with the price of tea in the Co-op? Doesn't mean I can't see, and I can't see where they're going to get the coal. All of Big Sandy's place and all the rest of the tail-ings, all of them places together don't have enough coal to keep this here fire here going. So I'm guessing they know something we don't."

"Yeah, they do. Joseph Collins at the museum was wonder-ing if all the seismic testing they've been doing turned up a seam nobody noticed before. But I agree with you. There's no coal to be reclaimed."

"You can say that again, isn't that right, Maddie? I bet you yourself was about the last person I remember doing it, digging through the slag for lumps of coal. Fill a burlap bag, potato bag, with coal and lug it home on your back. I remember Maddie here, couldn't a been any bigger than a first grader, bucking one of them bags home on his back. Your old man'd be sending you even in the rain. Say what you like about him yourself, Maddie, but he was a real bastard, your father. Sure you don't want to drink a toast to him?" Don Alex said, offering Maddie the bottle.

"I don't want to drink a toast to nobody, and leave my old man out of it. What did you know–"

"What do you think they're up to then?" David asked, diverting the confrontation.

"What you were just saying, David," Don Alex pointed out.

"What was I just saying?"

Don Alex took another drink, burped and said, "They're going to tear down the whole town, that's what Maddie and I were figuring. So it's just like what you were just saying, where's the coal? We worked it out, you know. If they can't find coal in the tailing then they're going to have to dig for it, probably under Big Sandy's, then follow the seam wherever it takes them. And since they won't be following the seam underground where we wouldn't even notice, they're going to be following the seam on the surface. Are you following me, David?"

"I'm trying to. Go on."

"So what I was saying was that there's the reason they stole Big Sandy's land. It's because that's where the seam begins. So they'll dig down there, but once they find the seam they're looking for, they have to chase it wherever it goes. I was explaining that to Maddie and know what he says? That they can't chase a seam out into the ocean so that means that the seam will have to go the other way, which, when you think about it, could go right through the middle of town – and anything standing in its way, don't you see. My being in favour of it, the mine, the way you said, is because it'll be good for some people even if it's not so good for some other people. Only trouble is, none of us knows who. The company knows right now, I bet, but they're not telling. But it'll be good for the rest of the town."

"What if the seam goes right through your house while you're watching *Hockey Night in Canada* or something, what will you think then?" Maddie asked Don Alex.

"Well that changes everything, doesn't it? They can shove their goddamned mine up their arse if they think for a minute they're getting their hands on my place," Don Alex said, sealing his determination with another syrupy mouthful of wine. "I'll do what Big Sandy's doing."

"Do you really think Big Sandy's doing it, Don Alex?" David asked.

"I seen him, didn't I? And I wasn't as drunk as I am now so I know what I seen. Big Sandy. I don't have to describe him to youse guys. You know what I seen. I'd like to scare somebody as much as he sacred me, that's what I'd like to do, so just let them come and try to take my house for their coal mine. Just let them."

"Don't you need to be dead to haunt people, David?" Maddie asked.

"That's the assumption."

"There's that to it, I suppose," Don Alex agreed, scratching his head over that particular problem, squinting across the fire, his tone suddenly changing to a whisper. "There's somebody out there and I don't know if he's alive or dead."

The three men stared into the night. The unmistakable approach of a human form brought on an epidemic of gooseflesh.

"Who goes there?" Don Alex asked in a voice that hadn't reached that same pitch since he was a thirteen year old.

"David, are you there?"

"Rita?"

Rita MacDonald emerged from the darkness, standing awkwardly on the far side of the fire.

"Gave us a bit of a start there, Missus," Maddie said. "You bout scared Don Alex to death."

"Didn't! I knew who it was. Who it wasn't anyway."

"We were thinking about the coal company, that's all it was what scared us, wasn't it David?" Maddie explained. "Aw, too bad we didn't think to bring some wieners, we could of offered the lady something to eat, fresh roasted. But Don Alex has some wine…"

"Maddie, will you shut up. Can't you see three's a crowd. We're not wanted here. Now come on."

"Why? It's our fire … oh yes." The situation was beginning to dawn on him. "We'll just be leaving then. Have to get back to work anyway."

Don Alex stood up, the wine bottle in his hand.

"You don't need to leave because of me. I'm the one who's crashing your party, Don Alex."

"Not a party, Rita, just a bull session. So you walked over the beach all by yourself. Aren't you brave? Didn't see anything, did you?"

"Nothing at all, Don Alex. Why, is Big Sandy prowling the beach now?" she teased.

"It's not a joke, not a joke at all. I seen him but you know that. You'll be saying hello to your father for me, or does he know anything about this."

"There's no 'about this' going on, Don."

"Don't worry, I won't mention it unless he does," Don Alex said, picking up a fabric Co-op grocery bag, two or three bottles clinking within, and stepping back into the darkness. "Come on Maddie. We better get lost."

"Shouldn't we have straightened the place up a little? Didn't know there was a woman coming."

"For the love of God, Maddie, you don't straighten up a beach," David and Rita heard Don Alex say as the voices faded away from them.

| 45 |

"Sorry for breaking up the party," Rita said.

"You did that all right. Thank you. There's plenty of room in the balcony here if you'd like to take a seat. Are you lost? The breakwater's thataway," David reminded her with a movement of his head.

"I felt like exploring new territory tonight. Yours. I didn't know you were holding seances over here or I would have stayed away," she said, taking his offer of a seat beside him on the driftwood log. "I suppose we'll be the talk of the town tomorrow."

"Probably be in the newspaper and everything," David agreed.

"How have you been?" Rita asked, her tone concerned. Professional nurse or concerned friend? It didn't matter, really. David found himself needing to talk.

"The children's mother called this evening," he began. "She'd seen the photo of Donald and the kids on the website and it frightened the hell out of her. Made me realize how fast I've been running away from that image myself, dealing with the insurance company, with the Fire

Marshall, with ideas for a new home, but now I've run out of distractions.

"Alexandra wants me to send the children to Toronto and I want them to go. Isn't that awful. Is that awful? I want them to be with their mother because I feel like I've already failed them as a father, but it's worse than that. There's some sense of guilt that if they go now to their mother, far from this place, they'll be her worry. That's small thinking, I know, but I also know that today would probably have been their burial day if things has not gone as they did, if Donald hadn't refused to give up inside that burning building."

David sat quietly then, a rising tide of tears in his eyes, flowing quietly, uninterrupted by Rita's presence.

"I'm a mess, Rita," David continued when he got a grip on himself. "I can't get the children out of my mind, or the image of Donald coming out of that house with them. Or the obsession that I'm having over this open-pit mine. Do you know that I was afraid for a moment there that the house had been set on fire intentionally to throw me off the story? How stupid is that? But it's gotten deep inside me, this story, the open pit, and I can't get it out of my mind. There's more to this than an open-pit mine, and I haven't a clue what it is and because of my own ignorance I've begun manufacturing my own evils. Gods and devils are born out of ignorance, have been since the beginning of time and thunder, but so help me God that's what I thought, feared, that someone wanted to throw me off the story, was sending me a warning. But the Fire Marshall's findings pointed to faulty wiring. And any sane assessment of my paranoia would have told me that if it was a warning it would have been something like a physical threat or a firebombing of the *Witness* office, not some corporate CEO trying to off an editor's family."

"And not Donald MacNaughton risking his life to save your children."

"No, not Donald."

"Are you still enemies?"

"Naw. We'll never see eye to eye but I think Donald has a blind eye when it comes to the mine. He's ambitious. Mrs. Big Sandy hit the nail on the head when she said that he'd sell out the town for a Cabinet post. Not in his eyes, of course. Politicians have a way of spinning gold out of coal. But that's what an open pit would do, change things here beyond recall, ripping up the dunes, and no matter what the Minister of Environment says, once this starts, this company is going to follow whatever coal they find wherever it leads. Once the investment is made and jobs are created, there's no turning back. And whenever whatever coal they're searching for is gone the company will go, and nothing here will be familiar any more. This town survived one collapse of the coal industry but another will doom it. The town's not like the sea. This shoreline can be destroyed by an August storm, and two days later it's healed and healthy again. I don't believe Shean has that kind of resilience. But tomorrow I'll have to forget about this for a while and drive the children to the airport, send them off to their mother."

Rita thought for moment before venturing, "I'm off tomorrow. Would you like company to the airport, especially coming back from it?" She sensed David's hesitation and made an immediate retreat. "I'm sorry, David. Of course you just want to be with your children. Please forget I even mentioned it. I understand."

"No, you don't understand, Rita. What I was going to say is that after I saw the children safely off, I planned to go into Halifax and file a stack of Freedom of Information requests with the Department of Mines and Minerals, and then go to the provincial archives and research their mining logs, see if there's anything from back then, back when Shean was still a mining town, to throw a light on what's happening now. I was going to get a hotel for the night. But I can delay all that if you'd like to come. Come, please."

A silence hung between them for the length of a wave or two lapping on shore.

"Actually, I'm off for the next two days," Rita said. And what happened next came as naturally as though they had been lovers for months or years, their passion undisturbed by the grittiness of the sand or the cooling predawn air. Afterwards, they swam in the large private pool that was the Gulf of St. Lawrence, dried and dressed, parting in the parking lot with David's reminder that he would be picking her up at her house in a few hours.

| 46 |

"**W**ell?!"

Rita MacDonald looked up from her cup of tea into the benign inquisition on Mrs. Big Sandy's face, the set of her mouth, the knowing in her eyes. Rita knew she was wearing last night like an aura over which she had no control.

"Well what?" asked Ronald MacDonald looking up from his prunes and porridge to glance from one woman's face to the other's for an answer to his question.

"It's women's talk," Mrs. Big Sandy answered without taking her eyes from Rita's.

"No it's not," Ronald replied. "Women's talk don't stop at Well! Women's talk begins at Well! Your mother never got it said, whatever it was, under the time it takes to boil an egg, and you're no different." He dropped his attention back to the fact that he was an old man eating prunes and porridge. When did that happen, he wondered, remembering bacon and eggs and buttered toast, and left the women to themselves.

Mrs. Big Sandy raised her eyebrows, silently repeating the question, and Rita could feel the blood welling up into her cheeks and could not will it away. Mrs. Big Sandy lowered her head then, a confirming nod that last night was just as she suspected, Rita trying to tiptoe in after four in the morning. What kind of fool did the girl take this old woman to be? I read more than tea leaves, dearie, she said to herself. Then she let the girl go and went to the stove to freshen her cup, going back too to her own thoughts of Sandy's ghost, believing she had willed him back into being.

While Mrs. Big Sandy's back was to them, Rita explained to her father that she was going to Halifax with David Cameron, that he had to take his children to the airport, and that they might stay in the city overnight.

Mrs. Big Sandy's bulk whirled like a ballerina, her face filled with suspicion, listening while Ronald said, "That's nice, Rita. Will you be staying with friends?"

"With a friend, yes, Dad," she answered diplomatically while the old woman snorted her personal judgement and turned back to the stove.

Tony and Mary were buckled into the back seat when David drove into Rita's yard but when Rita came out of the house and saw the two sullen children she opened the back door. "Tony, shouldn't you be riding up front with your father?" she asked, the boy's eyes brightening as he unbuckled the belt. Rita slipped into his place beside Mary, and caught David's eyes in the rear-view mirror. "Gender regressive perhaps, but the right thing to do under the circumstances." He answered with an agreeing wink.

Near Truro, an hour away from the airport and well ahead of the children's departure time, David veered the car into the off lane and into that town's gasoline alley.

"Where are we going to eat?" he asked his passengers.

"McDonald's!" shouted half the occupants in the car with unsuppressed excitement. "They have toys in their Happy Meals," Mary said, strengthening the argument.

David and Rita communicated via the rear-view mirror again.

"I can't not do this, Rita."

"Your children will be politicized enough just living in the same house with a newspaper editor, I imagine. No need of dragging them into Dad's clan warfare, but I'll need two things from you. A solemn oath never to mention this to my father and a bag to put over my head while I'm in there."

"And I'll need something from you, young man," David said, holding his hand out to Tony. "Your camera. I'm confiscating it for the duration of our time in there. There will be no digital documentation of this moral crime against Ronald MacDonald for you to post on your Facebook. I'll return it when we get out of there." For the price of a Big Mac, the almost-nine-year-old Tony surrendered the tool of his profession.

| 47 |

After watching the children's plane leave the runway, David and Rita drove toward Halifax.

"What will you be looking for in the city?"

"I want to go through the public archives. Coal reports should be logged there every year by mine inspectors and I want to see if there's anything I can use in the next issue that sets any kind of precedent for what's being proposed. I'd like to know if anything like this was ever considered or discussed before."

In the early morning hours before their departure, he had spent several hours downloading and printing Freedom of Information forms. He crafted his multiple requests to cover all the possibilities he could imagine in his attempt to unearth a document or documents that would reveal Resource Reclamations's intentions in Shean. Because he didn't have solid knowledge to guide him, the wide-ranging requests really amounted to a shotgun approach, the hope being that one of his requests would strike the mark, whether it was confirmation of an open pit, or a long-term plan for some other development disguised as an interest in coal or an actual mini-laboratory for experimenting with the concept of clean coal. His imagination had exhausted itself in producing more than twenty requests under the *Freedom of Information Act*.

Their first stop was the Department of Mines and Minerals where, after waiting for a few minutes, it was clear that no receptionist was going to greet them. David looked at his watch. Just past noon. Lunchtime. Rita and he were discussing whether to wait or return when a man noticed them through his open office door. "Can I help you?"

David placed the stack of FOI forms on the desk along with a company check, explaining that he would like replies as soon as possible. The bureaucrat flipped through the documents then placed his hand on them, picked up the check and examined it, looking at the signature. "Mr. Cameron, is it? Mr. David Cameron?" he asked. "Well, Mr. Cameron, you do understand that under section 6, article b of the Freedom of Information Act that your requests must have sufficient particulars to enable one of us in this office to easily find the information you want in order to provide you with the record. And that under Section 9, article 1, 9 (1) The head of a public body may extend the time provided for in Sections 7 or 23 of the act, up to thirty days, or with the Review Officer's permission, for a longer period if more time is needed. You can examine those conditions that can cause delays by referring to articles a, b, and c under Section 9, by looking up the document online. You do understand this, I assume."

David stared at the man's stony face, wondering where he might have seen it before. If he had seen it before, he was sure they had never met. "What I seem to understand you saying is that I may not get my information a.s.a.p. Is that what you're telling me?"

"My intention is to emphasize that these applications need to be specific as to the information you are requesting, or the issue you are interested in, in order for us to provide you with the documents you are requesting. Specificity is essential. I can't underline that sharply enough. Specificity is essential. Even then, the ultimate decision regarding the release of the requested information will rest with the deputy minister."

"And you're not him."

"No. Now is there anything else?"

David hadn't expected any more than he had received, the standard bureaucratic stick-handling, but his purpose had been achieved. It was a shotgun scattering of questions hoping to unearth information when he wasn't confident that he knew what he was looking for.

"Do you think Mr. Specificity will find your requests specific enough?" Rita asked as they walked away from the government building.

"Specifically speaking, I think that the answer may be specifically no," David replied. "Odd little man," Rita remarked.

By contrast, at the public archives the couple was courteously shown toward shelves of annual reports on mining activities throughout Nova Scotia dating back to the 1800s. Far from digitized, they required searching through to isolate those pertaining solely to Shean, and scanning what were often handwritten accounts and updates.

Between them they quickly acquired a facility for scanning the reports, David making notes when necessary and Rita pointing out to him any anomaly she encountered. The research, generally fruitless, moved along rapidly. They were working against the clock toward closing time when Rita, riffling through mine-related documents, suddenly caught her breath and brought a tome to David.

"Look at these letters, David," Rita said, pointing out two pieces of correspondence – from 1880 indicating that the provincial government had granted to two speculators a piece of land in Cape Breton not far from Shean.

"This one's dated March 29, 1880," he said, leafing through the handwritten pages, "from a Francis Ellershausen and a J. E. Burchell, written to Hon. Simon Holmes, Provincial Secretary. It was their intention to drain Nova Scotia's largest body of fresh water and drill it for oil. Listen to this, 'It's true that when we first projected the scheme of draining Lake Ainslie and applied for the grant we did not hesitate to say we did not seek the oil, we were led to do so for two reasons, first, we did not believe oil existed there in ... quantities, and second, we imagined the cost of draining the lake would not exceed the sum of fifteen thousand dollars.' It goes on to say that the new costs of draining the lake will exceed more than a hundred thousand dollars and asks the government to give royalty-free access to the oil when they do drain the lake.

"This second letter dated a few days later, April 2, 1880, is from a W. H. Blanchard of Windsor, also to Simon Holmes, and he says that he has been informed by Ellershausen that 'in the Attorney General letter certifying that the grant of Lake Ainslie will pass to him on completion if the ... special reservation of the oil rights in this whole area is made .... I take the liberty of urging that the government should assist in developing that oil region (if oil exists there) by making a free grant of a considerable area to the parties draining the lake on condition that the lake is drained.' He asks the Attorney General to encourage the government to give serious consideration to this matter."

"Matter? How can anyone reduce the draining of Lake Ainslie to a 'matter'? What did they even use oil for that long ago?"

"I don't know a lot about the history of oil, but I do know that by the 1880s the use of whale oil was declining in favour of processed oil, mostly for lamps and lanterns. And the first cars were starting to appear. But probably the significance of this date, this era, is that the oil was becoming more and more important. It was about then that the Rockefellers created Standard Oil, and perhaps our two speculators here saw themselves as the next Rockefellers."

"But why would they say at first that it wasn't oil they were after?"

"They were probably trying to protect their secret. Not unlike Resource Reclamations. But once the cost of draining Lake Ainslie escalated, the speculators wanted to keep all the rewards so they recommended the Nova Scotia government waive its right to royalties. Fortunately the government was as greedy as

Ellershausen and Burchell and refused, so the project died. We may not be that fortunate in Shean since the government and the corporation seem committed together."

"Lake Ainslie!" Rita said in disbelief.

"Lake Ainslie is twelve miles long, five miles wide," David said, adding nothing new to Rita's knowledge of the geography but needing to evoke the scale of what had once been planned for a lake whose waters fed part of the famous Margaree River, so valuable for its salmon and beauty that the federal government declared it a Canadian Heritage River. "What strikes me about the whole silly project isn't the oil. Speculation about that comes round every few years when prices rise through the ceiling. What strikes me is that these men thought they could drain the lake, destroy who-knows-what in the process, all on a possibility – maybe gas, maybe oil, or maybe something that was never there to begin with."

"They actually wanted to build channels around the lake to divert the feeder brooks until the whole lake drained down into the Southwest Margaree River. Then what, David? When they got the damned oil just let the water back in and fill the lake again? But would it ever have filled up the same way, I wonder, with fat trout and the feeding of that wonderful salmon river? What about the childhood boogeyman we used to hear about, the Lake Ainslie Monster? My guess is that none of it would have come back – the fish, the monster stories. It would have been a refilled lake that would have created a toxic brew that would have made Lake Ainslie a dead zone, probably to this day."

"Before or after supper?" Rita asked once David's arms had encircled her in the hotel room.

"We could do both," David reasoned as they undressed each other, entered the shower for a leisurely and tormented teasing under the cleansing spray, this time making slow, passionate love on the large bed, not hurriedly and hungrily as they had on the midnight beach. The whole night lay ahead of them, unencumbered by any responsibility except to each other.

Their appetites for each other temporarily abated, they scanned the menu of the Spring Garden Road restaurant they had agreed to try. While they talked, mussels and panfried haddock and medium-rare steak and un-tallied cups of coffee came and went. Whatever directions their conversations took, all led back to Shean's mysterious future.

"Constable Crimebuster! What brings you here today?" Two days after their return from Halifax, David's spirits were high as he cheerfully addressed Corporal Noseworthy's visit to the newspaper office.

"Investigating a crime, David, and hoping you can help me."

"My sources are sealed up tight within my ever-lapsing memory, but if there's been a crime, I'm always interested." David flipped open a notebook on his desk.

"Actually, I'm interviewing suspects."

"And we have some here at the *Witness*? Don't say you found out it was me and not Big Sandy who put sugar in the gas tanks of Resource Reclamations's machinery."

"If you want to plead guilty to that one too, it would do wonders for my crime clearance record," the corporal said.

"That one too'? What is it you're investigating?"

"Three days ago someone broke into Johnny Petticoat's basement and stole an estimated thirty bottles of wine he had recently set. I've already charged Don Alex and he vaguely remembers that he was drinking with you and Maddie Casey. He doesn't remember if both of you were with him during the break-in."

"For the love of Jesus, Corporal, are you serious? You are serious!"

"Just following up. I have an independent witness who will swear that she saw you drinking with Don Alex and Maddie, and that your breath smelled strongly of alcohol."

"Witness! Nobody saw me with them except..."

Noseworthy's face lost its self-control and broke into a smile. "I was having a coffee with Rita MacDonald at the Manor last night during my rounds and told her about the break-in. She told me about the fire at the beach. But I'm not here just to pull your leg, David. There was a break-in and I know it was Don Alex and I want to know if you can tell me anything about the circumstances surrounding it. He will be charged, and maybe Mad Maddie, and I hope you won't be."

"What I can tell you is that no crime was committed because nothing of value was stolen. I know. I had a mouthful of the stuff and I'd sooner swallow Listerine. Johnny Petticoat's wine couldn't have been more than a couple of days old. Maybe by Christmas it would be palatable but Don Alex must have been desperate to have to steal it. And I can't imagine that Maddie was with him. He was working, or AWOL from work, keeping Don Alex company on the beach, but he wasn't drinking."

"But Maddie does have a record."

"Yeah, about fifty Drunk on the Street charges."

"And at least one charge of theft over five thousand dollars..."

"Oh, come on, Harry. Did you read those charges? Maddie was charged with stealing property valued over $5000. He broke into the Dollar Store for Christ's sake. He had to make about two hundred trips from the store to his place with his pockets full and jacket stuffed with stuff. It took him so long to steal five thousand dollars' worth of inventory that he was still stuffing his jacket when the store opened in the morning. Even the judge was belly laughing, and Maddie got three months and restitution. It took him almost fifteen days just to carry all the stuff back to the store. That led to the largest fifty-cent sale in this town's history."

"Okay, so I'm not dealing with the crime of the century here, but I have a job to do and I will need to get a statement from you. I'd appreciate it if you'd stop by the office some time today. Can you do that?"

David nodded that he would, watched the officer leave, then dialled Rita's number.

"Dragging me into the Shean crime scene, are you?" he asked when Rita answered.

"I did mention the party at the beach, but you got off easy. I might have charged you with sexual assault except that I was afraid you might counter those charges with some of your own and I'd need to plead guilty. But I couldn't pass up the chance to involve you in a police investigation when I heard about Don Alex stealing John Petticoat's wine, so I told the policeman at the Manor last night."

"Oh, and does he stop by often?"

"Yes, when he's working nights and things are quiet Harry stops by for a cup of coffee and a chat."

Harry? "Most nights? Really?"

"Yes, David, really."

Tim Donovan strolled into the office and nodded to David, signalling that he had something to tell him.

"What've you got, Tim?"

"For this week's paper? There's the usual gossip we pass off for news around here, but Shelly Ross was telling me last night at the Five Bucks that Donald MacNaughton has called a special in-camera session of council for tonight. Did you know about it?"

"Nope. And there's been no notification. Not in the email. Nowhere. What time?"

"I didn't actually ask her since I was more interested in watching the way she moves to the music than probing ... well, probing for information. Do you want me to find out when? Am I going to have to go to that meeting?"

"Don't look so scared. I'll do it so we can leave your weekend intact. In camera? What does His Worship have to share that requires a closed-door meeting? Oh, that naughty MacNaughton."

"Are you going to use that in the paper? Naughty MacNaughton."

"No. Just playing with words, and you're not to use it either."

"Why bother? They're going to tell you it's in camera and the minutes aren't for public consumption. You're better off going to the Five Bucks. You might learn more about the meeting there than at the town hall."

"I can't let Donald off that easy. I'll be waiting for him when he comes out. By law, they have to open the meeting, even an in-camera one, with a public meeting, even if it's just for five minutes. And if they make a decision in camera, they have to pass a motion in the public session, which means I get to ask questions."

"Questions he won't answer."

"That in itself is an answer."

Donald MacNaughton was surprised to see David Cameron sitting in the public gallery when council met in open session long enough to get a motion to move in camera. The mayor stared at the editor until David finally said, "If you let me stay for the secret meeting, Mr. Mayor, I promise I won't tell anybody what I hear." Smiling, he picked up his camera case and notebook and retreated to the corridor where the public and press were always banished during behind-closed-doors sessions of council.

MacNaughton was even more surprised two hours later to see David Cameron still outside, busy scribbling notes to himself toward an editorial about closed sessions of council. Turning the notebook to a fresh page, David listened to the motion to adjourn, reminding the council that according to its own by-laws, the public and press had to be provided with a fifteen-minute question period after each meeting. David planned to use those fifteen minutes.

"Mr. Mayor, what was discussed in camera?"

"If I wanted you to know that, Mr. Cameron, I'd have invited you to join us."

"Will a motion be coming out of this meeting?"

"The meeting was for information only," the mayor said, David detecting a lack of the man's usual enthusiasm in sparring with the press. More important to the editor, he could sense James Jamison staring hard at him, as if willing him to read his mind, yet when he looked at Jamison, the councillor couldn't keep eye contact.

Leaving the meeting, David felt that if he was to learn anything, it would be from Jamison, but Jamison was a man of integrity who would not easily surrender council secrets – even when he disagreed strongly with them.

| 49 |

David opened the email from Jim Turner as part of his regular sifting of what's trash and what's news. It had been well over a week since Bethany and Jim had returned to Toronto but David's first communication with them came in an email while the editor was sifting through the daily download of trash and newsworthy press releases.

David, Just a reminder, in case it slipped your mind, that it's someone's birthday today. It is ten am Toronto time. If you get this in the next two hours call my desk – Jim

David looked up at the calendar. "Oh, Jesus," he said, reaching for the desk phone and dialling the number logged among a couple of hundred cards in his Rolodex, promising himself once again that one of these days he was going to enter them in his online address book. "Hello, Jim."

Their small talk laid aside, Jim handed the phone to Tony.

"Happy birthday, son. Doesn't Toronto have anything more exciting than Jim's job for a fellow to spend his ninth birthday?"

"I'm working, Dad. Half a day twice a week with Jim. Mary has a job with Bethany. She got to go out to Canada's Wonderland and everything. Bethany said she had to do a story but I didn't see it in the paper yet." Tony's voice dropped, and David could imagine his son walking a distance away from Jim for privacy. "It's called a desk job. Jim has to be here almost all the time. His job's not like yours where you don't have to do anything if you don't want to, just go to the beach. We're going to a place called Bay Street today. Are there any rides there, Dad?"

"Everybody gets taken for a ride on Bay Street, Tony. Look, I'm just kidding you, there are no rides there, but I'm sure Jim or your mother will get you out to Wonderland before the day is over. I wish I was there to take..."

"Dad!" Tony interrupted, remembering something. "You never gave me back my camera. Remember when we went to McDonald's? You said you'd give it back to me at the airport and you didn't."

"Tony, I forgot," David answered, recalling that he had stashed the small digital camera in the glove compartment before they went into the restaurant. "Do you want me to send it out?"

"No, Mom's letting me have hers while I'm here. It's bigger, like a real camera, like the one you use. But I wanted to show her my pictures that I took at home, the ones of you and grandma and the house where we're staying now and other stuff. Will you put it on my Facebook page?"

"Of course. But you'll have to walk me through it. How about I call you tonight when I get home and you can tell me what to do?"

"Okay, but you should learn yourself. I'm not always going to be here, you know."

"Well, there's no rush because I figure I'll have you lying around the house for at least the next ten years, and then maybe you'll win the Cape Breton lottery and I'll have you around for good."

"Huh?"

"Maybe you'll marry a nurse or a teacher ... oh, never mind. Can I talk to Jim? Have a happy birthday, Tony, and when you get home here to Shean we'll have another one."

The phone changed voices as Jim's deeper tone said, "Hello again."

"Bay Street? Jim, you're taking my son to Bay Street? Couldn't you take him to some place civilized? Where do the hookers hang out now? Or have they finally found their rightful home on Bay Street where all the mutual funds pimps hang out?"

Now it was Jim's voice that dropped to a confidential tone. "Don't worry, I won't corrupt the lad by exposing him to the seamy underside of capitalism. I'm only the boy's godfather, not his socialist-ranting editor and biological father. We're meeting Alexandra later, on Bay Street by the way, where the young man's mother has a meeting this afternoon, and then we're teaming up with Bethany and Mary and we're all going to Canada's Wonderland. But it's a surprise, so I'm whispering. Now tell me what's happening on the open-pit front."

"Still in the dark. Filed a score of freedom of information requests with the Department of Mines and Minerals but the bureaucrat I spoke with didn't leave me much hope that I would hear back in the next decade. Nobody in town is swallowing the coal reclamation story. Christ, this town was built on coal. People understand it and how much of it it takes to make an industry. You can't reclaim that much out of a few hundred acres of mine waste. I keep trying to dig into C.J.M. Lord's shady past, even assigned a researcher to scour the Internet, Rita's father, Ronald. You met him."

"Yeah, another anti-corporate like yourself, except that he has an actual cause that he's trying to rally his fellow clansmen around. But I suspect that giving him this job, a job I'm sure Tim Donovan could do in a single evening with his eyes closed, you get to go to Ronald's house and check up on him. When Rita is home that is. Mrs. MacArthur still chaperoning the two of you?"

"Ronald's good. He's got a gift in his old age for modern technology."

"I know, but Tim's good, too. I just wanted to say that. The week we worked with him..."

"For him."

"...for him, he impressed both Bethany and myself. If he ever decides to come this way..."

"I suspect he will. A bit of a Casanova Tim is, and it's a small town so eventually the pickings will get slimmer and slimmer and he'll be off to greener pastures."

"Not much pasture land in Toronto, but just about everything else he needs to indulge his reputation as a journalist and as a ladies man."

"Ladies man? Isn't that a bit outdated, or is it just us who are outdated?"

"Hell, David, don't be trying to age us. We're not forty yet and they say sixty is the new forty and so that makes us what – Tim's contemporaries? Although I don't think I'll share that thought with Bethany. Have to make a few calls and get a final draft to the editor before Tony and I set off for Bay Street."

David said goodbye to his son, feeling a loneliness at not being able to share this day with him. He buried the loneliness by returning to the sorting of the mail in his box, distractedly deleting online pitches for Viagra, thinking momentarily that feeling as impotent as he was about the Resource Reclamations story, perhaps he should order a bottle for himself.

Tony was at the far end of the phone line guiding his father through the steps to load the pictures from his camera onto his Facebook page. David knew how to unload the camera into the computer – he did it two or three times a week with his own camera at the office – but he had never ventured into the area of social networking, where the kids, both of them, were light years ahead of him. Tony was adept enough that from Toronto he could manage to get inside their home computer in Shean and bring up his own Facebook page and direct his father's unloading of the camera, more than 150 pictures, that he would then be able to show to his mother.

And because his father was already there looking at the page, Tony showed him the pictures of Wonderland that he had taken and posted for his friends to see. It had been a family affair full of birthday fun that probed like a tongue at the cavity of loneliness David had felt earlier.

The youngster was gone and David was alone in his home office, setting the boy's pictures to rotate through a slide show. The show had already begun by the time he returned to his office with a drink. A picture of the Beach Burger Palace was on the screen, followed by a picture of a foil-wrapped beach burger, then the burger itself undressed from the foil. The next picture was of the burger with a bite out of it, then one with two bites missing, and David silently congratulated himself on disarming his son of his camera before their visit to McDonald's. That subversive visit might also have made it to Tony's Facebook where Ronald MacDonald might have seen a photo of Rita biting into a Big Mac. Picture by picture, bite by bite, the beach burger diminished until there was only the empty wrapper and some traces of orange-coloured sauce that was the secret to the beach burger's appeal.

The slide show began again from the beginning, and David watched himself at the beach, wondering which time this was, thinking about how he had made time to get the children there as often as he could before they left for Toronto. He mused about how those efforts to be a single parent had been translated by his own child into a questionable work ethic. He recalled the conversation with his son, who described Jim Turner as having "a desk job," which in the child's mind translated to "real job." Nothing like his father, who could leave his job and go to the beach whenever he wanted. What was he teaching the boy? David really didn't care. He was confident enough that Tony and Mary would decide for themselves that their father had cared more for them than his job when they were growing up, never mind that they might be missing some vital information about him, such as the perhaps sixty hours a week of his time that was wholly devoted to the *Witness* in one or another of his multiple roles with the paper.

There was a nice photograph of Mary and her grandmother, obviously taken on a sunny Sunday afternoon at the race track, which his mother preferred even to her twice weekly bingo games when summer harness racing returned for its annual season in Shean.

And then there was a picture of Jim Turner behind the wheel of his car, then a strange still life of a coffee mug on a desk, not his desk, and not one from the *Witness* office, pictures of the whole desk, shots from distorted angles, a picture of three framed certificates on one wall beside a fragment of another picture, and then a picture of Jim in conversation with a man David recognized as the engineer at the open-pit mine site. The next picture was of the Beach Burger Palace.

David stopped the slide show and went back to the group of earlier pictures, bringing them up one by one, until he came to the certificates. He enlarged the top one, an engineering degree awarded to C.J.M. Lord. "When in the hell...?"

It was too late now to call Tony back, and there was no answer at Bethany and Jim's, so David fixed himself another drink and came back to the screen. He couldn't even get a call back from Lord, and Tony had wandered freely through the man's office, according to the visual evidence he was now looking at.

The certificates were for mine engineering, a business degree from a university David had never heard of and an honorary doctorate of humanities from the same university. Maybe this was a way into Lord's background.

And what would he find there that would be any more damaging than the news stories about the environmental damage already done, but profitably done, by earlier corporations he headed? Lord was a corporate CEO. News headlines had been filled since the beginning of the current millennium with CEOs and their scandals, thefts, unearned bonuses and hundreds of thousands of financially ruined lives while they continued to live off their questionable fortunes. The handful that had gone to jail were usually incarcerated in first-class conditions. If David or Donald had been sent to reform school in Shelburne for the shooting of Mrs. Big Sandy they would have had it a lot harder than any corrupt corporate CEO.

Something attached to the wall with push pins alongside the certificates drew David's attention. It was unframed, push pins at top and bottom corners. Only a small percentage of it had been caught by Tony's camera. It seemed to be a detailed blueprint. David went through his son's other pictures to see if a wider shot had caught the whole thing, but he was disappointed. Why? Because he desperately wanted it to be important.

He was on his third drink now. His mother was in bed, the children were screaming their absence with a deep silence and he was feeling desperately inadequate at a job he once felt he had mastered. He stared at the blueprint fragment, willing himself to see the rest of it, sensing that it was recognizable if he could just concentrate hard enough.

It was his mother's hand shaking his shoulder that woke him up, still sitting upright. The computer had gone into hibernation and the sun was leaking early light through the window. She removed the empty glass, told him to lie down for a couple of hours, that she would wake him.

At the office David plugged his flash drive into his desk computer and through it projected the image from Tony's camera onto the big screen that hung on the wall, as revered as a da Vinci painting. The office legend was that David bought it so that details of certain important pictures could be viewed on a larger scale, and he and Tim may even have used it for that purpose once or twice, but on the late nights of laying out the paper, baseball and hockey games seemed to bring comfort to Tim and his boss. By day, the rest of the staff were convinced that their own soap opera addictions were a secret. But for the moment the big screen was back to its original purpose. The mystery of the slice of blueprint his son had captured just grew larger with the big screen image of it, revealing nothing to David as he studied it over a cup of black coffee.

"Quick, Tim, look at the screen and tell me what you see."

Tim turned, looked. "A fortress?"

"Really?"

"Yeah. What is it?"

David explained.

"Still reminds me of a fortress. Doesn't this tall greyish mass here look like a fortress wall? Or a prison wall. Hell, maybe that's it. They're going to build a massive prison right here in the middle of Shean and the company and the government are working out the best way to spin it. Lot of jobs or not, not everybody is going to join the welcoming party when those inmates come marching it. Nightmares of serial killer escapes and all that. If this is a picture of it, then it's a done deal so it doesn't really matter what people feel. Protestors are just going through the motions. What do you think?" Tim asked his editor of his spur of the moment reasoning.

David liked it. "Want to fly that balloon? An opinion piece under your byline repeating what you just said to me? My gut tells me you're not right but it also thinks you're on the right track. I'm so tied up in open-pit mining conspiracies that I know I'm not thinking broadly enough. Whatever it is, people are being set up for it. I got a letter this morning," David said, holding up an official-looking page. "It's from the Department of Mines and Minerals rejecting every one of my Freedom of Information inquiries. Just a note saying there are no documents on file of an open-pit mine planned within the town limits of Shean.

"The bureaucrat who handled my requests said the forms generally weren't specific enough for staff to follow the leads and find the appropriate subject of the requests. We both know that even when they do find information it takes an average of several weeks or months. And when information does come along, it's usually long after you've forgotten why you were even asking for it. Or else they will send you pages and pages of stuff all blacked out because it's too confidential for you or me to know. But what they will not do, what they never do, Tim, is process FOI requests for at least a month of Sundays. Judging from the postmark, all mine were processed and replied to in three days."

"Gives you the feeling you aren't asking the right questions, huh," Tim said, turning back to his desk and settling in. "Did you know Simon Anderson died yesterday, three days short of his one hundredth birthday. Guess I won't have to go after his picture after all. Going to miss him. A hundred years old and sharp as a tack. He was my go-to guy when I needed a source for old age, or war memories, or what it was like to spend a winter in a pulp camp, stories I'll never hear again. What I'd like to do, if it's okay with you, is make something of his passing. Instead of the generic Centenarian Passes Away Peacefully I'd like to go through what I've already got and sort of reconstruct his life, a feature to make up for his falling short of the finish line."

David didn't even bother with so much as a nod of approval, swivelling his chair back to look at the picture on the big screen. He was already looking forward to reading what Tim had in mind, and so would a lot of other readers. David was so focussed on the image, trying to imagine the rest of it, evoke it into being like a reading from the bottom of one of Mrs. Big Sandy's tea-cups, that he jumped when suddenly Donald MacNaughton was there, bending down and whispering hoarsely in his ear, "What's that?"

"Jesus, Donald! You can't go around scaring people like that. We're not all like you, you know. Some of us have hearts."

"So what is it?" Donald asked again, staring at the image.

"C.J.M. Lord's office."

"Never been there," Donald said, looking closer. "What kind of an office is this?"

"It's not actually his office. It's a piece of blueprint pinned on his office wall. Thought maybe you could tell me what it is. You've never been there? That's hard to believe."

"Oh I've been to the trailer, met with Mr. Lord in the reception area. Never invited me into his office, the one with his name on it. Not really likeable, our Mr. Lord, but he's all we've got if Shean is going to get out of this goddamned lifelong depression. David, if you're going to be speculating about the in-camera session, well I'm not stupid enough to tell you how to run your newspaper, but I'm asking you to think hard about the choices you're making on this reclamation development, that's all I'm asking." Donald walked toward the door before David could turn his statement into a debate and maybe weasel some actual information out of the mayor.

| 50 |

Tim Donovan's speculative piece on plans to build a federal prison in Shean had the effect David had been hoping for: the park, the Grill and the Five Bucks were all hosting lively debates on what such an economic engine would mean for the town, which seemed equally divided on the issue.

The primary purpose of a prison, many argued, was to create jobs for people as guards, cooks and whatnots, good government jobs with pension benefits. Just supplying the prison with food and fuel and other whatnots would be good for local businesses, not to mention all those guards' wives shopping at the Co-op with their husbands' big paycheques. This chauvinistic position was soon assaulted by several women who wanted to know why women wouldn't be hired as guards. Because it's not a women's prison, came the retort. How do you know? Well, I'm just assuming... Well, assume all you want but there's women who need to be locked up too, you know...Oh, I know! I know! I can think of a few myself! What do you mean by that? Nothing, just saying you're right, maybe it will be a women's prison...

Others were more tepid about the prospect of a prison, even if the federal government had committed to a policy of building prisons as if they were fast food franchises, putting them all over the country. What kind of people would that attract to Shean?

Families of criminals are usually criminals themselves and how many of them would be moving here to be near their loved ones? But not all the families of crooks are crooks, others argued. Look at the Haleys.

From childhood, Buddy Haley, the youngest of the Haley clan, had wreaked havoc in Shean, a one-boy crime spree. From arson he graduated to breaking and entering, hot-wiring cars, drinking and assault. After several terms in the Shean jail, Buddy moved on to Ontario where he became involved in more serious crimes. Currently, he was serving several years in Kingston Penitentiary. His family was a fine one, well liked and never judged by their son's criminal meanness.

But what if they send him back here? Maybe that's why they're building the prison here, just to get him out of Ontario. They don't want Maritimers up there at the best of times and Buddy Haley can barely be called the best of times! But why do they want to build all these prisons anyway?

Because crime is good for the economy. When there's crime we need more police and more prison guards and more guns and more locks and more.... Okay, okay, I get it. So what if it comes? Will you be applying for a job? Well, if it's a women's prison like they're saying, I'm thinking that the wife would be a good guard. Can't sneak out of the house on her without a "Where do you think you're going?" coming at me from behind those beanbags she wears on her eyes when she's sleeping.

What did not materialize for the *Witness* reporters was a confirmation or denial of a federal prison planned for Shean. Nothing. No minister would comment. No councillor would comment. No one in C.J.M. Lord's office would comment. Tim Donovan's opinion piece had flushed out nothing.

James Jamison was in the Gulf Grill having a morning coffee as David had hoped. He wasn't always there, not a regular but patronage was a way for any politician to keep his pulse on the community, even if that meant putting up with people lobbying him for something, and this morning it was for jobs at the new prison, jobs for their sons, brothers-in-law and, in a few cases, themselves. He seemed almost to welcome David's presence in the booth.

"I've got nothing to say," he warned the reporter.

"I'm not asking you to say anything, James, but I have to admit I'm curious. Why hold an in-camera session without coming out of it with a motion? You couldn't have been transferring land to the MacNaughton clan or raising water taxes, so I have to wonder why council would spend two hours in a session in which nothing seems to have been accomplished."

"Oh, something was accomplished alright," Jamison conceded.

"But you can't tell me anything."

"There's nothing to tell, David. That's the whole damned problem!" Jamison's irritation was growing, not with David but with whatever happened in the meeting. David signalled for two more cups of coffee, sensing a crack in the wall of Jamison's caucus solidarity.

"People have a right to know," David said, feeling the emptiness of the words he had used so often in his professional life, knowing that in most cases people really didn't give a damn what politicians were up to. He thought of the Freedom of Information requests he had made and that some bureaucratic minion or Cabinet minister had determined he did not have a right to.

Jamison cracked a caustic smile. "Right to know, do they? And how is they have a greater right to know than I do?"

"I don't follow you."

"You running a tape recorder?" David shook his head, feeling the thrill of the chase coming to an end. "This is not for your newspaper, background only, okay? And it never came from me. What's going to happen in a few weeks, a couple of weeks maybe, is that there is going to be a major announcement made concerning the Shean project."

"What the hell is the project?"

"That's the tricky part. I don't know.

The purpose of the in-camera session was for MacNaughton to inform us, council, that the premier's office was placing an embargo of any information concerning the Shean project. Cabinet, caucus, bureaucrats, company officials, even lowly municipal councillors are forbidden from speaking with the press or anyone. No blogs, social networking, tweeting, whatever the hell that is, or any public discussion. The project will be unveiled by the premier and Mr. Lord when everything is ready. The federal government seems to be onside in this, too. So you see, David, I couldn't tell you anything even if I wanted to. You'll just have to find out for yourself because, as you said, the people have a right to know."

"MacNaughton is going along with this?"

"Yes, he is. Know why? Because he doesn't have any more of a clue about what's going on than you or me. He's been the local advocate all along, but it seems to me that he's been shut out along with everyone else."

"Any ideas, James?"

"Just that it's not an open-pit mine on the MacArthur property. It can't be. In fact, I spent a lot of time last night going through the source of that rumour and you know that your newspaper is the only place it has ever been mentioned. No one – no politician and not Lord himself – has ever used those words, except to refuse comment, whether politicians or Lord himself. You just manufactured it out of whole cloth the same way you did with the prison story this week. I know what you're doing. In the face of no information the *Witness* has been trying to guess what's going on down there. But you really need some cold, hard facts if you're going to get to the bottom of this David, or people are going to begin distrusting the paper." Jamison stood to go, leaving David feeling chastened. Coming from one of the people he most respected in Shean, the criticism stung deeper than he wanted to acknowledge, and there was no denying the truth of Jamison's words.

| 51 |

David Cameron gave what he was about to do considerable thought, but not one thought hinted in even the mildest way that what he was about to do fell within his own definition of sanity. The decision was made by an irrational, irresistible compulsion he permitted himself to be powerless to resist.

James Jamison's words had underscored the *Witness*'s ineffectiveness in breaking what was probably the most important story the paper might ever have to tell. The fact that everyone associated with the project was under embargo not to speak of it meant the provincial government was making an effort to control and spin the story on its own terms. What that meant to David was that there was a side to the story that could be damaging if it leaked out ahead of the premier's planned unveiling. The government was certainly one in trouble, months away from being forced to call an election, desperately in need of winning an economic lottery for the flat broke, jobless province before such time. Its political platform needed a concrete accomplishment if there was any hope of recapturing enough votes to win re-election. All its campaign eggs seemed to be tumbling into a single basket called Shean. David had no facts, but he was certain that he had a significant clue, a fragment of a blueprint hanging on the wall of C.J.M. Lord's office. It was his need to find out what that wall hanging was that led David to his next act.

The night was clear but moonless as David donned black jeans. He was thinking he should have a hoodie but had never owned one. His substitute was his only black sweater, a heavy winter knit. Toque served as balaclava. To blacken the face or not to blacken the face? He knew it was silly to take such a minor excursion into crime so seriously but he searched under the kitchen counter and found an ancient can of black shoe polish which he rubbed over his cheeks and nose, under his eyes and across his forehead before heading quietly toward the door.

He considered his car, decided that would add stupidity to stupidity, so began walking toward the mine site by back streets. When he reached Main Street he cursed his own editorials that had argued so successfully for new, bright street lighting. Only one car was on the street. Before he could scurry out of sight he recognized it as Rita's car. The tap of a foot on the brakes made the red rear lights flare, but because he had stepped back into the shadows the car accelerated again, the nurse heading home from work, leaving him to his plan.

Across Main Street, he followed the paths least travelled in Shean, especially at night – a maze of shortcuts and trampled-down bushes he'd been familiar with since boyhood – until he found himself standing outside the chain-link fence at the darkest corner of the mine yard. Fortunately no barb- or razor-wire rimmed the top of the eight-foot fence and David, the strap of his camera bag slung over his right shoulder and under his left arm, tested his grip.

David wondered at the popular appeal of rock climbing as the toes of his heavy hiking boots struggled to find purchase in the minute openings of the metal mesh, slipping and suddenly leaving him hanging by his desperate fingers, feet hopelessly clawing for a toehold. The effort seemed so loud that he imagined the whole town waking to wonder, coming in pyjamas and housecoats to watch the newspaper editor break into the mine site. But no one came to explore the sound, more amplified inside David's fearful head than in the air.

Soon his hands closed around the top bar and David pulled himself up, swung one leg over, hoisted himself to a sitting position and looked down. In the darkness the drop down the other side was a black chasm or the proverbial bottomless pit, but he needed to do something soon because if he straddled the fence for another minute he would surely castrate himself. He eased himself over the side, holding on tight while he let his body drop slowly, the toes of his boots scrambling like hamsters against the mesh, failing to find a foothold. After dangling for a moment, David let go. Both ankles reached the ground much sooner than he anticipated and twisted out of the way of the rest of his body so that he was lying flat on his back gazing up at the stars. He tested the damage to his feet and to the ankle once broken by a slap-shot. The doctor told him it would probably become arthritic in his old age. So this is what it's going to feel like, he thought as he waited for the pain to subside. Nothing was broken, he decided, as a star broke loose from the heavens and shot across the sky. Good omen or bad?

He lay there, his camera bag under his back, rough cinder ground eating into his shoulders, telling him to smarten up. Too late for growing brains now, too late for anything, even a change of mind, because that would mean getting right back up there on the fence, perhaps crushing his nuts this time – going home no better informed than before he decided to drop down to what was appearing more and more like the wrong side of the fence. David got to his feet, the ankle a limping casualty of his pending crime. He hobbled his way toward the centre of the mine site and the construction trailer that held secrets he needed to know.

Nicknamed Mad Maddie for once having held hot coal in his hand for the length of time it took him to chug a frothy, quart of ice-cold beer, Maddie Casey sat on the step of the construction trailer, listening to the slosh of liquid in the wine bottle (one of the stolen bottles for which Don Alex might be going to jail), and considered his own life – what was worth considering. A fog had enveloped him from adolescence through adulthood.

It wasn't all to do with booze, he knew that. He just couldn't remember much beyond the old man's backhanders and the old woman's fretful rosaries. He and Phillip had knelt night after night, mumbling responses to their mother's eternal novena that the police would bring word of her husband's untimely death: in a car accident, frozen in a snowbank, beaten to death.

Bessie Casey's prayers were answered when Angry Angie Casey was found frozen to death in a snowbank – a lot of good it did her, having died of breast cancer seven years earlier. After the funeral, Maddie told Phillip he was never going to get married so he could never have kids of his own to kick in the arse whenever he felt like it, because he often felt like it.

Phillip liked the logic and swore off marrying too, and they went on living in the house as always, Maddie drinking and Phillip working occasionally as a fisherman's helper and other jobs that kept the pogey coming. Just as well he was working, Maddie told him, since Phillip really didn't have any talent for drinking. Not really. He didn't have the stamina to keep on drinking through a hangover; he fainted like a woman once when he pissed blood after a binge. Phillip, Maddie conceded, didn't have what it takes to be a real man of the bottle.

Things for Maddie had been different now for three, maybe four weeks, him being sober for however long it was. Maddie has lost count of the days and weeks, and that was a good thing, Maddie reasoned, since somebody who was trying to quit smoking once told him that you haven't quit until you forget how long it's been since your last cigarette. Three or four weeks since his last drink. He had been done with it since the day Sylvester MacNaughton offered him seven hundred dollars to sign a piece of paper, something called a quick claim. Maddie scrawled his name on the lawyerly looking piece of paper and just like that had seven hundred dollars in his hand, mostly twenties.

With his luck changing, Maddie shunned the bar and its offerings, going straight to the video lottery terminals, flashing his wad at Joe the Bartender on the way. A few hours later he didn't even have enough money left to get drunk, so he went into the back room of the Legion where they kept the shovel and stuff for breaking up ice in the winter parking lot and found an axe and came out and began pounding the screens until he was wrestled to the ground, thrown out the door, and told never to come back. But that wasn't all. The RCMP, Corporal Noseworthy in fact, pulled into the parking lot and arrested him. Cuffed hands behind him, Maddie complained that he must be the first person ever barred from the Legion for being cold sober.

The judge didn't send him to jail, suspended his sentence instead and ordered him to pay restitution of one thousand dollars. So it was an expensive start on sobriety, one that might not have lasted longer than the time it would take to raise the price of a bottle, except that fortune continued to smile fondly on Maddie. Not long after the incident at the Legion, Don Alex had seen Big Sandy's ghost and quit the job just like that. As he was standing beside the engineer who ran things when that Mr. Lord wasn't around, Maddie was offered the job. That night he and Phillip turned up for work. When the engineer asked about Phillip, Maddie explained that with Big Sandy's ghost roaming around, nobody in town would work alone, and so Phillip was hired for minimum wage just like Maddie and that's how they worked it. Phillip was off on this night because he was this big baseball fan and the Toronto Blue Jays were playing the Boston Red Sox, an arch-rival match-up if ever there was one, so Maddie let him stay home.

Maddie's ears perked as he thought he heard the sound of something moving in the mine yard.

| 52 |

David limped over the slag heaps, depending more on boyhood memory than vision, until he was standing on a hill overlooking the working section of the site: two construction trailers under a pool of light from a temporary power pole, giant silhouettes of machinery and large stocks of supplies growing nearby. He grew conscious of the sweat filling his armpits and running down his back and it wasn't all fear, it was the damned black wool sweater, a Christmas gift that was out of season in this unseasonably hot summer. At midnight it was still well above 22 degrees Celsius.

Staring down on the trailers David became aware of how little reconnaissance had gone into this half-arsed investigative reporting plan of his, but sweating and sore, he was ready to get it done and be gone. Creeping down the slag pile toward the edge of darkness, he had no idea how he would get inside. There's the door, probably locked, and a few narrow slits of windows that may slide open, one of which he might be able to wiggle through, ignoring the image of himself being stuck halfway, his feet flailing outside the trailer, his hands scrambling for something firm to pull him through. Still stuck there when C.J.M. Lord arrived at the job site in the morning. Shaking that thought, David moved along the side of the trailer to the back, which the yard light left in darkness.

A sudden squeal made him think of a cat but the scream he heard was his own. Suddenly there were voices.

"Leave me alone!"

"Stop spitting on me!"

"Leave me alone!"

"Stop spitting on me!"

"Leave me alone!"

"Stop spitting on me!"

The struggle brought the two men out into the light.

"Is that you, Mr. Cameron?" Maddie asked of the intruder, the wine bottle raised in self-defence.

"Yes," was David's embarrassed reply. He held his camera case by the strap, threatening to swing it and wallop Maddie who held his wine bottle at the ready. "I thought you weren't drinking?" he asked more calmly.

"I'm not. What ... oh this," he said, indicating the wine bottle. "Holy water. Filled it up in that barrel in the church. In case I see Big Sandy's ghost, you see. What are you doing here, Mr. Cameron, sir?"

David's ankle called for a rest and he hobbled over to the step where Maddie had earlier been contemplating his life and sat down, Maddie squatting beside him. "What're you doing here, Mr. Cameron? How'd you get here anyway? I leave the gate open or something?"

David avoided Maddie's questions and jumped right to the truth. "I was hoping to take a picture of something if I could, but it's not likely I can. It's in Mr. Lord's office and I suppose that's all locked up."

"Yup! But hell, I've a key, haven't I, and it's not like you're here to steal something. Taking a picture isn't like taking somebody's booze or their money now is it? I'm just so glad you weren't Big Sandy...." Maddie rose to his feet and took out a small ring of keys. "Come with me."

Inside the trailer he snapped on the light, flooding the reception area with fluorescence. Barely containing his relief and excitement, David took the few steps to the door marked by Lord's name, turned the knob and gained nothing. He turned to Maddie. "What?"

"Your face, Mr. Cameron, it's all dirty."

"Must have rubbed coal dust on it when I twisted my ankle." Maddie's face clouded with doubt at David's explanation, but he didn't pursue it. "Don't have a key to that one, do I, that door. But that's not always a problem. Let's see here." Maddie searched the countertop that separated staff from visitors. Taking a ballpoint pen apart, he squatted before C.J.M. Lord's door and began digging at the lock.

"Is this how you got into the Dollar Store?" David asked.

"Heard about that, did you? Nope, not this way. That door was just left open. I turned the knob and oops! Next thing I knew I was inside. Charged with theft, if you were paying attention, not breaking and entering. Learned this trade while I was in jail. Three months in the basement of the town hall for the Dollar Store. Worse than a life sentence, some says, but I got fed three times a day. Shared the same cell as Buddy Haley. Could pick any lock, that fellow. Taught me how cause we both got sick of playing crib, and besides, when Sheriff Thurber was on duty watching us he was always watching television instead and that meant he was mostly sleeping and snoring, and I can't tell you how many times me and Buddy went out for a walk. Once we even went to the Five Bucks for a beer and nobody ever said anything. Buddy's not picking many locks now. Went to Ontario to go big time and now he's doing big time in the Kingston pen. You don't pick those locks is my understanding. There you go, take all the pictures you wants to."

David stepped through the open door as Maddie's hand ran along the wall and snapped on a light. The office was just as Tony's pictures had depicted it, including the three certificates on the wall, except for one difference: there was a large empty space outlined by blue and red stick pins. The blueprint was gone.

"Damn!"

"Problem?"

"What I was hoping to get a picture of isn't here. What about the engineer's office?"

"No problem long as you're just taking pictures and nothing else. Follow me." A moment later they were inside the second office. Nothing on the engineer's wall or desk suggested the nature of the project. David had the feeling that someone was one step ahead of him. "Nothing I can do about that," Maddie said and David followed the watchman's finger to the large green and grey safe in one corner of the office.

Outside, David sat again on the step to rest his ankle, Maddie joining him. "Did you really think I was spitting on you back there?" he asked, indicating the back of the trailer with a flick of his head.

"That's what it felt like. Glad you weren't though. Glad that you're not back on the wine too. It's been awhile now, hasn't it, Matt."

"Three or four weeks. All behind me now but I just take it one day at a time, like the real alcoholics say."

"Real alcoholics?"

"You know the ones I mean, the ones that can't go without it. Pitiful, that's what I say." David was almost moved by the compassion of a man whom, outside spells in jail, no one had seen take a seriously sober breath since he was fourteen. David guessed Maddie's age to be somewhere in the mid forties now, but really he was one of those ageless and forever presences in his and the town's life.

"Well, thanks for your help, Maddie, but I think I better start for home. Twisted my ankle and it's killing me. Would you mind letting me out? The gate slammed closed behind me."

"Now did it now? Never heard of a padlock locking itself," Maddie said, leaving David scrambling for an explanation while

Maddie continued. "Big Sandy, do you suppose?" looking off into the darkness, hefting the bottle of holy water in his hands, ascertaining that his weapon was loaded.

"Could be, Maddie, yes, it could be," David said as he watched Maddie open the padlock and swing the gate open for him. "Listen, I hope we can keep this between us, about me being here tonight. Is that possible?"

"Aw, well, geez, Mr. Cameron, sir, I don't know about that. For how long do you mean?"

"What do you mean, for how long?"

"Well geez, a story like this, you screaming 'Stop spitting on me! Stop spitting on me!' and all that it was in the wine bottle was holy water, that's a hard story not to be telling when a guy's got nothing else to say. I can keep it to myself for a little while if I need to but forever's asking a lot of a guy."

"Two or three weeks, maybe?" David suggested.

Maddie paused thoughtfully, considering the weight of the burden he was being asked to carry, then sighed. "Consider it done, Mr. Cameron. Take care of that ankle now."

"Thank you. I'll drop by the next time I need a blessing."

| 53 |

Mrs. Big Sandy was a nighthawk. She was also awake with the dawn, which caused Rita to wonder when the woman slept, or if she ever slept. At any rate, the old woman's endless presence rarely presented opportunities for solitude. That Rita could find only within the walls of her own bedroom, which was not where she wanted to be. Her long habit, going back to high school, had been the comfort of the kitchen. Her father was always early to bed or, if he was up late, preferred the livingroom. Long before his stroke, and long before his computer, his choice for solitude was the livingroom, and televised hockey games.

But there was a consolation prize having her aged friend there when she got home from work at night. The tea was always ready and hot, but tonight again there were no messages for her. "And why would there be?" demanded Mrs. Big Sandy. "Mr. David Cameron being so important if he does say so himself which maybe he doesn't say so himself but thinks it, I bet. And thinks that he has more important things to do than call the MacDonald house leaving messages with me to give to you when you get home. If the man had an ounce of decency in him, he'd be calling you at work, or picking you up there and bringing you home..."

Ronald's arrival from his office ended Mrs. Big Sandy's lonely hearts talk. The man was shaking his head. "That's not a nice man, that's what I'm finding out about our sweet Lord, if you can stand the blasphemy."

"It's not a blasphemy, Dad, it's a Beatles' song – George Harrison, "My Sweet Lord." You don't know how culturally astute you are, do you? So what did you find out?"

"Oh he's a mining engineer alright, our Mr. Lord, but that wasn't good enough for him, the big money being in owning coal mines, not engineering them or whatever engineers do in mines. They don't get dirty doing it, whatever it is they do. But what David said in his paper about Lord mowing down mountains in Virginia, that's all true, unimaginable but true, and I'm wondering if he's got the same plans for our own mountains."

"The highlands? Not likely, dad. If there was coal under them they would have found it a hundred years ago. I've read the reports in the archives in Halifax and nothing in them suggests that there's any coal at all there. But did you know that they used to believe there's oil under Lake Ainslie? One time, this was back in the 1880s, the provincial government gave two businessmen permission to drain Lake Ainslie to get at the oil."

"What were they going to do, suck it dry with a straw?" Mrs. Big Sandy asked. "That's just one of them there stories like the monster that lives in the lake."

"It's not story, it's fact, Mrs. MacArthur. I saw the paperwork myself."

"The monster! A fact! You're becoming as foolish as the rest of them."

"Not the monster, Mrs. MacArthur, the proof that there was a plan to drain the lake."

"What stopped them then?"

"Greed. They wanted the government to give them all the royalties from the oil, nothing for the province. The idea seems to have stopped right there."

"Nothing in it for the government so they stopped it, did they? Isn't that always the way? If there was something in it for them, votes or taxes, there'd probably be no lake there today, I don't suppose," Ronald observed.

"Well for the love of the Lord, the real one I mean," Mrs. Big Sandy said, "don't go blabbing that all over the place or the other Mr. Lord will be up there with a siphon hose sucking up trout and monsters and his own first cousins, the eels."

"David's already put it in the paper just to demonstrate the lengths to which some people will go to destroy nature for the sake of a dollar," Rita said. "He says that the same greed would think nothing of destroying a town like Shean either, which had no useful reason for being anyway, as far as corporations or governments are concerned. Rural places like ours are just going to waste when they should be contributing to the economy."

"Well, if you'd seen the stockpile of stuff that's coming onto the old mine site..."

"Onto Sandy MacArthur's property you mean, Mr. Mac-Donald. That's what the place used to be called and what it will always be called as long as I have anything to say about it, and I have plenty to say about it! What are they doing to his place? I haven't been out of this godforsaken house since the last time we went grocery shopping. What are they doing?"

"Nothing yet," Ronald, assured her, "but they've been bringing in lots of construction material. Looks like they have plans to make Shean contribute to the economy, whether we like it or not. It even looks like they're planning to assemble a cement plant. Don Alex says that's not it, not a cement plant, but that what they're going to build is a tiny coal-fired generator to practice cleaning coal. He got that from a secret source, he says, which means he made it up."

"Cleaning coal! Have they lost their minds altogether in this world? Nobody can clean coal. It's dirty. Scrub off one layer of coal dust and what you've got is another layer of coal dust and on and on it goes just like peeling an onion. And when you get to the very end, what do you have? A handful of coal dust just as dirty in the middle as it is on the outside. They may as well get down on their knees and try to scrub the tar out of the road. Never heard such foolishness in my life. Cleaning coal!" She slammed two cups of tea before Rita and Ronald and went to the stove to pour her own, allowing the father and daughter time to share a quick smile.

David was scouring his face in the bathroom the next morning with limited results. He took his problem to his mother, explaining that he had accidentally put shoe polish on his face and it wasn't coming off very easy. She looked at him as she hadn't looked at him since he was a boy, a boy she remembered rubbing soot on his face so he could go to a masquerade party as Muhammad Ali, and the next day it wouldn't come off. She told him then, and he was remembering what she was remembering.

"I know, I know," he said a step ahead of her. "I should have put something on my face, Noxzema or something, a grease base that would allow it to wash off easily. I forgot."

"I'm going to say I told you so, because it was thirty years ago I told you so, and you do remember but went ahead without thinking. Why, for God's sake?" She handed him the butter dish from off the kitchen table. He didn't answer, returning to the bathroom to scrub his face with butter, remembering the smell of butter in his hair when bubble gum stuck in it. Butter worked better with bubble gum, but the polish did grow slightly fainter, making his face resemble one large bruise.

It was his mother's second suggestion, turpentine, that sent David out of the house and down to the Gulf Grill for coffee and eggs, and inevitably a grilling at the grill, so Donald MacNaughton was the last person he wanted to see at that moment.

"David, did you learn anything ... what the hell happened to your face?"

"I was changing the oil in the car and got some grease on my face. It's hard to get off. Listen, Donald, I'm curious. When I showed you that slide from Lord's office, did you by chance mention it to him?"

"In fact I did. I had a meeting with him shortly after I left the *Witness* office. I can't talk about what we talked about but it's related to the in-camera session of which I am keeping you gloriously in the dark. Still never invited me into his office though, so I mentioned the photograph you had from his office, kind of a way of wondering out loud why you'd be invited in there but not me. He wasn't happy to hear it, I could see it on his face, not even when I said you didn't know what the picture was. What did you do, sneak a hidden camera in with you? Maybe I should get the municipal building swept for bugs, huh?" the mayor joked, but filed the idea away as not being too far fetched.

"Anyway, what I started to ask you was whether or not you had learned anything new about the plans down at the mine site. Hate to think you'd be printing them and placing the project in jeopardy, so do me a favour, will you. If you find out anything, give me a call so I can let you know if you're on the right track. Okay?"

"Will do," David said, aware that Donald was now as desperate as he was to find out what was taking place on the MacArthur property.

"Changing your own oil," Donald said, shaking his head. "You cheap bastard." He emptied his cup and left the grill, leaving David to wonder what his own imagination could conjure up regarding the project, just to play games with Donald's head.

"David ... what happened to your face?" He turned to see Rita standing behind his stool, his smudged face visible to her in the counter-length mirror against the wall.

He swivelled around and stared at her for a moment before saying, "Someday I'm probably going to tell you. You're in town early."

"Mrs. MacArthur says she's getting bushed living out in the boonies with only Dad and me so we're on a shopping expedition this morning. I left her at the hairdresser's."

"Is that safe?"

"The only danger is that Barb will turn Mrs. MacArthur's hair a cobalt blue. It was her idea, going to the hairdresser's. Our friend may be acquiring a touch of vanity in her old age. Or she may have noticed the three inches of roots buried under her auburn, which she says is her natural colour. It may well have been fifty years ago. Are you going to ask me to join you? And how long do I have to wait for you to tell me what happened to your face? You look like a clown who forgot to put cream under his makeup."

Drawing Rita to a booth free of eavesdroppers on either side, David explained his misadventure into the world of crime, emphasizing his hurt ankle whenever her laughter began to gather the interest of other customers. David tried to quiet her, pointlessly. "I bet even Mad Maddie didn't believe you. I think you're a good reporter but you're a lousy liar, David. But maybe that's what makes you a good reporter." David sat thinking that a good reporter was the last thing he was.

What did finally quiet her was the quizzical way she watched a customer enter the grill, look around, as though unfamiliar with the layout or searching for someone. "David, the man who just came in here, is he who I think he is?"

David turned but the man already had his back to him, going out the door. "Who was it?"

"I couldn't swear to it, but do you remember that bureaucrat, Mr. Specificity, we met at the Department of Mines and Minerals in Halifax?" Rita asked. "I think it was him."

"Possible. He is with the mines department and there is a mine pending here. He must have been looking for someone who wasn't here."

| 54 |

"That will never happen again!" Mrs. Big Sandy muttered to herself standing on the steps of Barb's Beauty Salon, trembling with a rage that imploded into one of her internal conversations with herself. Thirty-five dollars for dying and setting my hair! Not dying it, no, they don't dye these days. Colour restoration, she called it, a fancy name for a big price. I should have shown her a little colour restoration by choking her blue but the pathetic creature was so scared when she saw me standing in her beauty parlour that she started shaking like some fool coming off the booze and I've seen my share of them, trying to dry out and coming to Sandy for a bottle to help them get through it, hair of the dog they called it. Stupid idiots I called it, but she was shaking so bad the little creature would have pissed in her pants if I snapped at her. Colour restoration! Nothing but a dye job and a bunch of curlers. What would she do if she had to give me a perm? Faint? I was never in one of those places before and I'll never go inside one again. Fell for Rita's reasoning's what I did. She tricked me into it somehow but she'll tell everybody it was my idea. Well some people can't be reasoned with and she should know by now I can't be tricked by reason, but she reasoned with me all the same, said I hadn't had my hair done since Sandy died and I should have laughed in her face and told her the truth. I haven't had my hair done since Sandy got sick. What would she think of that, of me telling her that it was Sandy who used to give me my perms? He didn't like it much, closing the curtains tight and then locking them together with one of those giant safety pins they use on a horse's blanket, but he'd do it. Dyed my hair too when it was time, but it was the permanents that would make us giddy. It's the fumes, he'd say to me, it's like sniffing gas, and we'd giggle and then Sandy would say I hope to God nobody comes to the door looking for a bottle and me smelling of this stuff and he would be, he'd be just reeking of that lotion. But he gave me all my perms, and that pathetic thing in there couldn't hold a candle to Sandy's hands when he did it. He was good at it whether he liked it or not but he lived in terror of "the boys" finding out, and I could get what I wanted out of him then, tell him I'll tell them and then the things we'd do in bed just so he could be sure I'd keep my mouth shut and I wished when she was washing my hair that it was Sandy's hands doing that and it was all I could do to keep from crying thinking of him and that whimpering slut acting like she was washing an old dog full of fleas and scared to get bit but she doesn't know nothing about how to do it right. I've a good mind to go back to that place and tell her which twin has the Toni!

Mrs. Big Sandy stepped from the sidewalk into Memorial Park where Rita said she'd meet her in an hour although the hour had seemed like a week so she wouldn't have been surprised if Rita got tired of waiting and left. Rita wasn't there, and Mrs. Big Sandy, needing to rest her feet, scanned the park benches, none of which were empty, a situation she expected to rectify. When she saw Donald MacNaughton seated alone on a bench with one of those toy phones to his ear she decided he was sitting on the very bench she wanted to sit on. She dropped beside him and he shifted his back to her without even glancing her way, looking instead for privacy, still engaged in his conversation. We'll see just how long he can ignore me, thought the insulted

Mrs. Big Sandy as she closed the distance between them with a butt swing that nearly dislodged Donald MacNaughton from the bench. He turned glaring fire that quickly extinguished itself. "Listen, I have to go. But if you hear anything about what the premier is planning to announce, I'd like you to give me a heads up if you could. Be talking to you," he said and pocketed his phone. "How are you this morning?"

"Would you like to have a look at the scar you made on my arse?" said Mrs. Big Sandy, standing, threatening, attracting benches of interest.

"What are you doing?" Donald shouted at her as she threatened to hike her dress. "Will you please sit down? I know what you think of me but there's nothing I could do to save your home."

"Yes there was. You could've told the minister of whatever allows him to take another person's home that you wouldn't let him take away the home of one of your taxpayers. You could of told us he was going to do it. You should of told me. That's your duty as a mayor, and if I sound understanding to you, you little twirp, it's because these are the excuses Rita likes to make up for you not saving my home. That's the kind of person she is, I guess, but I think you just didn't give a sweet goddamned what the government or anybody else wanted to do to me, Mr. Sleazeball. Know how I know? Because you can lie just like a politician so there's nothing you can say that I can believe, so what I believe is you're guilty. You have no idea how miserable I can make the life of a boy who shot me and a man who stole my home. Wouldn't do it if Sandy was living!"

MacNaughton tightened his lips lest something lethally stupid slip through them. "Look, Mrs. MacArthur, it was the Attorney General who expropriated your property, not the town of Shean, not me."

"That minister's nothing but a name in a newspaper but you're right here and you can squeal and bleed like a stabbed pig, so just say oink, Mr. Mayor. I heard you on the phone asking somebody to tell you what's going on. Got sucker punched, didn't you? Gave them my house then they kicked you out of theirs. And now you're running around like a headless hen trying to find out what's going on. Do you know what you know about what's going on down there on Sandy's home? You know nothing, and that means you know everything because that's what's going to happen down there: nothing. Sandy won't let you. I won't let you."

"You're close to making a violent threat and I don't need to listen to this garbage," Donald said, passing Rita as she walked up the path.

"Not a very happy-looking man, but look at you! You're a delight. Your hair looks great. No wonder you're smiling. You must feel much better."

"What makes me happy," she said without taking her eyes off Donald MacNaughton's back, "is pulling the wings off that fly."

———

"Line two for you, David," Cheryl Horn informed him. David picked up the receiver. "David Cameron here."

"Mr. Cameron, you don't know me but I have something you might want to see."

"Who is this?"

"That's not important. But I may be able to help you."

"How?"

"I have something that might interest you as a reporter. But I can't come to see you. Will you meet me outside of town?"

"All this cloak and dagger stuff, how do I know I'm not walking into a sting, something to discredit me and the *Witness*? The paper's been asking some tough questions about whatever's going on and maybe somebody wants those questions to stop."

"It's not as sinister as all that, Mr. Cameron. I know I wouldn't enjoy the pressure of going undercover like some reporters do. I'm not a whistleblower either, but there are some things that go on in the dark rooms at the back of government house that make bureaucrats sick. We fantasize about letting the public know but it rarely happens. When it does, it is usually followed by a firing. If you don't keep my name out of it, that's what will probably happen to me."

The tumblers fell into place. "Were you in the Gulf Grill this morning?"

"I was there but I didn't stay."

"Where would you like to meet?"

"I've been driving around and I'm parked on an abandoned wharf maybe twenty kilometres north of your town. Know it?"

"I'll be there inside an hour."

| 55 |

David Cameron drove toward Lewis Wharf, which had been abandoned when the federal government consolidated most Maritime wharves, forcing fishermen from Lewis to move their boats to Shean. Having fallen into disrepair, the wharf had become a photographer's dream; tourists and local hobbyists snapping the wildness of the Gulf waters washing over it when the wind blew, or capturing serene sunsets on still summer and autumn evenings. David passed Ronald MacDonald's farm, crested a hill and slowed, taking in the summer view of the wharf, noting one parked car and a lone figure standing at the wharf's end.

Easing to a stop beside the lone car, David waited. A minute later, the figure turned and walked toward the cars, stopping to retrieve a briefcase from his own and opening the passenger door of David's Camry. David recognized the man, struggled again for the tip-of-his-tongue name, trying to remember if he had introduced himself to him and Rita. Nothing came but "Mr. Specificity." He nodded to his guest, half welcome, half uncertainty, and waited.

"This sneaky business, I'm not used to it but I need to be sure..." the man explained. His hands were shaking, his skin glistened with nervous dampness. "I'm not sure what I need to be sure of, to tell you the truth, except that if I'm found out I'll lose my job. You remember me, I think."

David nodded again. "I filed my Freedom of Information requests with you, right?"

"That was me."

"And I never received a response so quickly. Was that you too?"

It was the bureaucrat's turn to nod. "Nothing you asked about was relevant to what you were looking for. I guessed from all the unrelated inquiries that you were swinging in the dark, hoping to hit something. I hurried the response hoping you would keep trying, but nothing more came from you or your newspaper."

"Didn't think there was a point. Was there?"

"Not without the right questions. Right *question*. But even then the minister or deputy minister could have blocked it. But I know you're desperate to know. I found your newspaper online, and all the speculation about open pits and prisons, and I want to help you."

"How?"

"I want to give you something I think you need to know," he said tapping the briefcase in his lap. "Look, I'm just a bureaucrat pushing my papers and none of this should be any of my business and it probably wouldn't be except that it's you. I'd never even think of doing this if it was anybody else but you, but it's not anybody else."

"Me?" David interrupted. "Do I know you from somewhere?"

"No, we've never met, but I need to be kept out of it and I believe you'll do that."

"You know I won't expose you? Believe it why? Sure, reporters protect their sources but I'm not promising anything unless I know what I'm dealing with. And who."

The stranger opened the briefcase and removed a thick file, placing it on the console between them. David thumbed it quickly, seeing nothing but the large red stamp on every page reading Confidential.

"I don't get it," David said.

"Consider it a thank you. My name is Malcolm McVeigh."

McVeigh. Of course! The features of the man's face were finer, closer shaven, but it was the same face for certain. "You're Dougall's brother, aren't you?" David asked, recalling the face of the homeless man he had befriended in Toronto, a fellow Cape Bretoner whose help had turned David into an award-winning journalist, and who froze to death on that city's streets the same winter that the series had run in the *Star*.

"I'd always meant to send you a thank-you card or something, on behalf of the family, I mean. Dougall." he said, looking into the distance, or more accurately, into the past. "Dougall. He was the best of us, you know. Eight in the family but Dougall was the star. Bright! Jesus, he was bright. Scholarship to Dalhousie. Then he flunked out two years later. The bottle had him that soon, and it just wouldn't let him go, ever. We tried until we gave up and then he was lost to us, figuratively and literally. We didn't know where he'd gotten himself to, whether he was alive or dead.

"Those stories of yours, they got reprinted here, you know, in Nova Scotia in one of the dailies. I remember reading those stories and thinking at first that Dougall could be one of those homeless men, and then the more you quoted him, the more suspicious I got that it was Dougall. Oh God, if I had just contacted you then maybe.... And maybe you'd have just protected your source. Anyway, when he was found dead and you wrote about him there's no way to tell you what it meant to us, to all of us, especially my mother. Dad died several years ago. But in your story Dougall had all the dignity he would have had had his life not gone to hell the way it did. Or maybe I just imagined it, that your words restored him somehow. The most important thing though, was that you told the coroner who to contact as next of kin so we could bring him home and bury him in the family plot. I don't know how to thank you, but maybe this," he nodded toward the file, "goes some way toward saying it."

Talking about Dougall, David noticed that Malcolm's hands were no longer shaking, that his skin was dry. They talked for close to an hour about Dougall, about Toronto, about Dougall's burial, a grave David made a mental note to visit some day, about Halifax, and about the economic realities of urban versus rural living. They steered clear of politics, mines and confidential files until there was nowhere else for their conversation to go.

"There are only a very few people who could have given you this," Malcolm McVeigh said in parting, and David knew that whatever the files contained, it would never be traced back to Malcolm through David or anyone at the *Witness*.

Malcolm McVeigh's car pulled away, leaving David at the wharf with the file. Curious, he didn't wait to return to the office, opening the collection of documents to browse through them. Two hours later David was still seated in his car beside the wharf. He had read each of the documents thoroughly, some more than twice, studied the appended charts and blueprints with microscopic attention. Then he sat for another silent hour staring out at the Gulf, at Shean Cove.

When he did check his watch it was too late in the afternoon to stop at Ronald's house to see Rita. Instead, he phoned her at work, making a date for them to meet at the Shean beach when she got off at eleven.

"Is everything alright?" Rita asked, sensing a heaviness to David's voice.

"No, Rita, nothing is alright. Nothing, but there's no one I want to talk to about it right now but you."

David returned to the office, phoned his mother that he wouldn't get home for supper and, after the staff had left for the day, perked a pot of coffee that disappeared as was its habit while he waded through the documents once again.

Disappeared too was the evening sun and its flaring farewell beyond the horizon. A nearly full moon had risen in its place and under its soft luminescence he studied the world beyond the office window while the clunky rhythm of the copying machine reprinted and sorted several copies of the file. A soft breeze rippled the water in the sheltered harbour so that the fleet of crab boats bobbed and swayed against the wharf. The moonlight beamed a path directly down the channel that opened to the Gulf of St. Lawrence, and on either side of the channel was the undulating silhouette of the dunes. Beyond those dunes was what David believed to be Shean's finest feature, the beach that edged a deep cove along the Gulf of St. Lawrence. The beach was his refuge and he had never felt in greater need of its silence and solace. He placed the copied files in separate manila envelopes and put them in the safe until he could decide what to do with them, then left the office and drove to the shore to wait for Rita.

| 56 |

David sat on the same driftwood log that had been there for him all summer. It was a measure of how calm the summer weather had been since a spring storm deposited the driftwood upon the shores of Shean. The grey, stripped log had been a tree along some other coastline, knocked into the ocean by one of Nature's forces, and may have visited a dozen beaches before this one.

Every summer a new supply of driftwood provided fuel for bonfires, had been doing so ever since he was a boy, and should go on doing so for Tony and Mary and their children. There were no bonfires now, maybe later after the rock band at the Five Bucks shut down their sound. Tonight the beach seemed to be all his.

Driftwood was something he had come to appreciate over time, so many natural sculptures came from the carnage of someone else's shore. He was often moved to pick up a smaller piece and bring it home, find a place on the lawn to set it. They were certainly preferable to pink flamingos or garden gnomes, even for his mother.

In the moonlight, the two promontories of Noss Head and Hughie's Point sloped down from the highlands to form the cove. He wondered if there was a time when the land mass reached out to the far extension of those points before wind and water and ice etched the coastline into this and countless other coves. And how many drowned forests had drifted into this cove over the centuries, until the small ships containing the MacArthurs and the other founding families made their way here from Scotland by way of the already settled Prince Edward Island, where land had become scarce and land promised them was non-existent.

What did they see at first, those settlers who came blindly and trustingly across the Atlantic Ocean, a place an early Gaelic poet had gloomily sung about as being the Land of Trees? Did the shoreline then reach further out into the ocean than now? It had certainly been eaten away by erosion over David's own lifetime, portions of the sand dunes dragged away by retreating winter ice. The dunes had been slammed by large storms in the other seasons, none more damaging than the August gales, the tail-end of southern hurricanes. The face of the present dunes compared against photographs of thirty, forty, fifty years earlier allowed a measure of those changes. Yet the scars of those changes would heal quickly, the dunes seeming as unblemished and permanently beautiful as ever.

The first families began carving homes and barns and fields out of the land of trees for a century in Shean before the discovery of coal and then a new force made itself felt along the beach. Behind the dunes lay a deep pond formed from brooks that trickled out of those deep woods, and whose overflow waters trickled in a small stream across the dunes to add its pittance to the ocean's wealth. The first mining company put the mastery of engineering to work for itself, and soon the trickling stream was gouged out to become a dredged channel wide enough to allow coal boats to enter the pond. Local farmers supplemented their income or food supply by building small, hand-rowed fishing boats, using the channel to harvest the sea. With the eventual building of larger boats, they traded with Prince Edward Island, carrying cargoes of rough-hewn wood to sell or trade for island crops such as potatoes.

Those engineers of more than a century ago figured out how to pound wooden pilings deep into the dunes at the water's edge, constructing on top of them walls of creosote timber to fortify the channel. Those wooden walls became the wharf, fishermen tying up alongside at their designated spots to unload their catches. That wooden-sided channel lasted into the earliest memory of David's own childhood. From that wharf he and scores of other boys had leapt or dived into the channel's current.

Then construction technology advanced. The channel was stripped of its wooden walls and dredged, its entrance protected by hundreds of feet of breakwater stone pushing out into the Gulf, foiling the sandbars that had continually clogged the channel. Although the shipping of coal by sea from Shean had ended eons earlier with the arrival of the railroad, succeeding generations of fishermen had become professional, their boats larger, their catches greater as they began replacing the limping coal mines as Shean's economic backbone.

Eventually the tides found their way around that first breakwater to become a continual nuisance of channel-clogging sand. Half a decade ago, construction technology grew bigger trucks to carry bigger stones, a single armour stone weighing several tons to a truck, to make a bigger breakwater reaching further out into the Gulf, each phase of channel-building creating what the psalms sing about, what poets shout about and what politicians promise: a safe harbour. David Cameron's musing was interrupted by a movement along the water's edge.

"Rita?"

The movement stopped and the form all but vanished into the stillness of the night.

"David?"

"Up here." His voice drew her to the log.

Rita sat on the log beside him, murmured a few words about the beauty of the night, then asked, "What is it, David?"

"Full moon, a good night for horror stories. Want to hear one?"

"Big Sandy?"

"I wish."

Silence fell between them until Rita's voice broke it with, "Well."

David kept his silence, feeling that when he tried to put his thoughts into words they would come out sounding shallow or fanciful or silly, but he felt her patience waiting him out.

| 57 |

"You know about the Beaton Seam, of course."

"Of course. It's out there, isn't it? Some miners were killed, drowned, trying to mine it, I know that but not a lot more," Rita answered.

"It's a quality coal seam, low sulphur, many million tons of it apparently, too close to the seabed to mine safely, as we know. My great granduncle was one of those who drowned. But that's what this whole open-pit business is about, Rita, the Beaton Seam. It's got nothing to do with reclaiming coal from the mine tailings, but about going after the Beaton Seam."

"I thought it couldn't be mined? We've always been told that, that it couldn't be mined without the mine flooding like it always did before."

"Yes, but it's not underground mining they're considering. It's open-pit mining."

"Through the ocean? I don't think so."

"But what if you moved the ocean, Rita? What if you were to build a seawall, a dike, that arched from Noss Head all the way over to Hughie's Point, and then drained the cove? Then just a few shovelfuls with an excavator and you'd be into the Beaton Seam."

Rita looked out into the dark sea flecked with moonlight, her eyes bridging the distance from Noss Head to Hughie's Point, trying to imagine what David was describing, but it didn't seem physically possible. It wasn't possible, it couldn't be, and yet there was nothing of the storyteller in David's voice, no sense that he was entertaining or teasing her. "How?"

"Ever since Hurricane Katrina swamped New Orleans there's been lots of research into seawalls. The Dutch have been pushing the sea back for centuries, but this isn't exactly a dike we're talking about. I don't pretend to grasp the nitty gritty technology, but a lot of investment and research has gone into developments such as carbon fibre as a construction material. It's lighter and stronger than steel or cement, sometimes it's mixed with cement to lighten the load. They use carbon fibre in aeroplanes. There've been experiments in bridge building. One experiment I researched earlier this evening was in Michigan where a bridge was constructed in two days with carbon fibre technology. Normally, it would have taken forty. There are bridges in Canada constructed using the same stuff, something called carbon-fiber-reinforced polymer.

"The science of it aside, what laymen like you and I need to know is that they've been experimenting with lightweight panels using this kind of technology. One company – and this is what Resource Reclamations plans to use – has developed an interlocking panel with a watertight sealing. That's how they plan to construct the seawall."

"David, I don't know much about physics but you're talking about pushing back the ocean. That's an awful lot of pressure. Put that kind of pressure, relatively speaking, on one of my patient's arteries and it would burst like a balloon. The same thing would happen out there, wouldn't it?"

"That's what I'd think too, but the designers behind this idea don't think so. The wall would be anchored with huge bolts bored into the stone at Noss Head. At Hughie's Point where the earth is softer they will pour a concrete bulkhead against the cliff and anchor the wall there. They've even brought a temporary cement plant onto Big Sandy's land. When it's erected, they'll begin constructing the wall from each promontory. Normally it might be too deep out there for this project but Shean's cove meets the ideal conditions. The same geological upheaval that happened a million years ago or whenever, the one that pushed the Beaton Seam up against the sea floor, also heaved up what is now a relatively shallow stone ledge out there. Divers can drive anchor bolts into that ledge.

"Once the bulkheads and anchor bolts are in place, barges will bring the panels here, lift and lower them by crane, and divers will secure them to the sea bottom. Then, theoretically, the interlocking panels should move along fairly quickly, like Legos according to the reports I've read. And when the wall is completed the cove out there will be drained. They'll have all winter to do that, pump the water in the cove over the seawall. While this is going on, the wall will be tested against the pressure of the autumn storms and the winter ice floes. If it stands up to that battering, the mining of the Beaton Seam can begin as soon as the cove is empty, probably by spring. And when the mine has been depleted, the wall can be dismantled and moved somewhere else."

David went silent for a moment, then continued.

"And I played right into their hands with my story, with my speculation in the *Witness* about an open-pit mine at Big Sandy's. It created a diversionary debate that C.J.M. Lord and Donald MacNaughton were probably very happy about. I shifted the focus away from what was actually planned for Shean, created a lesser evil for them to deny with a straight face because my speculation was dead wrong. Mining Big Sandy's land was never the objective, Rita, but his land is ideally located to be the base camp for carrying out the mining of the Beaton Seam."

"I wondered about all the equipment that's been brought into Big Sandy's. I don't know anything about mining but it sure looked like overkill," Rita said. "This is going to cost a small fortune. How much coal is out there anyway?"

"Lots. That's where the provincial government comes in. They won't be investing a nickel of taxpayers' dollars in the venture, which will be popular with people. What Cabinet will do is provide policy or legislative support for the project when it becomes operational, enacting legislation that will force the power company to buy Nova Scotia coal exclusively unless there's not enough provincial coal being produced to meet the province's power needs.

"The power company might resist but then the premier would begin whispering words like 'essential service,' 'nationalization,' 'jobs for Nova Scotians,' – things any party would be willing to fight an election on."

"How do you know this, David?"

"I've seen confidential documents, agreements signed between the Department of Mines and Minerals and Resource Reclamations. It's thick and it has pictures, blueprints of what's planned for Shean."

"Don't tell me you broke into that safe in the mine office?"

"No, my cat burglar days are over, but some documents came into my possession."

"Don't ask, don't tell?"

"Yeah, something like that."

"Then I won't ask you about seeing Mr. Specificity in the grill this morning."

"Please don't."

David and Rita went quiet, staring at the moonstruck water, trying to imagine the unimaginable.

"My God, David, is this really going to happen?"

"Yes, I'm afraid it is. The papers I've seen make this a done deal as far as I can tell, and I don't know what can be done to stop it. Something, I hope, but I don't know what."

"But moving the ocean! It's madness."

"Madness, yes, but it's a possible madness. On the scale of the world's megaprojects it won't be that big a deal beyond Shean. Not compared to the destruction taking place in Fort McMurray or the rain forests or fishing out the oceans. It seems that everywhere in the world where we can destroy a forest or an ocean or desert for profit, we'll do it. It's always been that way, I suppose, the difference now being that we have the technological ability to pound the planet to death, and I'm afraid the plan for out there in the cove is another one of those crippling body blows."

"All this will be gone? Who knows about this? Are you going to tell? You need to. You said it can't be stopped but somebody has to try and the *Witness* is all we have here to help us. You're going to print this, aren't you?"

"Probably," David said, "but I'm asking you not to tell anyone about it. There can be no hint that I have the documents I've told you about. If word leaks out before the *Witness* comes out, the office will file injunctions so fast that not a word of it will ever be printed, not until our government controls and spins it like cotton candy.

"This particular kind of mining hasn't been tried anywhere else as far as I can find in any research I've done. Yet the environmental impact conclusion in the proposal for this mine, a conclusion apparently accepted by our own government, is mindboggling. When the life of the Beaton Seam has been fully exploited, the transportable seawall will be removed. The Gulf waters will then flow back into the cove, covering the whole mess. That would constitute their commitment to restoring the environment."

"Don't these corporations usually carry out these kinds of projects in other parts of the world, like the Third World or whatever it's calling it these days?"

"We are the Third World as far as our own governments and corporations are concerned. Cape Breton, Atlantic Canada for that matter, has been driving politicians and right-wing think tanks crazy for a century. We've even driven one of our prime ministers to call us a culture of despair, and so a megaproject with lots of jobs and good pay for a high unemployment area like this isn't going to meet a lot of resistance. Oh, the politicians will be expressing their concern for the environment, but when it comes down to a choice, the economy trumps the environment every time, so we can expect all the right noises to be made. Nobody in Halifax or Ottawa is going to stand in its way. It's too far advanced."

"What if it doesn't work? What if the wall breaks?"

David shrugged and went silent. David's online research into similar schemes had revealed widespread destruction disguised as construction. He could find nothing that exactly resembled the proposed project in Shean, but the resources to attempt it were in place – a corporate plan, financing, a compliant government, a desperate economy and a powerless rural town at the mercy of all those forces.

David's arm wrapped around Rita and he felt her willingly collapse against him. Slowly, wordlessly, in a world they both cherished, they made love in the sand. The first signs of dawn over the mountains led them back to their cars, where they stood holding each other and looking out into the lightening of the grey ocean. They kissed and parted, still cradling the silence between them.

| 58 |

Ronald MacDonald, followed by Don Alex, walked into the *Witness* office, a man on a mission who did not stop to have himself announced, certain that he was about to change David's life. "I've got this week's front page for you, David," he announced while still a distance away, allowing time for David to click the image and information on the front page currently being laid out into safety behind his screen saver.

Not in the mood for distractions, David barely acknowledged the two visitors. "What is it, Ronald? I'm kind of tied up here."

"This," Ronald said, holding out a piece of paper which his elder friend had printed off earlier this morning.

"This being?"

"Well, read it."

"You tell me, Ron, okay?"

"Okay. This I printed off this morning. You know I got a printer? Rita hooked it up for me this week. Proof. Not everybody in the Gulf Grill believes everything I'll be telling them about the things I find on the World Wide Web so now I print it off as proof."

"And you have proof of what?" David asked impatiently.

"Did you know there's a group on the World Wide Web calling for the retirement of, get this, Ronald McDonald. Not this Ronald MacDonald but my arch enemy. An organization called Corporate Accountability International said in *The Toronto Star* – isn't that the paper you used to work for? – that they're collecting names on a petition to have him retire. They don't want him selling fast food to children. They have thousands of names on their petition, they say so right here. Hell, all my own work got me fifty-seven names to sign up on my Lose A Quarter Pounder a Month Club, but they are all MacDonalds, I'll say that for them. I was in touch with these people and you won't believe this but I've been on the World Wide Web every day for a couple of years now, and lots of it trying to organize the clan into getting rid of the clown, and can you believe this, nobody at this organization here ever heard of me or my website. Must be Americans! But I signed their petition anyway, and they promised to have a look at my website and maybe even make a link to it. Think they'll do that, David? You never know who you're talking to out there. All you know's that you're strangers in common cause. So what do you think? You're not getting anywhere with this open-pit mine business I don't suppose, so if a mine opens here in Shean, then Sylvester MacNaughton and his franchise won't be ... wont' be ..."

At a loss for words, David was moved to see his friend was fighting back tears.

"Ronald, I promise you, we'll get something in the *Witness* about this. I'll get Tim to check it out and if it's legitimate we'll run a story about it. It won't be on the front page, and it will be information only, but once it's in the paper then you can use it to rally your clansmen, okay?"

Mildly appeased but certain that he had been gently brushed off by the man Ronald MacDonald considered his editor, he wondered if he should bother David with something else he had found in his research.

David had turned away, his back dismissing his visitors, but he sensed their lingering presence. "Is there something else?" he asked, not turning.

"It's this thing about insurance and the way some companies..." David swivelled and took the printout from Ronald, explaining that he'd have a look at it later but that right now he was busy with a story that was under deadline pressure. Don Alex tugged at a disappointed Ronald's arm and the two men left the office. David thought for a second about how he could have handled the situation differently, more diplomatically, but he was feeling far from diplomatic, his thoughts and stomach riding a roller coaster of thrilling fear.

"Is this for real, David?" Tim Donovan had asked when, in the sanctuary of his office, David shared with his reporter what he had discovered. "Look at this blueprint, the whole length of the beach becomes a strip mine. Over here, Big Sandy's old place, is where they'll set up their operations offices, weigh scales, whatever else they need to pull this thing off, but nothing can be done as long as those dunes are in the way. How many thousands of years for those dunes to form and a few hours with a bulldozer and they're history? Where's the Department of Environment in all this?"

"I think we heard their position at the public meeting, Tim. They're taking the position that it's a resource recovery process and that the restoration will happen when the job is completed."

"But then they were talking about an open-pit mine on the MacArthur tailings, not something this wild."

"Wrong, Tim. We were the ones talking about an open-pit mine on the MacArthur property. This," he said, indicating the maps and charts in front of them, "is what they were talking about. I think it was to their benefit that the *Witness* went ahead with predictions of an open pit in the middle of town. But all their answers about the Department of Mines and Minerals and

Environment were in reference to this project without ever having to elaborate on it. I think with our story in the paper we set ourselves up to be blind sided. They were able to do a good job of selling the town on the idea I had proposed, or opposed, in the paper. There was never a denial, never a confirmation. One of the consequences of not checking our facts."

"So we're checking these facts for sure?" Tim asked, pointing to the documents.

David sat back in his chair and twirled it around so that he was looking out the window at Shean Cove and the Gulf of St. Lawrence. He was silent for a long time while Tim waited. Then he swivelled around to face his reporter.

"No, Tim, we're doing no such thing. Not a single phone call, not an inquiry. A man should learn from his mistakes but obviously I'm a slow learner. What I believe though, know, is that if we begin phoning Resource Reclamations Limited or the Department of Mines and Minerals or any other department, or even Donald MacNaughton, we'll tip our hand to what we have here. The *Witness* will be hit with a paralyzing storm of injunctions forcing us to keep what we know out of print, possibly have the documents seized and ourselves discredited through leaked reports to the other media so that what we have will become meaningless, an industry joke. I don't doubt the capacity of Resource Reclamations or C.J.M. Lord to try to hurt us, even physically. Despite his pro-labour, pro-safe workplace rhetoric, his history is one of union-busting, and there's substantial rumours but no proof that organizers have been hurt on his job sites, beaten by thugs.

"These documents are my source for the story, and these will be the only source. Until press time I need you to sit on this. You're only the third person in Shean to know about this and no one needs to know until they read it in the paper."

"David, I'd like to do a sidebar for the story, maybe with pictures of the dunes as they are now and what's in store for them, try to make it as personal as we can for our readers."

"Before you go ahead with that, you should be aware that our world can come crashing down on top of us when this hits the street, and that the legal reaction could throw a broad net not just over the paper and its editor and publisher but any reporter who was involved in spreading the story. It might have consequences for you."

"Yeah, a sidebar about the dunes, and maybe an opinion piece about the whole sleazy affair," Tim said, as if he hadn't heard a word.

"Okay, but we do need to fill the *Witness* with some fluffy midsummer stories, and Ronald MacDonald brought in a web piece, somebody's blog or something, that I'd like you to turn into a story that appeases the man," David added.

| 59 |

"Have you got time to look at something?" Tim asked a couple of hours later, beckoning the editor out into the main office by pointing at the big screen. "Those blueprints aren't going to be dramatic enough for the story we're telling this week," he explained.

David studied the picture as Tim went on. "I took the four -by-four up to the top of the Cape where I could get a good shot of the town," he explained as a photograph filled the screen. Tim's camera had caught a panoramic view of the town in magnificent light, looking down from the Cape across the church steeples, the canopy of trees, the blocks of houses, then across the open land where the mine pitheads had once been, then the MacArthur land and beyond to the golden strand of shoreline and out to the Gulf of St. Lawrence. The photo captured the Gulf in a sparkle of sunlight reaching out to the horizon. David was impressed by the quality of Tim's photograph but not surprised by it. The man had a gift.

"Then I Photoshopped it and got this." Tim pulled up a second photograph showing the same steeples, trees, houses, but that's where the similarity ended. A seawall had been superimposed across much of the sparkling water, an arc reaching from promontory to promontory. Inside that wall Tim had dropped a photograph snagged off an online site of an open-pit coal mine. The area was filled with massive trucks and excavators, the breadth and black ugliness of it brought into sudden context.

"Jesus!" David said. "Holy sweet Jesus! Is this what we're looking at a year from now?"

"Something like it," Tim assured him. "What do you think? We can bill it as an artist's concept of the Beaton Seam Project or something."

"Nice work, Tim. I want it to run full colour across the middle pages for maximum size and impact, the original on top, your artist's concept below. We'll also put a small print of your concept on the front page promoting the spread, and get that image on our website. Now back to work, we have a paper to get out tonight."

———

"David, have you lost your fucking mind!"

Donald MacNaughton charged through the *Witness* office waving the newest edition of the newspaper, its headline, Seawall to destroy Shean cove! over a story that filled the paper's front page with Resource Reclamations Limited's plans for Shean's shoreline, supported by photographic reproductions of key passages from the confidential files and Tim's graphic Photoshop work.

David stood up from Tim Donovan's desk where the two reporters were discussing the very issue that had enraged the charging mayor.

"When did you start writing science fiction? This Stephen King shit is going to land you in jail. Libel! Does the word mean anything to you, you poison prick? You'll have half the town believing this garbage and trying to convince the other half. What in the name of Christ are you trying to do?"

"Come into my office, Donald," David answered. "I want to show you something."

MacNaughton waited until David closed the door before unleashing again. "Where in the Jesus did you get this garbage from? The Beaton Seam! For hell's sake, David, get a grip on yourself. This thing is obsessing you and you're making a public fool of yourself, as if I care, but you're ruining the only thing Shean has going for it. Okay, so an open pit's like any armpit, ugly and smelly, but it's jobs. We'll be lucky if Resource Reclamations doesn't pack up and move out of here. Maybe then I can talk Council into giving you a medal. There's more at stake here than what you do or don't like, David! There's people's lives and their right to make a living."

David watched the mayor curiously while waiting for him to go quiet. "You really don't know what I'm talking about, do you? Not a clue about what this issue is exposing? Holy shit, you really were sold a bill of goods about Big Sandy's, weren't you? Is that what they told you? An open pit? Maybe a small generator to do research on low-emission coal? Or did they tell you they were opening an underground mine? Whatever C.J.M. Lord told you is a lie. Now read this before you say another word."

Donald hefted the package David handed him, as if the weight of the file would tell him the weight of the issue. He took the papers out, began rifling through the first few pages with angry indifference until words and phrases began to catch his eye. The leafing grew slower, the mayor lingering a little longer over each page while David waited.

He had not slept yet. The day before, he took out the copies of the file he kept in the safe and mailed a set to each of four newspapers and television stations, one copy special delivery to Jim Turner at the *Star*. It was hard to say what would come of it, but he was acutely aware of what could come out of it for him.

He hadn't told Rita at all about what his newspaper association's lawyer had said to him, that he was advising David not to print the material he had, that possession of it was probably illegal. The few pages David faxed him as a sample was enough for a legal mind to see a minefield of guilty verdicts. If he did publish the files against legal advice there was the possibility that the newspaper association's insurance company would refuse to defend the *Witness*. David would be out there alone and lucky to get away with paying out just tens of thousands of dollars. Since ruthless corporations can be far more merciless than that, David had to decide which type Resource Reclamations Limited was. He retained his own lawyer.

It all seemed such a romantic waste of time, David and Goliath, but this wasn't the same David even though all Goliaths look alike. The single illegal aspect of it for this David would happen when he printed the story and reproduced the confidential information. Nothing about the covert agreement between the provincial government and Resource Reclamations was illegal. But the papers themselves were confidential because all the ministers involved, including the premier, and C.J.M. Lord believed that it was in their best interest to keep the agreement to themselves.

They had obviously been spending months preparing their presentation, anticipating objections, protests, aiming their story at the majority of voters who don't really pay a lot of attention to politics, to the environment, to social issues. They undoubtedly planned on bringing in a battery of public relations consultants to design and unveil this important industrial project in a way that would ensure that the public's first encounter with the concept would be positive: job creation, innovative engineering, prosperity where no real prosperity had existed for more than half a century. The information would be confirmed by a team of well-paid scientists whose assessments and opinions went to the highest bidder.

The Dutch have been doing it for centuries, reclaiming land from the sea but Resource Reclamations would be touting the use of the latest development in dikes or seawalls, assuring everyone that although the technology has advanced, the principle was the same. Farmland or coalfield, it was all about productivity, about bringing back to Nova Scotia one of its oldest and still its richest resource – coal. Throw in a few lines about "clean coal" and carbon credits and no one would really notice the destruction of a town.

If he couldn't endure it, those coming changes, where could he possibly go? He had been among the lucky few to learn that you can go home again, but the hometown he'd returned to was in danger of vanishing into something else, if not altogether.

As he had sent the newspaper's pages across the Internet to the paper's printer, David felt like he was sending a message in a bottle: Town in trouble. About to prosper. Help!

The environmentalists could be counted on. The Ecology Action Centre would issue press releases and hold news conferences and reporters would turn up and editors would use both the releases and the press conferences to plug any news hole. But Shean needed more allies than a bunch of people perceived to be anti-sealers or tree huggers. The town itself, no the province, would need to rise against plans to mine the Beaton Seam with parades and protests and familiar arguments, but the overall attention span for resistance to anything was short, shrinking down eventually to a barely audible grumble. Without leadership any opposition would fizzle.

The file hit David's desk with a thud that David felt sure woke him from an eyes-open nap.

"Any more Glen Breton buried in those drawers?" Donald asked to a negative shake of the publisher's head. "Where did you get this stuff, David? If this is real..." His eyes moved to the window behind David and its view of the harbour and dunes and the wide cove beyond.

"You really didn't know anything about this?"

"About this? Nothing. Look, I've been talking with Elmer Monke off and on for most of the winter. He was the one who introduced me to C.J.M. Lord and to the Mines minister, Jim Singer. You know, the actual plans were pretty vague from the beginning. An environmentally friendly way to recover coal and probe below Big Sandy's place for accessible seams. But the diamond inside that small gift was hints, that bastard, hints that finding a way to reach the underground coal still wasn't out of the question. I'm thinking of a pithead, not an open pit. Those hints came with a lot of maybes and confidential information that couldn't be shared at the moment. Ha! Hell, C.J.M. Lord even talked about how, when the coal recovery was finished, the reclaimed land would be seeded and developed as a golf course. That was going to be my ace for getting James Jamison onside if I needed his support. Buddy MacMaster never played a fiddle the way those bastards played me. What I think you might have done was screw with their timing."

"With the open-pit mine story."

"Yeah. At first the minister and Lord were pissed off, and according to them so was the premier. The premier wanted to reveal the plan only when everything was a go – not a word before that. Same with Lord. I could see the premier's point. Politicians are all about controlling information, power-hungry bastards. But none of it could begin without getting Big Sandy's property. I thought that part was a no-brainer. Who in this town gives a damn for the bitch? We offered to buy it and when that didn't work..."

"Your jaw didn't work for quite a while after that, either."

"When that didn't work Singer coaxed the premier into taking the expropriation route. Again, who'd care? And who'd expect shotguns and dynamite and newspapers and television cameras? Then your story came out about the open pit. At first they were pissed off. I was pissed off. You jumped their announcement plans by a few weeks but then when the whole province didn't rise up in arms over the idea of an open-pit mine in some remote corner of Cape Breton, it played into their hands again because it was never about an open pit at Big Sandy's, was it? And I played right into their hands too. It was about this," Donald said, tapping the files, "always about this, and this is nothing I'd ever support. I'm going to phone the minister and tell him it's a no go."

David laughed harder than he had in days.

"What?" the mayor asked.

"You're going to phone him and cancel the whole deal, are you, Donald? Just like that? Get a grip, for Christ's sake. You're a part-time mayor of a small town that's got no future. I don't know what your personal ambitions are but I suspect that Mrs. Big Sandy hit the nail on the head at the public meeting about you wanting to go to Cabinet. But she also told me about your phone conversation in the park just before she went aboard you for stealing her home.

"Face it. You've got a corporation that doesn't give a damn, not about Shean and not about you, and a government that couldn't care less about either. They've got the publicity machinery to make this project sound like Nova Scotia's shot at becoming Alberta, and I don't see anything that's going to stop them. So make your phone call, then let me know that the project is stopped and I'll lead with that story next week." David could feel anger rise with the frightening truth he felt in each word he spoke.

A silence filled with futility fell between them. Finally, it was broken by MacNaughton. "David, whatever's behind us is behind us now, forever I hope. If you need anything from me next week for the paper, let me know. Hell, you can make up whatever you want me to say. I think you do that anyway, but whatever happens, keep in touch. I'll take your calls. Promise."

"That may happen sooner than later because as you can see here on the front page," David said, pointing out a shaded, boxed story, "thewitness.ca edition will be updating this story daily from now on, hourly if necessary."

| 60 |

David's covert dispatches to the province's other media – dailies, weeklies, radio, television – remained anonymous for about fifteen minutes after thewitness.ca posted its version of the story with Tim Donovan's unholy vision of the future. Reporters across Nova Scotia began their hunt for a story angle that would stand out beyond the Beaton Seam information already on their desks. The place to begin was with the source of the story itself so the *Witness*'s phones were in a frenzy of ringing. The documents behind the story, where they came from, what they foretold for Shean's and the province's economy, was suddenly the only story in play. David handled each of the inquiries with professional patience when all he wanted to do was get on with continuing to cover the story himself. Still, he drew comfort from the calls. It meant that the rest of the province's media, while they had not gotten as excited as David would wish over earlier accounts of what had happened in Shean since Mrs. Big Sandy took herself hostage, had been quietly watching. They considered the stories in the *Witness* a local issue, but an issue with potential provincial overtones. David and Tim's efforts hadn't been utterly ignored, merely monitored. Now the *Witness* had blown the lid off a very real story, an economic bonanza or an environmental disaster or both. David was no longer alone in asking questions, trying to pin down evasive politicians and speculators. Given a five-minute lull in phones ringing, David made his escape.

The Gulf Grill was as loud as sober people allowed themselves to be when sober, arguing the stupidity of it, the ingeniousness of it, the jobs. Fuck the jobs, they've already put the fishermen out of business. Why? So they can hire them for the mine. Or maybe they'll just let the fishermen wander around the mine site in all their fishing paraphernalia picking up dryland lobsters, stuffing crabs in their pockets. Maybe that's what they'll do. You didn't read the whole paper, my friend. The documents say that the federal Department of Public Works has agreed to rehabilitate the Lewis wharf and move the fishermen up there. Half of those fishermen were forced to come here when the federal Department of Fisheries closed most of the wharfs along here anyway so they won't mind going back. And if the Shean fishermen don't like it, well, what can they do about it? They're already divided among themselves. A good piece of strategy that, divide and conquer. So you think we've already been conquered, do you? They're going to destroy the childhood of any kid who is ever going to be born here, poor bugger won't even know what it's like to... Well I'm not saying I like it, just that it's a fact and we have to accept it. Besides, you're too old to go swimming.

"You looking for a kickback on all the coffee I sold this morning? God, I wish the *Witness* was a daily, I'd a been retired long ago,"Theresa Gulf, as she was commonly called, lamented as she filled the editor's cup. "That's about the ugliest thing I ever saw. How did they do that, David, that's what I don't understand, just walk in and say this is the way it is. If the whole town resisted, said no, refused to comply, object, even obstruct, do you think they'd send in the troops? Used to do that when the miners in this town tried to get a piece of the coal boom pie. But there is no piece of this pie, is there? Some asshole somewhere's got the whole damned thing.

"Hey David," Georgie MacLean called from a booth. "This picture – when did you take it? It's not even there yet, it's like one of those pictures of people who aren't even born yet, that's what it reminds me of. How'd you get it?"

"It's Tim's picture. It's not actually taken, it's Tim imagining what the seawall will look like using a tool called Photoshop."

"A tool, like a hammer?"

"No, it's a computer tool, digital, you know. It's a digital... thing...that you can do with a computer to make one thing look like another. You know how it is."

"No. No, I don't know – that I *do* understand. But if I do understand you, what it is I'm looking at here on this page, it's not real. It's not a real picture, you just made it up and put in on the front page of your paper and scared the bejesus out of everybody and it's not even true, this picture. Who's a guy suppose to believe?"

"Believe what's written in the paper," David told Georgie. "The picture is just trying to give an idea of what the words say, that Resource Reclamations has plans to change the environment we live in into something huge, destructive, ugly and profitable."

"Oh I don't know about that. That's an awful lot of words for anybody to be reading. Mostly I just look at the pictures, read what's under them and here I was thinking I was getting the truth like I'm suppose to expect and all the time I was being digitized by some goddamned technology. Here take this paper. I'm going to think about whether I'll ever buy another."

"He's not happy," Theresa said. "Must be awful to be like him, not to have enough imagination to get a joke leave alone how to read the news. I think you have a visitor." She nodded toward the Mountie standing behind David.

The Beaton Seam wasn't Shean's number one news story for long, being bumped out of position by the news that David

Cameron had been arrested by Corporal Harry Noseworthy and taken to jail for revealing state secrets.

In the park, in the Gulf Grill, in the Five Bucks, the response was argumentative and excited, everyone in possession of his or her own copy of the *Witness*, including Don Alex, who had been swatted on the nose by Ronald MacDonald when he tried to read the paper over his friend's shoulder. It probably wouldn't have mattered except that Don Alex, upon reading about the seawall and the Beaton Seam, slapped Ronald on the back in celebrating the good news.

"Good news!" Ronald replied, cringing under the backslap. "It's almost as bad as that franchise whose name shall not be spoken in my presence opening up shop in Shean. Buy your own paper you cheap arsehole." Don Alex did and retreated to a park bench of his own to read the good news.

The rumoured arrest remained unverified but grew to such proportions that it overshadowed the Beaton Seam story and consumed so much attention that if Big Sandy's ghost had walked through any of the three most popular debating forums he would have probably gone unnoticed.

Mrs. Big Sandy did not go unnoticed.

When she got home from work the night before, Rita had told her houseguest what would be in the *Witness* the next day when it hit the stores. The old woman was slow to grasp the concept, even when Rita drew it out on a piece of paper, showing the town, the cove, the planned seawall. In her frustration of not getting through to Mrs. Big Sandy, and her horror at what she believed Resource Reclamations was planning to bring to Shean, she summed up by saying, "This mining company could ruin the whole town, Mrs. MacArthur, pollute it and destroy it!"

The scale of what she was trying to impress upon the woman finally got through, taking the shape of a huge smile. "Will it now? Will it, indeed!"

And the next morning instead of preparing breakfast for Ronald and Rita in the kitchen she was sitting at the table with a cup of tea when they got up, wearing her going to town clothes and waiting to be driven into Shean. Rita drove her father and Mrs. Big Sandy, the former glumly grasping his daughter's sense of pending disaster, the latter spurting giggles like a little girl. Rita dropped them off at the park and they wandered off their separate ways, Ronald to wait for the *Witness* in the Gulf Grill where he needed to buy his morning's breakfast. Mrs. Big Sandy began to stroll around in a disturbing manner, humming and whistling, a persona no one in Shean had ever witnessed before. The newspaper, the arrest rumours were meaningless to her. She just walked and waited for the shock to set in.

Mrs. Big Sandy moved like the *Queen Mary* through Memorial Park where men sat about on benches, some chatting to each other here, some arguing with each other there, some stubbornly silent with each other. A single theme dominated all the moods and emotions being expressed or suppressed, the Beaton Seam.

"There is absolutely no goddamned way this company or any other company can push the ocean back to get at the Beaton Seam. David Cameron's pulling our legs. Who are they going to hire to do it, Charlie, I ask you that? Who are they going to hire? Moses to part the sea?"

"No, Danny, it's technology. They have that now, you know, technology. They didn't have it when we were young but they have it now, technology."

"And what technology are they going to use to push the ocean around like a puddle?"

"Well, they're going to use just what I said, technology."

"And I asked you what technology. But now what I'm asking you is what is technology. What in the hell do they mean when they say that word? Technology! We didn't have no technology in our time, just shovels and picks and steam shovels and bulldozers. That's all we had but now all they have is technology, so tell me what technology is."

"Well, it's what it is. Technology – you know, computers and stuff. It's in the papers all the time, technology."

"And that's what they're going to do, is it, use computers to push the ocean back..."

Charlie Mackay and Danny Sampson felt the shadow fall over them from behind their bench and fell into frozen silence.

Mrs. Big Sandy harrumphed into the back of their balding heads. "A lot you know about it, either of you, a janitor and a...a...what, a waste of your father's semen is what Sandy used to say about you, Sampson, the way you used to question his burnt-out checks, lording it over him in that stupid government office where you pretended to work! Oh the party they had when you retired. Did you know that? The widows and the burnt-outs and the other people you used to make beg for a tank of oil in February. Didn't invite you to it, did they? That's because they were celebrating the sight of your fat arse going out the door for the last time. And you were just as stupid then as you sound now. That's what they spent their measly checks on that month, booze to celebrate getting rid of you like you were head lice.

"Why Sandy ever let you live this long! But what's going to happen to you now, the two of you, and all these other fossils sitting around here making fun of everybody who walks by. She's a goner, you know, this park. The MacNaughtons have plans for it that don't include you in their fancy pancy restaurant. Just as well. All you'd be breathing here would be coal dust. You'll be doing that in your livingrooms anyway, just like before. Revenge is mine, sayeth the Lord."

Mrs. Big Sandy's arrival at the Gulf Grill had three men jammed in the washroom doorway, not giving an inch to each other while she stood in the middle of the restaurant looking around like a census-taker at the mostly empty booths. Those that were occupied were holding the *Witness* high, absorbed in the lead story or the obituaries or whatever page would keep them from making eye contact with the woman whose glaring silence sought out the most likely candidate for an assault. Theresa Gulf poured a coffee for Mrs. Big Sandy and placed it at the counter and directed her attention toward it, but the old woman was having nothing to do with the peace offering, ignoring the cup and the grill's owner until her search located the odd coupling of James Jamison and Ted Clarke in a booth, each with a copy of the *Witness* and huddled in conversation. Jamison, owning a respected dining room in his hotel-motel complex, was a rare sight at the Gulf and rarer still was the councillor's sidekick on council, Ted Clarke. She had them cornered, and moved in for the kill.

"Well Mr. Jamison, what do you think of that news?" The question merely rhetorical, she charged on. "You're Mr. Vision of this dump of a town, aren't you? The new sidewalks, the new fancy lights all over the street. Wanting to dress this town up in cheap paint and pavement just so more people will stop at your bedbug hotel and make you richer than you already are. That's what you want. A golf course! Ha! Sandy always used to say about your golf course that there'd be nobody swinging no golf clubs down there, just Canadian Club like always. And now along comes Donald the Bastard and his crew and his rich friends and they're going to turn Shean back into what it always was before you came along with your big ideas about rich tourists flocking like seagulls to the beautiful beach. Well, where's your beach now, Mr. Jamison? It's going to be pushed over to Prince Edward Island, that's where, and we'll all be covered in coal dust again, and the only thing dirtier than coal dust is half the minds in this stupid little town." As she turned to leave, Mrs. Big Sandy caught Theresa's eye, holding the younger woman in her stare for a moment before her gaze grew more sympathetic and she released her without a word. The elderly woman, like Theresa, had had her head filled with nightmares of business failure when the MacNaughtons built their big restaurant in the park.

Mrs. Big Sandy had two more stops to make before making her way to the Co-op to catch her pre-arranged drive home with Rita. She stood in front of The Five Bucks, deep breathing before her entry, stoking her engine, which was ignited by the memory that she was not allowed inside this establishment. Patrons were always being barred from The Five Bucks, including Sandy from time to time for pounding the piss out of this waiter or that drinking partner. It was a simple code: the bartender told a patron that he was barred for a week or a month or a year, and most abided by the ruling, meekly waiting out their sentence. Mrs. Big Sandy, in her drinking days with Sandy, was the only Five Bucks customer who required a restraining order. That had been a forgotten number of years ago and she wondered if it was still in place. She hoped so as she opened the door and stepped inside the darkness of the morning tavern, barely able to discern people from tables, the only light seemingly provided by the terminals of the video lottery machines. As her eyes adjusted she was able to take in the whole place. Only a few tables were occupied, mostly by the hair-of-the-dog crowd that needed an early morning fix and who would be fixtures there until closing time.

"It's all over gentlemen," she yelled, loud enough to vibrate already fragile heads, roil unstable stomachs. "It's all over. There's jobs coming to Shean and every one of youse is going to be sent down to the open-pit mine with a pick and shovel to steal the Beaton Seam right from under the ocean. Because the ocean," she explained, anticipating that reading the morning paper wasn't a high priority with this crowd, "because the ocean is going to disappear. Did you know that? They have the technology to do it, that's what they're saying, and so they're going to do it, and there's not a damned thing you or anybody in this town can do about it. But the best part is that you beggars and thieves, that's what Sandy called you, beggars and thieves, is going to have to go to work because the government won't let you live off hard-working people like the rest of us when there's work to be done. You'll have to pay your own goddamned way.

"Sandy always said that most of youse here in Shean would shit yourselfs if a mine or factory came along because Shean has been a pogey heaven for so long, people going away to earn your stamps or whatever they're called now and coming home and drawing unemployment insurance for the rest of the year without anybody ever having to be afraid of the Manpower Office calling them, telling them there's a job right here in Shean they're being sent to. Well that's all over gentlemen, your big pogey scam is as good as over. That's what they're out there protesting, most of them. So why don't the whole bunch of you go home and pack your lunch cans because it's over! It's all over!"

In the corner, a video lottery machine sounded the bells and whistles of a major win. That someone had been playing while Mrs. Big Sandy was talking upset the old lady. She went over to the machine, dumped the player off his chair then caught the top of the display terminal and, with a massive heave, crashed it to the floor. The bartender went to the phone but Mrs. Big Sandy called to him on her way out. "There's already an injunction against me in here somewhere. Just look around under the counter and you'll probably find it."

Her final stop took her to what had once been the McArthur land. The torched house had already been hauled away. There were "No Trespassing" signs on the gate but it was open and she felt a desperate need to go home, to walk along the changing landscape of the property where they had lived for so many decades along with Sandy's centuries-old roots, which he both cherished and despised. The construction yard, for that's what it clearly was now, was a hive of activity, although everyone on site ignored her as she made her way to the highest point of the land, which was really the highest point made by years of mine tailings dumping, and stood and looked out at the Gulf. It was here that she and Sandy would come from time to time, not often, and stand and watch the sun set. They preferred the autumn sunsets with their blast furnace reds and violent purples swirling as the sun hurried down past them in the shortening days. Sometimes Sandy's hand would find hers and they would stand there watching, pretending that nothing was happening between them, that their fingers weren't clinging to each other, and stay until the last ray of light left the sky. If Sandy was still here walking his land this is where he would expect to find her, and as she stood there alone she felt less lonely than she had since the day Sandy died and left her.

| 61 |

"I need to know where those files have come from," Corporal Harry Noseworthy told the newspaper editor.

He had picked David up at the grill following a phone call from Halifax. Before the newspaper was even back from the printers to be distributed throughout the town and county, the online version had been posted the night before. It had been read by someone, presumably in Halifax, who appreciated the bombshell nature of the story and informed his or her superior, who probably notified the minister of Mines, who probably contacted the premier, who probably contacted the attorney general who, no probable about it, contacted the RCMP demanding an investigation into the leaking of confidential government documents.

"David, I'm going to ask you again, how did you come into possession of those documents? I'm asking you to hand them over to me. Better for you that you do it now than when investigators arrive from Halifax to grill you. You can stonewall me all you want but they'll find out, they'll find out because they don't give a shit for you or what they'll need to do to you, but they'll find out. You can save yourself and everybody else a lot of trouble by telling me now. How long do you think it will be a secret? It's a small province and the Department of Mines and Minerals is a small department and eventually we'll find the culprit, so you may as well tell me now."

"I made a nine-day novena to St. Jude asking for help in uncovering what Resource Reclamations and the government are up to and on the ninth day these documents appeared on my desk," David answered.

"And what does St. Jude call himself when he's not in Heaven?"

"I don't know, but I know my own name isn't Judas. If I've committed a criminal act, corporal, charge me."

"Criminal act? Oh, you did commit one, but don't be naive, David. This isn't about criminal acts, this is political, and you've pissed off some very powerful people in this province. Politicians don't like whistleblowers in their midst or journalists sniping at them from the pages of their newspapers."

"And the RCMP is at their beck and call?"

"No we are not! Regardless of the Attorney General's motive for calling us in, a crime has been committed, and you committed it."

"Corporal, I have nothing to tell you. I had an awful lot of news to tell people in Shean about what's going to happen to their town and their lives if this project goes ahead. How they react to it, I can't predict. Maybe most people will embrace it. Maybe most people will be outraged over the stupidity of going after the Beaton Seam. What I do know is that the corporation and the government have been keeping information away from the people here, and I'll tell you why. Because they don't believe that this is something people will willingly accept. It may already be too late to stop it. It's gone too far, I'm afraid. I can understand the secrecy of Resource Reclamations and the creep who heads the corporation, he's beyond the ability to care about anything, but Jesus, Harry, our own government...

"You know what's sad? That there's no way to measure the destruction that's coming. The project promises a lot and will even deliver on a lot of those promises. Good jobs, economic prosperity — rare things that people around here usually hear about happening elsewhere, Alberta or the Northwest Territories. But the cost, the cultural cost, the loss of identity, the destruction of an environment that Shean has cherished for as long as the town's been here, there's no way to measure the loss of a community's soul, Corporal, and that's the price of the coming prosperity. I'm able to tell people about it because someone had the courage to let me in on the nastiness of some members of our own government. I have nothing else to tell you."

"Do you think I don't know what you're talking about? I come from Newfoundland, or perhaps I haven't mentioned it to you before." Noseworthy said this with a small smile, a fleeting touch of the friendship that existed between them beyond the parameters of this professional encounter. "What we know in Newfoundland about the destruction of communities is legendary. I was raised in St. John's by parents who, along with thousands of others, were forced out of their outport villages and dumped into the city. There was never a day that the outport wasn't mentioned by my father, and never a day, I don't think, that my mother didn't cry over the loss of her home and all her family buried there.

"And when it comes to silly government-backed projects, even the Beaton Seam can't top Newfoundland's great cucumber conspiracy. Do you remember the Newfoundland government's plan to grow cucumbers in the middle of Newfoundland? Going to market them to the whole world, we were. Greenhouses, acres of them, you could see them glow like ghost towns when you flew over. Millions of dollars wasted, but I suppose millions were made by Cabinet ministers and corporate CEOs and whoever else helped sell that harebrained scheme.

"Personally, I think what's proposed for Shean is every bit as stupid, and will probably be just as disastrous as you predict, but none of it is illegal. What is illegal are the files themselves, your having them. Maybe you look on your source as a hero but the fact is that he, or she, has broken the law, and my duty is to uphold that law. If that sounds ideal or silly to you, that's your problem. I have some commanding officers above me that I may not respect, maybe don't even trust, but I do respect and trust the law, and it's been broken here in a serious way. This is a person I believe would betray his country as quickly as he betrayed his minister or the coal company and I have no use for him. He's a criminal, David. We'll find him."

David refused to answer, finally asking if he was under arrest and if not was he free to go. He was, at least until it was time for Corporal Noseworthy or an investigating unit to question him again.

"David, you might want to see this. The premier is giving a press conference on *News World*," Cheryl said, a couple of hours later, not adding that they had stumbled on it clicking around the big television in search of *Coronation Street*. David hurried away from his writing.

"...because much ado is being made of nothing regarding the proposed mining of coal in Shean. Or let me rephrase that, much negative ado is being made about something important in Shean. All you reporters present know what I am talking about. Nova Scotia has been in an economic struggle for decades. The innovative proposal by Resource Reclamations Limited, virtually a Nova Scotia company, holds that key. If Resource Reclamations Limited is successful then Nova Scotia coal may once again compete in local and international markets.

"Much has been said about the environment, as always happens when two or more anti-capitalists gather to criticize the hard work, investment and even the prosperity that that hard work and investment bring to others. I reject the insinuation that people like myself, that a government such as ours, elected and trusted by the people of this province, don't care about the environment, but it seems to me a poor way to protect a pristine environment in any place, by keeping people unemployed.

"Here are some cold, hard facts for all Nova Scotians to consider. Eighty per cent of the population of this country now lives in urban areas, in cities. When people living in rural communities look around them what they see are roads crumbling, infrastructure collapsing, schools in need of repair, hospitals losing beds every time there's a new budget. Shean, like every town its size, needs massive investment. How long can people living in rural environments go on believing they have some inherent right to demand new roads, new schools? Someday, some politician is going to stand here, in front of this legislature building right here in Halifax or maybe in Ottawa, and ask the people of those and other cities, 'Are you willing to pay higher taxes so people in places like Shean can have better roads or a new school?'

"Shean may well be one of those communities about which those questions will be asked. And if that economically troubled town turns down this golden opportunity to pay its own way because of a handful of environmentalists and radicals and a left-wing newspaper, I think people in the rest of the province are going to remember a time when Shean had the opportunity to help pay its own way, and refused that opportunity. They'll think twice about their tax dollars going to infrastructure and services in Shean. But in Shean, economic opportunity exists now, and the people of Shean are going to be able to pay their own way despite the current dissent because Resource Reclamations Limited gives them that chance.

"By supporting this economic development, in this case the development of the long-elusive coal field that we know as the Beaton Seam, this government is reaffirming its commitment to development. We need to make ourselves energy independent."

"I'll take a few questions. Identify yourself if you do have questions."

"Briggs with the *Metropolitan News*. Mr. Minister, the Ecology Action Centre has launched a large campaign to see that the development in question never happens. They quote the damage to the fishing industry in Shean as well as other potential dangers such as coal dust, a resurgence of asthma and TB, black lung and the loss of sensitive reefs. How do you respond?"

"Mr. Briggs, the Ecology Action Centre occupies a building in Halifax that if it wasn't there, the building I mean, might be a nice green space within this city, a park or a playground. Are they prepared to move their offices into the trees along Robie Street to convince us of their sincerity? But more seriously, I understand that Resource Reclamations Limited and the federal Department of Fisheries have reached an agreement on how the fishery in Shean will continue. In fact, that information has already been made available in the media, illegally I might add, through stolen documents.

"To address your second point, the health of the community is at no greater risk with the development than it is at risk by maintaining the status quo. The very first determinant of a community's health, as identified by the federal Department of Health, is unemployment. Supplementary to that, we are not talking about underground mining where miners are trapped in a cycle of breathing bad air. The current statistics concerning asthma among Nova Scotia's children is alarming and there are no coal mines operating. Public health is a bigger issue than this one industry, an industry that isn't even operating as we speak, but the health of the people in Shean will be closely monitored.

"Your third point, Mr. Briggs, the destruction of the sea floor or reefs. We have the assurance of C.J.M. Lord and Resource Reclamations that those reefs will be restored. It's being done all the time all over the world, the sinking of decommissioned war ships and other redundant items that form reefs within a few years, become alive with coral and other life forms. A similar approach will be carried out in Shean, possibly leaving a Mecca for divers from around the world that will make Shean a diver's paradise."

"Sheila Gunn, CBC. Nova Scotia is presently Canada's worst coal polluter. If the province encourages this production, what incentives are there to discontinue the burning of coal when newer, safer, more efficient technologies become available?"

"One of the world's great misconceptions, Ms. Gunn, is that coal is a dirty source of energy. It continues to carry the blame and the sins of the past, but clean coal technology has been in the works for a long, long time..."

"Isn't clean coal research funded by the coal industry?"

"The source of funding should be irrelevant. Results are what matter. And results are being achieved. What this government and I are encouraging is for the province's power plants to move as quickly as possible to the development of a circulating fluidized bed for power generation. It's not new technology. South Africa developed it during World War II and recent research in Poland demonstrates that coal fluidized-bed units show significantly satisfactory emissions levels. C.J.M. Lord, CEO of Resource Reclamations Limited, has already indicated that his corporation could become the vehicle for the development of that technology in Nova Scotia.

"That's all the questions I have time to answer right now. Any further questions can be directed to my communications official."

| 62 |

Rita MacDonald saw that David's car was still parked at the *Witness* office and pulled in beside it.

David had been lost amid the multiple paths along which the Beaton Seam story led him, and what it meant for Shean, and what it meant for his newspaper and how he might combat the premier's press conference on the front page, but his confusion was rescued by the knock on the door, the one he had been expecting, hoping for, feared might not come.

He let Rita into the office but she pulled him by the hand out onto the doorstep. His gaze followed her finger into the sky where a full moon with Jupiter at its side pointed out to them an illuminated sea, sparkling all the way to the horizon with the excitement of the late summer night.

David pulled the door closed and didn't bother to lock it, letting himself be led by Rita's silence to her car and then onto the sand. They kicked off their shoes to walk along miniature waves lazily lapping yet filling the golden darkness with the phantom roar of an ocean thrashing widely against a resisting shore. They moved smoothly together with a single destination, a single longing.

Rita was first to speak. "What do you think is going to happen, David?"

"Nothing that people won't adapt themselves to, unfortunately. I suppose when the MacArthurs and the other families first landed here a couple of hundred years ago the changes they made to the place must have appalled the Mi'kmaq who were already here, seeing the forests vanishing into ploughed fields, wooden houses and barns and fences that said, 'This place is ours now, go away!' Unrecognizable to them. This was one of their summer camping grounds, you know, then they'd move inland for the winter. Our own ancestors probably felt they had been moved often enough and were sinking roots here. Their success was the Mi'kmaq's loss.

"And I suppose that when the coal company came, there were people who saw it as a similar devastation, the farms emptying because there was work and cold hard cash to be had in Shean, a boom town drawing miners from all over Europe and the United States, who were often violent strangers brawling in taverns that were built on what had once been farm fields where, because of the smoke and ash, not so much as dandelions grew any more. But it's also the place where we grew up, where we want to live out our lives, some of us anyway, and I suppose people will just adapt to the new facts all over again."

"Thank you for the history lesson, but what I was asking was what do you think is going to happen to you. You were arrested today."

"Not arrested. Taken in for questioning. The arrest may come later, though. Will you come to see me in the Dorchester pen?"

"It's no joke, David. The stories are spreading, stories that you're being sued, that you'll lose the *Witness*, that you'll lose everything over this. You seem to have pissed off a lot of important people, or people who think they're important. You must be worried about it."

David walked beside her, recalling that he had uttered those exact words about pissing people off several hours earlier. "Did Noseworthy stop by for coffee tonight?"

"Yes. Why?"

"Just wondering," David answered. "I don't know what's going to happen, Rita. The fire at the house is a good lesson in how quickly anyone's fortunes can change so I'm not taking anything for granted. But about Noseworthy, he wanted to know where the files came from and that's the line in the sand for me. Only three people know where those files came from, the person who gave them to me, myself and you with your intuition, but I need you to promise me that no matter what happens, no matter what charges there are, if there are any at all, you will keep what you suspect to yourself. We're friends and something more, but the other person is a stranger to you. He's not to me, not any more. So promise me that under no circumstances will you come to my defence at the cost of his identity unless I ask you. Will you?"

"Promise."

They continued to stroll along the beach, David lost in legal thoughts. His privately hired libel lawyer didn't hold out much hope since David acted against legal advice from his newspaper association's lawyer not to publish the document he had submitted for an opinion. After reading the news story, his lawyer told David that the *Witness* would have a hard time mounting a defence if the Department of Mines and Minerals or the Attorney General decided to come after him with both barrels blazing. His suggestion to David was that the publisher's only defence might be an all-out offensive in hope of shaking loose some rotten apples. Most politicians have their pockets full of rotten apples they want no one to learn about.

Rita stopped, kicked off her shoes, socks and carrying them in her hand stepped into the wet sand at the water's edge, the wavelets rolling against her toes. "These after-work visits here have started to feel like pilgrimages," she said, "like if I miss coming here one night after work it will vanish like that village, what was it called, the one in the movie..."

"Brigadoon," David answered.

"Yes, Brigadoon. I suppose we all live in a place called Brigadoon, a place that's forever disappearing. All those changes you were just talking about? Shean today isn't anything like it was when our parents were young, which was probably different from when their parents were young. It's not even very much like it was when we were children, is it, David? And what did you mean, 'and something more'?"

Her question lost David, left him scrambling to remember what he'd said, to wonder what he'd meant.

Rita rescued him. "When you said we're friends and something more. What's 'something more' to you? And don't think about it, just tell me."

"I guess I meant that we've become lovers," David answered, "Sort of. I mean we are but we haven't really talked about it, and maybe we shouldn't. Not now. Not yet. We're both being swept along by circumstances we don't seem to have any control over, and I've been in circumstantial relationships before. Those circumstances could change the world we live in into something unrecognizable. Maybe into a place I won't want to live in any more, a place where I won't want to raise my children. Maybe I'll become like you, someone who wants to escape a life sentence here. I can't analyze it, not really, and I don't want to. I just know that if you weren't here at this time in this place, I'm not sure how I would be handling this madness." He made a sweeping gesture with his hand that took in the entire bay. "With the paper I mean. I'm not sure I wouldn't just shut up and go along."

"You'd never do that, David. It's got nothing to do with me, that part of you. That's just who you are, and that's why ... yes, you're right. Let's not examine our lives right now, let's just live them," she said, turning to him, feeling the press of his lips on hers.

| 63 |

Donald MacNaughton came to David's office to learn what he'd missed during his absence.

"Absence. I didn't even know you were gone."

"Halifax. Annual gathering of municipalities, meeting with the minister. Standard stuff. Did I miss anything I should know as mayor?"

David smiled. "Catch the premier's press conference by any chance?"

"Nope. We're off each other's Christmas card list. What did he have to say."

"Lots. Give a listen," David said, cueing up a CBC podcast link, turning up the volume. "I won't subject you to the whole thing, but there are a few points he makes that you may be interested in."

"Here are some cold, hard facts for all Nova Scotians to consider. Eighty per cent of the population of this country now lives in urban areas, in cities. When people living in rural communities look around them what they see are roads crumbling, infrastructure collapsing, schools in need of repair, hospitals losing beds every time there's a new budget. Shean, like every town its size, needs massive investment. How long can rural people go on believing they have some inherent right to demand new roads, new schools? Someday, some politician is going to stand here, in front of this legislature building right here in Halifax or maybe in Ottawa, and ask the people of those and other cities, 'Are you willing to pay higher taxes so people in places like Shean can have better roads or a new school?...'"

"The sleazy bastard!" Donald said.

"That's a given, but what's new about what he said, Donald?"

"New? Nothing's new about what he said because it's already been said, by me. If you remember the public meeting, well those are my words almost verbatim. Rural communities, pay our own way, all of it. Now he's using my words to make the town, and me, look stupid."

David waved a copy of the *Witness* containing the mayor's words from the weeks-old public meeting over the open-pit mine. "You're being bit in the arse by your own teeth, you mean. It happens. It's politics. But there was something else the premier said that made me curious, Donald. Earlier in the speech he claimed that Resource Reclamations was 'virtually a Nova Scotia company,' so I did some digging and the company is registered in Nova Scotia. The registry also makes available the executive and board members of the company," he added, passing a paper to Donald.

Donald scanned the page. "Lyonel Briggs, that's Elmer Monke's former law partner. Thornton Jones here is a brother-in-law to Ted Singer. Sylvan McKnight is a contractor and the largest contributor to the party's last campaign. Jeanette Sole was the premier's campaign manager. And some of these other names are serious party heavyweights. But there's a name missing here. Mine! Why wasn't I offered one of those seats?" Donald flushed with anger. "I worked hard for those bastards and besides, there should be someone from Shean on the board."

"I suspect C.J.M. Lord could see right through you to that perverse sense of integrity of yours," David offered.

"Meaning?"

"Well, whether you like it or not, you aren't a wholly corrupted politician. Not yet, anyway. Sure, you signed on for an open-pit mine that I think indicates that you would do almost anything to help yourself politically, to the point of making yourself believe an open pit is a good thing because it means jobs. But if you had been asked or appointed, or however they do it, to the board of directors, then Lord would have been required to lay out for you Resource Reclamations's entire plan, including the seawall and the Beaton Seam. Probably he thought you'd balk at that."

"Probably? No probably about it. Look, David. On the record. I was approached by Singer and C.J.M. Lord about a proposed resource-based development for Shean. You know that's where my focus has always been as mayor, to find a year-round means of putting this town to work. I'm not much on tourism or government services as sources of sound employment. While James Jamison and his committee were exploring seasonal stuff like tourism, golf courses, resorts, whatever, I was talking to people who try to get the greatest value out of wood products. Instead of pulp they wanted to build a lumber mill making construction-grade material. It fizzled, but that's what I've been interested in. Then one day I received a visit from C.J.M. Lord, accompanied by Singer and Monke, envoys of the premier, and they had a proposal to run by me. Was it possible, they asked?

"What they described was reclamation mining, an open pit. How would I or the town feel about that? I told them that if there were enough jobs with decent pay, it could be sold to people. Not you, perhaps, but to enough people to pull it off. You'll be able to do it, I told them, acting like some stupid adviser, as long as the mine doesn't reach the sand dunes and the beach. My words, David. *As long as it doesn't reach the sand dunes or the beach.* I may not be a big fan of tourism but I'm not stupid either. That beach, that whole shoreline, has value. Jamison's right about that; it's not enough, but tourism coupled with industry is good for everybody. So my only condition to Lord was that it be protected. No problem, he assured me. No problem. If he had showed me this blueprint I'd have punched the little fat fucker's lights out! But he didn't and so I went along with it.

"Now this next section I'm going to tell you isn't for the record because I plan to stay alive, but I told them not only was it possible but the general area they were looking at belonged to Sandy MacArthur, and he was dying. The property was in arrears, it was a toxic site as far as the Department of Environment was concerned, and it was suggested that with his death the land would be available for a song. At that time they were giving Sandy a couple of weeks but it stretched into more than a year, stubborn old fucker, but that worked even better in their interests, Lord and the premier's. It gave them time to put all sorts of things into place so that it was a go almost from the moment Sandy died. I thought Mrs. Big Sandy would be easy to buy out since she probably had no money – she wouldn't even be able to pay the property taxes. I got that part wrong, but I was sure she'd take the expropriation offer. Well, as you know, she didn't, and my own offer to buy her place had me ending up in the hospital. But there was no stopping the process.

"Now back on record, David, I made a mistake getting involved with these people. The process should have been more open but it's too late for that now. What I think, and what I'm telling you based on what I've heard and what I've learned – and I do have my own sources too – is that these plans for the Beaton Seam have been in play for a long time, and I think that Lord and the province have been setting everything in place so that the seawall construction can go ahead without a hitch. They've sold it to Cabinet. They got federal Fisheries to go along. It was going to be a big economic win for Shean, for the whole province and for a government facing an election, and the ticket to that win is the Beaton Seam. But Christ, this is a disastrous development for our town. You once wrote in an editorial that rural towns like ours, in looking for an economic solution, need to be careful that they don't become so blinded by jobs and money that they lose the nature of the very place they're trying to save."

"I wrote that?"

"Yeah, but if you can't remember, then it's something I said ... feel free to quote me. And I also want your readers to know that if the Attorney General follows through with a lawsuit or court case against you or the *Witness* over those confidential files, we will seek intervener status in the courtroom. I've polled council informally and we're agreed on this. This project needs to be stopped!"

"Those statements will pretty well sink your chances at a Cabinet post, or even a nomination, won't they?" David asked.

Donald smiled at him. "Off the record again, I had a chat with the leader of the opposition while I was in Halifax. His party would really like to get rid of some of its aging deadweight and they plan to talk to our Grady Snow about retiring, maybe getting him a party perk or a provincial one if they can defeat the government."

"And of course..."

"And of course, your paper is going to get me that nomination and, I love telling you this unhappy news, it's going to get me elected, because I'll be giving you other quotes, all warm and woolly and critical of the people who are trying to wreck this town, a town in need of leadership at the provincial level, Cabinet material in the new government. That's what the leader of the opposition and myself chatted about and none of this is printable. But when it does become printable you're going to hate saying the things about me that you're going have to say, but I'm the right person and you know it."

With Donald's departure David sat at his desk exploring a question that hadn't been asked yet, not by the paper and not by him because his assumption had been that once he ferreted out the board of directors for Resource Reclamations, he would have his answer. He didn't. The Beaton Seam was the mining company's first undertaking and it was a massive one, hundreds of millions of dollars perhaps. Where was the money coming from? Chasing that question across the Internet led him to a venture capital group called Coastal Futures. But there's a firewall there around the seawall here, David mused.

Intelligence, a *Star* editor once told him, wasn't knowing something but knowing where to find it. He dialled Jim Turner's desk.

"Jim, David here. How are things in Toronto?"

"Like you care. What's happening? I've been following your story online. The daily updates are a good idea. It's getting more and more interesting, so much so that I'm scraping together my own version."

"Well, if you want the whole story, your version or mine, you're going to have to help me. I'm trying to find out who the major investors are in the Beaton Seam. The company's board of directors is a bunch of political slugs. No investors of scale. But I have traced Resource Reclamations Limited back to a venture capital fund, Coastal Futures. It seems the fund is providing the seed money and apparently whatever else is needed to get the Beaton Seam up and running, but I can't crack that nut, the one that would tell me who those investors are, who these people are behind the development. It seems strange, suspicious actually, considering the amount of money involved, that no investors are represented on the corporation's board, just local political pigs with their snouts in a new trough.

"I don't suppose I need to explain venture funds...," David continued.

"No, you don't. I know how they work. Investors spread the capital from the funds among several business, playing the odds that some will fail, others will stagnate or be stillborn, and some will succeed, reaping huge rewards for investors."

"Thanks for the lesson, which was about the same as the one I was going to give you. You know this isn't what I normally do for a living, so I want to ask you if it's curious that Coastal Futures is putting all its eggs in one basket, the Beaton Seam. What do you make of that?"

"You're right that putting all their eggs in one basket is a curious way for a venture capital group to invest.

"Aside from that, if this Coastal Futures fund isn't publicizing its investors then they clearly don't want any publicity. Venture funds aren't like nickel and dime mutual funds. They usually have serious capital within them, capital that comes from major players, especially on the investment scale that the Beaton Seam needs. If it's a sealed fund, then it won't be easy. Frankly, David, if there is a way for me to find out, it's going to cost me some pretty serious capital. I don't mean cash but I'll have to call in a lot of my own chips to get the information, if it can be gotten at all."

"I'm not asking you to break any laws here, am I?"

"No, much worse. You're asking me to be a journalist daredevil which isn't my natural state of self preservation but..."

"Jim?"

"Give me a minute."

David waited through the pause until impatience got the best of him. "Look Jim," he said. "I'm asking for your help only as far as you can give it. I don't have a hope in hell of getting any further with this, but then I think, 'I know the heart of the story lies there, in knowing who the investors are and why they're so shy about letting you, me or anyone know about it.' If you run into a brick wall..."

"Or a seawall?"

"....wear a helmet. Protect yourself, but you're the only hope I have."

"Actually what I was thinking is that I may not be your only hope. Would it be okay to bring Bethany into it?" Jim said. "She's a skilful investigative reporter, but if you're reading the *Star* online you know that. She has contacts way beyond anything I've cultivated. They're not necessarily in the field of high finance but one or more of them have worked for her before. She describes these nameless people – and even with me she protects her sources – claiming a couple of them have the qualities of a digital jewel thief, the means to break into somebody's corporate mainframes and pilfer confidential files. She may not want to touch this with a ten-foot pole, but it won't hurt to ask."

"Look Jim, anything you or Bethany can do to help me with this, I'd appreciate. But I'm not asking either of you to put anything on the line for this or for me. I don't want either of you to become collateral damage in my story."

"Well, if we do wind up unemployed, how are you fixed for reporters?

| 64 |

Mrs. Big Sandy wasn't happy that Rita was dragging her back into town to take part in a protest against the proposed seawall and coal mine development. "Where were all these people when the government was stealing Sandy's land? Did they give a fiddler's fu– "

Rita's upheld hand stopped the woman mid tirade. "Mrs. MacArthur, I agree with you. People should have been more involved when your land was expropriated but they ... we weren't ..."

It was Mrs. Big Sandy's turn to stop Rita and have her say. "Don't you dare include yourself with that riffraff. If it was up to them I'd be in jail or worse, in that old people's home where you work. I'm going to this protest because you asked me, not because I give a good goddamn what they do to the rest of the town since they've already destroyed the only place Sandy could call home in this world. Destroyed by men with balls so small they couldn't screw a gnat, all they could do is screw an old widow out of her husband's home. They can bulldoze the whole place for all I care, but you care, Rita, although I don't know why. You told me yourself that you want to go away on one of those big ships, but that's why I'm going through this nonsense, for you, but don't tell me to be on my best behaviour. If I'm going to do this I want to have a little fun while I'm at it."

Ronald MacDonald stayed wisely quiet in the back seat where he had been relegated at some forgotten point since Mrs. Big Sandy came to live with Rita and him. He was trying to ignore the empty place within him that was slowly filling up with fear. Everybody was talking about the seawall and the mine and what it would mean, and they argued with each other about having jobs at home instead of going away, or the destruction of the shoreline that would no longer make Shean a coastal town. Instead, the town would have a black abyss in its midst that would spurn visitors looking for beautiful places to rest or swim. Its only appeal might be to those looking for work. Nobody was talking any more about what the mine would mean to local businesses. There were a few that might benefit from the mine, but most were small businesses providing services like tea and coffee in tiny restaurants like the Gulf, good food even if the menu was heavier than bunker oil in grease and lard.

But with the mine would come more people and bigger businesses, the kind of businesses that had big signs and television ads and killed little businesses like the Gulf with their fancy looking food. He remembered what David Cameron wrote in an editorial one of the few times he took up Ronald's cause regarding corporate food outlets. David called Shean "franchise-free but flat broke," writing that it was an indication of how desperate the town's economy was that it couldn't support even one of those Canadian shrines of "fat food," Tim Horton's. It was hard to tell from David's article whether he actually celebrated or lamented Shean's economic condition, but what Ronald knew now in that rumbling stomach of his was that when the mine was developed the franchises would arrive, and among them would be the name he had stopped uttering because it blasphemed his own. Ronald MacDonald also knew from the most recent issue of the *Witness* that David Cameron and his newspaper had let him down, really let him down.

———

The sunny Saturday afternoon weather favoured the protest organized by Carmen Langille, and David thought it was noteworthy that a young high school teacher could inspire half the high school population to get out of bed on a summer morning and join her on the picket line. She was dispatching them in groups to follow along the periphery of the mine's chain link fence, instructing others to walk the shore, documenting with cellphone photos the grassy dunes, types of sand formations and shells, seaweed or other coastal treasures, all of which would be lost to them, to everyone, she explained, once the mine began. Although school had yet to begin, the students were already embarking on a science project to create a virtual Shean shoreline online, a permanent memorial in the wake of the mining madness.

Less energetic or less mobile protesters wouldn't or couldn't make the arduous walk of the vigorous young, standing instead at the mine gate stopping or slowing the flow of trucks. The protest was a large one by any measure of Shean's usual lethergy, but opposition wasn't a universal town opinion. The protesters were being heckled by a significant number of people who felt the mine was in their or the town's best interests.

David Cameron watched it through his lens before making his way to where Rita and Ronald and Herself stood with the group at the gate, Donald standing a wise distance away.

"Good turnout," David said, still snapping pictures of protestors and placards, jotting notes to himself. He felt confident enough in their changed relationship to approach Mrs. Big Sandy about a quote, he no longer being the person who shot her in cold blood. He had even felt, around Rita's and Ronald's kitchen table playing cribbage or auction, a resentful sort of liking coming from her, although the smile could just as easily be the result of a quietly released fart. Still, she had only been tangent to the Shean story since her eviction.

"What do you think this protest will accomplish, Mrs. MacArthur?" he asked.

"I'll tell you what it'll accomplish," she started, her words trailing off as she stared at a long white Cadillac that was trying to nose its way through the protesters and toward the gate. "Is that the Lord himself, the antichrister?"

"Who else would it be," Ronald noted.

"I can't tell. His car is wearing sunglasses," Mrs. Big Sandy said, pushing people out of the way and taking her place directly in front of the car. Arms crossed she glared into the tinted windshield and waited. Other protesters, smiling, smirking, gathered around the confrontation. The Cadillac inched threateningly forward. "Just you try it, buster! Just you try it!" The car made a few more mock movements toward her.

The driver's side window slid down quietly and C.J.M. Lord stuck his head out. "Would you mind moving, please? I have a right to go onto my own property!"

"Oh, the wrong choice of words," Donald whispered to David.

With the agility of an athlete the elderly woman was beside the car, her two hands pressing down on the half-opened window far too powerfully for whatever automatic gizmo raised and lowered car windows, forcing the electronic mechanism to whirl wildly somewhere inside the door. "Your own property! I dare you to step out here, you baldheaded little weasel, you worm of a thing you are. Get out or I'll pull you out through the window!"

"I phoned the police," Lord said, holding up a cellphone as proof of his threat. Mrs. Big Sandy wrenched it from his hand and flung it over her shoulder, then reached inside to grab the driver, who slid across the seat out of reach. She wrenched the door open and leaned inside. The protesters heard a whimpering sound when suddenly Mrs. Big Sandy was sitting inside the idling Cadillac and before anyone could grasp what was happening the car gears ground into reverse, backing up at a deathlike speed before wheeling the car around, its bottom crunching as the car left the makeshift road and was up onto cinders and rock before landing back on the road. Pointed in the opposite direction, it drove away while the awed protesters erupted into a wild cheer.

The RCMP arrived moments later in response to a 911 call from the mine. When the constable on duty learned what had transpired he contacted Corporal Noseworthy, who arrived in his civvies and his own vehicle.

"Kidnapped Lord! Jesus Christ!" Noseworthy looked from David to Donald to an ashen-faced Rita MacDonald, stepping toward her. "Where would she go?" he asked, not mentioning the agreed-upon peace bond and Rita's willingness to take responsibility for an arsonist who burned down her own house.

Rita's face collapsed almost to tears as she raised her eyes to meet the Mountie's. She inhaled deeply as she composed herself. "I don't know," she said, slowly recovering from shock. "But it's early to be calling it a kidnapping, isn't it, Harry? Maybe she just borrowed his car..."

"With him in it?"

"He might have said yes. It was hard to make out what he was saying..."

David turned away from that conversation, flicking open his phone and dialling Tim Donovan's number.

"Huh," a voice thick with a Five Bucks hangover asked after many rings.

David explained the situation and suddenly Tim's hangover was flushed in a rush of excitement. "Kidnapped Lord!"

"Well, we can't call it that at the moment, but that she's wanted for car theft should be okay. I want you down here asking questions, then get to the office, write it up, post it on our site then send it out to every media contact we have. Do whatever you do with social networking, blog it if you want, Tim, but flog the shit out of it."

"What about you? You're already there."

"I'll be chasing the follow-up."

"David, do I have to put my byline on this? Mrs. Big Sandy, you know, can get pretty..."

"I'll tell you a secret, Tim. Mrs. Big Sandy can't read. That's not for any news story, by the way. Now jump in the shower, rinse off the stink from last night and get down here."

| 65 |

David rejoined Donald and Ronald, the Corporal and Rita and the conversations swirling around the mine gate, while in the background a dozen other speculations were happening. The Mountie paused, his questions stopped for the moment by the ring of his Blackberry. He listened, nodded, spoke. "No, don't do anything alone. Just stay at the foot of the driveway and keep any cars from going in and especially from coming out." He hung up. "That was Constable Smith. There's a white Cadillac parked in MacDonald's yard." A convoy of MacNaughton's SUV, David's Toyota and Rita's Ford followed the RCMP officer to the outskirts of Shean and on up to Ronald MacDonald's farm.

In the yard, Noseworthy examined Lord's Cadillac, including popping the trunk. No sign of the company CEO. The Mountie eyed the barn a short distance away, then lifted his head higher and sniffed while his entourage watched. He shifted his interest to the house.

"Something's cooking." An observation that caused a smile to pass between Rita and David, both having had the same thought – that Noseworthy's nose was certainly worthy. Like a crowd of school kids behind a teacher they followed the policeman into the porch, watched him turn the knob and look through the open door while standing aside, just like in the movies. No armed fugitives fired at them and they stepped inside.

"What's all this?" a surprised Mrs. Big Sandy asked, turning to the crowd coming through the door. In one hand she wielded a knife, in the other, a half-peeled potato. "Are you all staying for supper?" she asked, giving Rita a look that said the younger woman could have warned her of company. She remained oblivious to the fact that she was the very person they were there to see. Noseworthy spoke.

"Mrs. MacArthur, where is Mr. Lord?"

"We're having him for supper so there's plenty to go round," she replied, raising the knife. When her remark brought no response she shifted directions. "Oh, you expect me to tell you where I buried the body, do you. Cough it up just like that?"

"Yes, I expect you to cooperate," the Mountie continued. "There's a matter of a broken peace bond you signed with the magistrate, and since Rita is the person who vouched for you, the person who guaranteed you'd stay out of trouble, I think you'll find she's in a bit of trouble herself."

"You wouldn't!"

"Oh, but I would, Mrs. MacArthur. Kidnapping, grand theft auto, and that's just the beginning of the charges that will be brought against you, against both of you if need be. If you've harmed Mr. Lord in any way, you're looking at assault charges and maybe..."

"Rita had nothing to do with it. You don't lay a hand on her and I'll tell you."

Corporal Noseworthy nodded an agreement to his bluff.

"He's out in the barn. I put him there because I couldn't stand the sound of his voice, the things he was calling me! He's lucky I'm not boiling his nuts in this here pot to feed to him when he gets hungry. That's what he is — lucky. I sent him out there to shovel cow shit, see if it smells any better than his own bullshit."

Noseworthy and Constable Smith, trailed by David, Donald and Ronald, made their way toward the barn.

"Mrs. MacArthur, I didn't know you could drive. Do you have a licence?" Rita asked when the men had left.

"Licence! Ha! Didn't I say the same thing to Sandy. Didn't I ask him if I needed licence. And he said if I don't have a licence I can't very well lose it if I'm caught driving, he said. So Sandy learned me, said I'd need to know how to drive his truck and I did because I can't tell you how many times I drove that thing home when we had it, with Sandy passed out beside me. So I drove the car home and it's out there if he wants it back."

C.J.M. Lord was leaning on a shovel used for shovelling manure out of the stall normally occupied by the half dozen heads of beef that Ronald MacDonald raised for whatever meagre profit it brought. David suspected a case of labour of love trumping labour of profit. Lord was staring into a dark distance, no indication he had used the shovel as anything but a prop for his intense thoughts. As the four men approached, led by the plainclothes Mountie, Lord threw the shovel aside, its clattering to the floor sending up a spray of manure flecks toward Lord's trouser leg. If he noticed, he ignored it.

"Are you okay?" Noseworthy asked. Lord replied with flinty-eyed contempt for both the question and the men listening for his answer. It told David a lot about how C.J.M. Lord commanded such confident investments. Physically, he was a political cartoonist's dream, short, rotund, hairless, traits that successfully camouflaged the evident ruthlessness swimming to the surface at the moment. They were getting an up-close look at the CEO of Resource Reclamations Limited, stripped of his public relations persona.

"Of course I'm okay. That woman and I went for a drive. That's all I've got to say about this now-closed subject." Lord passed through them as if they weren't there, making his way toward the barn door.

"Take those boots off, all of youse. You can't expect to go tracking cow shit all through the house."

Seething with rage, C.J.M. Lord walked straight through Mrs. Big Sandy's words and stood in front of the old woman, glaring at her. The old woman retaliated with the "evil eye" that had terrified generations of children and adults in Shean.

While the others watched, David studied the exchange. Lord was used to having people do his will whenever his corporate fly-casting snagged a likely political ally. Fly fishing in Nova Scotia, David suspected, had been as easy as jigging smelts for a man of Lord's experience. A naive and desperate government hungry for economic success would be common fare for Lord. Mrs. Big Sandy was someone who fell outside the realm of power within which the CEO was used to dealing, but somewhere in this very early afternoon he had finally taken her measure and wouldn't be taken in or taken away by her again. If Mrs. Big Sandy realized this, she gave no hint.

"Don't think for one minute you're staying for supper," Mrs. Big Sandy chided, but Lord thrust out a fierce hand so that all the men in the kitchen made a sudden movement to protect the widow, but she merely sneered at the out-held hand and reached into her apron pocket and produced a set of keys. That explained why Lord hadn't simply driven away from the farm the moment she left the car. They remained in a bitter staring match, Lord's hand still extended. "You've got all you're going to get from me!" Mrs. Big Sandy said. Lord let his stare linger a few seconds longer, then turned and strode toward the men who had eased themselves into chairs around the table.

"That meaningless little rag that you publish had better put a lid on the lies and innuendos its been spreading or I'll litigate you right out of business. Don't flatter yourself that you're the only person doing research in this town. I know more about you and that newspaper of yours than you'll ever learn about me, and I know that you couldn't afford two days in court with me. You'd be wise to keep that in mind. And keep this in mind:

that seawall is going to be built, the Beaton Seam is going to be mined and there's nothing your paper or this half-arsed mayor here can do about it. You'd be wise to stay out of my business, to stay out of my life, from here on." With a final look back at Mrs. Big Sandy, an unspoken communication zinging between them, C.J.M. Lord left Ronald MacDonald's kitchen, his car roaring a moment later down the driveway.

"Did you come here thinking I stole his car?" Mrs. Big Sandy said to the Mountie. "I don't know why anyone would want to steal his car for anyway. The damned thing's colder than Sandy's truck in February." This puzzled her audience until Rita said, chuckling, "the air conditioning."

Checking on thewitness.ca with his Blackberry, David saw that Tim Donovan had already uploaded his story of the confrontation and kidnapping at the mine site. David phoned the office, catching his young reporter there on his day off, telling him that the story had been resolved without incident and without charges.

"Ah, shit!" Tim said. "I sent it off to every contact we had. The phone here's been ringing wild."

"Well, Tim, you'll just have to get the truth out there, so as soon as you go home, have lunch, do whatever else it is you need to do, get back to the office and get the right story out there."

"Kinda tabloid, chief, but I like it. Will do!"

A smaller convoy of David's and Donald's cars returned to Shean, one behind the other all the way to that oasis of peace they called the Five Bucks. Donald bought the first round and returned to the table with Victor Mason in tow.

"Victor." David said with welcoming surprise. "I thought you shipped out to Alberta."

"Yeah, well," Victor answered, almost embarrassed. "I was packing when I got a call from Resource Reclamations. They needed a heavy equipment operator right away and had my application on hand. I took the job," he added, making it sound like a confession.

"That's great," David replied sincerely.

"The truth, David, is that I've been avoiding you, knowing how you feel about the development, but Christ, I can't tell you how good it is to have breakfast with the wife and kids, head off to work and be home for supper."

"You don't need to explain anything to me, Vic. Did you know about this, Donald?"

The mayor nodded, noting to his editor friend, "That paper of yours doesn't keep up with the news very well, does it?"

David returned his attention to Victor. "What do they have you doing down there?"

"Unloading trucks mostly," Victor answered. "Later, with the actual mining underway, I'll be out there," Victor added, his head nodding toward the Gulf of St. Lawrence, visible through the tavern window. All three men turned their attention to the sea for a moment. "What are you hearing about it, David? More than you can print or what?"

"Not enough to stop it if that's what's worrying you, buddy, but there's something amiss about this whole thing. No evidence of it that I can find or print. Just a feeling."

"He feels the same way about me, Victor," the mayor said. "Suspicious of anything that doesn't think like him."

"But he is printing things. I thought there was an injunction against you or the *Witness* printing anything about the story," Victor said.

"An injunction against using any of the information in the files they're investigating. That story about the board of directors up on the website now doesn't come under the injunction. There was nothing in the files about the company make-up or naming of the directors. It was fair game."

"What bothers you exactly about the board of directors? Sounds like just another bunch of political pals gathering at another trough. Happens all the time."

"Yeah, but for the most part, these are all political nobodies, Victor. None of the major investors is represented on the board of directors, just a bunch of provincial flunkies. Yet there are investors who have hundreds of millions of dollars at stake here, and they're letting people with nothing at all at stake form the board of directors. I don't get it. We don't even know who those investors are. Yet."

Victor signalled for another round of beers. Donald passed, needing to leave for a commitment at home. Victor's gaze returned to the window, giving thought to David's words, or so David hoped.

"I think you're scaring somebody," Victor said. "There's been a huge push to get this thing underway for the past couple of weeks now."

"How so?"

"Trucks are rolling in and unloading everything needed for the seawall anchors. The wall itself will be coming on barges once the anchors are set at Noss Head and Hughie's Point. A lot of cement to be poured at Hughie's Point. They're erecting a temporary cement plant on the MacArthur property, and there's been a lot of drilling and soon there'll be blasting at Noss Head to get the anchor bolts in place over there. There are a couple of carpenters on site at Hughie's Point prefabricating forms for the cement pours. We've been racking up a lot of overtime, and there's talk now of a second shift. Still only a handful of us working there but that will change once the construction starts."

Victor fell silent again, drained his beer and ordered another round. David's instinct told him to let his friend find his own way along the conversation they were having.

"I was in the engineer's trailer the other day asking about where to lay the inventory that came in on one of the trucks. There was a map of the project on the wall. Never saw it there before. Impressive, I said, telling the engineer it reminded me of the layout for a job I once worked in a strip mine in Alberta. Not the seawall, but the excavation plans seemed the same. Turns out he was one of the engineers for that same job. He was with Gardener Mines at the time. He just left that job a few months ago to come over to Resource Reclamations. Pretty exciting challenge from an engineering point of view, was how he put it. He was glad to talk to somebody who spoke the language.

"It's impressive, David, very impressive what they have in mind. From a construction point of view, that is. He was showing me his proposal to speed up construction of the anchors at Noss Head and Hughie's Point. Right now, the trucks, cement trucks, gravel trucks, whatever, will have to load up on MacArthur's land, then drive through the town, and that'll be a lot of truck traffic every day which we locals – don't you hate when people from away call local people 'locals,' like we're a separate species or something? – won't much like. And when they do get through town they have to go a ways up the Highland Road then down a road yet to be constructed to the edge of Noss Head. The same on the other end of town for the work at Hughie's Point.

"His plan cuts out eighty percent of the travel time. What he wants to do is drive a road from MacArthur's property across the sand dunes and build a bridge across the harbour channel. They'll be at Noss Head in a fifth of the time without disrupting town traffic. Same at Hughie's Point. Thoughtful, huh? Waiting right now for the Department of Environment to okay the plan but nobody's expecting problems.

"In fact, Lord came back from wherever he was today – and you're going to tell me that story when I finish mine, right? – and told us all to go home for the rest of the weekend but plan on a day and night effort to get this road across the dunes finished *tout suite.*"

Victor lifted his bottle again and drank deeply.

"Why are you telling me this, Victor?" David asked.

"Telling you what? We're just a couple of buddies shooting the shit about work over a few beer. The dunes are going to go anyway once the mine's underway. What's a few months one way or the other? So tell me, what happened with Mrs. Big Sandy?"

| 66 |

David ran Victor's story through his memory time and time again, fingers itching to type out the rhythm of its telling on the keyboard. Victor had to have known how easily the "leak" would be traced back to him, and what that meant. David knew what it meant – getting one of his friends fired in the interests of telling a story people needed to know, that destruction was imminent. But Victor had given him nothing, not a knowing nod, no wink of complicity, just a story as chilling as any ghost story that had ever haunted the Celtic place where they lived.

David deliberated what to do and heard himself humming, "The answer, my friend, is blowing in the wind," growing gradually conscious of where that inspiration was coming from. He heard it whistling through an open window somewhere in the *Witness* office, felt the jarring of it against the building's wall. The wind signalled the arrival of the first of the August gales, under whose command the waters of the Gulf rose against the land. Trees could fall, basements might flood, an unsecured mobile home might be shredded, but it was from the hammering of its huge waves against the shoreline that the fearful thrill came, drawing an audience to the shore to watch in the beams of a dozen sets of headlights.

Looking out into the premature darkness, David saw the sunset smothered under a blackness of cloud. He picked up his camera and left the office.

At the shore, David left his car to join the others. He felt he was experiencing an ancient moment, the crowd silhouetted against the eerily lit sky, and he was one of them, had been since boyhood. They gathered for this annual ritual of wild ocean watching, the first of the August gales, reminding each other of stories from the past, memories of childhood, their own or their parents' or their grandparents'. They were the same people every year, gathering as for a solstice at Stonehenge. It wasn't as if the whole town of Shean poured down to the shore, it was nothing like that, but that's how it would be remembered in the telling, "That year during the August gale the whole town headed down to the beach in the storm…"

With or without a camera or an excuse he knew he would still be here, part of something that he was only vaguely beginning to understand in the almost certain knowledge that it was going to disappear.

David had no idea how long he had been there, wind-whipped, wet and delighted until a voice rose above the ocean's sound. "I thought I might find you here," Rita said, a transparent raincoat covering her nursing uniform. "Do you think their seawall will be able to withstand this?"

David needed to lower his ear to her mouth to catch the words.

"This is as bad as I've seen it in a long time," David answered, his voice filled with excitement, sensing more than seeing the raging rise of black waves pounding their way to the shore. The waves became visible only when they broke in a white froth that formed an apron that rushed from the normal tidemark to the very banks of the dunes.

Some of the damage was already strewn about them, pieces of the small boardwalk and stairway that led people from the parking lot down onto the beach and, inexplicably, several large stones that had been on the beach were now on the parking lot. Tomorrow, David thought, all will be "changed, changed utterly," words from a poem, the title and author of which evaded him. He thought of the driftwood tree that had been his pew all summer when he came to the shore to sit and think or meditate or pray. It was being picked up now by the same waters that had deposited it here, and sometime in the future, weeks or maybe years, it would settle for a summer on some other beach somewhere. He felt the loss with bittersweet acceptance.

"Look!" Rita screamed into his ear, her hand pointing toward her own sanctuary, the breakwater. These waves would not be moving that stone bastion anywhere, but even from the distance of the parking lot the furious sea's efforts to do just that could be seen in the form of white water rushing across the top of the armour stones like a galloping stallion's mane. Not tonight, seemed to be the breakwater's answer to the destructive anger that was otherwise ripping the coastline apart.

Around them the stories were circulating, always arriving at the clan memory of a washed up body, a young girl, oh, a hundred years ago maybe, longer – yes longer, because she was buried in the dunes right up there, along with those settlers who didn't make it through that first winter, including two of the MacArthur family and two or three from the other families. There was no graveyard at the time because there had yet to be a death, and in the deep winter frost the sandy dunes offered the most sensible burial site. But it was during the August gales that the young girl washed ashore, whether from a sunken ship or washed overboard, no one ever learned. And it was during ensuing gales that people claimed they saw the girl walking the dunes.

"This was the kind of weather she washed up in, see, and she was still wandering around, looking for something, for someone. Maybe she didn't even know she was dead was what my mother said. Saw her myself, you know, not a word of a lie. It was that storm back in 1974, a real piece of work. Ten feet of shoreline went in that blow. August 17, to be exact, and I was standing here on the parking lot because just like tonight there was no shore left, just that high tide there, and I saw this person all in white floating across the top of the dunes like she was in a trance or something..."

David and Rita eavesdropped on the telling, and David joined in on the sharing of storm tales and ghost of the dunes sightings, remarking that his was probably the last generation of kids to go looking for the beautiful ghost on stormy nights.

"Last generation?" Rita teased. "You're only thirty-six."

"And you're what, thirty-three?"

"Around there."

"Did you ever go looking for her?"

"Actually I don't remember ever hearing about her."

"I rest my case. History, like these dunes here, can vanish in a hurry."

They stood and watched and got wet and grew tired and one by one the cars drifted away until Rita and David were left alone with the slowly waning storm. "Come with me," David said, making his way up the highest dune, and the tall structure topping it, a story forming itself as they climbed hand in hand.

The cairn had been dedicated three years earlier, erected by descendants of those first families. The names of those buried there were inscribed on the plaque and below was a brief description of the young girl who had washed ashore and was buried with those already at rest there.

David recalled dedication day well. The speeches themselves were generally forgotten but not the crowd that had gathered and certainly not the parish priest who had offered prayers for the dead and, more importantly, had consecrated the ground, making it an official Catholic cemetery.

———

In the stillness and sunshine of early morning the same people returned, and along with them scores more, walking along the shore, pointing out what was changed. The ocean continued to roll in wildly, driven by a now-distant force, and not venturing, despite its violent energy, beyond the natural tidemark.

David had barely slept. Having parted from Rita, he returned to the office where he wrote the story he wanted to tell, posting it on the *Witness*'s website, hoping to excite the town's imagination. At home, he napped a couple of hours on the couch, rose to have breakfast with his mother, then went back to the beach with his camera. The storm and its aftermath were in themselves a story.

The shoreline was almost unidentifiable in its changes. There were places along the dunes where five or six feet of sand and its underlying mud had gone missing. Snow fencing, which had been erected by the town following a storm a few years earlier and which had done an admirable job of trapping the sand back onto the beach, now stood in a twisted puzzle of laths and wire, having no will to act again as efficiently as it had before.

He walked past people who pointed out areas of destruction they felt the newspaper might be interested in photographing, and David followed their leads although he had a firm idea of what he wanted. Through his lens he framed his shots, but at one point lowered his camera to see if what he was seeing was real. With a smile one preserves for the meeting of an old friend he walked toward a familiar length of driftwood, his own tree. It had been lifted, shifted but ultimately left on Shean's shore. David sat down and stared out to sea, choppy with whitecaps, and whispered something like thank you, as though the ocean had personally decided to leave him a gift. Grace and gratitude.

While David was celebrating the survival of his favourite driftwood, his decision for the *Witness* to become a temporary online daily was catching on. The daily hits hinted at a modest habit forming in Shean, a couple of hundred early morning visits, people checking out the site to see what, if anything, new had happened in the Beaton Seam saga. But the *Witness* hadn't become a single issue newspaper. David and Tim, along with a couple of stringers hired to cover and submit stories, kept the regular news flowing on a daily basis as well.

On Sunday morning after the storm, readers clicked in and found themselves reading about the Ghost of the Dunes, the August gale that evoked her, the burial of Shean's first citizens, the dedication of the cairn and the consecration of the cemetery. Accompanying the stories was a front page editorial built on the theme of the ever-healing nature of Nature, and how the damaged dunes would repair themselves. That had been the way for centuries, but those same dunes would not heal easily from the coming destruction before the giant bulldozers owned by Resource Reclamations Limited. What if, David speculated, the company decided it would be efficient and profitable to drive a road across the dunes to reach Noss Head? That the dunes wouldn't see the coming autumn was a certainty, the editor noted, but that they might not see the end of summer, perhaps not even the end of the coming week was also within the realm of the possible. The editorial ended predictably by calling for the provincial government to undertake a full environmental impact assessment of so rash an act.

While David half-nodded, his head resting against the driftwood tree and his body stretched along the sand, other people in Shean began talking about what they had read that morning, sending friends home to read it for themselves. Readers edited into fact a single idea from the *Witness's* editorial: "The bastards are going to plough the dunes away starting tomorrow."

People began wandering down to the beach, drawn now not by the aftermath of the storm but by the sudden awakening of what it all meant, all this development. Among them was Carmen Langille who, after reading David's words, packed her camping gear and a week's supply of food and backpacked to the shore, where she set up her one-woman occupation of the dunes.

Father Eddie Walker, abandoning his prepared homily, spoke publicly for the first time on the issue of the seawall and the Beaton Seam, reminding the congregation that the Shean dunes constituted a consecrated cemetery. People who carried the same genes as some of those buried there were present in the church at this very moment, he noted. Their forefathers were at rest in the dunes awaiting the Resurrection. But understand, the parish priest told his parishioners, that it is not just the ground around the cairn that is blessed. The cairn, he reminded them, was placed on the most prominent height of the dunes but there was no evidence, factual or anecdotal, that suggested the exact location of the deceased. Wherever they lay, he said, is the sacred ground of those heroic first settlers who undoubtedly died in a state of grace. Theoretically, the entire stretch of dunes was a consecrated Catholic cemetery that should not, could not, be desecrated by bulldozers, unearthing bones in the most ruthless fashion. Next Sunday's Mass, Father Walker announced, would be held on the Shean dunes.

David, exhausted and semi-conscious on the sand, wondered what would happen when C.J.M. Lord read the editorial. Had his editorial succeeded in burying the fact of a source within Resource Reclamations's workforce or would Lord read between the lines and know that David wasn't speculating at all about a road across the dunes? He'd quickly find his way to Victor Mason. Then what? Fire him? Or perhaps pretend ignorance and assign Victor to the lead machine that would assault the dunes as the planned road construction started. David didn't envy Victor the decision he'd need to make in that moment.

Tim Donovan, surprisingly awake early on a Sunday morning after a night at the Five Bucks, read David's story at home. Another ghost story! These old people and their superstitions, he thought. Good stuff though, the way David was raising the dead in his war against the seawall. Tim wanted in on it. Day off or not, he drove to the beach, notebook and camera for company, and collected the stories taking place on the dunes. Carmen Langille was a stand-alone story, as was Father Walker's plan to hold next Sunday's Mass on the dunes. Other dune walkers he interviewed helped form a sense of what the destruction of the dunes would mean to them, and from those diverse reasons Tim wrote a profile of Shean's relationship to its environment, supported by a score of photographs.

David grew aware of a sound above the still rolling sea, recognizing its industrial hum coming from the MacArthur property. Sunday morning and men at work, probably finishing the erection of the cement plant, checking the machinery and inventory, preparing for the first major step in constructing the seawall: the building of a road where no road had ever been. He imagined it through his children's eyes when they returned from Toronto, the gutted shoreline where they had spent all their young summers, where they had once walked, shocked, in midwinter among decapitated seals, where their father could go any time he wanted because he didn't have a real job like Jim Turner. Perhaps he just had too much memory of his own, and perhaps Tony and Mary would eventually have no memory of it at all.

More recent memories matter too, David decided, thinking that less than twelve hours earlier, alone in a sheltered corner of the dunes, Rita and he had made almost desperate love, their passions finally subsiding as the wind itself, which had howled high above them, had eased. It was as if they had broken a wild mustang, David thought but didn't risk sharing with Rita, finding himself delightfully shocked at her words, "That felt as if we were riding the storm into exhaustion."

It was barely eleven. David phoned his mother to say that he wouldn't be there for their traditional Sunday morning brunch of poached eggs and sausages and bacon and fried ham and reservoir of tea. He could sense her disappointment but it was Rita he wanted to see before she had to work.

Mrs. Big Sandy's fare wasn't quite what his mother would have served him, but he was grateful for the tea and biscuits and time in the kitchen. It occurred to him that Ronald MacDonald's farm kitchen was becoming command central for a core group gathered around the *Witness*'s efforts to get to the truth of the Beaton Seam. Even Donald MacNaughton had found a comfortable place at the table, he and Mrs. Big Sandy staying in their neutral corners despite her intention to eventually make him pay for shooting her.

What David noticed this morning was that beyond nodding an acknowledgement of David's arrival, Ronald had remained in his livingroom office, surfing the web, challenging crib players around the world.

"Do you think your father disapproves of me seeing you?" he asked Rita quietly, lest Herself hear and decide what answered was required. "No!" Rita answered with certainty. "Why would you even ask that?"

"Perhaps you haven't noticed, but he's been distant with me for a few days now."

"Then talk to him," Rita said.

David entered Ronald's sanctum and sat in a chair beside his older friend, watching him lay down sixteen points and peg across the winning line. Another pin for his global map.

"Ronald, is anything the matter?" David asked when the game finished.

"Why would there be?" Ronald responded curtly, his manner clearly conveying that something was wrong.

"Well, for one thing, you haven't even said hello to me in days. That's not like you, so I'm asking if I did something to offend you. If I did, tell me and I'll apologize."

Ronald was quiet for an eternity before deciding to speak. "It's just that you've become so obsessed with this Beaton Seam thing that nothing else matters. There's other stories people are interested in reading in the *Witness*, you know."

"What stories am I missing, Ronald?"

"I brought you a good story and it wasn't important enough for you."

"What story?"

"Huh! You don't even remember. I brought you the story about the group that is trying to get up an online petition to get that clown to retire, and you didn't even print it."

"What do you mean? I assigned that story to Tim, asked him to work the information you brought in into a news story for the paper. I assumed it went in. I don't always remember every story that gets printed. You should have said something."

"Well I'm saying it now."

"And I'm saying this now, Ronald. I'm sorry it didn't get in when you were expecting it, but it's still news and I guarantee you it will be in this week's paper."

"You're sure?"

"Ronald," David said, his inflection asking to be trusted.

"Okay then, let's have a cup of tea and some of those biscuits, and then I got to get back here. There's somebody from Yemen thinks he can teach me a thing or two about cribbage. Ha! Where the hell is Yemen anyway?"

At the kitchen table David raised the lobby calling for the clown's retirement. "Would that bring an end to your boycott, Ronald, if the other Ronald McDonald retired?"

Ronald gave the question some thought. "Yeah," he decided, "except for one other little thing."

"Which is?"

"Well, they could change their name to Campbell's," he said, evoking the 1692 massacre of the MacDonalds of Glencoe by the Campbells of Argyle, causing an animosity between the two clans that lingers through the next three centuries.

"I'm afraid another company's already got that name tied up."

"It's okay with me if they sell soup alongside their hamburgers. I got nothing against their soup, even have a couple of cans in the cupboard there."

| 68 |

"Tim, Ronald MacDonald was asking me why we didn't run the information he brought in for the last issue. I asked you to work it up into a filler piece to keep him happy. Didn't you do it?"

"Yes, well I am doing it, but it's taking a bit of research."

"Research?"

"Yeah, but it's interesting."

"With all that's going on around here you think it's interesting to be researching the retirement of a clown?"

"What clown?"

"What clown? What other clown is there? Ronald McDonald. Know him?"

"The old guy in the kilts? Sure I know him. Don't know if I'd describe him as a clown though, but odd, really odd."

"I mean Ronald McDonald the clown, Tim! Do you know him!"

"Oh yeah, that one. But what's he got to do with industrial insurance?"

"Industrial insurance?"

"That thing the old guy printed off, you asked me to look into it. I picked it up off your desk where you said it was. It was about insurance. But first, I want to ask you, do you have any insurance policies on me, you know, insurance that I don't know about, so that in case I die or something you'd get the money and not my parents?"

"Now why would I do that?"

"Well, then, do you know what a COLI is?"

"Yes, Tim, I do. COLI is an acronym for company owned life insurance policy. They also call it Key Man Insurance, so that if the company president or vice president gets killed, the company collects the insurance to cover the costs of finding someone to replace that key man."

"Good, boss. You're scoring a hundred percent so far. Next question: do you know what Dead Peasant Insurance is?"

"Dead Peasant Insurance? Got me there, Tim. Never heard of it."

"Then let me tell you how it works. There are companies that buy insurance on their own regular employees without telling them, a half million, maybe a million dollars, and the company pays the premium. If the guy is killed on the job, the company gets the insurance, see. He's just a working joe, right, a dead peasant to use their jargon, and they don't even have to tell the guy's family. I'm not talking about key man insurance on company presidents or vice presidents, David. I'm talking about corporations that buy life insurance policies on their own employees without telling them. The companies collect the death benefits, and its all tax free to boot.

"That's what Mr. MacDonald brought in here but when I read it I knew I couldn't work it into anything like a filler the way you asked me, not without risking us getting sued, not without some backup information, especially since what he brought in mentioned our good Lord."

"Lord!" David was beginning to understand his reporter and that might mean having to give him a raise. "Tell me."

"What I'm telling you is true. It's happened lots of times, corporations buying dead peasant insurance policies on their own employees and not telling them, then collecting the insurance if somebody got killed on the job. Nothing illegal about it either. Most states and provinces in North America have banned it, but not all of them, including Nova Scotia. The news story Ronald brought in was about three miners killed in a coal mine in Virginia. The families sued for compensation and in the process learned somehow that there was an insurance policy on each of them, but when they inquired about it, it wasn't they who were the beneficiary, it was the company. The company collected the insurance money, and guess who was a company vice president? Our very own C.J.M. Lord. Not his first time collecting, according to the story, but nothing illegal about it either. What do you think?"

David remembered Ronald bringing in the item about the petition to have Ronald McDonald retire. His friend had also mentioned a second item he printed off but David, up to his ears in work, had only half heard. Between Ronald and Tim, David sensed that the *Witness* had a new angle from which to continue its assault on Resource Reclamations and its co-conspirator, the Nova Scotia government. He wanted to wrestle the story out of Tim's hands but it was his, not David's. Instead, David sifted through a box of discarded press releases under his desk that were waiting to be recycled. He found Ronald MacDonald's retirement piece and went to work as copy editor, rewriting it. Secondary and un-local as the story was, he planned to post it on the front page of thewitness.ca.

Corporal Harry Noseworthy phoned David at the office to inform him that on Thursday coming, two RCMP investigators would be in Shean to interview him about the documents he had been in possession of when Noseworthy seized them. "There seems to be a push to get to the bottom of this, David. I've said before that you've royally pissed off some important people. They're coming at you so keep your guard up and your lawyer handy. It's those online updates of yours from what I can gather.

They, whoever they are, thought that threatening you with stealing confidential government files would shut you up, but you're not very good at that, are you? See you Thursday ... unless you find another way to break the law before then."

David didn't have time to worry about what was coming later in the week, whether it was a lawsuit, an arrest or jail. But he was grateful for the heads up from Noseworthy because it told him that the friendly Newfoundlander himself had also been trying to ferret out just why so much artillery was being trained on the small town editor of a newspaper nobody paid much attention to beyond its twenty miles of circulation.

But David was more interested in the copy Tim was sending him as he worked exclusively on the insurance story. He had documented the details of the three miners who had been killed, insurance policies on their lives held by Gardener Mines, the company C.J.M. Lord had been vice president of at the time. As designated spokesman for the company, Lord was quoted in news articles pointing out that nothing illegal had taken place. His statement was underscored a short time later when the court ruled that a company holding insurance on its employees was not illegal.

David had designated himself Tim's research assistant and scoured sources for other examples of companies that had held dead peasant insurance on employees. He learned that while it wasn't a common practice, it was hardly a rare occurrence. These facts he forwarded to Tim.

When Tim finished with the story and David with the editing, the insurance tale was uploaded to the Internet, but it left David Cameron feeling unsatisfied. He still believed in newsprint and ink, facts and typos, and he knew that most of his readers did too, preferring the tactile experience of turning the page, scanning the headlines that dared any of them to stop and read the story. But he was a couple of days away from publishing the newsprint copy of the *Witness*. All his best stories were finding their necessary way online – without the digital reality of the Internet these stories would be still waiting to be told, possibly too late. He hoped he'd have an original and new news story worth telling when publishing time came.

At Ronald MacDonald's house, Mrs. Big Sandy was breathing hard, heaving like an old horse while Ronald read aloud stories from thewitness.ca that he had been refusing to read before he and David reached their understanding.

"Did you ever hear of the Lady of the Dunes, Mrs. MacArthur?" Ronald asked, hoping to nudge his houseguest away from the mounting rage, not realizing that he was pouring gasoline on an open flame.

"Hasn't everybody!"

"Not me," Rita said. "I lived here all my life and I never heard of her until Saturday night's storm."

"Well, we all did," Ronald interjected. "We all took our turns going down to the dunes to look for her. People who said they saw her said she was beautiful and she would be reaching out to them like she was looking for help. But I haven't thought about that in years. It was only during storms like the one we had last night that she used to appear, I guess. Maybe her soul thinks every storm is the one that drowned her. Funny, but one time there used to be more ghosts around this part of the island than living people, I swear. Where have they all gotten themselves to, I wonder?"

"Have you ever seen her, Mrs. MacArthur? You lived close to there."

"I haven't and if I ever do she'll not be a ghost much longer, I can tell you that. She'll be dead, that's what she'll be. Traipsing around those dunes wearing a flimsy thing, I've heard, and she only comes out on stormy nights, just stormy nights in August if you believe some people, but if Sandy thinks he's going to get up to that, well he's got another think coming. Stormy nights are what he likes too, you know, the way they rip and tear at things and he'd get all excited and I liked it too, when he got all stormy like that... What are you people listening to? It's none of your business, is it? This is just between me and Sandy and that tramp down there. If I thought for one minute that that's what he was getting himself up to I would have been down there in a minute to stop it. If I found him with her I'd wring her scrawny neck, that's how I'd stop it! Don't look at me like that. I might go down there and dig her up myself and throw her bones back into the ocean where she came from, that's what I'll do. Did anybody in that newspaper there say they saw Sandy last night? Did they?"

"No. Please don't get yourself all worked up over nothing."

"Nothing! That slut getting up in the middle of a storm and going looking for my Sandy and you say it's nothing! I'll nothing you! Sandy's not one to be cheating, not when he's sober anyway, and he's been sober now for months, hasn't he, but he's a man and you know how weak those poor pathetic things are with their poor pathetic things always sticking out looking for attention. Well if she gives Sandy any attention she'll get some attention from me. Believe you me!" Mrs. Big Sandy let herself collapse against the back of the rocking chair. She'd had her say. Rita walked out of the kitchen holding the *Witness* to her face and Ronald was off to see to the calves. In the window of the front room, with Mrs. Big Sandy still heaving but beginning to subside like last night's sea, father and daughter caught each other's eye and crumpled in laughter, a laughter they tried, for the sake of their very lives, to keep silent. The laughter was more difficult to suppress when Rita read her father's silent lips: "I think I'm going to miss Herself when she leaves."

Rita had a different thought. Mrs. Big Sandy's description of her and her husband's behaviour in the fury of a storm reminded her of her own stormy night of love in the Shean dunes.

| 69 |

Monday morning Tim photographed surveyors on the dunes marking out the path the road would take, their work constantly harassed by the small colony that had gathered around Carmen Langille.

"Just kids sucking up to the teacher so they can get good marks next year," was Don Alex's take on the protest, sharing his observation with Ronald and David in the park.

"And maybe they just care, Don Alex. Did you ever think of that, that maybe there's people who just care a lot about something, enough to do something about it, sand dunes for some, fast food restaurants for others? And maybe people who don't care about nothing don't know how other people can care about anything."

"I care about a lot of things, Ronald, and you know that yourself."

"Oh yes, you care so much you're the president of the Caring People's Society of Shean, that's what you are, caring the way you do about everybody's business but your own."

"Well I'm glad you noticed, but there's caring and there's silly caring and what's sillier than sleeping in the eelgrass at the beach trying to stop jobs from coming to town?"

"And you had one of those jobs, didn't you? Retired after one night, which is more work than you did in all the other nights of your life."

"You know why I quit. It was Big Sandy's ghost got to me or else I'd still be down there looking after things a lot better than Mad Maddie and Phillip, and if I was still there I'd get on one of those there bulldozers there and shove those protestors home to their mamas, that's what I'd do."

The two men seemed headed for another falling out. David tried to head it off by asking Ronald if he had read the story about companies insuring their employees without telling them.

"Terrible thing that."

"What's so terrible about insurance?" Don Alex asked, still spoiling for an argument. "It's a good thing if you ask me. Where would this town be without unemployment insurance, tell me that, so don't go knocking the hand that feeds you is what I always say."

Ronald tossed an exasperated look David's way then turned back into the fray. "Listen Mr. Man, do you own your own computer? No you don't, so you don't know what we're talking about. When this story comes out in the real *Witness* next Wednesday and you read it over my shoulder like the cheapskate you are, then you tell me it's a good thing for a company to be insuring its employees and hoping they get themselves killed so they can collect a million dollars."

"You don't know what you're talking about. You never seen a million dollars in your life, Mr. Ronald MacDonald with your silly kilt, making fun of that other Ronald McDonald with his red nose."

"His nose isn't as red as yours, Don Alex, and at least he didn't get his from drinking..."

"It's your nose'll get red if I break it with this here fist right here," Don Alex said, holding the closed threat in front of Ronald's face. Ronald waved it aside and stood up. "I've got more important things to be doing than looking at the dirt in your knuckles, and I'll tell you what's more important than you and that's what's going on down at those dunes. I'm going to walk down there myself and talk to that Langille girl and stand beside her if those bulldozers come."

"Ach! You're not fooling anybody, Ronald. If she wasn't about as pretty as a kitten you wouldn't be standing anywhere near her but you're just like the rest of them there protestors, falling for her pretty face and that figure she likes to show off with a waist about this size and those nice, firm little milkjugs of hers. The only difference between you and the rest of them is you're old enough to be all of their grandfathers, including the teacher."

"Milkjugs! My God, man, did you really say that? Milkjugs! Oh, you're one romantic human being, aren't you? Did you ever hear the like, David? You're just a dirty old man and I don't mean your filthy knuckles. If you ever say anything like that about my Rita, I'll...I'll..."

"You'll get David to punch me on the nose. You think the whole town doesn't know what's going on with those two?"

"Whoa! Whoa!" David shouted.

Ronald stood in front of Don Alex and said in an even tone, "Rita could do a lot worse than this fella here, a hell of a lot worse but she'd never do worse with any man than your wife did!" He turned to David. "Come down to the house for a visit this evening, David. There's things to talk about when fools aren't around." With that he strode soldier-like across the street, making his way to the Beach Road.

David sat silently beside Don Alex absorbing Ronald's words, wondering if Rita's doing worse than him meant that Ronald thought she could do a lot better. He wondered too what the whole town was saying. Not daring to ask Don Alex he quietly left the man's side and made his way back to the office, curious about what Ronald had to talk about.

David's day had been spent researching corporate insurance on unsuspecting employees, following Tim's stream of updates from the dunes where he was writing an onsite blog. Various photographs of Carmen Langille accompanied Tim's words, and David suspected something more than professional dedication kept him on location. He wondered if Tim was aware of the competition posed by Ronald MacDonald's presence, also colourfully reproduced on the website.

The provincial dailies were also monitoring the *Witness* website. Not with the fervour David hoped his paper's stories would instil, but they were taking note of the occupation of the dunes and speculating as to whether a Catholic cemetery would hold the same legal and emotional intensity as First Nations' sacred burial grounds when threatened by desecration.

After supper with his mother, after speaking with the children about their return, he drove down to Ronald MacDonald's farm, surprised and grateful to find Donald MacNaughton's car parked in the yard. Whatever fatherly conversation Ronald might or might not have been planning would be put on hold. He recognized as well that he was pleased for another reason. Slowly and without comment from either, Donald and he were finding their way back to the friendship that had existed before the shooting. They were less guarded with each other, argumentative as ever but not in too personal a way.

Inside, Donald was at the table with Rita, Ronald in the rocking chair with the fiddle, Mrs. Big Sandy at the stove.

"It's easier to find you here than at the office," Donald explained, and David could feel it, a blush, a goddamned boyhood blush, filling his face with the redness of Don Alex's nose, but Donald moved right along. "So how's it looking for our town? Is it life for us, or a living death?"

"Oh, I'm quoting that one, Donald. Life or a living death. Headline with a question mark," David told him. "But the story so far is the story you know, unless you've learned something new to add to it. They're surveying the dunes. The road will go ahead as soon as the stakes are set, although those survey stakes are having a hard time staying in the ground, and the surveyors are getting a hard time whenever they try to reset them. But the fact is that it's sand, nothing but sand and eelgrass and I doubt C.J.M. Lord will hesitate to shove it out of his way. He's pissed off for one thing, and he probably wants to get as far along as possible before our ghost stories and long ago dead start to sway public opinion. Certainly there hasn't been any indication that the premier or Cabinet is prepared to back down on this. My guess is that they are still hoping to build an election on it."

David's recapping was interrupted by the ringing of his cellphone. He looked at the display and excused himself, going into Ronald's study.

"David, how goes it," Jim Turner's voice asked.

"Good, Jim, and with you?"

"Good. Look, I'll get right to it. Somebody we know happened to know somebody who knew how to do what you needed done. I've got some names for you."

David pulled the notebook and pen from his always-armed-for-emergencies journalist's pocket and began writing the names of the investors in Coastal Futures, the investment fund backing the development of the Beaton Seam.

"Whew!" he whistled more than once as he wrote.

"I hope that helps."

"Oh, it helps, but it helps cloud things more than clarify them. What do you make of it yourself, Jim? Of the low profile these corporations have kept. Hell, a couple of them have enough clout to start wars all over the world and then get the contracts to go in and rebuild those countries once they've been blown to smithereens."

"I've been thinking about it too," Jim said. "Clearly they don't want a public face on this project, but why? My guess is that's it's environmental. We're talking about coal, and in the current political environment increasing carbon dioxide emissions in North America isn't something that will sit well with a lot of groups and organizations. It may be as simple as a low profile for high profits. The less even some of their shareholders know about fossil fuel investments the better for the company. It's not uncommon for environmental activists to buy shares in corporations like any of these so they can attend the annual meetings and ask embarrassing questions in front of the media."

David listened to Jim's assessment. "That's one possibility. This isn't a popular development. We're getting lots of encouragement and moral support from all corners of the country but not a lot of help in preventing it from happening. What do you make of the board of directors, all Nova Scotians with no representation from the investor? That's not normal, is it?"

"No but the reason's probably the same, to keep a low profile. And it's a perk for a compliant government to reward its friends. Board members on a company the scale that Resource Reclamations is shaping up to be, can get a damn good per diem. But don't kid yourself David, the investors are watching their money. If it's not at the board level, then I'd look on site itself. Who in the management or planning of the seawall has a history with the investors?"

David recalled his conversation in the Five Bucks with Victor Mason, talking about the engineer who had come over to this job from Gardener Mines.

"That's it, Jim. That's how the investors are watching their investment. They're providing the executive talent for Resource Reclamations. I know that for a fact. There's an engineer there from Gardener Mines. I imagine other key management positions have gone or will go to people from the other corporations. They're probably on loan or leave of absence. That puts a bit more of the jigsaw puzzle together. Thanks."

"I don't know if any of this gets you anywhere, but good luck. If I come across anything else I'll be in touch. Meanwhile, I'll see how this plays out in the *Witness*. Bethany sends her best."

"She certainly does, Jim. Thank her for me."

| 70 |

Ronald had put aside the fiddle and was drinking from his cup of tea at the table when David returned to the kitchen and an audience of curious faces.

"We could hear bits and pieces of that," Donald said.

"Yes, we could," said Mrs. Big Sandy, "because that fellow right there made Ronald stop playing the fiddle so he could eavesdrop on your conversation. The rest of them were no better, but not me, David. I'm too deaf to hear you from the other room so I decided that it was your business and none of mine. Not like some people," she added, glaring at MacNaughton.

"But if you could hear?" Donald asked.

"You shut your face or I'll shut it for you with rat poison the next time I get to make a cup of tea for you."

David sat at the table holding his hand up for peace between the warring factions, and peace fell between them because both Donald and Mrs. Big Sandy, as well as Rita and Ronald, wanted to hear what the reporter had to say. He flipped through his notebook until he had the page he wanted.

"The investors in the Coastal Futures venture capital group are – are you ready for this? – Gardener Mines, Maecenas Construction, LKT Construction, Seawall Innovations, Mount Sage Oil, Simile Oil & Gas, International Industry Insurance."

The momentary silence was in part because most people at the table were unimpressed by the names, but not all. The first to speak was Donald. "Maecenas Construction? That the largest construction company in the world. And LKT isn't far behind. Construction companies and energy companies and insurance companies. What do you make of it?"

David repeated the conversation he had had with Jim Turner, the speculation that the companies wanted to keep lows profiles while the Beaton Seam was being developed, avoid publicity and criticism from their own shareholders. He explained Jim's theory behind the non-entities who formed the board of directors.

The August evening had become a late night but Rita was still refreshing the cups from her teapot while Mrs. Big Sandy added biscuits and molasses and strawberry jam to keep the informal brainstorming committee alert and energized.

"Let's take these players on one by one," David suggested, returning to Maecenas Construction. "This isn't a corporation that apologizes for anything. I can't really see them hunkering down because a coal mine is being developed in Shean, regardless of the circumstances. The company's official position on global warming is denial. It's not happening. Whatever changes may be taking place are happening naturally, part of the planet's cycle from ice ages to civilizations. This project isn't a big operation compared to ninety percent of the projects they have going on all over the world in places where they have to hire armies of mercenaries to protect their workers. It just doesn't fit."

"The same can be said of LKT," Donald noted. "A bit of lip service to the environment, then bulldoze it away."

Rita looked at David's scribbled notebook. "What would Seawall Innovations be doing keeping company with the rest of the investors? It's their wall, isn't it? They're going to do alright just by selling the seawall."

"In kind?" Donald asked. "No matter who comes looking for money from our town council – arts groups or community groups – they always seem to weasel out of putting up any cash themselves by offering 'in kind' contributions – manpower, furniture donations, what have you. Maybe the wall's their in kind contribution and they share in the coal profits."

"In kind works at the municipal level but not at this level, Donald," David suggested. "These companies have invested what we can guess must be hundreds of millions of dollars in Coastal Futures. I'm thinking that Seawall Innovations sees their wall being used to make a major coal mine happen in Nova Scotia and want in on the profits. They're a relatively new company and this is a way to begin to diversify early."

"What about the oil companies?" Ronald asked. "Aren't they the same as coal companies? They're all after the same things, aren't they?"

"Yeah, profits," David sneered.

"My socialist friend shuns the dirty word 'profits' while running a business in which he hopes to make profits."

"Hope being the absolutely right word," David answered.

"And such is the hypocrisy of socialists," Donald pointed out.

"Donald, when profits impoverish half the world..."

"Don't begin arguing about those things. There's plenty of time for that when this is all over," Rita chided. "From what you said, I can see why most of the partners are investing in this, but what's in it for an insurance company, Industrial Insurance International?"

"I heard of that company somewhere," Ronald said, trying to recall where he'd encountered it.

"Yes, you have," David interjected with excitement. "You brought that information into the *Witness*. That story about that company being sued for insuring its employees. The company was Gardener Mines and C.J.M. Lord was a vice president at the time. The insurance company issuing the policies was I-3, more formally known as Industrial Insurance International.

"So what the hell is going on here?" David continued. "We're pretty well agreed that these companies don't duck and run from the media or environmentalists or even governments. So why the low profile? The secrecy?"

"Liability!" Donald said, the word sliding across the table like a puck across the ice to be scooped up and driven home by David with a sudden snap of his fingers. "The seawall!"

"Of course it's the seawall! That's what this whole operation is really about, isn't it? The Beaton Seam is ... what?"

"A potentially profitable windfall if the seawall works, and I underline the word 'potentially'," David said.

"Take the rest of us through what you two seem to have figured out," Rita asked.

David and Donald fell into silent silos trying to articulate, each to himself, what they had intuited together. David was the first to speak.

"In those files I obtained from the Department of Mines and Minerals the research, the science around the mobile seawall was sound. Theoretically sound. That was repeated several times. Now I'll need to go back through them with a fine-tooth comb to be certain, but I don't believe it ever mentions testing the seawall on anything but computer models and in laboratory tidal pools. If that's the case, what's being planned for the Shean cove is a real-life experiment of a technically unproven technology. Unproven in the conditions that this seawall will be tested in this coming fall and winter."

"And if I'm right," Donald added, "the reason for the low profile is liability. David, you can check this out with your secret business source up there in Toronto, the one none of us knows about, and see if I'm following the money the way I think it's flowing. When we do a municipal project with provincial or federal funding, then the money committed to those projects dribbles out in phases. We get some up front to get started, then another portion of the funding when, say, the sidewalk cribbing for a cement pour has been finished, then another ration of money when the concrete is poured, and then when the finish work is completed, the cement finishing, the planting of grass or flowers, we get the rest. If we don't complete the project we don't get the rest of the money.

"What I'm willing to bet on is that Coastal Futures is doling out the money for this project in a similar way. If anything goes wrong, then the venture capital will stop flowing, the investors will save some of their money and the project will end."

"But what are they afraid will go wrong? They seem to practically own our government," Rita asked.

Donald and David composed a scenario between them.

"Suppose the seawall is completed and it works. It works for say two, three months, then the ice comes heavier than any computer program imagined and the wall collapses. Then the experiment will have failed. The funding stops," Donald explained. "Now suppose we move the success of the seawall up another few months or even a year and they are actually mining the Beaton Seam. Then some flaw or unpredicted force of nature missed by the computer models lets the ocean push through the wall. It would take a matter of seconds, minutes at the most, for the Gulf of St. Lawrence to reclaim its lost cove. How many miners and workers is Resource Reclamations Limited predicting it will employ? How many of those men, or women, would have any chance in hell of getting out of there alive?

"Liability," Donald repeated.

David continued with the scenario. "As long as the companies involved are simply investors with no direct ownership in Resource Reclamations Limited then they get to shrug and walk away. Resource Reclamations, being funded in the kind of increments Donald described, would have only its hardware assets, no hard cash, and most of those assets in the form of machinery, would be underwater. C.J.M. Lord and his company might have to go to court to face lawsuits from miners' families, but it's a blood from a rock situation. Nobody gets hurt but the people of Shean. Possibly hurt tragically."

"Then why are they doing it?" Mrs. Big Sandy asked, "if they're only going to drown people?"

"Because," David answered, "if it works, if the seawall endures the August gales, the autumn and winter storms, the polar ice floes, and obviously they believe it will, then the mobile seawall being tested here will have a market all over the world. Some predictions about global warming claim that we can expect sea levels to rise anywhere from five to fifteen feet, higher in some places. Imagine all the coastal cities just here in North America. Oh, there'd be a market alright, a multibillion dollar market. The wall is strong, lightweight, can be assembled in a fraction of the time it takes to build a regular dam or dike. And then there's that other market, temporary dams, levies, coastal exploration for any number of resources and treasures. If the seawall works, there will be massive profits made from the Beaton Seam and the proven seawall technology. If the seawall doesn't hold, well not one of these corporations could care less what happens to Shean or the people of Shean who might wind up going to work for them."

"Print that and you'll be dealing with more than the Attorney General," Donald said.

"I'm going to run this by my secret source that everyone seems to know about, talk it through, but I think we've dug down to the financial bedrock the seawall is standing on. I need to get to the office, phone Toronto, and have whatever I can of this information up on the website before its morning visitors begin to arrive."

"I suspect some of your morning visitors will be arriving by computers located far from Shean. Some people with a vested interest in seeing this seawall happen will be taking a peek from Halifax, maybe even from some corporate headquarters in Toronto or New York, and they're going to be very unhappy to have even scraps of this information made public."

| 71 |

The ongoing updates by the *Witness* did draw the attention of the provincial dailies, radio and television. Some sent reporters to cover the occupation of the Shean dunes, the town that was becoming a household word in the province, the place where that crazy old woman held herself hostage, where the local press carried regular reports of ghost sightings, where residents, most of them anyway, were trying to stop the development of an open-pit coal mine in the middle of the ocean, and where, if rumours were true, that same crazy old woman had kidnapped the company CEO, although no charges were made and even though the RCMP claimed the rumours were based on a misunderstanding, there were scores of eyewitnesses who told a different story.

Shean's resistance to development set off no serious alarms, protests or outraged editorials across the province. The reports treated the story more as entertainment than hard news. The town's late summer tourism spiked mildly due to interprovincial traffic.

The *Witness's* online reports of the industrial practice of insuring employees for corporate benefits earned a brief story and minor editorial calling for the province to enact legislation making such exploitation of workers illegal in Nova Scotia. Still, none of the stories coming out of Shean triggered the kind of concern for which David hoped. They did bring a handful of fervent environmentalists from across Cape Breton and the mainland to take part in Carmen Langille's occupation of the dunes. Through all the week's reports the premier and his cabinet stayed silent, with media questions referred to public relations people whose job it was to say nothing as nicely as possible.

The most recent revelation – making public the names of the corporations investing in the Beaton Seam project – finally did bring a response from the premier, who told Halifax reporters that the companies backing the project were among the world's largest and most successful construction and energy giants, a fact that only served to strengthen his government's resolve to continue with the project. The statement seemed to fuel activity in Resource Reclamations's beachhead, the former MacArthur land.

Despite disruptions of the surveying of the dunes in preparation for a road, plans for the road were going ahead.

David knew with sickening self-assurance that the building of the road, or, more precisely, the destruction of the dunes wasn't an immediately necessary step in Resource Reclamations's development plans. There was still much work to be done to ready Hughie's Point for the arrival of the convoy of cement trucks that would pour the bulkhead needed to anchor the southern section of the seawall. This wasn't business as usual. This was personal. This was C.J.M. Lord giving the finger to David Cameron and the *Witness* with an action far more devastating than any legal suit against the newspaper or its publisher.

David sat at his terminal. The eternity that had seemed to exist between the last hard copy edition of the *Witness* and the copy that would be hitting the streets of Shean in the morning felt anti-climactic. The next issue would be a general repetition of all that had been posted online the previous week, a last appeal to deafened ears. The edition of the *Witness* that would be published a week from tomorrow would, David knew, carry photographs of the bulldozing of the dunes and the reality of the seawall, all leading toward the inevitable mining of the Beaton Seam.

David was staring at the lash of rain on the window, wondering if Carmen Langille was still in her tent, determined to stop Resource Reclamations's bulldozers. The only purpose of these thoughts was to help him avoid the last stages of the paper's preparation. "Line two for you, David. It's Rita," Cheryl Horne called across the office. David winced at the informal way she had passed along the information about the caller, as if it was common knowledge they were seeing each other, which it was, he knew, but still...

"David, can you come down here?" Rita asked when he picked up the receiver. He detected a hint of desperation in her voice. "I can't go into it here. I know you're getting the paper ready, but if you can spare just an hour..."

David looked at the half-written editorial on the screen, the time on the wall clock edging its way toward the moment when he would have to click the send button, dispatching tomorrow's *Witness* to the printer. What the hell was the difference.

David entered the MacDonald kitchen to the absurd sight of Rita and Ronald seated at the table while beside the stove Mrs. Big Sandy held Maddie Casey in a headlock, rapping him on the skull with her knuckles every time he moved or moaned. David raised his hands in a question, seeing that Rita was somewhere between hysterical laughter and pure hysteria. Ronald was pale and still as a plaster statue.

"Be still, you worm, before I snap your goddamned neck," Mrs. Big Sandy threatened when Maddie, aware of David's arrival, began to squeal with something like relief, while Rita composed herself to explain to David what was happening.

"We went to the concert in the park, the rally against the mine, but the rain wrecked it and we came home early. Mrs. MacArthur…"

"I went up to my bedroom and look what I found crawling out from under my bed! This thing!"

"I was going to call the police but Maddie begged me to call you instead," Rita went on. "He said you could explain."

"Me? Mrs. MacArthur, would you please let him go so he can tell us what he's doing here."

Mrs. Big Sandy eyed David suspiciously. "If I let him go don't you let him run out that door. I'm too old to be running after him but if I have to I will, and you know yourself that if I have to run after him it'll only be to kill him."

"He won't run, I promise you."

Mrs. Big Sandy lifted her arm and Maddie Casey dropped from under it to the floor, grasping his throat and coughing in exaggeration. David guided him to the table. "What are you doing here, Maddie?"

"Well I can't tell you that, Mr. Cameron," he said, at which Mrs. Big Sandy made a move toward him. "Ahhh! Keep her away from me."

"It's me or her that's going to get the truth out of you, Maddie. Your choice."

"You, Mr. Cameron. I'd rather you tried to get the truth out of me. But I can't tell you."

"Then why did you want me here?"

"'Cause you'd understand, you know, me being here where I'm not suppose to be, and you'd help me out so I wouldn't, you know, tell anybody about you-know-what."

"About what?"

"About you know, 'Stop spitting on me! Stop spitting on me!' Remember?"

David sat at the table and looked hard at Maddie. "I'll be telling that story myself, Maddie, right in the newspaper if I have to, and then it wouldn't be your story to tell to anyone. Besides, it's not that important to me now, but what you're doing here is. Tell me or tell Corporal Noseworthy." He took out his phone.

"Okay! Okay! I'll tell you but you have to promise me you won't tell anybody, just like I promised you, and I kept my promise, remember."

"Who don't you want to know?"

"My boss."

"Lord? He sent you?"

"You guessed? Just like that? I guess that's why you're a newspaperman, just like Superman."

"Maddie!"

"You know I have to make resti..resti...pay back money for that machine I broke. A thousand dollars. Mr. Lord told me that if I did him a favour he'd pay me five hundred dollars. That's a lot of money, Mr. Cameron, almost half of what I need."

"What favour?"

"He wanted me to get him something from this house. He said it was taken from him against his will so I wouldn't actually be stealing it, see. I'd just be retrieving it is how he put it."

"Retrieving what?"

"What she took from him," Maddie said, pointing toward Mrs. Big Sandy.

"That little suitcase?" Mrs. Big Sandy said.

"Lord's briefcase? You took Lord's briefcase?" David asked turning toward her.

"His *brief* case. You mean that little prick has a suitcase just for his underwear? The pervert!"

"Do you have it?" David asked.

"I do! I took it out of his car and he made such a fuss over it that day we went for a drive that I decided to keep it, told the bastard if he didn't make trouble for me then I wouldn't make trouble for him, and if it was so important then he shouldn't be leaving it lying around on the front seat of his car where anybody could just take it if they wanted to. Finder's keepers, as Sandy always said."

Rita asked the elderly woman to get the briefcase.

"David, I'm sorry to have taken you away but as you can see, this isn't your average break and enter, is it? It looks to me like Maddie has been taking lessons in that profession from you. And Maddie, if you don't go to jail, you have my permission to tell that story about David to anybody you want to."

"Thank you, Miss."

Mrs. Big Sandy returned, slapping the expensive-looking leather briefcase on the table. David examined it, noting that it was locked with a combination lock at each latch.

"I'd love to know what's in here," he said to Rita while shaking it like a Christmas gift, as if whatever racket it sent out would tell him what he wanted to know.

"Why don't you look in it then?" Mrs. Big Sandy asked.

"Because it's locked and private and forcing it open would be a crime," David explained.

Mrs. Big Sandy eyed him with withering contempt and grabbed a bread knife off the kitchen counter, inserting it under each tab and snapping them. She opened the briefcase. "Nothing in here but papers," she reported, disappointed at the absence of whatever C.J.M. Lord wore for underwear. She picked up the contents and dropped them on the table in front of David and Rita.

David leafed through a stack of documents related to the project. They told him nothing new. Rita fingered her way through a separate folder of documents with indifferent curiosity.

"David!"

David looked up. An ashen Rita passed him a folder. He opened it and began reading. "Jesus Christ!" he said, reaching for his phone. He entered the *Witness*'s number. "Tim," he said a moment later, "I never thought I'd get to say this in my lifetime but, Stop the presses! I'll be there in twenty minutes."

| 72 |

The Shean Witness reached the streets on Wednesday morning shouting the headline,

DEAD PEASANT INSURANCE:
Company insures unsuspecting employee for $1M.

Under the headline was a photograph of Victor Mason, the gentlest one David could find in his archives – Victor with his two-year-old daughter in his arms watching the annual Shean Gathering Parade.

> Victor Mason, an employee of Resource Reclamations Limited, learned just last night that the company for which he works has taken out a life insurance policy on him worth one million dollars ($1M) without his knowledge, and without his family being named as beneficiaries. Resource Reclamations Limited was the only beneficiary named on the policy. Along with Mason, the company held similar policies on seven other employees. This type of policy is referred to in the insurance industry as dead peasant insurance, and is taken out on unsuspecting employees with the company as the sole, tax-free beneficiary if the employee is killed on the job.

Contacted last night, Mason was asked if he was shocked to learn about the policy.

"Shocked?" the heavy equipment operator asked in reply. "No, I'm not shocked! I'm pissed off and if I see that little creep [meaning company CEO C.J.M. Lord] I'll rip his frigging head off. That's about as polite as I can be with my daughter here in the room," he added.

Mason, a lifetime resident of Shean whose professional life as a construction worker has seen him on some of the country's and the world's largest projects, thought the Heavens had reached down and blessed him when his credentials found him a well-paying job here at home, where he could be with his family daily.

The popular Mason, father of Timothy, 6, Angus, 4, and Theresa, 2, and who is still referred to locally by his high school nickname, the Gentle Giant, was anything but gentle when asked if he would be reporting to work this morning. "No. But I'll be on the job site," he said. Told of the seven other employees who are also insured by Resource Reclamations Limited, none of whom could be reached for comment last night, Mason asked for their names. "I'll let them know," he said.

The Shean Witness came into recent possession of copies of the insurance policies. While a proposed open-pit, offshore mine in Shean is Resource Reclamations Limited's first project, the practice of insuring employees' lives and reaping tax-free profits is not new to some of the people and companies involved in the development. Company CEO C.J.M. Lord was vice president of Gardener Mines, an international coal mining operator, when it was sued by families of miners accidentally killed while employed with that mining company. Gardener Mines, the Witness learned earlier this week, is a major investor in the proposed seawall and open-pit mine through the venture capital group Coastal Futures. Industrial Insurance International (I-3), the company holding the policies on Mason and the others, as well as the company that insured the miners in the aforementioned suit against Gardener Mines, is also among the investors in the project.

Resource Reclamations Limited's planned project is to erect a seawall to push back the Gulf of St. Lawrence waters that fill Shean Cove, exposing the bottom of the ocean shore for the development of an open-pit mine to get at the legendary Beaton Seam coal deposits just below the surface. Efforts to underground mine that seam were tried several times before being abandoned, the last attempt claiming the lives of four miners in 1917.

In its prospectus, Resource Reclamations Limited claims that it expects to employ as many as 200 people in its mining operation. Assuming those figures are accurate, and that those employees are at work if the experimental seawall (which has never been tested beyond computer simulations and laboratory wave pools) breaks down under the pressure of the sea, the rush of ocean back into Shean Cove could come at an alarming speed, calling into question the ability for everybody, if anyone, to escape the deluge.

If the company follows through with its current precedent and takes out life insurance policies on all mine employees, then in the worst case scenario where all employees are lost at the mine site, the company would stand to collect an estimated $200 million.

Resource Reclamations Limited is expected to begin construction of a road as early as this week that requires the destruction of the sand dunes along the Shean shore. Protesters against the proposed mine have occupied the dunes and hope to stop the environmental devastation.

It was the same picture and much the same story in the dailies. Editors at the dailies had caught the story amid the late press releases just as their deadlines bore down on them, but each one made front page space for the Shean story in the hope that the other papers had missed it. Victor Mason was being discussed in coffee shops and call-in radio shows across the province with the familiarity of an old friend. Shean's saga had a face now, and Victor Mason was potentially its first victim – if you didn't count the old woman – of a company that planned to profit from employees' deaths.

The *Witness*'s website groaned under the unfamiliar burden of so many visits, readers leaving comments filled with an anger that transcended the usual public cynicism and the kind of indifference that allowed politicians and corporations to take advantage of opportunities that increased their power or profits.

They wouldn't actually plan to get them killed, would they?

I doubt that, but if making money's all that matters then you can get pretty reckless about the way you make it, even careless about safety, see, or indifferent. So if something happens, well the company's covered, see.

And if the family doesn't even know, like it says in the paper?

Doesn't matter, none of their business really, just business, that's all, nothing personal.

So you mean the company would take the million bucks when Victor here gets killed and let that poor little girl starve?

That's about it, I guess, and even if the family sues for wrongful death or whatever, well the company might settle for a quarter of a million, a half million, and the company's still in half a million dollars. Great work if you can get it, collecting, I mean, not the getting killed part.

Reporters already on the dunes were joined by more of their profession, and David Cameron, who was interviewed in person, by phone or on camera as the publisher of the paper that broke the story of an all-too-legal but ghastly and immoral corporate practice, was regularly introduced to readers and viewers as "a nationally award-winning journalist." As interest in the seawall deepened, media examinations of the experimental nature of the mobile seawall and its potential consequences for miners, along with the environmental destruction necessary to get at the Beaton Seam, grew more intense. Combined with the breaking of the corporate insurance story, public understanding of what was proposed blossomed into appall. Reader and viewer hunger for more details forced the media to root through earlier reports in the Shean weekly and examine them through a more analytical lens than they had used before.

Among those news people calling *The Shean Witness*'s editor was a Toronto business reporter with the country's largest newspaper. After the familiar banter Jim Turner asked David what was currently happening in the Beaton Seam story.

"I think it's less a Beaton Seam story than a mobile seawall story, Jim, but right now things are at a standstill. I don't know if it's the calm before the storm or not, but what seems certain is that the project won't be going ahead as planned for this week. Tim's been down at the mine site since early morning. The employees are all there but they're not in much of a mood for working. They're waiting for a long, white Cadillac to arrive. I suspect they'll be waiting all day. They have lots of company though. Reporters are here from all the media. *The Globe and Mail* has someone on the ground here, and I'm hoping the television networks will pick up the local broadcasts for their national news shows. Victor Mason is the man of the moment. He has the whole stage because the company and the politicians seem to have evaporated."

"Do me a favour, would you, David? The *Globe and Mail* reporter – why don't you set him up with an interview with your friend, Mrs. Big Sandy. Let him get mauled a bit."

"You know him?"

"No, but I hate the idea that he's there and I'm not. Need to sign off for now. Hope this works out the way you want it to."

| 73 |

Cyril Bender, Resource Reclamations's engineer, drove down to the mine site, saw the anger in the eyes of the men waiting for someone from the company to show, put his car in reverse and drove away. Beyond that, there was no sign at all of company activity. Tim Donovan stayed with the protest at the mine site gate, returning to Carmen Langille's tent frequently enough to inform the whole town of his intentions. Well, his hopes anyway.

By late afternoon the protest shift had ended, Victor and his fellow strikers going home. Maddie Casey showed up with Phillip, wondering if he still had a job, and exchanged a few words with Tim Donovan. "Don't know if I'm supposed to be working or not now. Or who's going to pay me. Tell the truth, I don't really care if Big Sandy steals or ruins every damned machine in here cause your boss told me that my boss never insured *me* for a million dollars. I wasn't among those guys who were and that's a piss off because I could use a million bucks as much as the next guy. Aw, to hell with it," he said as Tim was leaving. "I'm going home. How's about a lift."

There was a supper being served at Ronald MacDonald's, no hamburgers involved, he told David when he extended the invitation. "It's kind of a farewell dinner for Herself who'll be leaving our castle in a few days for one of her own. We finally got that settled. Rita's cooking the meal and she's a fair hand at it as well, David. Wouldn't hurt you to sample what you might be getting yourself in for, if you know what I mean." David was beginning to think that everybody in Shean was in on the news except him and Rita. They'd been keeping themselves far from the kind of discussion that could lead to conflicting expectations and dissolving interest in each other. But he was game for any chance to be in her presence, so he accepted the invitation.

"So how will you like living on your own again, Mrs. MacArthur?" David asked.

"Well it's about time's all I can say. I wasn't born to live in the middle of the woods like these people. I need civilization around me, not those damned deer you see jumping through the pasture every morning, and all those damned birds in the morning are more annoying than a mine whistle with their singing, and it's always the same thing over and over when those birds sing, just like this fellow when he plays his fiddle. He just knows one tune as far as I can make out."

"Bless the ear that can actually hear," Ronald said without offence, merely and wistfully wishing for an audience that could tell the difference between a strathspey and a reel.

"This is very good, Rita," David said, the compliment well meant but also meant to veer the conversation away from its possible collision course. And the conversation remained polite and pleasant until half way through the apple pie dessert, when a loud knock hammered the door. Before Rita could answer it or Ronald call out a "Come in!" the door swung open and an uninvited but glowing Donald MacNaughton was standing there. "Not watching the news?" he asked, striding across the kitchen into the livingroom, turning on the television.

"Look at that fellow, no manners at all. Just walks in here and takes over. He was always like that. Where's my frying pan?" Mrs. Big Sandy was saying but Rita quieted her while Donald stood beckoning for them to come see. But all they could see was an advertisement for secondhand cars.

The six o'clock news started with a live broadcast of a press conference with the premier.

"This government has been committed to economic development in this province. That's what we have been elected to do, create well-paying jobs that will strengthen this province's fiscal profile and allow all Nova Scotians to share in that prosperity. It is my belief, this government's belief, that the more deeply rooted in the province's natural resources our economy is, the more control we have over it.

"The information technology industry is becoming the world's most influential industry, and we do all we can to recruit and welcome that economy. But the IT economy, as has been demonstrated over and over again, is a fluid one, able to move its operation from one part of the world to another at the click of a mouse, leaving unemployment and hardship in its wake. Nova Scotia's economic sustainability needs more stability than that."

"What in God's name is that man saying?" Mrs Big Sandy asked, winning smiles all around but not distracting attention from the screen.

"...and it is possible that in our pursuit of an economic pillar for this province, the resuscitation of our historic coal-mining industry, this government may have been a bit over-enthusiastic to get started. We entered into an agreement with Resource Reclamations Limited to develop what is commonly referred to as the Beaton Seam in western Cape Breton. In our zeal to get people back to work it is possible that we overlooked certain criteria. On a project of this scale and environmental sensitivity, our own laws call for an environmental impact study. That might have been a mistake had the oversight not been caught in time. I am here this evening to announce that our government is placing a moratorium on that particular development, effective immediately, until a full environmental impact study can be carried out. It is important to us that Nova Scotians know that while jobs are important, the health and safety of our citizens, of our children, is a priority..."

A cheer rose in the MacDonald livingroom while Ronald pointed the remote control at the television set before a standby panel of experts could begin explaining what viewers clearly heard and understood.

"Well that's the end of that!" Ronald MacDonald said with satisfaction. "No McDonald's coming to Shean in the foreseeable future. We fought them off tooth and nail, us and the *Witness*. The Gulf Grill lives to serve its hamburgers another day."

Back around the kitchen table a jubilant silence held sway until broken by Donald MacNaughton. "It'll take five years to carry out the impact study, maybe longer. Resource Reclamations will be gone from here by the end of the week because I know we were right. This wasn't about coal. Never was. It was about the seawall. They'll find somewhere else to test it, somewhere where the oceans are filled with coves and hurricanes or cyclones. Lord and his company aren't going to wait around. They're as good as gone and good riddance as far as we're concerned. No such luck for the government though. I bet lawsuits are being filed by Resource Reclamations as we speak for tens, perhaps hundreds of millions in lost investment and lost profits. But they're gone."

"I just hope nothing like this ever happens again," Rita remarked, and catching the look that passed between David and Donald, asked, "What?"

"It's over for now, Rita," David agreed, "but the Beaton Seam's still out there, and so is the technology to get at it. It's over for now but in five, fifteen, fifty years' time there'll be another C.J.M. Lord and another Resource Reclamations Limited wanting to try again."

"Maybe, but for now the truth is that you beat Resource Reclamations, the two of you and the *Witness*," Rita said.

"This is an awful lot of self-satisfaction and not much on the thank you side of things," Mrs. Big Sandy interrupted. "My Sandy could use one of those slaps on the back that you're passing around amongst yourselfs. I told you he wouldn't let it happen just like he told me and now you have the proof so don't go forgetting what he did for this town that always hated him. It was the MacArthurs that found this place, and it was the MacArthurs saved this place so my Sandy's a hero and you better remember that in that newspaper of yours, Mr. Reporter! You better not forget that this stupid town of yours has a guardian angel, and I'm going to talk to that crazy priest that's going to say mass on those dunes next Sunday about canonizing my Sandy. Saint Sandy, Patron Saint of Shean, and he better do it if he knows what's good for him or I'll squeeze that collar of his tighter than that there Lord's necktie! All of youse down on your knees praying to him. Oh, he's going to love that, my Sandy is," Mrs. Big Sandy said, clearing the table and carrying the cups away.

"So now what, David?" Donald asked.

"So now what what?"

"So now what? We stopped progress but we still have a flat broke town losing population, living for the most part on unemployment insurance and welfare, raising food for the food bank – all signs of the poverty we live in. Yeah, we stopped progress but we haven't changed a thing."

"There's Jamison's development plan," David reminded the mayor.

"Oh, that's going to get a good hard look, I assure you, but I stand by what I've always said. Tourism isn't going to save us. I always thought that tourism should exist so people can come to places like Cape Breton to see how we live here, not so we can live here."

"What I'm guessing," David said, "is that the premier's attempt to disassociate his government from the bad taste Resource Reclamations's insurance scheme has left in people's mouths won't work, and there'll be a change of government in the near future, and that you'll be part of it, Donald. Then you'll have all the answers, and one of them better be the right one or your local newspaper will hound you all the way to hell."

"But first the *Witness* has to get me elected. Look, I need to drive to Halifax in the morning to meet with the opposition leader about just that, getting elected, so I better get going."

"Before you go, Mr. Mayor, there's a condition on the *Witness's* support. While you're still mayor you can expropriate the lots in the park owned by your brother and vest them to the town. But during that process, while you're paying your brother market value in return for those properties you can see that Maddie Casey gets full market value for his property too. Your brother paid him seven hundred dollars for a quit claim on the property but it's worth at least ten times that. Whether Sylvester pays or the town pays, Maddie gets his money. We all owe him that much."

"Why?" Donald MacNaughton asked, his hand still on the doorknob.

An hour later, still howling gales of laughter at the image of Mrs. Big Sandy with a hammerlock on Mad Maddie Casey, Donald MacNaughton left with a few parting words. "Oh, Maddie'll get his money alright! Oh I'll see to it that he does!"

| 74 |

"Victor Mason to see you, David," Helen informed David.

Victor was standing at the front counter, shaking off the editor's invitation to come into his office. "Just wanted to renew my subscription and say goodbye," he explained to David. "I called the union hall in Alberta. There's a job waiting for me. Sixty bucks an hour, living allowance and a camp. And no dead peasant insurance policy on me. Why do you suppose Lord took out that policy on me and the others so soon? We were months away from being in any actual danger on the job."

"Probably assessing who would be staying employed for the long haul, people like yourself. Buying a few policies at a time. Trouble is, thanks to Mrs. Big Sandy, he bought those policies too soon."

"Came back to bite him in the arse, didn't they? I'm renewing my subscription, but I was wondering if I can ask a favour of an old friend."

"Anything I can, Vic. What is it?"

"Well, the paper takes a week or more to get out to Fort McMurray. The news from home is always good to get but the advertising section is usually stale by then. What I was wondering, and if there's a problem with doing this just say so, you've got a business to run, but sometimes ads come in here way ahead of the paper printing them, right? Like maybe a few days before you come out on Wednesday? If I give you my cell number and something comes along in my line of work, heavy equipment mostly, would it be possible to let me know ahead of the paper coming out?"

David reached for the recent edition on the counter but Vic stopped him with, "I've already looked. There's jobs for a couple of term teachers, a director of nursing, a part-time short order cook at the grill and a dozen ways to get rich sitting at my kitchen table stuffing envelopes or some such foolishness. But is there a chance…"

"Of course there is, Vic. There's every chance. I'll check the ads out as they come in, put the staff on watch. There's never much, but you know that. But anything that can help bring you back here I'll be glad to do. Good luck, Vic," David said with heaviness.

"Thanks, David, and look, whenever there's a chance of getting my mother's picture at the Manor and sticking it in the paper, it's always a nice surprise. Makes a guy lonesome as old hell to see her, or the kids in a hockey game or even the wife winning a quilt, but it lets a guy know there's still a home to go home to. 'Til I get back then," Victor Mason said, reaching out his hand to his friend.

David had returned to updating the online edition of the *Witness* with the news about the environmental impact study when he was interrupted again, this time by a phone call from Corporal Harry Noseworthy. "This is your week for good news," the RCMP officer told him. "Just had a call from Halifax and you won't be receiving a visit tomorrow from those investigators I told you about. The Attorney General has called off the investigation into the leaked files. Probably afraid an investigation will find out far more than the name of the person who leaked it, considering the kind of scum the government has been dealing with on this seawall business."

Sunday morning broke sunny and warm for early September. David woke to the excitement that he was leaving for the Halifax airport late in the afternoon to pick up Tony and Mary, and tell them about the decision he had reached about their new home. He would be building on the lot he had purchased from his mother. She'd tried to give it to him but he insisted on paying fair market value, which would give her enough of a bank account to do things like join friends on a bus tour to Maine to shop when the Canadian dollar flexed its occasional muscles or join friends in Florida if she wished. But this morning they were going together to Father Walker's Mass at the memorial cairn on the dunes.

The whole town seemed to have turned out for what itself turned out to be an ecumenical service that included all of Shean's clergy. David guided his mother to a place near Rita and her father. When the service ended, his mother left him for the company of her friends and Ronald cornered a group of churchgoers to regale them on how he had single-handedly fended off "that clown."

Rita and David strolled along the beach, part of a widely scattered crowd sharing the same idea. For both of them, possessive of the beach and unused to sharing it together in sunlight, it was too crowded. Passing the closed-for-the-season Beach Burger Café, David was struck by sudden hunger, and so suggested a late breakfast at the Gulf Grill.

Seated in a booth, David asked Rita, "When you were a kid, did you ever go looking through haunted houses?"

"A couple of times."

"We used to do it a lot, me and Donald, especially. Sometimes Victor was with us, or we'd be in a crowd, but usually it was me and Donald. There were half a dozen old abandoned places with reputations for being haunted, and we'd go inside.

I'll never forget the feeling, it was always the same. You'd go to the house after dark, places like what they used to call the Old Castle up near Lake Ainslie, with nothing but a flashlight and courage borrowed from the person with you, who was probably borrowing his courage from you. You'd go inside and right away that courage would give way to fear, imagination, even prayer. Everything made you jump, a scrap of curtain still hanging in a paneless window moved by a breeze, a sway of shadows along the wall if the wind picked up, the scurry of a mouse, the squeak of the stairs as you went up them to check the bedrooms and the attic. No matter what convictions you had about no such things as ghosts, it was impossible to utter such a denial while you were there. It possessed you, that fear and that belief, and all you wanted to do was be out of it. And when you did come out the back door into the orchard or the yard and the moonlight and the stars, it all seemed so imaginary, that haunted house.

"That's what I feel now, as though I've just passed through a summer-long haunted house filled with threats that in the end never materialized, but I'm left with one unanswered question, Rita. I still don't know what I would have done if Resource Reclamations Limited and C.J.M. Lord had come at me with the lawsuits they threatened. It's one thing to be a small town newspaper fighting for or against the local issues you know, but I was picking a fight in which I was way out of my weight class. I just don't know."

"I do," Rita answered without elaboration. "But it's been a different kind of summer for me, too. Do you want to hear what I've decided?"

"Maybe. It depends on what it is you've decided," David answered, smiling faintly, uncertain if this was goodbye to the nurse who hoped to roam the world. "So tell me."

Rita's words died on her lips when Donald MacNaughton opened the café door, spotted them in the booth and made an enraged charge in their direction. His hair was uncombed, his eyes bloodshot. "This is your idea of a joke, isn't it, the both of you?"

"What?" Rita asked straight-faced.

"What? What? What? I got back from Halifax about three this morning, barely got any sleep and needed to get down here to town to … never mind. I walked out to my driveway and realized the empty lot beside my house was no longer empty. There's a goddamned dilapidated old trailer on it, and who's standing on the doorsteps swinging that goddamned cast-iron frying pan of hers with one hand into the palm of her other hand like she wished it was my head? This is your doing."

David's arms rose in innocent surrender while he struggled to keep a straight face, but he lost that fight in a hurry.

"So you think it's funny?"

"Do you know what I think, Donald? I think this newspaper could use a good political cartoonist. I should have had Tim up there this morning hiding in the bushes to get a picture of your face."

"Funny, is it? Know what I think is funny? That I don't think it's one bit funny. That's funny, David."

"That doesn't make any sense, Donald, but what you've said is funny. We'll both get a good laugh out of it once you get over the shock of having a new neighbour, but it's none of my doing."

"Of course it isn't. You haven't got the goddamned guts or imagination to pull off a prank like this. So it had to be you," Donald said, turning his attention to Rita, who feigned innocence. "Oh yes, this has your fingerprints all over it. You and that old quiff hatched this thing up between you. Did you see the goddamned trailer she's living in? It's unsightly and unfit for human habitation and I'm going to have it removed."

"I wouldn't move too fast on that, my friend," David cautioned. "Remember your political ambitions. You could get blamed for evicting the same old woman from her home twice."

Rita waded in with her explanation. "The poor woman just wanted to be close to you in appreciation for driving C.J.M.

Lord off her Sandy's land. Oh, and yes, she also mentioned that she wanted to be a daily reminder that you once shot her in the arse and she is never, ever going to let you forget it. Oh, Donald, there is a God!"

Donald MacNaughton sizzled, looking from one to the other, knowing that he needed to get out of there before his own face broke into the smile he was determined wouldn't be allowed to assert itself. He turned away, throwing his final words over his shoulder. "What this town needs are some seriously new zoning laws!"

"Won't help," David called after him. "She'd still be grandfathered in as an existing home."

"That worked out better than I ever imagined," Rita said as their food arrived and they allowed their laughter to subside.

"Can we return to your decision now?" David asked.

"Yes, we can. I wanted you to know that I've applied for a new job."

"Cruise ship?"

"No, something less romantic. The director of nursing job at the health care complex. Maybe you saw the ad. It was in the *Witness*."

"I heard it mentioned," David said, quelling a surge of excitement. "Why? That kind of position sort of calls for a long-term commitment. I thought you were keeping your options open."

"It is a long-term commitment, David. I've given it a lot of thought since the position was advertised. Whether I get it or not, it's still about a long-term commitment."

"What's changed since we last had this discussion?" David waved his hand toward the shore.

"A lot. I guess it began to change the night you told me about the seawall. That image, it's never going to leave me. Even when I was away, whenever I wanted to just sit and think about something, or if I was feeling low or depressed or whatever, the place I would always go in my mind was to the breakwater, my breakwater. It's been a magic place for me since I was a teenager. I sat there alone many, many nights, escaping from my friends, to stare at the stars and think about travelling the world.

"When it became clear that this breakwater, this shore, this ocean, could be taken away from me in a single act of greed, I began to rethink what it was I wanted to leave behind, and so I guess I feel that if I don't stay here and keep an eye on things along with you, it will disappear. We can't let that happen."

David was slow to respond, and Rita seemed in no rush to hear what he wanted to say. Finally he made the effort.

"Does this mean that if I tried to say some of the things I've been feeling and thinking, about us, if I try to say them out loud instead of pretending that you and I are simply thrown together by circumstances instead of by some other mysterious force, that if I said some of those things, we might even survive them and still go on seeing each other like this, out in the sunlight with no shadows, no secrets, just us telling each other the truth?"

"If I followed that convoluted, near admission of deeper feeling, then I'd say yes. In fact, you're free to say whatever you need to say. And who knows? If you say just the right combination of words, you might even end up winning the Cape Breton Lottery."

Frank Macdonald, is the award-winning author of *A Forest for Calum*, long-listed for the 2007 IMPAC International Dublin Literary Award. A long-time and award-winning columnist, Macdonald is an accomplished writer of short stories, drama, poetry and songs. His humorous, often satirical columns in the *Inverness Oran* have twice been anthologized; *Assuming I'm Right* in 1990 became a stage production that has toured Nova Scotia and elsewhere in Canada. His play *Her Wake* won Best Canadian Play at the Liverpool International Theatre Festival in 2010 and, also in 2010, he authored *T.R.'s Adventure at Angus the Wheeler's*, a children's book, illustrated by Virginia McCoy. Frank lives in Inverness, Cape Breton. *A Possible Madness* his second novel was runner-up for the Dartmouth Book Award.

Thank You

I would like to thank Cape Breton University Press, for their encouragement and confidence in bringing this book through its many stages.

Thanks also to Sandra McIntyre, editor, for her guidance, advice and many "teachable moments," which I appreciate greatly.

I would like to thank Mark Green for sending me off in the right direction in my search for a seawall that would work, at least in theory and in this story. Any faults engineers may find with this theoretical wall are failures of my own imagination. Thanks also to Lawrence Ryan for just listening, which he has been doing for decades.

Thanks also to my partners and friends at the *Inverness Oran*.

I would like to thank Virginia McCoy, my reader and so much more, for being there through it all, and staying anyway.

CPSIA information can be obtained at www.ICGtesting.com
Printed in the USA
LVOW07s0521081214

417730LV00001B/45/P